GATHER THE DAUGHTERS

GATHER THE DAUGHTERS

A Novel

JENNIE MELAMED

Little, Brown and Company

New York Boston London

Melamed

Copyright © 2017 by Jennie Melamed

Hachette Book Group supports the right to free expression and the value of copyright. The purpose of copyright is to encourage writers and artists to produce the creative works that enrich our culture.

The scanning, uploading, and distribution of this book without permission is a theft of the author's intellectual property. If you would like permission to use material from the book (other than for review purposes), please contact permissions@hbgusa.com. Thank you for your support of the author's rights.

Little, Brown and Company
Hachette Book Group
1290 Avenue of the Americas, New York, NY 10104
littlebrown.com

First Edition: July 2017

Little, Brown and Company is a division of Hachette Book Group, Inc. The Little, Brown name and logo are trademarks of Hachette Book Group, Inc.

The publisher is not responsible for websites (or their content) that are not owned by the publisher.

The Hachette Speakers Bureau provides a wide range of authors for speaking events. To find out more, go to hachettespeakersbureau.com or call (866) 376-6591.

ISBN 978-0-316-46365-2
LCCN 2016950142

10 9 8 7 6 5 4 3 2 1

LSC-C

Printed in the United States of America

For my amazing, talented,
magnificent Mom and Dad

PROLOGUE

Vanessa dreams she is a grown woman, heavy with flesh and care. Her two limber, graceful daughters are dancing and leaping on the shore as she watches from the grass where the sand ends. Their dresses flutter chalk-white, like apple flesh or a sun-bleached stone. A calescent sun shatters on the surface of the water, luminous shards slipping about on the tiny waves like a broken, sparkling film. One daughter stops to turn and wave wildly, and Vanessa, her heart aching with love, waves back. The girls clasp each other's forearms and spin in a circle, shrieking with laughter, until they collapse on the sand.

Rising and conferring with their heads close together, they hike up their dresses to wade into the sea. *Don't go too far!* calls Vanessa, but they pretend not to hear. Walking wide-legged like awkward herons, wetting their hems, they peer into the water for fish and crabs, until the younger one turns back and yells, *We're going to swim, Mother!*

But you can't swim! Vanessa cries frantically. Heedless, they crash into the water and begin paddling away, kicking their slender legs and thrashing with their hands. Swiftly, borne by a powerful current, they grow smaller and smaller. Vanessa tries to run to the edge of the sea, but her feet are stuck fast, woven into the ground like tree roots, her legs paralyzed as dead stumps. She opens her mouth to call them back, but instead of urging her daughters back to shore, she finds herself screaming, *Swim faster! Get away from here, get out, now!* The sun vanishes and the sea turns dark, roiling and spitting, and their beloved faces shrink to motes. Vanessa clenches her fists, closes her eyes, and shrieks, *Never come back here again! I'll kill you if you come back here! I swear I'll fucking kill you both!* The girls disappear into the horizon, and Vanessa drops her face into her hands and weeps.

Thief, whispers a voice that seems to come from everywhere, echoing and groaning in her rib cage. *Blasphemer.* The ground softens, and she falls through a sea of dark slime into the raging black fire of the darkness below. Her bones snap like sticks. Rotating her head violently on a broken neck, she sees her daughters writhing next to her, their straight, slim legs bending and shattering as their white dresses burn.

Then Father is there, shaking her, holding her. "Vanessa, relax," he says as she trembles and whimpers. "It's just a dream." She loosens her fists and sees, in the gray dawn light, that she has cut small, dark crescents into her palms.

"What were you dreaming about?" asks Father sleepily.

"I can't remember," she replies, and no matter how often the dream comes back to haunt her, smearing and dissolving hotly in her brain as she gasps and claws her way to consciousness, she always tells him she can't remember. She knows instinctively it is not something to be freely given away to adults, like a flower or an embrace. This dream, the dark embodiment of blasphemy, is a shameful secret rooted strongly as a tooth or a fingernail. And Father, muttering vaguely as he kisses her sweaty brow, never tries to wrest it from her.

Sometimes, in the drowsy mornings after, she gazes at Mother and wonders what she would call out if Vanessa were swimming away from her, toward the wastelands.

SPRING

CHAPTER ONE

Vanessa

The long spelling lesson is done, and Mr. Abraham is now talking about soaking and curing leather. As he rambles on about techniques for concentrating urine, Vanessa inhales lightly and cautiously, as if her lungs are about to be scalded by the acrid smell of leather curing in its vats. The half-vinegar, half-musk scent hangs in the air for weeks in early spring, and she's already decided she will never marry or even live near a tanner. Keeping her eyes open and her face attentive, she drifts off into daydreams of summer. When Letty reaches back to scratch a shoulder blade and drops a note on her desk, Vanessa jolts into the present. Using her bitten nails to pick open the small package, she reads:

Do you think it was her first time?

Half an hour ago, Frieda Joseph burst into tears while trying to spell "turnip." They weren't tears of frustration, but big, dry, gulping sobs like she'd been punched in the throat. Mr. Abraham took her out of the classroom for a while. He must have sent her home, because he returned without her.

Frieda's chair sits naked and prominent. All the girls around it are carefully looking in another direction. There's a bloodstain on the wood, bright and ragged, with a dark, crusting drop on the floor. Everyone knows it wasn't there yesterday.

Vanessa is silent, lost in memory, and Letty shifts in her seat and eventually turns to cast her a questioning look. Annoyed, Vanessa shrugs curtly at her.

Letty faces front again and flakes off a tiny corner of paper. She writes something with the thin charcoal pencil, stretches extravagantly, and drops it on Vanessa's desk.

Vanessa snatches the paper and cradles it in her lap, squinting. The charcoal is smudged and she can barely make out the words: *What a baby. I didn't cry my first time.*

Vanessa bites her tongue in exasperation. Carefully separating a piece of paper from her sheaf, she writes, *Liar.* Stretching forward, she drops it on Letty's lap like a little yellow butterfly. Letty shoots Vanessa a hurt look and then assiduously turns toward Mr. Abraham and fakes interest. Vanessa begins winding the ends of her braid through her fingers, wishing she were outside, running.

All the girls wear braids, smooth and sinuous over their shoulders, and they toy with them when nervous or excited. It's a deeply ingrained fidget, and when girls turn to women and put their hair up, their fingers flutter uselessly in the air as they try to remember what is missing. Hems are another favorite target for irritable fingers, and it is a rare girl's dress that bears a neat, well-stitched edge. Today they are dressed in whatever their mothers saw fit for May, which leaves some chilly and some sweltering. A few of the dresses are pink from berry juice and others yellow from roots, while some are simply the undyed off-white of light wool. The dresses are smudged and stained, darkened at the armpits and splattered with the remnants of messy eating. Summertime is for intensive weaving and sewing, and the dresses will either be let out or let down, firmly scrubbed and reused, or given to a family with a younger girl. While the older girls often wear new, fresh dresses, the younger ones are always swimming in threadbare smocks ready to fall apart.

As Mr. Abraham drones on, Vanessa wishes there was enough paper for drawing, but the wanderers decided a few years ago that the island should produce its own paper, instead of relying on leftover sheaves from the wastelands. Mr. Joseph the arborer has been experimenting, but this year's batch is an extravagant failure; the paper crumbles and separates almost at a touch. Even so, they know better than to waste it. When Bobby Solomon drew a sheep breathing fire on one of his sheets, his teacher Mr. Gideon whipped him so badly he limped for days.

The clock seems to run slower when three o'clock approaches, the hands creeping and stuttering. Vanessa wonders if Mr. Abraham remembered to wind it this morning. It's a beautiful thing, beaten from wasteland copper and full of the tiniest gears and wheels possible, like infinitesimal tawny beetles, so small they could fit on a forefinger. As much as Pastor Saul likes to talk about sin and war, Vanessa can't help but think that they were doing something right in the wastelands if they invented such miraculous devices.

Gabriel Solomon brought some parts to school last year, filched from his clockmaker father, who received the precious objects from the wanderers. The children gathered around, always impressed by wasteland goods, begging to touch the miniature glimmering shapes. Sometimes when Vanessa sees the stars, she imagines little sprockets and gears from a broken clock, flung up into the black. She wishes her father were a clockmaker, even though a wanderer is much more important. *The holy wanderer walks the wastelands without becoming part of the disease,* Pastor Saul likes to say. Vanessa once asked her mother which disease he was talking about, but Mother didn't know. She asked Father, and he talked of the diseases that ravaged the wastelands after the war. He wouldn't tell her about the war itself, though; he never does. Vanessa has attempted various charming ways to ask Father questions—he likes her cleverness, but despite her efforts, he refuses to discuss it. She can't find anything about it in their library either. Everything that ever happened must be in books, somewhere, but none of the ones she has access to have proved helpful.

Finally the clock reaches five to three. Mr. Abraham erases the large slate in the front of the classroom, wiping clean the chalky detritus of learning, and the children stand automatically with their heads bowed and hands clasped. Ceremoniously, Mr. Abraham takes down a copy of *Our Book,* the only book ever written on the island. It's handwritten on wasteland paper and bound in the strongest leather, but he still has to use a finger to keep loose pages from fluttering to the ground like dead, holy leaves.

"From the fires of wickedness we grew forth, like a green branch from a rotten tree," he reads. *"From the wastelands of want came the hardworking men of industry and promise. From the war-stricken terror came our forefathers to keep us safe from harm."* Like everyone else, Vanessa mouths the words along with him. *"From the cleansed and ravaged dust of the scourge came the flowerings of faith and a new way. With the ancestors to guide us, we will grow and prosper on a straight and narrow path. O ancestors, the sanctified first ten, plead with God on our behalf, and save us from impurity. Amen."*

"Amen," repeat the girls. They file quietly out of the room and then scatter, their heels clacking on the wooden floor like a handful of pebbles tossed to the ground. The girls mingle with the other classes, streams of boys in ragged pants and long shirts, younger children shrieking and running happily ahead. Sarah Moses catches Vanessa's arm as they run down the stairs and into the humid air.

"I bet it will rain soon," Sarah says, squinting up at the hazy sky. Her hair is frizzy with moisture and outlines her head in a jagged halo.

"It's not even June," Vanessa replies crossly. "It never rains before June."

"The woodbirds are burrowing into the trees already," Sarah says gleefully. "Mother says that's a sign. Tom's been sharpening rocks all winter."

Vanessa rolls her eyes. Tom Moses has dreams of making weapons, but so far all he's ever done is throw rocks and dart away, hooting. "Shouldn't he be helping your father weave?" she asks Sarah pointedly.

"He does," Sarah says. "We've made lots of cloth this winter, Mr. Aaron's thread is good this year. We'll have mountains after summer. The new sheep they brought from the wastelands really helped. Sometimes the lambs are speckled."

"I know," Vanessa answers. Everyone went to stare at the spotted lambs when they emerged from their mothers. Grown, they look like they're splattered with mud, although the rains haven't started yet. "Does that mean the thread is brown?"

"Kind of tan," Sarah says. "Not dirty-looking, just different." Vanessa nods thoughtfully, wondering if the wanderers had to round up each sheep separately, or if they'd stumbled across a whole pen of them. New animals are rare, but this was a stroke of luck; about half of the lambs on the island had begun dying from some unknown illness, and the wool had been brittle and weak for years.

Despite the damp warmth, Vanessa enjoys her walk home. Blackbirds are muttering in the trees, and the tall, slender grasses shiver with unseen animal life below; the rhythmic swoop of a rabbit or the whispering rustle of a hunting cat. Dodging the fields of shorter green pasture, she walks in the amber, knee-high meadows, letting the blades brush her legs with swift strokes.

At home, Mother has made cookies. Ben, Vanessa's three-year-old brother, looks like he's been eating them all day. Amused, Vanessa brushes golden crumbs from his blond ringlets and is rewarded with a wet, milky smile. Mother comes up beside her with two honey and corn cookies on a clay plate, and fresh milk in Vanessa's favorite lacquered cup. Intently, Vanessa stirs the milk with a finger and watches as blobs of tawny cream rise to the surface. She dunks in a cookie and carefully licks each drop of cream clinging to its sweet, crumbling mass.

Eight years ago, when Vanessa was five and her grandparents drank their final draft, the family moved to this house, leaving the old one for Mother's sister. Like most of the island houses, it is built almost entirely with wasteland wood, treated with a water-repellent tincture from the dyer Mr. Moses. While the house itself is well constructed and sturdy, the Adams' kitchen is the finest on the island. Father, who likes to build things, set to work on the kitchen as soon as his parents were buried, adding special drawers that could be filled with flour or grain, and metal rods at different lengths from the hearth fire, with a clay door to shut so the room wouldn't fill with smoke. He laid dove-gray and lavender stones fanning out from the oven door, the closest of which could be used to keep food hot. Vanessa remembers Mother walking around the new kitchen in a daze, smiling and giving Father joyful glances filled with a strange longing Vanessa couldn't quantify.

The crowning jewel of the entire house is the kitchen table, also made of wasteland wood, but shimmering with rich, iridescent tints of gold and crimson. Father's family has passed it down over the decades, and it bears the stains of use: a burnt-black spot in the middle, scratches along the legs that scar blond. To protect it from further injury, Mother has covered it almost completely with a rough woven mat, but Vanessa likes to lift up the edges and run her fingers over the blushing wood, watching as the oils of her skin make a greasy film on top.

"Watch you don't spill," says Mother as Vanessa presses her fingers into the table. "Father wants you to go to bed early tonight," she adds. "He says you don't sleep enough." Vanessa looks at her, but Mother is busy scraping burnt crumbs into a bucket by the wall. Sighing, Vanessa dips her fingers into the milk and presses them into the remaining cookie crumbs, making a paste. "Oh, and Janet Balthazar is birthing soon, so we'll be attending that. Probably in the next couple of days."

Vanessa winces. Janet Balthazar has had two defectives, born blue and slimy and dead like drowned worms in a puddle. If she has a third defective, she won't be allowed to have any more babies. Her husband, Gilbert, will be encouraged to take another wife. Occasionally, women choose to take the final draft rather than live childless. Pastor Saul likes to commend those women.

Vanessa can't imagine quiet, boring Gilbert Balthazar making any big decisions. He and Janet will probably grow old and sad, and then die quietly and without fuss when he is too useless to do anything. Hopefully he'll have taught someone else how to forge by then. All the boys want to learn, betting that he won't manage to have children and will have to train someone's second son. He is constantly swatting them away from his fire and yelling at them to go play.

"Do we have to go?" says Vanessa. She remembers Janet's birthing of her last defective, which was horrifying and repulsive.

"It's our duty," says Mother, which means yes.

"Can I go into the library?" asks Vanessa.

"If your hands are very clean," says Mother. Vanessa recites the next phrase under her breath with Mother: "I want you to remember how lucky you are to have books at your fingertips. Nobody else on the island has that privilege."

All wanderers are also collectors. How could they not be, wading through the detritus of civilization past? Each wanderer family not only inherits a pile of treasures, but adds to it each time the wanderer visits the wastelands. Sometimes it's all a jumble: delicate flowery plates and glittering jewels and pieces of machines. Sometimes there's a theme; the wanderer Aarons have pictures and sculptures of horses, their strong legs unfolding while their delicate necks arch forward, eerie to island children who have never seen anything larger than a sheep or faster than a dog. Father, like all the Adams back to their original ancestor, brings back books. Their library is nearly as big as the rest of the house's rooms put together. Father hid some books in a secured chest, saying they are only for the eyes of wanderers, and Vanessa has never been able to budge the lock. But most of the books are just stories, and these he keeps standing proudly on simple shelves that run around all four walls. The books are staggering in their variety: some as tiny as the palm of a hand, some so big Vanessa has to prop them on her stomach to lift them. They are covered in buttery leather finer than she's ever seen, or cloth woven so tightly it hurts the eyes to pick out the warp and weft, or thick paper splashed with illustrations that never flake off. Vanessa thinks the prettiest is the book that has a very thin layer of gold on the peripheries of its pages, so when it's closed, it looks like a shining treasure. Despite its outward

11

glory, *The Innovations of the Holy Roman Empire* has no pictures to tell Vanessa what the Holy Roman Empire was, and no definitions to tell her exactly what it invented.

Father scratches out the publication dates of all his books, saying wasteland years are meaningless, but he leaves in the names of the authors and everything else. The names bowl Vanessa over with their strangeness. *Maria Callansworth. Arthur Breton. Adiel Waxman. Salman Rushdie.* On the island, everyone bears the family name of an ancestor. First names are approved by the wanderers, the names of someone on the island who is already dead. Vanessa thinks her name is boring; she'd much prefer to be named Salman.

They have books at school, huge ones that students share during class time. At school they don't scratch out the dates, but that doesn't mean much because nobody knows what year it was when the ancestors touched shore. As in Father's books, the names of the publication locations are exciting and impossible to pronounce. Philadelphia, Albuquerque, Quebec, Seattle. The students have made up stories about what these places were like before they all became the wastelands. Philadelphia had tall buildings of gold that shone in the sun; Albuquerque was a forest always on fire; Quebec had such cold summers that children froze to death in seconds if they went outside; Seattle was under the sea and sent books up to land via metal tunnels.

Vanessa finds many of the books in Father's library dull. Father once gave her one he said was good for girls, but it was all about people who wouldn't call each other by their first names and never thought about anything except getting married (the process of which seemed alarmingly complicated). Father was amused at her report and gave her *The Call of the Wild,* which she's read eight times. There are dogs on the island, but not massive and ferocious and strong, like in the book. She learned so much from it; all about sleds, and competitions, and outdoor fires, and wolves. Sometimes she dreams of herself alone in the cold, striding through snowy emptiness with bristling, savage wolves at her side.

Today, Vanessa picks out a book called *Cubist Picasso* and flips through the pictures. The first few pages are torn out, and the rest are only images. Father says he doesn't know what Cubist or Picasso are. She likes the strange pictures showing things that don't exist, grown people with eyes on one side of their head like defectives. Lindy Aaron once let her touch a painting, even though she wasn't supposed to, and it felt rough and thick under her fingers. These images look like they would feel that way, but under her skin is just paper.

After a while, Vanessa tires of lying around, and goes outside. Farms and gardens spread green in ragged patterns under the hazy sun, and the Saul orchards are a faint, dark line on the horizon. Since Father is a wanderer, he receives regular tribute from every island family of the freshest, most delicious food that the fields, gardens, and sea have to offer; Vanessa's family thus only needs a small vegetable garden, and creamy grasses sweep and lean in the wind around their home.

A dog is trotting around, brown and thin. Vanessa calls to her, and the dog lopes over happily. It's Reed, one of the Josephs' dogs. Reed puts her big head on Vanessa's breastbone and grunts, and wriggles around like she is trying to bore through her rib cage. Vanessa scratches her ears, and the warmth from Reed's forehead spreads through her. Vanessa wishes she were a dog; all she'd ever have to do is run around and eat things. Although so many litters of puppies are drowned that she would need luck to make it to doghood.

Dinner is mutton and potatoes. Vanessa dislikes mutton, although Mother always tells her to be thankful for any meat they have. Her attempts to be thankful have failed; the mutton tastes like dirt. Father eats it with gusto, closing his teeth over the fibers and chewing lustily. Looking around, she sees chewing mouths, closing on flesh and turning it into slime, and she clenches her jaw against the turn of her stomach. She nibbles at a potato with butter and some burnt, crunchy mutton skin. Eventually Father notices and says, "Vanessa." Forcing the mutton down, Vanessa barely chews, pretending she is a dog. Dogs don't chew, they just swallow.

"Would you like something to help you sleep tonight?" asks Mother. Father frowns. He thinks the sleeping draft is unnecessary and is always disappointed when Vanessa takes it. Vanessa nods at Mother, careful not to look at him. Her evening glass of milk has a bitter, acrid undertaste.

That night, Vanessa barely awakens. When she does, the wind is making everything move rhythmically and tree branches are slamming into the walls. *It's almost summer,* she thinks, and then darkness overtakes her once more.

CHAPTER TWO

Vanessa

The church is halfway underground. Mother says that when she was a child, it was mostly on top of the ground, but it's been sinking ever since.

When the ancestors came to the island, they built a massive stone church before they even built their own houses. What they didn't know was that such a heavy building would sink down into the mud during the summer rains. The enormous church slowly disappeared below the surface, its parishioners unconsciously hunching their shoulders lower and lower as the light filtering through the windows became obliterated, like a black blind drawing upward. Undaunted, the builders added more stones, and the church, in response, kept sinking. Every ten years or so, when the roof is almost level with the ground, all the men on the island gather to build stone walls on top of it, and the roof becomes the new floor. Vanessa asked Mother why they couldn't just use wood, but Mother said it was tradition, and it would be disrespectful to the ancestors to change it. All the eligible stones on the island are long mortared into vanished church walls. The wanderers have to bring new ones in slowly from the wastelands; if they tried to bring them all at once, it would sink the ferry.

Vanessa can't help but think that if she were in charge, she would build it just a little bit differently, so it might last longer. But she suspects that when she is a woman, she will see no problem with the current method of church building. She's never seen an adult express anything but enthusiasm for the process of building up and then sinking the church.

The stones the wanderers bring in are beautiful and multicolored, and Vanessa finds the texture pleasing, the way they stick out from the clay walls. She likes to run her hands over the smoothest rocks, the same way she likes to rub a perfectly round pebble that she keeps in her pocket. One stone has the fossil of a small eel imprinted on it, and all the children enjoy staring at the graceful patterns of its bones.

It's disappointing to go down the long set of stairs into the dim building. The windows are carefully constructed from larger fragments of glass, which makes them appear fractured, like someone smashed them and then sealed them up again. Currently they are half buried in black mud. Sunlight hovers faintly near the ceiling, spreading in delicate veils. Vanessa always watches the windows carefully, even if she's listening to the sermon. Letty swears that once a huge animal, like a big worm but with teeth, swam up against a pane until its white belly was flat against it, writhing and biting until it wriggled away. There are many legends of enormous underground creatures, bigger than the church itself; they glide through summer mud, curling around children in a soft, muscular embrace and then swallowing them whole.

The pews are polished wood, the smoothest to be found on the island. Although they are worn with the imprints of hundreds of buttocks, Vanessa still slides around uncomfortably; she can never find a place to settle. Pastor Saul is at his lectern, framed by the massive stone wall behind him.

As usual, he is speaking of the ancestors. "They came from a land where the family had been divided, where father and daughter were set asunder, where sons abandoned their mothers to die alone. Our forefathers had a vision, a vision that could not be satisfied in a world of flame, war, and ignorance. The fire and pestilence that spread across the land were second only to the fire and pestilence of thought and deed hovering like a black smoke."

There is an old tapestry, fragile as a moth's wing and colossal as a cloud, hung with care on the wall behind him. It depicts the founding of the island, each ancestor delineated by slightly different hair color. The ancestors alight on shore, build the church, build their houses, have children, have meetings with different children under fruit trees, stride around taming nature or yelling at birds (it's hard to tell), comfort old men, die, and rise into the sky. The cloth used for the tapestry, while faded and tattered, is still gorgeous: furry green material with golden threads winking through it, water-spattered maroon cloth thick and slippery as a cut of meat, a pale yellow that Vanessa knows was once golden and luscious as a setting sun.

Alma Moses, another wanderer's daughter, once told Vanessa that her father mentioned a machine that went awry in the wastelands and turned everything to flame. That pretty much the entire world caught fire. A lot of what the pastor says sounds like it. Fire first, pestilence after. The scourge. But then, wanderers go to the wastelands all the time and come back with cloth, metal, paper, even animals, none showing any sign of immolation. Perhaps everything burned up and then grew back again. Hannah Solomon, another wanderer's daughter, said her father told her it was a disease, a disease that rotted flesh and killed people where they stood. Another girl, June Joseph, said that then the dead people rose and shambled around, setting things on fire with their eyes until their corpses rotted, but June is known to exaggerate and her father is a goat farmer anyway.

Now the pastor is talking about women, which as far as Vanessa can tell is his favorite subject. It gets him more worked up than anything. She pictures him striding about in his bedroom at night, lambasting his wife when all she wants to do is go to sleep. He has two sons, so she would be the only woman available to upbraid.

"When a daughter submits to her father's will, when a wife submits to her husband, when a woman is a helper to a man, we are worshiping the ancestors and their vision. Our ancestors sit at the feet of the Creator, and as their hearts are warmed, they in turn warm His. These women worship the ancestors with each right action, with each right intention. Surely the ancestors will open the gates of heaven, and our grandfathers' grandfathers will welcome us with open arms." Vanessa feels Father staring at her and reluctantly stops gazing out the window.

"Only when these acts of submission are done with an open heart and a willing mind," the pastor continues, "only when this is done with a spirit of righteousness, can we reach true salvation." Vanessa knows that if you don't get saved and go to heaven, you slip into the darkness below forever. Once, before she started having her nightmare, she asked Mother if that meant going underground, where the monsters lived. Mother laughed, but then sobered and said maybe. Thanks to her dream, Vanessa is now intimately familiar with the darkness below and the terror it brings. She struggles to be righteous all the time, especially in her thoughts. She imagines her ancestor, Philip Adam, scrutinizing each unworthy thought that comes into her mind and making a black mark on a piece of paper.

"Men, we are not without task in this," warns the pastor. "We must treat our daughters with kindness and sensitivity. We must not hurt them at a whim, or damage them, but engage with them as the ancestors contracted when they left a forbidding land. We must deliver them safe, wise, and loved to their husbands. We must allow our wives to feel cared for, as cared for as they felt in the arms of their fathers as young children."

Vanessa turns to look back at Caitlin Jacob, who always has fingerprint bruises on her arms, just as the people sitting near Caitlin turn their heads to look at something else.

"Our society is built on our women," says the pastor, "on dutiful daughters and dutiful wives, but we must help them and protect them. We must be good shepherds. We must remember the teachings of the ancestors, and why they came to this land."

There is movement in the corner of Vanessa's vision, and she realizes with a start that Janey Solomon is staring at her from a few pews over. Vanessa and Janey are the only girls on the island with red hair, which gives them a certain status they would enjoy even without their other attributes. Vanessa's is a clear, dark brown-red, which she finds boring next to Janey's hair, which burns like fire. A red that is almost orange, it glistens and sparks, its coppery strands crackling outward. She seems to give off her own light from where she sits.

Vanessa hesitantly meets Janey's eyes, which are gray to the point of colorlessness, and suddenly their pupils dilate until her eyes seem black. Frowning, Vanessa remembers the last time Janey stared at her, years and years ago, and what happened afterward with Father the same week. Her heart beats faster. Can Janey see the future?

Everyone is afraid of Janey. She hasn't reached fruition at the age of seventeen, which is unheard of. They say she eats almost nothing, to keep herself from it, only just enough to keep her eyes open and her blood flowing through her veins. Vanessa tried it once, to see what it would be like to eat almost nothing. She got tired and hungry by the afternoon, and ended up eating two dinners.

Part of Janey's aura of intimidation stems from memories of summer. When summer arrives, Janey and her younger sister, Mary, are unstoppable. Even the boys are scared of them. They say Janey gouged Jack Saul's eye out and then made it look like an accident. They say her father is so scared of her he doesn't even talk inside the house. They say nobody's ever laid a hand on her without regretting it.

And now she's staring at Vanessa. Breathless, Vanessa glances back, then away, unable to meet the black gaze. What does she want? Vanessa looks away until she feels dizzy and then looks back at her. But now she sees Janey's staring past her, looking at somebody else— or maybe looking at nothing and running in circles in her strange, fiery head.

Vanessa watches Janey's incandescent braid, so brightly colored it seems to move, writhing and snaking over her shoulder. When it's time to stand, Vanessa forgets to get up until Father touches her shoulder. She jumps.

19

It's time for the reading of the island laws, which the pastor calls the ancestors' commandments, and everyone else calls the shalt-nots. *Thou shalt not steal. Thou shalt not listen at thy neighbor's walls.* Vanessa's mind drifts lightly as her mouth forms words so familiar that she could recite them in her sleep. *Thou shalt not disobey thy father. Thou shalt not enter another man's home uninvited. Thou shalt not raise more than two children. Thou shalt not fail to give thy wanderer proper bounty.* There are plenty of shalt-nots, but she can't remember a time when she didn't know them. Father told her once that there used to be only ten or so, but the numbers rose as the wisdom of the wanderers increased. The voice of the congregation swells to support her absentminded murmur. *Thou shalt not forget thy ancestor. Thou shalt not touch a daughter who has bled until she enters her summer of fruition.*

Vanessa wonders, as she always does, why the commandments use words like "thou" and "thy" when she has never heard anyone talk like that. other than when reciting the shalt-nots. Even the pastor doesn't talk like that. She imagines saying to Fiona, "Shalt thou invite me to thy house after school, that I may play with thy dog and eat thy cookies?" and has to bite her tongue to keep from snickering. A baby starts shrieking, a long howl that turns rhythmic as her mother starts bouncing her, cooing the shalt-nots into her face like a lullaby. *Thou shalt not allow thy wife to stray in thought, deed, or body. Thou shalt not allow women who are not sister, daughter, or mother to gather without a man to guide them. Thou shalt not kill.*

After the shalt-nots, the collection plate is passed, and the needle. Father has it in his lap and is sucking blood off his finger. You don't have to do it until you reach fruition, but Vanessa, always precocious, started when she was eight. She carefully takes the needle, inserts it into the pad of her finger, and squeezes a drop into the red, gelatinous puddle. Afterward, the clotted blood will be poured over a crop field that's struggling. To Vanessa, whose family has never had to farm, the crop fields are huge holes all waste goes into: animal dung, human waste, blood, dead bodies. She tries not to think about the fact that her food comes out of those holes as well.

Talking is forbidden after the service, until the home worship is complete. Her fingertip tastes like metal. Getting up, people file out of the pews and up the long steps to the doorway. Vanessa glances hopefully at the sky, but it's a bright blue. She smells heat in the wind. The last few weeks before summer are always the worst.

They walk home quietly, nodding at other families processing toward the church; services will repeat all morning. Once they reach their house, Father opens the altar room, which has a separate entrance. Most houses don't have special rooms for their altars, but Father built one when Vanessa was a baby, and soon the other wanderers followed suit. Mother cleans it faithfully, with a rag and soapy water, but it always becomes dusty. Motes twist and whirl, glittering in the sun like tiny weightless birds.

The altar is made of a light wood, polished and carved in a way that Vanessa has never seen an island carver achieve; it's a piece Father found in the wastelands. Propped up on the altar is a tattered copy of *Our Book*. The originals have dwindled to dust, and part of the pastor's duties is carefully scribing new ones. Next to *Our Book* is a beeswax candle speckled with tiny black dots—gnats must have found their way into the wax as it cooled—and a picture of the first Adam, Philip Adam, and his family. Father says it's not a drawing, but a way to capture a moment in time that people used before the scourge. Like the pictures in the schoolbooks, but glossy and vivid and alive. Vanessa assumes this means that people back then were almost gods. How else could they capture time on paper?

Philip Adam stands tall and strong and blond, smiling like he's about to laugh. His dark-haired wife is partly turned toward him, gazing at him with adoring eyes, her hands placed lightly on his side. Next to them is a lanky boy, tall but without breadth, grinning awkwardly and showing too many teeth. On the other side is his daughter, thin like his wife, too thin. She's dark as well, her shadowed eyes like holes in her head, her mouth a dark line. At their feet a baby with an impossible tuft of blond hair looks wary. You could have more than two children, back then.

On the island, worshiping God is about as useful as worshiping the sun: words of praise or words of pleading are unlikely to move either. God sits high and untouchable, a creator with nothing more to create, a father who lost interest in his children ages ago. It is the ancestors, those godly men of yore, who watch over the mortals on the island. It is their strong, capable arms that greet the dead into heaven or strike them into the darkness below. Any prayer is passed from their lips to God's ear, as well as any lapse or blasphemy. "The ancestors see everything, everywhere on the island," says *Our Book,* and for a time in her childhood Vanessa felt like she was defecating for an audience of thoughtful ancestors.

Each family will be worshipping its ancestor right now. Other families are gazing at drawings or relics of Philip Adam, one of the first ten ancestors, and offering him their words of worship. It seems somehow licentious that more than one family can call Philip Adam their own. When Vanessa marries, she will praise a different ancestor, which will be strange; she has spent so long gazing at the miraculous picture of the handsome blond man that she worries the next ancestor will be a disappointment. They say Philip Adam was a genius. He wouldn't sleep for nights on end, scribbling copious notes that would eventually be condensed into *Our Book,* then lapsing into trances, having to be fed and cleaned while he wept. He gathered the other ancestors and urged them to the island before the apocalypse he foretold. He was the first pastor too and planned the first church.

"In your name, Philip Adam," Father says, kneeling in the dust and touching the picture with a reverent finger. "In your name."

"In your name," parrot Mother and Vanessa, while Ben says, "In name."

"First ancestor, bring us strength. Teach us wisdom. Reach to God with your arms, bring Him into our lives, wind Him around our thoughts, bury Him within our breasts. Let the men be strong like trees, and the women like vines, the children our fruit. And when we sink into the earth, gather us into your arms and take us to God's domain, and let us not look downward into the darkness below."

"Amen," say Mother and Vanessa. Ben has gotten distracted by a small shimmering moth. Mother pinches him, but this only makes him yowl and clench his small fists.

CHAPTER THREE

Amanda

Mrs. Saul the wanderer's wife, with her pinched face and tart tongue, is not whom Amanda would have chosen to perform the ritual, but she was available and Amanda was impatient. They step into the birthing building, Amanda's candle flickering and dancing lightly over the tightly hewn walls. The wood is swollen with the stale, metallic smell of dried blood, the leavings of hundreds of squalling infants and wailing mothers. Amanda wrinkles her nose; Mrs. Saul notices and snaps, "Haven't you been to a birthing before?"

Amanda doesn't answer. She has, one time. Mother took her in order to show that she was doing her maternal duty, although Amanda suspects she didn't fool anybody. They sat silent and morose as Dina Joseph, the goat farmer's wife, screamed and thrashed and delivered a dead infant, deep blue streaked with scarlet and white slime. Dina sobbed, and Amanda felt irritated that she was forced to witness this raw, bloody grief. She glanced at Mother, who looked bored, and suddenly thought, *We are utter defectives. At least, when we're together.* As if reading her mind, Mother glared at her, and Amanda glumly returned to staring at the blue pile of flesh and gore in Dina's heaving arms.

Mrs. Saul sighs. "Do you know the ritual?"

Amanda has heard the stories at school, about babies being sliced out of screaming women, examined, and placed back inside, but she doesn't trust her informants. "Not really," she says.

"Well, no matter," Mrs. Saul says briskly. "It won't kill you, and then you'll know. But take care it is kept secret. Men do not know of this, nor should they. This is women's business. We are the ones who need to prepare ourselves."

Amanda nods. "Mrs. Saul?" she asks.

"You're an adult now," Mrs. Saul replies, "and you can call me Pamela."

"Um," says Amanda. The idea of calling Mrs. Saul by her first name seems blasphemous. "Why does it have to be a wanderer's wife?"

"You would prefer someone else?" inquires Mrs. Saul icily.

"No, no, it's not that," lies Amanda. "I'm just wondering. Why."

"Because as wanderers' wives, we hold power, and we are as wanderers among the women," says Mrs. Saul grandly, and Amanda nods, although she's doubtful about the accuracy of this comparison.

They are silent, breathing in the bloody air, and then Mrs. Saul says, "Are you sure you want to do it? Many don't. There's nothing wrong with waiting until the birth."

"Yes. I'm sure." Amanda pauses. "What do I do?"

"First, take off your dress."

Amanda grabs the hem of her skirt and pulls it over her head, then for good measure unties the cloth binding her swollen breasts, so she stands naked. Mrs. Saul squints at her and says, "About four months along?"

"About," says Amanda.

"You are thirteen? Fourteen?"

"Almost fifteen."

"A good age for your first child. Lie here, let me get some straw." Mrs. Saul scoops up a pile of hay in the center of the room. "Lie back, legs straight." Amanda obeys, peering at the dim ceiling. "This will be painful."

"I can handle pain," replies Amanda stiffly.

"I believe you can," says Mrs. Saul, and Amanda stares at her, suspicious. Is Mrs. Saul paying her a compliment?

Reaching into the pocket of her dress, Mrs. Saul pulls out a small knife, instantly ablaze with candled reflections that leap and twist in the rippled metal. Bringing it to Amanda's breastbone, she begins singing.

She doesn't sing words, but rather a tune with nonsense syllables, a melody that wavers like the candlelight. She has a low, husky, beautiful voice that Amanda never dreamed could emerge from Mrs. Saul's sour throat. The knife lightly traces downward from Amanda's sternum to where the swell of her belly curves upward. Taking a deep breath, Mrs. Saul begins cutting. She doesn't cut to muscle, but enough to break through layers of skin, and blood begins to bead and swell in glossy vermilion spheres. Amanda is mesmerized by the slow incision, the freezing-cold line on her skin that turns boiling and steams with agony in the knife's wake.

"Breathe," says Mrs. Saul, breaking off midsong, and Amanda does.

Once Mrs. Saul is done, Amanda gazes down at herself. Mrs. Saul has cut an impossibly neat, straight line down her rounded stomach, all the way to her pubis. The song lulls her, carries her to and fro, toward and away from the pain. Cool blood trickles down either side of her belly, striping her ribs and turning her into some strange animal in shadow.

Mrs. Saul pauses in her tune, and Amanda takes the opportunity to whisper, "Now what?" But Mrs. Saul only glares at her and resumes singing. She opens a small, thick cloth bag and takes a breath as if to steel herself. Her ropy hand rises with a handful of something white and crystalline, and she quickly, violently smears and pushes it into Amanda's wound.

Screaming, Amanda arches, feeling cracked open, the torment burrowing deeper and deeper into her flesh. The line of pain blossoms, a searing crimson flower, sheds arcane patterns on her belly that burn bone-deep. She can't get enough breath to wail all her agony, and she pants, sobs, chokes.

"Breathe," says Mrs. Saul.

Amanda tries to turn, but Mrs. Saul's hands are firmly on her abdomen, pressing on each side. She's not sure how long she lies there, writhing and gasping like a beached and gutted fish. As the pain begins to recede, wave upon wave softening and retreating, her attention fixes on Mrs. Saul's hands.

"What do you feel?" she whispers.

She can tell from Mrs. Saul's face. Clenching her eyes shut, she tries to move something inside her gut, shove her baby into life. After a few minutes she opens her eyes once more and sees that Mrs. Saul has tears streaming down her face.

"It's a girl," Amanda says accusingly.

"It's a girl," says Mrs. Saul, nodding, her song done. "She didn't move at all. She just stayed silent and still, despite the pain. It's a girl, may the ancestors help her."

"The ancestors don't help anyone!" shouts Amanda, and can tell by Mrs. Saul's face she's gone too far.

"May they forgive you," Mrs. Saul says loudly, punctuating each word.

"May they forgive me," repeats Amanda meekly. Her blood-smeared belly aches and twinges, and she bursts into tears. Mrs. Saul moves to her head and strokes her hair soothingly.

"It's all right, Amanda," she whispers. "We were girls. We are here now. Our daughters will endure. Think of the summers, think of the love you will have for her."

All Amanda can think of is a filthy winter, time spent trapped in her bed by bonds of flesh, clenching her teeth against a scream, over and over and over.

I won't do it, she thinks. *I won't do it.* And then, *By the ancestors, I have to do it all over again.* She weeps with a grief so strong it flows through her veins like a sickness. Mrs. Saul puts her arms around the recumbent Amanda and lays her head against Amanda's throat. Her hair smells comfortingly of goat's milk and dust and salt.

"Weep now," whispers Mrs. Saul. "Weep deep. When you are through, rise and return to your husband with a cheerful face. Endure. I have done it and so can you."

Amanda's daughter, too late, kicks and circles in her womb.

CHAPTER FOUR

Caitlin

Caitlin has a recurring dream that she dreads, of a world without summer. A world where the rains never come and everything goes on the way it did before. A world where there is heat without freedom. Sometimes she worries that she's going crazy, like the Solomon boy who gabbled and banged his head against the walls. His parents patiently waited for him to die so they could have another, more useful child, but he stubbornly survived for years, and when he suddenly vanished everybody knew what had happened. Caitlin would rather not have that happen to her.

When she wakes from the dream, she grabs her ears and pulls until they hurt. The thread of pain running through her head brings her back to being Caitlin, who is not crazy, who knows there has never been a world without summer, and there won't be one now.

Caitlin is almost to her summer of fruition, but with any luck she won't bleed soon. Some of the girls look forward to the summer of fruition, and she knows she should. Afterward, she'll get married and live somewhere else. Joanna Joseph says that everyone enjoys it, but if you don't you can drink things that help you enjoy it. Caitlin isn't sure what scares her more, going through it as Caitlin or becoming not-Caitlin, and waking up afterward with no idea what happened to her.

In Caitlin's mind, the summer of fruition is as terrifying as the wastelands and the darkness below. Father talks about the wastelands a lot. Caitlin's father is not a wanderer, but he claims they tell him terrible things. Late at night, Caitlin mulls over his stories, lengthening and embellishing them until a nightmare blossoms from the grisly seeds. She pictures scenes so horrifying that sometimes she cries for the wasteland children, even though she's not completely sure that there are wasteland children. Although there must be, since she was one. But that was long ago, and she can't remember it.

As for the darkness below, Mother says she won't have to go as long as she is good. And so Caitlin tries her best to be very, very good.

Mother is very, very good. Sometimes at night, if they can tell by Father's snores that he won't wake up, Caitlin crawls into bed with her. Mother curls around her like a warm, sheltering blanket. They can't sing songs or talk the way they would during the day, but Mother hugs Caitlin so tight and safe that she almost can't breathe. It feels good, the pressure. Sometimes she can sleep, then. Caitlin has heard there is a syrup you can drink that makes you sleep through just about anything. She's afraid to ask about it and hear a firm no, preferring to dream of a golden-thick world where sleep comes like a breath, unconscious and inevitable.

Every day after school, she tries to help Mother as much as she can. The house chores must be performed quietly, unobtrusively, never bothering or annoying Father. It's hard to keep up with what needs to be done, as Caitlin's house is falling down around her. Mother is skilled at quietly scrubbing and sweeping so that dirt and dust are collected and discarded, but Father has forgotten to rebuild soft spots in the wood. Every couple of years, men must apply a tincture made by the dyer to prevent mold from blossoming, but Father has forgotten that too. The walls are a luxurious riot of black and brown, plumes branching from a spot on the bottom of the wall and flaming up to lick the ceiling in swirls of tiny dark spots. She and Mother will sometimes take cloths and patiently scrub, or even use their fingernails to scrape off the stains, but their efforts never do any good. Caitlin can see pictures in the mold, the way people see things in clouds. A tree. A butterfly. A monster.

Other buildings sometimes seem almost too clean, too intact, the walls uncomfortably dry and staring and bare, the frightening freedom of not needing to know what parts of the floor to avoid. Stairs that she can run up and down with abandon, instead of deftly skipping the rotting steps.

Life must be lived this way because of Father, who does not like to be disturbed. He takes the instructions of the ancestors to keep patriarchal order in his home very seriously. It embarrasses her that everyone thinks Father beats her, but she knows that it's just because she bruises so very easily. Father sometimes jokes that she'd bruise in a strong wind. If he lays a hand on her leg, it bruises. If he pulls on her arm to punctuate a point, it bruises. Sometimes she doesn't even feel it. Caitlin hates the marks; it's like her body is a tattletale, blabbing everything that everyone else's body keeps silent. Her body is so garrulous, with its bruises and pink marks and maroon spots, that she rarely talks, not wanting to add to the din. If she can't be smart or pretty, she can be quiet. And good.

Caitlin is a rare first-generation child. Mother and Father came to the island when she was a baby. A lot of the children used to ask her what she remembered from the wastelands, but the honest answer is nothing. She asks Mother, who says she doesn't remember either. It would seem odd to someone else, but Caitlin thinks she is telling the truth. Mother is so wonderful, but she's different from other mothers: thin and pale and curling into herself. If by a miracle there is nothing left to do, sometimes she'll just sit at a table for hours, staring into space. If Caitlin asks what she's thinking about, she'll half smile and say, "Oh, I'm just…" and never finish the sentence. When Father is in the room she instantly reverts to shadow, skittering around the edges, magically removing plates and wiping counters without actually being seen.

It's a little easier to get Father to talk about the wastelands, especially if he's drunk on mash-wine. The problem is, Caitlin can't find the right questions. She'll ask if there was a big fire, and he'll laugh and say "Was there ever!" in such a way that she can't tell if he's joking or telling the truth. She asks why he and Mother came, and he says something about the ancestors and the shalt-not about listening at walls. She asks if there are still horses, remembering the sturdy, leggy giants from pictures in schoolbooks and the Aarons' paintings. He says, "Horses! Why do you want to know about horses?" She asks if there are children in the wastelands, and he says, "Keep asking questions and there'll be one."

She never asks him questions if he's not drunk, or if he's too drunk. She has to time it just right. Once she got him to admit that there were dogs in the wastelands, and she was popular at school for two whole days, but then everyone started ignoring her again. Caitlin knows they wish she was smarter and could ask better questions. It's hard with a father like Father, but she doesn't know how to explain that to anyone else.

During times of quiet, afternoons when Mother is staring at the wall and Father is snoring in the bed, her mind is always running, running. She can't shut it off. Strangely, the only place that seems peaceful is church. Despite the pastor's grim warnings of the darkness below, and the inevitable sinking disappointment at how bad she is, church is predictable. People sit in the pews while the pastor strides and thunders. She doesn't have to say anything or answer any questions, and she knows every single person in the pews has to sit there and stay quiet, like her. Sometimes she closes her eyes and falls slightly into a doze, so she still hears the pastor but sees colors and flashes of faces behind her eyelids.

On this Sunday, she is slipping off to sleep in the pew when suddenly a movement in front of her flips her eyes open so wide they feel lidless. Janey Solomon has turned and is staring at Caitlin, who nearly shrieks. Of all the people in the world, Janey scares her the most. More than Father, more than the wanderers with their secret meetings and sweeping decisions, more than Haley Balthazar, who once punched Caitlin in the stomach at recess. It's not just Janey's unique appearance, with her shining hair and bounteous freckles, or all the rumors about what she's like in summertime. It's that Janey herself isn't scared of anything, which is the most terrifying thing about her.

Caitlin looks down at her lap, at the rough-woven dress with a moth hole. She looks up at the ceiling as if she's found something interesting there. She even tries a jumpy little wave in Janey's direction. Janey's gaze doesn't change, she just tilts her head like a dog hearing a faint noise. The light gray eyes with wide black pupils travel over Caitlin's forearms, which have mottled bruises peeking out through the long sleeves. Caitlin feels a sudden urge to shout, "It's okay! I bruise really easily!" but of course she'd rather die than yell anything in church. Janey's freckled lips pull to one side. Caitlin is considering crawling under the pew when Janey turns around and faces front again. Heart racing, Caitlin slowly creeps her hand down the side of her thigh, finger-walks it across the wood like a hesitant spider, and seizes her mother's fingers. Mother squeezes Caitlin's palm briefly, like a reflex, and smiles vacantly toward the front.

CHAPTER FIVE

Amanda

Amanda goes into one of her staring spells in the root cellar, while she is examining carrots. She's holding a bunch in her hand, deciding which to use in a salad for supper, and then suddenly something shifts. There's a quiet weight to her shoulders, lost hours settling over her like a mantle. Walking slowly upstairs, she checks the clock. About two hours this time. She hesitates, then sighs and goes back down into the cool dimness.

Amanda once told her neighbor, Jolene Joseph, about the lost time. Jolene laughed and said it was "pregnancy crazy," and that the same thing happened to her. Amanda laughed too, and didn't mention that she's had these spells as far back as she can remember.

Her episodes of lost time have gotten worse since the baby started kicking. At first Amanda thought her digestion was off, but then she realized that the flutters were too regular and quick to be gas. A moth beating against a window frantically, then settling with a shiver onto a windowsill. The first time she recognized its trembling, Amanda pressed her hand deep into her belly and thought, *Hello, baby girl.* Then she ran to the outhouse and puked into the miasmic pit. She lost time then, staring into a mosaic of sewage through a faded, lime-smelling wooden opening. When she came back to herself, she slowly walked back to the house, thinking, *There's no way to know. It could be a boy.* Now she knows for sure.

Amanda is terrified that, upon having a daughter, she will turn into her mother. Mother hated Amanda from the moment she was born. Amanda found out later it was Father who fed her, using goat's milk and a cloth, when Mother refused. Father had diapered her, cleaned her, and played with her while Mother sat in bed, staring at the ceiling and crying.

When Amanda was two, Elias was born, and Mother adored him instantly. Father was always busy repairing roofs during the day. At first, Amanda tagged after Mother and Elias, but they pulled into a shell made only for mother and son, leaving her lost and confused. Eventually she stopped seeking their company. She only laughed and talked when Father was home, when he would take her on his lap and rub her feet between his hands, and curl locks of her light brown hair around his fingers.

Amanda even slept with him in her child's bed, with Mother and Elias sprawled out in the bed meant for two adults. As she grew, she started butting against him with her kneecaps and elbows and hips. When she was six, Father's body stretched across the bed made her wakeful, and then she couldn't sleep at all. Even if Father was sound asleep, she jerked at every twitch, tensed at every snort. Eventually she started sleeping curled in an impenetrable ball by the fireplace if it was cold, and sprawled on the roof like a limpet if it wasn't. Father teased her at first, then pleaded, and then commanded her to sleep in bed at night. But as soon as he fell asleep, she slipped away.

When the other girls at school found out that Amanda was sleeping on the roof, they thought she was different and brave, a fearless rebel. She didn't mind that designation at all. Given her threadbare clothing and disintegrating shoes—Mother only mended Amanda's clothes when they were at the point of falling off her—it was better than being known as pitiful.

Soon even sleeping on the roof was too much proximity to Father, and she began roaming around in search of other places to sleep. She learned she could sleep in the cold, although not in the snow. Eventually she began sleeping at the edge of the island, where the brackish water lazily cozied up to land. The morning horizon was always foggy, and she could never see very far, but she liked the way the light filtered through the fog like a gentle touch, the way the outlines of trees and driftwood glowed and sharpened as the sun rises. She liked the little hermit crabs, scuttling around with one fist triumphantly thrust into the air, and the sound of fish leaping and plopping in the water. She even liked going back to Mother's scowls and Father's glum, sickening affection, because she knew that a few hours had belonged just to her.

Amanda doesn't want her daughter to sleep in the cold because her mother hates her. But Mother probably didn't plan to hate Amanda. It just happened.

When Andrew comes home, Amanda is still holding a bunch of carrots in the root cellar. Her candle has almost burned to a stub. The cellar is stone, carefully built and mortared so that muck doesn't seep in during the summer. The fading light jumps and flickers on the smooth walls, so that the hanging chickens and piles of potatoes seem alive and threatening, things with teeth.

"Is that dinner?" he asks, laughing. He puts a hand on her swollen belly and kisses the back of her neck. For the first time in Amanda's life, she wants him to go away.

"Dinner will be late," she says. "I took a long nap."

"That's fine," he answers. "On Thursday there'll be half a rack of mutton ready at Tim's, all smoked and ready for the cellar. I should have asked for a whole one; his roof will hold for decades. Longer than the rest of the place." He is covered in sawdust and twigs, and she wonders if he was crawling under a tree.

Amanda can never quite believe she married a man who does the same work as Father. Now the reminder makes her gorge rise, and she tries to force it back down her throat and focus on the conversation.

"I don't know," she replies. "A whole rack could go a bit off before we eat it."

"Not with the appetite you've been having," he says, grinning at her.

"Not me," Amanda says, touching her belly. *Don't say "her."* "The, the baby."

"The baby," Andrew agrees.

"I'm actually not very hungry tonight," she says.

"Would you like me to go to George's?" he asks. George is Andrew's older brother, another roofer and an overall cheerful man. He has two daughters.

"Would you?" says Amanda, forcing a smile that feels like a lie. "It's just that I'm...so tired."

"Of course," he says, taking her hand, and she loosens her fingers from her palm one by one so that he's holding a hand and not a fist. That night she eats unwashed carrots for dinner, squatting on her haunches in the root cellar, savoring the metallic taste of the dirt as much as the sweetness of the vegetables.

Late that night, she hears sobbing from the house next door. From the pitch of it, she can tell it's Nancy Joseph, who recently started bleeding and so is facing her summer of fruition. Sighing, Amanda rolls over fretfully, frustrated at her inability to block out the sound. Eventually she dozes off, but the soft weeping clings to her mind and follows her into her dreams. She dreams of a child crying desperately, skinny and hunched over, and Amanda is frozen and unable to say or do anything to comfort her.

CHAPTER SIX

Vanessa

Mother keeps telling Vanessa her turn will come, but she still finds birthings disgusting. She's seen a lot of them, animal and human, and the actual event itself doesn't bother her anymore. It's the thought of *her* having to do it that is awful. She doesn't want all that stretching and fluid and odor to ever have anything to do with her. Mother says she'll feel different when she's older, and Lenore Gideon told Vanessa she doesn't have a choice anyway. Vanessa suspects they're both saying the same thing.

Janet Balthazar is breathing hard, and at every contraction her belly turns to stone. Mother is rubbing Janet's stomach with oil, and Killian Adam is holding burning herbs under her nose, to dull the pain. The sweet, musty scent of the smoldering plants cuts through the heavy smells of blood and sweat. There's always at least one wanderer's wife at a birthing, and despite Vanessa's protests, Mother drags her along to a few every year. The small wooden birthing building— which holds up to three laboring women at a time, just in case—is crammed full of daughters, brought to learn about their future tribulations. They range in age from Hilda Aaron, who just learned to crawl and has now fallen peacefully asleep on the straw with her rump in the air, to Shelby Joseph, who is having her summer of fruition this year and looks aghast. Birthings are the only time unrelated women past fruition can gather together without men, and Vanessa has seen laboring women completely ignored as a cluster of women talk rapidly, shooing the children away. But Mother never ignores a woman in pain, and the others are taking her cue. She keeps dipping her head toward Shelby, muttering instructions and explanations. Janet screams, the cords in her throat vibrating against her skin.

Vanessa is huddled with the younger girls, a loose aggregation on the straw that is trying to move farther away from Janet Balthazar but is already bumping up against the walls. "This had better not be a defective," says Nina Joseph to Vanessa, stating the obvious. Nina's only seven, so Vanessa doesn't snap at her.

"I'm sure it will be fine," Vanessa says.

"How do you know?" asks Nina, and Vanessa realizes she doesn't, she's just parroting Mother.

"Well, if it's not fine, then..."

"My mother had a defective before she had me and Bradley," says Nina.

"I don't think my mother had any defectives," says Vanessa, although she's not absolutely sure.

The two girls are positioned where they can see right between Janet's legs. The candles, placed in bowls of water, gutter and flicker and paint undulating patterns on Janet's naked skin. There's a rush of blood and water and a resultant rich smell, and together they get up and move to one side, where all they can see is a straining, trembling thigh. When the birthing is done and the hut empty, the daughters are responsible for cleaning out the soiled straw and spreading fresh bundles to await the next deluge of blood. Vanessa is not looking forward to it. It makes her remember the time, about a year ago, when she found a pile of rags in the kitchen soaked through with blood, maroon and stiff, stinking of copper. Mother was in bed recovering from a headache. When Vanessa asked Mother if she had started taking up butchering, hoping to turn it into a joke, Mother's face hardened. "In a way," she said, and Vanessa had been too frightened to ask anything more. For the next few days, Mother dragged around the house, irritable and weak, and Father sat staring into the fire, his eyes shining too brightly. Uncharacteristically, Vanessa was too disturbed to ferret out what was going on.

Inga Balthazar skips over. She is a plump ten-year-old with glowing brown curls who always looks smug and satisfied, like she just ate an entire cake. "Mother says it's alive, she can feel it kicking," she announces. "I wonder what they'll name it? Jill Saul just died, so they might name it Jill."

"Does that mean it's not defective? If it's kicking?" Nina asks Vanessa.

"No, sometimes they're born alive," Vanessa says thoughtfully. She heard that last year Wilma Gideon had a baby that looked like a gutted fish.

"There haven't been any defectives in my family for three generations," Inga says proudly, obviously reciting something she's heard. "Our bloodline is spotless."

"No it's not, your brother is stupid and ugly," replies Nina. Inga bunches her small fists, but then Janet squalls, and they turn to look.

"Daddy says that they could bring things from the wastelands to make the pain better," says Inga, "but that's unnatural."

"They make the pain better for other things," Vanessa points out. "That's not even from the wastelands, they grow the plants here. Remember when Mr. Saul the fisherman broke his arm and it bent backwards?" She didn't see it, but part of her wishes she had.

Inga nods, looking doubtful. "I don't know why it's different. Maybe if you don't have pain, the baby won't live."

"That doesn't make any sense," says Nina.

"I wonder what it's like in the wastelands," says Vanessa. "Birthings." Both Nina and Inga turn to stare at her, their brows furrowed.

"I thought there wasn't anybody left?" says Nina.

"No, there are people left but it's only a few defectives," corrects Inga. "I mean, mostly defectives."

"Then why would it be different?" asks Nina.

41

Vanessa says, "I thought everything was different."

"Everything's worse," hazards Inga. "I bet you have no friends around you and no herbs, and if you take too long somebody cuts your belly open and takes the baby and leaves you dead."

"Why would somebody take the baby?" says Nina, wrinkling her forehead.

"Father says that children are precious in the wastelands," Inga answers. "Ones that aren't defective. They're worth more than gold. There aren't many of them."

"Why not?"

"Because of war, and disease, and murder." Inga ticks the items off on her fingers briskly. "He said that I would live about two minutes in the wastelands, before someone murdered me."

"If you're so precious, why would they kill you?" contends Vanessa.

Janet screams again, louder. Another gush of bloody water, laced with black. The straw beneath her wilts and darkens like the fine hair around the edge of her forehead. She is glistening with sweat, every muscle writhing under her skin, her lips stripped back from her teeth. In the close, warm air of the shed, mended every time even a whisper of cold air drifts through the boards in winter, Vanessa can smell Janet's breath; it's sour, full of pain and panic.

"Why can't they give her a sleeping draft?" Vanessa murmurs. "Mother gave me some last night. I barely woke up at all."

Nina looks wistful. "Daddy says I shouldn't ever take it."

"Why not?"

"I don't know."

They all turn as Janet shrieks high and reedy, like a trapped sheep. "There's the head!" cries Sharon Joseph, who is kneeling between her legs. "Push!" Janet pants in short, moaning gasps.

Something slithers into Sharon's lap. She hands it to Shelby, telling her to suck the slime out of its throat. Shelby makes a face, and Sharon slaps her. Leaning forward, Shelby gives the baby a dramatic kiss, spits blood and white muck into the straw, and retches.

"It's alive!" says Inga with surprise. "I wasn't expecting that."

"You're the one who told us it was alive," responds Nina.

"Yes, but I didn't expect it to *stay* alive."

"It's a girl," says Sharon, glancing at Mother and Janet, and the three women burst into tears.

Laughter for a boy, tears for a girl. Everyone at the birth is supposed to weep if it's a girl, and now everyone is dutifully crying. Sharon's shoulders shake rhythmically. Surprised, Vanessa feels her eyes fill and tears slide hotly down her cheeks. She glances at Nina, who has hidden her face in her hands. Nina blurs, then sharpens, then blurs again as tears spill down Vanessa's face, gathering at her upper lip and jaw, dripping onto the already damp and salty straw. The room is so full of noise that she calculates nobody will hear her if she scrunches up her face and yells as loud as she can. And so she balls her fists, licks the briny tears off her lips, arches over at the waist, and screams like she's being slaughtered.

Vanessa once asked Mother why everyone cries for girls. It doesn't seem fair that boys are greeted with celebration, but that everyone cried when she came sliding into the world on a river of salt and blood. Mother told her she'd understand when she was older.

CHAPTER SEVEN

Caitlin

Tonight, when Caitlin closes her eyes, instead of seeing a scowling ancestor or terrifying monster, she sees Janey Solomon. She's looking at Caitlin, and her mouth is askew, and Caitlin realizes that she's not angry or disapproving, just thoughtful. Burying her face in her pillow, Caitlin smiles a little.

A few hours later, as Caitlin is dipping in and out of a doze, she hears little *plink*s against her windowpane, which means Rosie is awake. Carefully creaking open the window, trying not to make any noise, Caitlin slithers out onto the roof. It groans loudly but holds her weight. It makes Caitlin sad to know that someday she will probably get so big she falls through the roof—although in truth the roof could give tomorrow. She also can't bring herself to tell Rosie Gideon to stop throwing pebbles at her window, even though window glass is more precious than almost anything on the island and Father would be furious with her if the window broke. Besides, if she told Rosie to stop, Rosie might start leaping onto the roof and banging loudly on a wall—or worse, ignore Caitlin altogether.

Slimmer and lighter than Caitlin, Rosie is perched on the edge of her roof expectantly, waiting. Caitlin guesses the Gideons rue having a house so close to her family, but she likes the proximity to Rosie. Scooching and shinnying, she inches down the flaking shingle roof until they are squatting across from each other, inches apart, mirror gargoyles. Rosie took out her braids for the night, and her hair falls over her shoulders in tight ripples of brown.

"I heard a drop of rain," Rosie whispers.

Caitlin stares up at the sky, which is clear and black and strewn with stars. "I don't think so."

"I did!" Rosie is nine and very headstrong. Caitlin often reflects that if they were the same age, Rosie would be more likely to punch her than talk to her. But Caitlin's extra four years earn her a grudging respect. "I think summer is here."

"I don't think quite yet," says Caitlin, the words bitter in her mouth. She swallows to clear the taste, but it lingers like a film. "Almost, but not quite."

"I don't want to wait any longer," complains Rosie. "My shoes are too tight. Mother spanked me for pinching Gerald when he deserved it. I hurt."

The *I hurt* shivers through Caitlin's bones in sympathy.

"It will come," she whispers. "I promise. Maybe only a few days?"

"Listen," begs Rosie. "Tell me if you hear rain coming."

The two girls are silent, inhaling the sultry night air and each other's breath. Caitlin hears crickets, a dog barking, a branch cracking, Rosie's light, expectant breathing. She hears her own heartbeat, industriously tapping against her ribs.

"I don't hear any rain," says Caitlin finally. "I wish I did."

"I hate it in my house," mutters Rosie. "Whenever my aunt comes over, she and Mother fight and break things. It's loud."

They squat there for a little longer, and then Rosie whispers, "Last night I prayed to the ancestors that Father would die."

A flash of panic runs through Caitlin's groin to the pit of her stomach, like she's just caught herself from falling off the roof. "You can't pray to the ancestors for that. They'll hurt you. You have to follow the shalt-nots. I don't pray to the ancestors for that, and..." Caitlin doesn't finish the sentence, but they both know what she's thinking: *My father is ten times worse than yours.*

"Why not?" Rosie looks offended, like Caitlin just confessed to something obscene.

"I can't pray for that, I wouldn't. It's the way it is, the way it's supposed to be. Daughters submit to their father's will, it's in *Our Book*. It's what the ancestors *wanted*."

Rosie narrows her eyes like she's going to argue and then shrugs guiltily. Her shoulders rise and fall sharply in her nightdress, dipping her collarbone in shadow. "I know. It didn't work."

"Of course it didn't work. And you had better stop, or you'll go to the darkness below. You might even get exiled." Caitlin tries to keep her face as stern as possible, feeling like she should impress on the younger girl the gravity of her transgressions.

"They can't exile me for what I'm thinking. They don't know what I'm thinking."

"Thoughts become words," Caitlin quotes from *Our Book*. *"Words become actions, actions become habits. Tend to your thoughts, lest you find yourself fighting for something you never really believed in."*

"How do you know it all by heart?" Rosie says.

Caitlin shrugs. "I just do. I can remember things sometimes."

"But not what really counts," says Rosie, referring to Caitlin's failure to remember the wastelands.

"But not what really counts." Caitlin sighs.

After a moment, Rosie says quietly, "The ancestors don't answer any of my prayers anyway."

Caitlin glances at Rosie and sees that she is near tears. "Well, someday they will, maybe," she says soothingly.

"Yeah, if I pray for what they want me to pray for."

"Well...isn't that what you *should* be praying for?"

"That's not fair. That's like...like telling me I can have anything I want to eat and then only letting me pick from three boring things I've already had a hundred times."

Caitlin frowns, trying to digest this. "The ancestors love you," she says finally, limply.

"No they don't. They love my father. That's why he's still alive."

"They love everybody."

"Don't be ridiculous. Everyone knows they love the men more."

"Then why were women chosen to be the holy vessel for babies?" Caitlin says, parroting Pastor Saul's logic.

"Have you ever *seen* a woman have a baby?" snaps Rosie. "You call that *holy?*"

Caitlin is quiet, hugging her knees. The sound of crickets swells and recedes, swells and recedes, like shining ocean waves bringing in a tide. Rosie is an irritable child, everybody knows that, but Caitlin has never seen this lucid bitterness. "What else do you pray for?" she asks softly.

Rosie bends her head to Caitlin's. "I wish that it was summer all the time," she whispers back. "I wish that Father was dead, all of them were dead. I wish that I could live all on my own, with nobody around except some dogs and cats and goats. I wish that I could turn into a man."

Caitlin bows her head as well, so their foreheads almost touch, and she feels the short, silky hairs growing out of Rosie's temples tickling her skin. For a long time they listen to the faint night noises, taking deep breaths and sighing them out with longing so palpable it wraps around their throats.

Eventually Rosie rises. "I should go back to bed." Then she squats down again. "Does your father let you have the sleeping draft?"

Caitlin shakes her head. "No. I mean, he's so... well, he probably wouldn't notice if Mother gave it to me. But if he found out, he'd be angry."

Rosie narrows her eyes. "My father won't either. I don't know why. I don't know what it hurts."

Caitlin shrugs. "Most girls I know don't get to have it."

Rosie sighs and they are quiet for a moment. Then she says, "I hope Father doesn't come looking for me."

Caitlin nods. Then the thought that her father might come looking for *her* floods her brain, and she scrambles up the creaky roof and into her room breathlessly. It's not until she's huddled under the covers that she remembers he never comes this late. Still, she's so worked up that she stares out the window for hours, listening to her heart pound in her chest like it's clubbing her for her misdeeds. The next day she falls asleep in class and gets her palms slapped.

SUMMER

CHAPTER EIGHT

Caitlin

A thousand hands clapping once, a boot on a hollow rain barrel—the sound slithers over Caitlin and she jolts awake, sitting up in bed. She can't breathe. Slowly she realizes she's alone and safe, and her breaths lengthen. A finger drums the top of the roof, multiplying into a handful of fingers, bored boys in church, restless schoolgirls. Soon the beats are hard and fast and ringing. A laugh bubbles up in her throat, and she bites down hard to break it. It is raining. Summer is here.

For a while she doesn't move, afraid somehow that if she wakes Mother or Father, they will stop her. She knows they won't stop her—they can't—there's even a shalt-not. Every child has a summer, except Ella Moses, whose legs don't work because she fell off a roof a few months ago, and the really little children, on the breast or freshly off. But somehow she fears a huge weight coming down on her, to lie on her and keep her in her bed, slowly crushing the breath from her lungs until she is flattened like grass underfoot. Caitlin listens hard and hears Father snoring. He's not even awake. Slowly she creeps out of bed and opens the window.

Darkness and water mix to form a thick, whirling mass. She hears a scream, and then another, and then a chorus far off, the sound of escape. She holds a thin arm out the window and feels a rain so thick it's like putting her hand underwater. Standing there, she tries to think, tries to prepare, but there's nothing to prepare. She can just go.

Caitlin grabs her quilt, which is beautiful and pink and will be ruined before the night is through, and wraps it around her shoulders. Stepping quietly out of her room, she sees a black figure hunched before her, a ravening monster, and claps her hand over her mouth to catch her shriek. "I hope you'll be careful," says the beast, in Father's voice.

She nods, although he can't see it in the dark, and stands there. If he doesn't move, she may have to creep back into bed and pretend she didn't hear anything, that she's not even alive. But then he melts backwards, saying, "You know you could stay, if you wanted to..." In response, she simply gathers the ends of the quilt off the floor and runs so fast she almost falls over.

The rain hits her like a shovel. Standing still, Caitlin feels sheets of water pound her head and melt into her bones. The quilt immediately becomes sodden, weighing heavily on her shoulders. She takes one step, and her foot sinks into the newly formed muck. Memory kicks in, or some primal urge, and soon she is racing into the darkness with no idea of where she is going.

"Oof." Caitlin hits something soft and falls over. A body, small and wet like hers. A hand probes her face, feeling around her cheeks.

"Who's this?" a girl's voice says.

"Caitlin Jacob. Who's this?"

"Alice. Alice Joseph."

They pause for a moment, as if saying grace before a feast, and then simultaneously whoop and take off running, hand in hand. The quilt falls off one of Caitlin's shoulders and bounces along the ground, equally gleeful. Caitlin and Alice bump into the sides of buildings, into trees and fences, and finally collapse on the ground, laughing. Caitlin lifts her face to the sky and feels the water beat soft the fearful expression she knows she always bears.

"It feels like the end of the world!" says Alice, following Caitlin's lead and staring up into the source of all the water and joy.

"Maybe it is," says Caitlin. "Does the island attach to anything at the bottom, or does it just float?"

"I think it floats," Alice replies, and then laughs because her mouth is filling up with water.

"Let's run some more!" cries Caitlin, and they scramble up and run through what feels like an orchard, falling more times than she can count. She knows that she will be a black-and-blue mess tomorrow, but the mud will cover it. The quilt wraps around trunks and rocks, like it can't go any farther and is begging for rest, but Caitlin yanks it along to the sound of ripping wet cloth. Eventually Alice runs smack into a building and says, "I think it's a barn!"

"How do you know?"

"Smell it!" Caitlin sniffs but all she can smell is rain. "Should we go in?"

Caitlin wavers between visions of a warm hay bed and the thrill of running farther. Before she can say anything, they hear whoops in the other direction and dart toward them.

They play at finding one another, exchanging wild calls with the other group and running toward the sounds, figuring out when they've gone too far and running back. Eventually Caitlin bangs into someone and they go down in a tangle of arms and legs.

"Got you!" crows a voice she recognizes as that of Richard Abraham.

"No, I got *you!*" she corrects him, and starts trying to pin him down in the dark. He squirms and wriggles out of her grasp like a panicked fish, and his "Chase me!" drifts back to where Caitlin is lying. She rolls and slips and runs in his direction while he calls "Chase me! Chase me!" Finally she lunges and he falls down in front of her with a loud, wet smack.

"Not fair!" Richard cries happily, and tries to yank her quilt away. Caitlin yanks back, and they play tug-of-war in the rain until Caitlin wins, sliding backwards and falling on her rump. Richard slips by her, his cold wet flesh sliding on hers and disappearing.

"Mine!" she roars happily. She takes off running nowhere in particular, flailing her arms wildly in the dark and laughing louder than she would dare scream at home. It's summer, and the quilt is hers, the lavish rain is hers, the brimming joyous night is hers. And there are many more days and nights to come.

CHAPTER NINE

Janey

Janey feels slowly breathing flesh curled inside the curve of her sleeping body. She is draped around her sister, Mary, like a blanket of bones and skin. Opening her eyes, she sees a grassy sea, drenched and aromatic, splotched with dark puddles. Blinking, she glances down at Mary's body. Her nightgown is half torn away like she was mauled by a monster, her legs painted garishly in mud and bruises and grass stains. Stretching her hands toward the sunrise, Janey sees they are scratched brown and laced with blood. She is naked already, her graceful, freckled legs and arms caked with dirt and coagulating scabs. Closing her eyes again, she yawns and shifts her body like a satisfied dog settling in for a nap. Janey looks peaceful when she sleeps. When her eyelids veil her restless eyeballs, she looks like what she is: a too-thin seventeen-year-old, stunted and overgrown at the same time, with flaming orange hair. When her eyes open, she turns into something else completely. Her eyes kindle with fire, one that is warm and inviting but is just waiting to shoot lines of flame across the wooden floor and burn your house down.

"Good morning, sleepy." She hears a whisper and opens her eyes to see Mary's lovely green ones beaming into hers. Smiling, she settles her head against her hands and gazes at Mary's face. Mary is thirteen, still a child, but not for long. Her cheekbones and full mouth hint at womanhood, and her body is soft and slender, but rounding. Janey tries to keep her from eating, to yank her back from falling into the

57

abyss of adulthood, but Mary can't cope with hunger like Janey can. Janey absorbs hunger into herself, riding the wave of white-hot pleading in her body until it fades to a glow that warms her blood. Mary gets hungry and eats apples behind Janey's back.

Janey's not sure how long she can go without coming to fruition, but she hopes it's forever. She can't imagine herself with a husband, cooking dinner, looking up into a man's face, or lying with her legs spread apart, screaming a new life into the world. Just thinking about it makes the world darken a few shades. *Never. Death first.* She glances at Mary, who has fallen asleep again, breathing deep sighs, her eyeballs roaming under their lids.

She turns her gaze to the sodden yellow field, where countless small feet have made holes and puddles. There is always a strange peace the morning after the first rain, when all the children are asleep and the island is swimming in rainwater. Morning fog hangs creamy and thick, a cool quilt pulled over the treetops. Occasional butterflies float by in lapis and gold and orange, clapping their wings together briefly and sailing on unseen currents of wind. Birds cheep tentatively, like they're asking a question, unsure if they'll be answered by another downpour.

Janey and Mary will find some of the other children later, band up and figure out who their friends will be this time, but the first night of summer they always spend by themselves. Janey likes to run until they reach the shore, then plunge into the water and splash around. "I'm leaving!" she'll cry. "I'm swimming away!" Mary only goes in up to her waist, even though the water is pleasantly cool and seems to suck at her slightly, drawing her in. Everyone knows that there are monsters lurking under the deeper water, hungry for girlflesh.

Last night Mary stayed half underwater, half deluged by rain. Janey finally emerged from the water, panting, her skin blushing with chill, and flopped onto the wet sand. "Someday I will," she breathed into the rain hurling at her face.

"You'll swim." Mary laughed.

"I'll hold a knife to the ferryman," said Janey. "I'll kill him unless he takes us across."

Janey and Mary have both spied on the ferryman from the rushes near the dock, watching while the wanderers board. He has a face like a stone, cracked and sharp and pitted, sprouting white hairs like a strange moss. His odd hat is perched low and hides his eyes in shadow, but his hands are strong and tense, roped with gray veins. Most of the children don't think of him as alive the way everyone else is alive. Janey can usually make people do what she wants them to, but she is stymied as to how she would ever force him to do anything.

Banishing such a grave thought on the first summer night, she opened her mouth and drank the rainwater, coughing and sputtering, then swallowing and talking wildly about finding her own island to live on. "I'll swim and find a better one," she said. "Only you and me."

"What will we eat?" asked Mary, smiling at one of her favorite games.

"We will eat chicken and apples," Janey said grandly.

"What if there are no chickens and apples?"

"Then we'll eat . . . goats and spinach."

"Ugh. What if there are no goats and spinach?"

"Then we'll eat fish and potatoes."

"What if there are no fish and potatoes?"

"Then we'll eat . . ." She paused. "Dogs and corn."

Mary started giggling. "I don't want to eat a dog!"

"Eggs and corn, then."

"What if there are no eggs and corn?"

"Then we'll eat dirt and stones."

Mary's giggling increased in pitch, in anticipation. "What if there are no dirt and stones?"

"Then I'll eat . . ." She drew it out. "You!" When Mary heard the word she leapt up and ran, screaming, and Janey chased her into the water.

While Janey is smiling widely, remembering their splashing

struggle, Mary begins moaning and grumbling, flipping over and shoving her back into Janey again. "I have so many bruises," Mary informs her, stretching.

"I have more," Janey answers, yawning and twitching her skin like a goat shedding a fly.

"Not true!"

"True!"

They bolt up, examining their legs and pointing out bruises that could easily be patches of mud. Mary reaches over to wipe the mud off Janey's legs to prove her point, and Janey starts wiping at hers. They start giggling, since their hands are equally filthy, and Janey hears Mary's stomach rumble.

"Let's go see what they left," Mary says. "I want some breakfast."

Janey sighs inwardly, but doesn't want to ruin the peaceful morning. "Fine," she says tautly, trying not to snap at her sister. Reaching up, she takes a piece of bark off a nearby tree so she can shred it with her fingernails. It peels off with the grateful ease of sunburnt skin.

The nearest house is the Sauls', tucked behind a boulder and shaded by a few larger, white-and-black trees. As they approach, the Saul dog Goldie lopes over to lick Mary's face with his paws on her chest. Janey pats her stomach happily, and Goldie throws himself on her with glee. Running her fingers behind his ear, she carefully pulls a flea off his neck and crushes it.

"Soon there won't be any dogs out," says Mary.

"No," says Janey, who is now scratching his rump so he twists back and forth with pleasure, ears back and tongue lolling. "We should enjoy them while we can." She kisses Goldie's nose, and he snorts and bathes her face with his tongue.

The Sauls' doorstep is of no use, as Goldie or some other hungry creature pushed over the dish cover and ate whatever was there. They walk through their fields and to the Abrahams', who have a plate lying under a deep, inverted clay bowl. On the plate are small, cold boiled potatoes. Mary eats two with her dirty hands. Janey plays with

Goldie's ears and gives him a potato, then reluctantly gulps half of one as a concession to her ever-brewing hunger. Janey likes that the adults have to feed them during summer, even if she won't eat much of anything. It makes her feel powerful, like she's an ancestor who has to be appeased, or a wanderer receiving tribute.

"You have to eat more, Janey," Mary says.

"I'm fine," Janey replies absently, finding another flea. "I had a bite."

"One bite," retorts Mary.

"I'll eat Goldie's fleas," Janey answers, smiling, and then wanders to the Abrahams' rain barrel, using a bucket to take a few swallows.

Mary rolls her eyes and accepts the bucket, gulping down the fresh water. "Come on, let's keep going."

Hand in hand, they walk through fields bent from the rain, the crops inclined backwards like parishioners observing a sky-bound miracle. The acrid, weighty scent of human and animal fertilizer has long since melted into something sweeter and dustier. A pen of goats is already netted over by a responsible farmer, and they pass by shut-up houses with empty dishes on their front steps. Janey spots a figure moving, and points, and then she and Mary are running. It's only Melanie and John Joseph, but soon they're chasing after them.

It's the second summer since Amanda became a woman, and Janey still feels the strange void left in her absence. She is furious at Amanda for abandoning her, although part of her knows she's being illogical. She begged Amanda not to eat, to make her childhood last, to stay with her, but Amanda shrugged and said, "How else am I going to get out of my house?"

Janey hasn't spoken to Amanda since her summer of fruition. When she passes her, Janey looks away sharply, almost violently. As Mary's pace increases, Janey tries to forget Amanda and focus on chasing other friends, who are filthy and full and ready to run.

CHAPTER TEN

Amanda

Summer is here, and Amanda is indoors, hating herself for sniveling about the heat and insects like the rest of them.

More than a year ago now, Amanda had, like Nancy, lain in her bed and cried as her summer of fruition approached. In a stroke of luck, she'd started bleeding just before the prior summer ended. Dark blood had spotted and then streaked through the black mud on her thighs, terrifying the boys, fascinating the girls, and calling forth every mosquito in creation until she rinsed herself and slapped on more mud.

With this fortuitous timing, she had an extra year to mature and prepare, much more than girls like Janice Saul, who had started bleeding in May and was still small as a child when she went off to her summer of fruition. It also meant a year of peaceful sleep in her bed, for now Father could not touch her. But she was still terrified, for her body was about to be loosed into a world of men and motherhood and blood. She didn't dare talk of her fear with any of her friends, worried about seeming weak, or discovering that everyone else she knew was thrilled about the whole thing. She raised her head and pretended a lack of concern, and at night lay awake, her hands wringing and her teeth peeling strips of flesh, delicate as onionskin, from her lips.

It was tradition for a girl's mother to escort her—or drag her—to the house where the summer of fruition began. Amanda's mother may have hated her daughter, but she also insisted on upholding appearances. That morning, as Amanda performed her usual ablutions with trembling hands, brushing her hair until it shone and scrubbing her teeth with salt, stopping to empty her bladder every five minutes, Father sobbed in his bedroom. She hated the sounds he was making, childish and raw and intrusive, and had to bite her tongue not to scream at him to shut up.

When she emerged in her church dress, Mother was staring out the window, her arms crossed around herself. Elias was nowhere to be seen. Amanda wondered if Father was going to dry his tears and come give her one last embrace, but the sobs from the bedroom continued. Mother turned to examine Amanda, letting her flinty eyes travel from the neat braids to the clean leather clogs, and sniffed. "Well," she said. "Let's go."

As Amanda began walking silently a few paces behind Mother, she wished for the hundredth time that she had a normal mother, one who might whisper words of encouragement or wisdom. Amanda knew that if nobody was watching, Mother would skip with glee like a summer child to finally be getting rid of her—but then again, maybe not. Amanda's summer of fruition was Mother's first step toward death. When Amanda had children, her parents only had until the wanderers deemed Father no longer useful, and then they would drink their final draft and be buried in the fields. It usually didn't take long, particularly for those who made their living with their bodies. Father never complained, but she saw him limp sometimes and knew which shoulder was his bad one. Sometimes old men, terrified of leaving the world, worked even as they cried and screamed with pain, until a wanderer came to counsel them into a quiet death.

Amanda saw muddy children streaking across the horizon like fish leaping, and closer, two children ran past and then stopped, so suddenly that one bumped into the other. "It's Amanda," whispered one of them, and they took hands and stared at her as she slowly passed, as if she were an otherworldly being or exotic beast. They were probably thankful they weren't her. She would be thankful to be them.

When they neared the Aarons' house, Mother took her arm tensely as they walked. Amanda half expected Mother to bend her head and begin muttering gibberish, pretending to offer support she had no inclination to give. Unused to the feel of Mother's skin, Amanda was surprised at its slackness and dryness, and had to fight to keep from pulling her arm away. They stopped near the door.

"Good-bye, Amanda," said Mother primly.

"Mother?" said Amanda, and Mother turned to face her. Fighting not to let her fear show itself, Amanda felt a tear slide down her cheek and said despairingly, "Do you have anything to tell me?"

Mother's mouth tightened. "What would I have to tell you?" she asked, her eyes narrow and dismissive.

Amanda shook off Mother's arm like she might a stinging insect. Taking a deep breath, she lifted her chin and left Mother gratefully behind.

She opened the door slowly, hoping she wouldn't cry or scream or otherwise embarrass herself while everyone else sipped tea and stared in astonishment. Taking a deep breath, she walked into a group of about fifteen girls her age, some huddled on the floor, some embracing bravely, and one vomiting in the corner.

Looking back, Amanda admires how Renata Aaron handled them. She cleaned them up, calmed them down, and sat them on the floor with cake and milk.

"I want all you girls to know that none of you will be forced to do anything," said Mrs. Aaron. Some of the girls sighed in relief, but Amanda didn't quite believe her. "I also want you to know that for the first month there is to be no physical contact whatsoever. I mean it. You will get to know these fine young men through nothing more than conversation."

"What happens after a month?" asked Ursula Solomon, her mouth ringed with crumbs.

"We will meet again and decide what to do," said Mrs. Aaron cheerfully.

At their age, twelve and thirteen and fourteen, a month was still a lifetime. The girls shifted and glanced at one another, seeking permission to relax their posture and unclench their teeth.

"Now, remember you can't marry someone with the same last name as you," said Mrs. Aaron, "so you might not want to waste time talking to them, although it's always nice to be friendly. And nobody who is a father, son, uncle, or brother to anyone in your family. That's the rule. Even if you love them and want to marry them. So don't love them."

"What if we can't help it?" said Jennifer Abraham, and someone else giggled faintly.

"Well," said Mrs. Aaron sweetly, "I suggest you ignore them. There is no point in fanning a fire which must be put out."

There was a pause, and she continued. "I want you to know that all the young men who have come of age and are ready for marriage are kind and gentle men. You don't need to worry about anyone hurting you, or being cruel to you." Nobody looked at Paula Moses, who had fresh fingerprint bruises around her wrists. "Kind and gentle men," repeated Mrs. Aaron emphatically.

If they're all kind and gentle men, then how did Paula Moses's father get married? thought Amanda, and Mrs. Aaron glared at her as if she had spoken aloud.

"As you know," said Mrs. Aaron, "you will be spending each night in a different household, moving from house to house during the day. Everyone is thrilled to have you. I am but the first of many women who will help and guide you.

"You will travel as a group, always having each other, and the men will join you at the end of the day when they are finished working. You will spend the whole night together. I want you to be respectful of other people's homes and not break anything, or try to hurt anyone."

Amanda wonders who, in the past, has broken things and hurt people.

"Now, are there any questions?" asks Mrs. Aaron.

The girls glance at one another. The idea of raising a hand and asking a question when faced with such a massive, enormous unknown is laughable. Where would they start? But then Ursula pipes up, "What if I don't like any of the men?"

"Well," said Mrs. Aaron, "I find that unlikely. Every girl who goes through her summer of fruition finds a husband."

But they don't necessarily like them, thinks Amanda.

All the girls, at one time or another during past summers, have hoisted themselves up to a window to watch a summer of fruition. Even in the first month of summer, they'd seen what happens, which completely belied what Mrs. Aaron was saying. But they wanted desperately to believe her. They had a month, and anything could happen in a month. They could run away, change, die. So they let themselves be soothed, and accepted seconds of cake, and put their heads close together to whisper.

There seemed to be a collective intake of breath upon the entrance of the men, brought in early on the first day. Some of the girls huddled close as if preparing to defend themselves, but the men were so polite and quiet that even the most frightened girls soon relaxed. Andrew told Amanda later that Mr. Aaron had given them a speech beforehand, comparing the girls to frightened mice. "You need to calm and charm a frightened mouse," he told them. "What are you going to do? Stomp in there and grab the one you want? They'll bolt in a second. They might even bite you! You need to tiptoe in there and barely even look at them. Offer them food and drink the way you might offer your ancestor a meal if he showed up at your door. Lie down on the floor and show your belly, if it helps them think you're not there to eat them."

The first night was all gentle talk as the men ceremoniously and submissively offered the girls more slices of honey cake or cups of milk. Even more surprisingly, they seemed to be genuinely interested in the everyday details of the girls' lives. The youngest of the men was at least seventeen; having an adult so fascinated by their childish chatter was like being drunk for the first time. All the men were so handsome, tall and bright-eyed with luxuriant beards. Soon some of the braver girls were giggling and playful.

That night, after the men left, the girls huddled together, whispering about who they'd liked and who they hadn't, what they'd talked about, who would make the best husband. The next day they walked en masse to Callan Moses's house, shrieking at the rain and blackened children, and then delighting in the desserts that awaited them. Honey was precious on the island, and they'd never experienced such an explosion of sweetness. Janice, who couldn't stop crying and vomiting and curling up in corners, was given a special drink by Mrs. Moses to "help her relax." It made her calm and cheerful and unable to walk quite straight. When it wore off and she started sobbing again, she got more. She was the first to lie down under one of the men, giggling and hiccupping, her eyes glossy and dark. It was Thomas Joseph who took her, caressing her like she was something precious and new, while she stared at the ceiling in a syrup-sweet haze. The girls, talking to the other men, were too embarrassed to watch outright. They threw quick, fascinated glances toward the rutting couple, while the men shifted and stared and stepped a little closer to the girls they were looming over.

By the end of the first week, Amanda sat on Dale Joseph's lap and kissed him. By the end of the second week, she was running through a room of Byron Jacob's house with no clothes on, laughing at four pursuing men and promising herself to the one who caught her. The girls had discovered the power they had, the power to make men crawl and beg. They could say yes or no and the men would listen; they could play with them like pets or puppets. The men wanted to please their future wives, make them desire their strange male bodies with swelling muscles and heavy, dark, almost comical genitalia. The girls crawled over the men like curious animals, experimenting, examining, sniffing, biting. A couple of girls found the act of love repulsive and submitted with the stiff, resigned faces of old women shouldering a heavy load. To Amanda's surprise, a few men actually seemed to prefer this sullen submission.

Amanda found sex with the men intoxicating, whereas before her summer of fruition sex had only been wearisome. There were certain aspects, however, she could not stand. She hated a man's full weight on her and she didn't like being touched on her throat. The worst was being surprised out of sleep by a lustful hand. She bit Garrett Jacob badly when he tried to slide fingers over her breast in the night, waking to him cradling a bleeding palm and glaring at her. Embarrassed and guilty, she apologized and let him do whatever he wanted with her later—acts she was pretty sure the ancestors would have disapproved of.

One night she awoke to sobbing. This had been a common sound during the first few days, but most of the girls had gotten over weeping for their lost childhood. Those who did were quiet, curled up on their sides to sleep, a few tears running slowly from their eyelids to the floor. Crawling naked, Amanda found the source of the sound: Janice was wedged into the corner of the room, trembling like she used to.

"Janice," she whispered. "What is it?"

Janice tried to speak, but couldn't. Some sleepy man mumbled a protest at the noise, and Janice plastered shaking palms over her mouth and nose like she was trying to suffocate herself. Amanda crept next to her and pulled Janice's body to hers. It was strange, the feeling of a girl's skin on her own instead of a man's, the softness and smoothness and comfort of it. Janice put her head on Amanda's collarbone, and her hot tears gathered in the tiny hollow there. "I can't do this," she said.

"What do you mean?" said Amanda. "You're doing a wonderful job. You were the first one, don't you remember? All the men love you."

"I don't remember, not really," said Janice. "I've been drinking whatever they've been giving me, and everything seems all right, but

69

then it wears off and I'm back to being me again. And I can't do this. I just can't."

"But Janice," said Amanda, "I mean, how did you...before? I mean surely you have before." She flushes in the dark.

"I have never," said Janice. "I mean, not like this."

"Oh," said Amanda, too surprised to pry further. "Well."

"I just," said Janice, her voice rising, "I need to leave, I need to get away." She put her hands on Amanda's. "Will you come with me? Can we run away?"

The urge that rose in Amanda's throat was choking in its bright impossibility, its vivid promise. "But, Janice, where would we go?"

There was a long silence, and then Janice said, "I need more of that drink. I need it now." Amanda could feel Janice's heartbeat, thrumming into vibrations like the wings of a hummingbird.

"Wait," said Amanda, and although she was pretty sure she wasn't supposed to, she woke Mrs. Solomon, their current host.

"What is it?" asked Mrs. Solomon blurrily. "Is someone hurt?"

"It's Janice," said Amanda. "She's...not well."

"Oh, the one who's being dosed," said Mrs. Solomon. "Surely she's over it by now?"

"She's not," said Amanda, and again, "She's not well."

Mrs. Solomon rose with some grumps and grunts, and walked with Amanda to Janice's corner. She took Janice's clenched fist in her capable hands.

"Janice," said Mrs. Solomon quietly. "You're a woman now. This is what women do. This is how you get married, and have babies."

"I don't," said Janice, hiccupping, "think I want to be a woman."

"My goodness, dear," said Mrs. Solomon. "As if you had a choice."

Janice burst into fresh tears, and Amanda saw exasperation on Mrs. Solomon's face, but also sadness and concern. "Darling, were you hurt? Did one of the men hurt you? You need to tell me if they did."

Janice shook her head rapidly. "I barely even remember most of it."

"Then why the tears?"

"I just...I just..." She trailed away, hunting for an explanation for her distress. "I just want things to be like they were before. I want a normal summer."

"Soon you will have children, who will have the summers you once did," said Mrs. Solomon.

"Do you miss it, Mrs. Solomon?" asked Amanda suddenly. "Summer?"

A flash of pain darted across Mrs. Solomon's sun-lined face. "We all do, dear," she said, sighing, "but one can't be a child forever. Wait here, girls, I'll be back. You're lucky I have the ingredients; some men don't even like it in their house." Janice lay against Amanda quietly, her muscles twitching. Soon Mrs. Solomon came back and quietly offered Janice a cup filled with strong-smelling liquid.

Janice stared at it, her child's face suddenly looking thin and old, and then grabbed the cup with both hands and gulped the contents down. Taking a deep breath, she closed her eyes, waiting for the drug to take over. Amanda reached for the cup, sniffed it, and licked out the bitter dregs.

By the end of the summer, they were tired. Tired of moving between houses, tired of sleeping curled up next to the other girls, tired of wildness and play. Their nights with the men had moved from frantic sex to gentle conversations and even shared naps. The men had to go back to their regular lives during the day, farming or potting or whatever their families did, and their faces were drawn from lack of sleep. It was in this drowsy time that Amanda and Andrew started talking. She found him shy and funny, and liked the crow's feet he was already developing, the shocking white streak in his dark hair.

She remembers lying parallel to Andrew—she can't remember which house they were in—breathing in each other's breath and exhaling it back to its birthplace. His callused hand stroked her slowly, tracing the arc of her hip and the trough of her waist, perusing her ribs one by one to her damp armpit, and then starting its way back again. His fingers left a surge of pleasantly prickled skin in their wake, her nerves purring and calming. For Amanda, this was the most pleasurable act of the summer so far.

His smell was alien, brutal, intoxicating: notes of soil, copper, leeks, and the fine dust that gathers on the coats of animals. She raised a finger and ran it down his cheek. He smiled and kissed her fingertip, then closed his eyes.

Looking into his face, Amanda tried to imagine him as her husband. The summer had been so frenetic and tumultuous that it had barely occurred to her that she would be someone's wife when it ended. She had pictured herself in free fall, in a dizzy tangle of sex and sweets that would last forever.

Soon frost would come and muddy, red-eyed children would start returning home. She would put up her hair—she knew how, the girls had practiced endlessly the entire summer—and walk out into the world an adult. Her metamorphosis was complete: she already felt more staid, heavy, treading firmly on the ground.

What would she do as a woman? Have children, of course. Care for the house. Lie under her husband. Talk about boring things that didn't mean much. Suddenly, despite her years of desperation to escape him, she missed her father keenly. He was the only one who ever really talked to her. He was the only one who ever knew her.

Feeling her muscles tense, Andrew opened his eyes. "What's wrong?"

"I don't want to get married," she confessed in a revelatory whisper.

A frown drew a divot between his eyebrows. "Well, we don't have to," he replied slowly.

"No, no, I mean at all. I don't want to get married at all."

He raised himself up on one elbow, and she rolled onto her back. "What do you want to do, then?" He put a hand between her breasts, as if to feel her heartbeat and ensure she was hale.

She thought. The silence crawled up her ankles, lapped at her knees, enveloped her waist, and then drew itself tightly over her face like a suffocating sheet. There was no sensible answer to his question. She just stared at him.

"Do you know what I'm looking forward to about being married?" he asked.

She shook her head dumbly.

"Waking up in the morning," he said, "with my wife next to me." He put his hand on her cheek and she could feel herself trembling.

She wondered, *Do I want to marry him? I don't not want to marry him. I'd rather marry him than marry any of the other men.*

She groped for her voice and gasped softly, "My parents didn't sleep in the same bed."

"Well, later, I suppose." He shrugged. "So much to do. Children to distract you."

She blinked.

He reached out his free arm and drew her to him. She felt his taut, hairy body graze her naked skin.

"Imagine, we could wake up like this every morning," he murmured. And even though she knew it would never be the same, that they would lack the soft, sweltering warmth of summertime, the faint breathing of sleeping friends, the sweetness coating their teeth, the blissful and ragged weight of sleeplessness, she still leaned toward him in agreement.

They weren't the first to agree to marry, or the last. There was a wanderer's daughter, Flora Saul, in the mix that year, and she was almost immediately won over by the handsome, quick-witted Ryan Joseph. The two girls with swollen breasts and morning nausea were also sought after early. Proven fertility was a valuable asset, worth never quite knowing who fathered your eldest child. Several girls had been picked out by the men long before at church or neighborly dinners and were doggedly pursued until captured. The men left over had to decide between the girls nobody else had wanted. In the end, the three unengaged men looked at drugged Janice, hideous Wilma, and Beth, whose sister had had three defectives, and they made their decisions. There was a man for every girl, and even if they weren't thrilled at picking through leftovers, it was better than having no wife at all.

When Amanda finally said good-bye to the other girls, with whom she had bickered and embraced and laughed and whispered, she felt lucky. She hadn't been forced to settle for someone she disliked; Andrew was strong, capable, and affectionate. Most importantly, she could finally escape home. While she waited for the wedding day, held when the first leaf turned, she simply pretended she wasn't there. When Mother yelled, she didn't hear it, her thoughts full of her future with Andrew. If Father tried to gather her up in his arms, just for a quick hug, she barely acknowledged him.

When Andrew carried her over his doorstep, she laughed and kissed his forehead. It took several anxious months to get pregnant, but when she did, his joy was her joy.

Now the memory of his joy has a dirty sheen clinging to its surface, a dark tone she can't scrub away. Back then, vomiting and tired and full of new life, she thought she'd had everything she ever wanted.

She was wrong. She feels so consumed by terror, she's not sure if there's anything left of her. She lies still and limp like damp straw. Inside of her, her daughter is rolling around, swimming happily in a pool of blood and seawater. Her daughter knows nothing but wetness and darkness and muffled sounds. Her daughter keeps her awake. Summer is here, and she is trapped in the bed, trapped under the weight of her child. Amanda thinks of Janey, three years older than her, dirt coating her straight, blameless body. She feels a stab of envy so sharp she curls up against herself and tries not to scream.

CHAPTER ELEVEN

Vanessa

On the fifth day of summer the mosquitoes come sudden like the rains, except instead of falling from the sky, they rise up from the ground. In veils of humming gold they sweep the landscape, falling to feed from anything with blood in its veins. The good farmers have already netted the sheep and goat pens; the lazy ones are running and cursing, slapping themselves with one hand and hanging nets with the other. The dogs yipe and whine and run indoors, shaking clusters of insects from their eyes and noses. The cats disappear to the mysterious airtight nooks and passages where cats go, or those who are more tolerant of people lounge indoors, accepting pats of butter and scraps of chicken with a resigned and deserving air. The children throw themselves into the puddled mud, rolling and shrieking and rubbing it on their faces and hair. They end up caked with clay armor, which they endlessly reapply to the creases of elbows and knees and buttocks.

They laugh at themselves, rolling and wriggling in the mud like worms, baring their teeth white against dark faces. Mosquitoes dive into them and probe uselessly, clinging to filthy skin like tiny iridescent feathers. Vanessa often wonders what the mosquitoes live on, since all the people, dogs, and livestock are either indoors or protected, save for mad dashes to empty summer pots into the outhouse. Perhaps the rabbits and rats. She asked Mr. Abraham once, but he had no idea. Father would know. But it's summer, and she doesn't have to think about him for months.

Father always has an air of cheerful resignation before summer. "I ran about like a maniac, so you might as well too," he says. He teases Mother about bloodying some girl's nose when they were both children, and she shakes her head. His voice switches to his lecture tone, slightly louder with brassier vowels. "Summers are the cornerstone of our society," he says grandly. "They keep the family working. If you didn't get a taste of freedom, you would break down in a year."

"James," Mother says, frowning, her gaze on the floor.

"Don't eat rotten food," Father warned Vanessa right before the rains came. "Drink rainwater only. Don't fight too much, you'll get hurt. Don't get mud up inside yourself. Come home if you get sick."

Vanessa nodded obediently. Nobody goes home when they get sick. Last year, Alicia Solomon got a cough that turned into a fever, and then she started hacking up bloody phlegm. She lay shivering for days, tossing and calling out, and sweated so much the mud ran off her in rivulets. Her brother had to slap off the mosquitoes and endlessly pack the mud back on. One of Alicia's eyes turned scarlet. She looked so terrifying that the youngest children ran off screaming when she looked at them. But she didn't go home, and nobody tried to make her go home. Eventually she arose, shaky and headachy, and her eye faded to shell-pink and then to white again.

With the dogs and people and animals all huddled behind barriers, the world outside seems much bigger. The houses shrink to small boxes, while the fields stretch and yawn wider, and the trees unfurl toward the sky. Even the horizon seems longer somehow, with more sea and shore. The children are the only ones who can walk free, and they grow too, towering over their domain.

Chelsea Moses makes the best cake on the island, and every morning she puts one out, frosted with butter and honey and apple cider. She says she does it for the children, but Vanessa is convinced she does it because she loves watching them fight. Many children hunker down to sleep within view of the doorstep so they can be on alert in the early morning, and after her skirt swishes back inside they wait a beat, then run for it. With twenty or so children aiming for one cake, it quickly turns into warfare. A few mornings Vanessa participates, not only because she loves sweets, but because she loves the fury of dragging at arms and legs with bare hands, punching slick faces, leaping over bodies to grab a handful of frosting. She eats more mud than cake, but it's sweet with rich crumbs, and sometimes salty with blood from a split lip. Vanessa knows she should start starving herself like Janey, but the thought of going without that amalgam of dirt and honey and blood is too much to bear.

After the children disperse, Vanessa runs to the tallest tree on the island, a sycamore, and climbs it. She likes its three-pronged leaves, and the patchy bark that looks like it has a rash. She hopes that someday it will grow tall enough that she can see the wastelands. Father says it must have roots that go miles deep, because otherwise it would fall over in a storm. As it is, when the wind blows, it sways as gently as a hawk on a current, rustling like a faraway river.

Vanessa adores climbing. She likes to pretend she's a monkey, which she's never seen in real life, but Father has a book with pictures of them. She imagines they move like her, arms and legs held wide, paddling up the branches. The monkey is her favorite animal except for the horse, with its long comical face, and graceful neck arched like a rainbow.

Father made her promise not to tell anyone about anything she reads, but Vanessa finds it boring to talk about her forbidden knowledge only with him. Sometimes she'll try to draw a deer in the dirt, and explains to other children how it runs fast and flips up its tail, but when she goes back home and looks at the real picture, she realizes none of them would know a deer if they saw it. They would be envisioning an animal with wavering legs, two eyes on the same side of its head, so fat it would collapse immediately under its own weight.

At the top of the tree she stretches and strains her neck, but all she can see is water and a cloud bank. The problem with waiting for the tree to grow is that she is growing too, putting on weight and building bone. Soon she'll become a woman, and then she'll never be able to climb trees again. She's never seen an adult climb a tree. Perhaps they would break the branches away and plummet to the ground in an ungainly heap.

Vanessa watches the fog flow and dance and fray, slow and thick like blood in water. She hears her own heart beating, and her breath, and realizes there are no mosquitoes up here to whine their summer song. She starts imitating their hum in her highest voice and then sings a psalm from church, substituting nonsense words because she doesn't want to think about Pastor Saul. "Oh, for the fooooog," she calls, "and the dog, and the mosquitoes on a log. Someday it will snow but now, oh no! Cake and potatoes, potatoes and cake, not for a defective, so nice to make! Up all alone, so far from home, singing a song, wish I could stay long, sing my summer song." She stops singing and listens to the faint echoes of children playing. Gathering her courage, she raises her voice gleefully and sings Father's favorite swear word, which would get her smacked if any adult heard her say it. "So fuck! Fuck! Fuck you, Father and Mother, fuck you, little brother, fuck all the others, fuck the ferry and the fog, fuck school and fuck church and fuck the ancestors and fuck fruition, fuck you, fuck the island too." She pauses, waiting for wrathful ancestors to swarm forth like angry bees, or for the tree and the ground to fall away while she hurtles into the darkness below. A bird chirps. Heartened, she swears and sings until her voice becomes hoarse. Then she inches out on a smaller branch, squats, and patters urine down on the lower branches, half hoping nobody is below her, but also half hoping they are. Creeping back, she settles her hips into a curve on the tree and stares at the open sky. She won't have to leave until she needs something to eat, and that could be a long time.

CHAPTER TWELVE

Amanda

Amanda never paid enough attention to what her mother did at home. But after marrying Andrew, she found herself in a house—*her* house—that she was meant to sweep when she'd never used a broom, with dinners she was expected to cook when she didn't know how to build a fire. Other girls learned these things soon after they learned to walk, but Mother had scorned to teach her, preferring to take care of the house herself while Amanda wandered wild.

Everything she did after her marriage, even everyday moments, seemed strange. She had to wear calf-length dresses and walk instead of run, had to gather and knot her hair on her crown—not in practice, but for real—had to smile and greet adults instead of heedlessly passing them by. When she saw her old friends who were her age, but hadn't yet had their summer of fruition, she had to smile at them like an adult smiles at a child. She hated it, and could tell that they hated her.

Not that she wanted to go back to Mother's hatred and Elias's blank stares and Father's heavy embraces. She loved Andrew and wanted to be his wife. But she wanted to run and shout, and sling her arms around her friends, and sleep on the shore too.

The nights were strange and hectic, Andrew's touch familiar yet strangely foreign and confusing. After he went to sleep, she often had trembling fits, waves of shivering bowling her over like a strong wind. They'd had lots of sex during the summer of fruition, but now, in a marriage bed, it felt wrong. Sometimes she went outside and walked in the cold dirt barefoot, staring at the white moon shining through the fog. For the first few months, she only slept after she felt Andrew get up and go to the kitchen in the morning. Then she was slammed face-first into a dark sleep like someone shoving her into the dirt, and didn't arise until the early afternoon.

Uncertainly, she'd push the broom around the floor until dust was moved from one corner to another. Then she'd try to mend something, or cook something, and Andrew would come home to find her lost under a pile of cloth or vegetables. She loved that he always laughed and pulled her to her feet, and wore the badly mended clothes, and ate the inedible dishes. She loved him until they blew out the lanterns, and then she wanted to creep away on her belly like something boneless and primitive.

Three months after she married Andrew, Father came to visit. He had stayed away, which surprised Amanda, who had expected more contact from him. (She didn't expect anything from Mother and Elias, and they barely even acknowledged her at church.)

Then, just when it was getting cold enough to frost over, Father showed up at the door with a smile and a dead rabbit. Amanda had never skinned a rabbit before, and Father sat at the table and watched as she sawed and winced and pulled the pearlescent sheets of membrane, which stretched taut and snapped into dull white gristle as cold maroon blood ran thickly over the edges of the table and onto the floor.

"I miss you, Amanda," Father said as he got a cloth and knelt to wipe up the florid spatters. "I have nobody to talk to anymore."

"You know you can always visit," she replied, her fingers sliding over slimy ribbons of vein and tumescent, slippery muscle. "I'm surprised you haven't before."

"Your mother doesn't like it."

"That's not surprising."

"She says that now you're out of the family, I should treat you like anyone else."

Amanda frowned. "But people still visit their children, and everyone has their mothers help them when the first baby comes." She paused. "Although I'd rather get advice from a goat."

"Are you pregnant?" His voice quavered a bit.

"I don't think so." She and Andrew were starting to be concerned, after three months of regular bleeding every time the moon went dark.

There was a long silence. Amanda had stripped the skin from the rabbit's back and belly but was having trouble getting it to detach from the joints and tiny paws. It writhed and pulled wetly in her fists. She wondered if she was supposed to cut the head off, and felt a wave of irritation at Father for not offering more help.

"It's so strange to think of you having a baby," he said. He was staring at the carnage heaped on the table, his hands twisting between his knees.

"It is strange," she agreed, and sat at the table with him. Her dress was stained crimson at her waist, her arms encased in sleeves of dried gore. "I'll have to scrub this dress with soap. Hopefully the stains will come out of the floor," she said, trying to speak lightly.

Father nodded, looking away and shifting in his chair. "Couldn't Andrew show you how to butcher a rabbit?"

Couldn't you? she wanted to snap, but said, "I don't know. If not, one of the wives can."

"I suppose." He took the cloth she was wiping her hands on and played with the edges, reddening the tips of his fingers. The sight made her stomach turn. "It's a shame your mother didn't show you more, before you left."

"She hates me," said Amanda. "You know that. I'm out of the house now, though, so I don't have to care about her anymore."

"I wish you weren't."

"Weren't what?"

"Out of the house."

"I'm glad I am."

He winced like she'd slapped him. His forehead creasing, he stared at her. "You're glad?" he said. "You're happy? Completely happy?"

Amanda's mind drifted to nighttime, and how she snuck out of the house to see the moon, standing until her feet went numb. "Not *completely* happy, but I love Andrew, and I'm sure I'll get better at all the things I'm supposed to do."

"You look so much older with your hair up."

"It feels strange. Like I was wearing the same clothes for years, and somebody took them away from me."

He nodded. "That's how I feel without you."

"How is Elias?" she asked, suddenly wanting to change the subject. "Has he started working with you yet?"

"Somewhat. I don't think he likes it. He told me he wants to be a fisherman."

"Well, fishermen have sons too," she said flatly. She had to fulfill her destiny as a woman, and Elias would have to fulfill his destiny as Father's son.

"He's smart. He could have been a wanderer if he'd been born to one." Father's voice was admiring but detached, like he was talking about someone else's child. "Before I know it, he'll be ready to leave the house. He doesn't want to leave your mother, of course."

"Of course."

"I don't know what she'll do when he leaves. But if I can survive losing you, she can survive losing him. Though she'll feel lonely. I do."

Amanda nodded, unsure what to say.

"I didn't want to come see you. I wanted to let you settle in, but I also knew it would make me miserable."

Amanda shrugged. "I'm sorry. I don't know what I can do. Children grow up and leave."

"It's life, it's life. I've watched others lose daughters and felt sorry for them. Now they can feel sorry for me."

"Not too sorry," she said, half laughing. "With me running around the island all the time and sleeping on the sand, they probably think you're better off rid of me."

"It hurt every time I woke up and you weren't there."

"I was—" Amanda tried to think of what she was. "Young. Angry."

"But you're not anymore."

"Angry? I don't think so. I'm just...tired." She sighed. "Maybe I've grown old enough now. I don't know. It is nice to see you." This is only half a lie; the familiarity of his face warms something in her.

"Have you ever thought what it would be like if we could live together forever?"

Amanda looked up sharply. "No. Of course not."

"I've thought about it. Just living together, you greeting me every evening when I came home and waving good-bye in the morning. You tending to the garden, the rain barrel, the chickens. We could stay together forever."

"No, we couldn't. Nobody does that." Her voice rose more quickly than she wanted it to, and its volume intensified with her pulse. She didn't remember standing, but now she towered over her seated father. "You can't do that. It's against the shalt-nots."

"I'm not saying it should happen. I know you have to marry, and have children. Andrew is a good man. You chose well."

"I did." Her voice echoed around the kitchen, and she realized she was nearly shouting. Embarrassed, she quickly sat down and looked at the blood on the floor. "I don't know what you want, coming here and talking like this," she said quietly.

"It's just wishes, Amanda. Silly wishes. I'm an old man now, I won't live much longer. Long enough for Elias to have children, I hope, but once you have a child...well, I feel like it will be the beginning of my end."

"Maybe I'm barren"—her voice hitches—"and Elias's wife will have defectives and you can live a good long time."

"You know I don't want that." They were both quiet, a bird punctuating the silence now and then with a quickly ascending *whoop*. Amanda felt stupid and clumsy and unreasonably aware of her breasts hanging free under her housedress. Bulbous, ridiculous, shameful. She rose, arms across her chest, and Father rose too.

"Come." He held out his arms, and she moved into them by rote memory, not even thinking about the movement until his head was on her shoulder. Her nostrils were filled with the scent of his hair, and she shuddered without meaning to. Father didn't seem to notice. "My girl," he murmured, rocking her back and forth.

Eventually Amanda pried herself away, disentangling herself carefully but hurriedly from him. Father's arms remained open, hanging in the air like they were suspended from strings, his face revealing an awkward mix of hope and despair.

"I should go," he said quietly, his arms still extended. "I'm a foolish old man."

She cleared her throat. "I won't let you distract me anymore! I have to figure out how to turn this rabbit into food," she said, as gaily as possible, as if they had just had a pleasant conversation over some cake and tea. "Come by for dinner soon, so you can see Andrew."

"Yes," Father said, giving a strange little bow she'd never seen, and he walked out of the house still holding the bloody cloth. Amanda sat down in the chair, feeling like her bones had turned to water. Putting her head between her knees, she stared at the red smears on the floor until they seemed to mean something, as if they were written in a language she could almost, but not quite, decipher. Her arms wrapped around her head and she pulled her hair loose, her tears making rosy, blood-veined splotches in the splattering of red below.

CHAPTER THIRTEEN

Amanda

Amanda wakes in blackness, sitting neatly on her heels, a sphere of cold, milky light gleaming down at her. Choking with surprise, she lets out a small quavering scream and her hands begin groping her face, her belly, her legs, to confirm she is whole. Her daughter is restless, striking at the inside of her womb as if to rouse her from her fugue.

Reaching down, Amanda feels her hands sink into cool, satiny mud and realizes she is outside. There are hulking forms in the distance that, as her eyes adjust, morph into dark houses and crooked trees.

Suddenly she becomes aware of the mosquitoes assiduously drinking her blood, their threadlike, saber-sharp snouts nosing below her skin. Heeding an instinct from the summers of her childhood, she plunges from her seated position to lie flat on her back in the mud. Holding her breath, she begins writhing like a suffocating fish, coating her limbs and torso in cool muck, and then, pushing up to her knees, takes two handfuls of sludge and claps them to her face, spreading the chill mud over her eyelids, down her cheeks and neck, letting it creep down in between her swollen breasts.

She reaches under her nightdress and slides mud upward from her thighs to her groin, over the full-moon swell of her pregnant belly. Her baby spins in bliss. Spent, Amanda collapses onto her back once more. The mud not only fends off most of the shrill, humming bloodsuckers, but soothes her raw and stippled skin. How long was she sitting bare-skinned and absent, like a supplicant cowering before a bright hole sliced out of the night sky? Suddenly Amanda is sobbing, salty tears burning away the mud on her eyelids. Rolling onto her side, she curls up and howls rough and gibbering sobs into the darkness. In the past few weeks, she has done so much muffled weeping, tears rolling down her temples and pooling in her ears, trembling slightly in the effort to breathe evenly and not disturb Andrew, who snores benignly in his safe, blithe dreams where there is no reason to struggle. Now her wails feel as if she is tearing something loose, a scab over a gash that, once liberated, commences to bleed and bleed.

Her daughter begins to revolve in her watery cage, faster and faster. She thumps Amanda's bladder sharply, and Amanda, not caring, urinates hotly into her wet, rumpled dress and the mud below her and keeps keening.

When her throat is raw and her lungs weakened, she remains curled around herself, the tops of her thighs pressed against her firm belly. *I can't do this to you,* she tells her daughter silently. Her daughter pauses, twitches, begins swimming in loops in the other direction. Amanda lays her right hand above her pubic bone, feeling the underwater whirling and dancing in the small, waterproof bowl of the womb that is no longer her own. Her tears have dried and the mosquitoes are hovering ready, and she rubs her face through the mud like a dog with an itch. *I'm so sorry,* she thinks, pushing herself up with her hands and staring fearfully at the cold moon. Amanda sets off toward one of the slumbering houses to try and make her way home.

Will Andrew wake when she throws buckets of cold rainwater over her skin and stands naked and shivering in the moonlight? Will he feel the dampness of her hair on his arm when she crawls back into bed? If she begins sobbing, will it simply color his dreams with the calm, rhythmic rocking of a winter sea?

Light footsteps in the distance: the children of summer, roaming in search of excitement, or a comfortable place to sleep.

CHAPTER FOURTEEN

Janey

Leading the way, with Mary behind her like a smaller, darker shadow, Janey crashes into battle. She's not exactly sure which children she's fighting, although she recognizes Brian Saul's curls under a paste of mud, and Lisa Aaron's jet-black, tangled braid.

The children are battling for a prime location on the shore, where the sea roaches like to nose around in the glinting shallows. To Janey, they resemble alien, jointed monsters that could be found in the darkness below—although at the size of a small plate and the speed of a snail, they're almost cute.

Slightly clumsy and with poor vision, Mary never fights as well as the others, but she follows in Janey's path and lashes out laterally at any moving bodies. It's difficult to properly injure anyone, because they all become very slick in a matter of seconds. Clenched fists slip off to the side instead of thudding solidly into skin, nails skitter down muddy limbs without ruffling skin to shreds, even teeth slip over mud-caked flesh and click shut with an unpleasantly electric snap. No matter how a fight starts, it always ends the same way: dirty children writhing and wincing in a tangle of torsos and limbs, like they've fused together into some filthy, many-legged abomination.

Fighting makes Janey feel alive in a way that nothing else does: not hovering alone in the black night with her whirling thoughts as company; not running until her heart heaves and her lungs turn to silver, glowing and intractable; not cradling Mary in her arms as she stares at a star-smeared night sky, knowing she will watch them wheel in their slow path until morning. Fighting makes Janey's blood sing. It's not the promise of harming others, for she rarely intends genuine injury, nor is it the prospect of revenge on her enemies, as Janey has few enemies she takes seriously. It is something about the heat in the contraction of a muscle, the speed and split-second calculations, the impact of intimate physical contact when, apart from young children and Mary, she lets nobody touch her. Deeper in her is the realization she avoids: it is the only time in her life when the violence of her thoughts are made flesh. She screams, thrashes, lunges as her mind goes still, as her fists and teeth and nails become a churning mass illuminating the turbulence within.

She knows there are rumors that she likes to bash people with rocks or break their bones, but they are unfounded. She is a good fighter, however, perhaps the best on the island, and she never, ever, ever gets tired. She might get dizzy, and her vision might flicker around the edges like there are masses of dark birds homing in on her, but fatigue, giving up, is anathema to her.

Howling with rage and pain, the losing children retreat in a ragged group and squat scowling farther down the beach. Patty Aaron, Lisa's little sister, starts inching toward their lost territory, but Janey hisses at her, snapping her teeth like an angry dog, and Patty flees again. Drawing herself tall and upright, Janey stares regally out into the water. She relaxes and smiles as Mary wades in and gazes delightedly at a sea roach, then touches a smooth, cold shell and shivers. Four-year-old Greta Balthazar, in the water next to them, looks askance at the sea roach, her expression dubious. When it moves irritably, she squeals and smiles, revealing tiny sharp teeth. Her brother, Galen, is packing mud back on her skin where it's fallen off. "Wash the hair, Greta!" he says cheerfully, plopping two handfuls of dove-brown clay on her head and smoothing them down until they drip over the back of her small neck.

Janey feels something cold on her back and realizes Mary is doing the same. The salty clay by the sea smells different than the red veins that run through the dirt. This clay smells like seawater and freshly slaughtered fish. She reaches down and smooths muck over her skin, squishing it between her fingers. Helping Mary repatch the coating over her smooth back and legs, she then pats it carefully around Mary's green eyes so it won't fall in. By the end of summer, everyone's eyes are scarlet with irritation.

Later the other children, victors and losers alike, drift off. Janey moves closer to the brush lining the shore and begins building a fort. She breaks twigs and long, flexible branches off the bushes and erects them in the sand for the frame. Then she and Mary weave branches into walls, going over and under in a soothing rhythm until she's not thinking about anything at all. It gets dark and Mary yawns, totters, and falls asleep, but Janey keeps working. She is too happy, too energetic to sleep, and time slips past as the stars burn their way across the sky and the sun rises again. When Mary wakes at dawn, the fort is almost done, and the walls have been packed with clay, thick and smooth.

Janey grins when she sees Mary awake, the mud on her face cracking like a large, hideous egg to reveal soft freckled skin beneath.

"Did you forget to sleep?" asks Mary.

"Isn't it beautiful?" Janey says.

It is. Janey's always been good at doing things with her hands. The small patches of wall Mary built are rough and uneven, wood poking through the mottled clay. Janey's are perfect, tight and uniform.

Mary rolls onto her belly and yawns. "Now what?"

"Now we live here forever."

"But I want breakfast."

Janey rolls her eyes. "Sea roaches are probably edible."

"Ugh."

"Oh, come on," says Janey. "We can stay in here forever. We'll never come out." She can't think of a more perfect future. Her, Mary, the beach, a house they built themselves.

"That would be boring."

"It would be perfect." Janey lies back on the sand, staring at the porous roof over their heads, the milky, seeping chinks of sunlight. "We'll tell each other stories all day, and watch the stars at night. We'll live on fish and water." She yawns. "We'll never get any older."

CHAPTER FIFTEEN

Amanda

Amanda hates summers now. She knows why the adults let the children run free: they're too tired to do anything else. When the temperature spikes, the sun bullies the plants until they wilt and are only refreshed by the warm afternoon rains. Amanda is sheltered from the sun, but she wilts too. She can't open the window or the doors unless she wants to invite a ravenous cloud of mosquitoes into the house. Netting is too precious to waste on houses; it's saved for men working outside, and animal pens, and walls or roofs that fall in during the summer. In her house, there are tiny cracks in the walls and the windowsills that let in a small, steady stream of golden bloodsuckers. She is forever slapping her arms and legs, leaving bloody smears and ruddy handprints, setting out to hunt down the source of the whining, hungry hum and giving up before she goes two steps. The backs of her knees and creases under her breasts drip with sweat. She doesn't mind giving food away to the muddy children outside; in this heat, eating itself seems repulsive. When Andrew reminds her that the baby needs to eat, she chokes down bites of cold porridge. She naps in the summer heat, rolling over slowly in a pool of sweat like a piece of meat being basted.

Sometimes when the downpours start, Amanda loses her self-control and races outside to stand in the rain, letting the warm torrents wash over her. The mosquitoes set forth hopefully, but raindrops smack most of them off her flesh before they can draw blood. The children shy away from her, unused to seeing a summer adult stand still in the rain. She'd love to tear off her dress, slap mud all over herself, and sprint toward the nearest tree. But the mud would drip in globs off her breasts and belly, cake in the hair between her legs, spatter when her flesh jiggled as she ran. She would disgust everyone.

Andrew comes home to find her with her arms out and head back, inviting the rain to further soak her clothes and skin. He manhandles her inside. "You can't do that, Amanda," he says, his brow creasing. "Everyone can see you."

It's true, and she has no doubt that news will spread across the island in a matter of days. Amanda Balthazar, gone crazy. Women have very little amusement during the summer besides gossip.

"But it's so hot," she whines, hating herself.

"This is not the way to fight it," he answers, putting a gentle arm around her soaked belly. He doesn't offer suggestions for the right way, she notes irritably. "I'm sure you're so uncomfortable and acting so...oddly because you're pregnant. It will be better next summer." She doesn't say anything, allowing him to blame her behavior on pregnancy.

Andrew brings Amanda into the kitchen and offers her a dry dress from her cupboard, but she shakes her head. She sits at the table, dripping onto the stained floor, while he slices a dried apple for her and pours her lukewarm water. Amanda doesn't feel hungry or thirsty, but she nibbles at some apple to please him. His face relaxes. "Imagine telling this story to our children," he says, laughing. "The day Mother went crazy and stood out in the rain."

The apple is sickly-sweet and leathery on her tongue, hard to swallow. "What would you say if I said I wanted to leave?" she says suddenly, too loudly.

"Leave the house? Now? You'll get eaten alive."

"No, leave for the wastelands."

He laughs, then frowns when Amanda doesn't change expression. "You're serious?"

"Yes. What if I wanted to leave the island?"

"Well, you can't. I mean. How could you?"

"I don't know. But pretend I had a way to leave."

"Like what?"

"I don't know, just pretend. Would you leave with me?" She leans forward and clasps his hands in hers.

"Leave the island?"

"Yes."

"Amanda," he says, putting his hands on her damp shoulders, "why would I want to do that?"

"Just to see what it's like out there."

"Why would I want to see that?"

"To see for ourselves. To live by ourselves. There must be food there, otherwise what do the people who give things to the wanderers eat? They bring in rice, don't they, we don't grow rice. Who grows the rice? The netting. Someone makes *paper*, and it's much better than ours."

"They take what the dead left behind," says Andrew, shrugging.

"But not everyone is dead. I mean, I've heard there are defectives and freaks that walk the wastelands. And families come in from the wastelands, sometimes, which means at least a few people aren't defective or freaks, right? At least a few. Caitlin Jacob isn't a defective."

"Okay, fine. But why would you want to raise our baby there?"

She pauses. "I just, I need to go."

Andrew is staring into her eyes confused, as if trying to catch a glimpse of sense in them. He takes her forearms lightly. "Amanda, we can't go. I don't want to go. We have a house here, and food, and family, and a whole community. This life is a gift from the ancestors— why would you want to throw it all away?" He frowns at her.

"You're just quoting from church. I feel like...things might be different there."

"Of course they would."

"I think maybe this isn't right."

93

"What isn't?"

"The island. The way we live. I just really, really need to leave." She shakes off his touch, then grabs his wrists and holds them tightly, hoping he can feel the desperation flowing through her veins. She moves closer to him, wondering how to convince him. Should she kiss him? Should she melt into sobs? Should she fall to her knees?

He puts his palm on Amanda's cheek, and she feels the calluses brush her skin. "Is it the baby? Is being pregnant scaring you? I remember Mother said she had something similar when she was pregnant with me. This feeling that she had to get out."

"I just feel like our baby might be better off if we lived somewhere else."

"But we have nowhere else to live." He pulls Amanda into a hug, his gentle, muscled arms squeezing her breathless. "I know it's frustrating sometimes, the same chatter, the same people, the same food. It's boring. The summers are too hot and then almost right away it's winter, and spring is too short. I don't blame you for wanting to escape sometimes. But we're safe here, we have a life here. We can raise our child in a place that's safe and protected."

"I need to get out of here."

"I feel the same way sometimes." He laughs, running a hand through his sweaty hair so it stands up in sandy spikes. "Especially when the children are running around like crazy and you're either running through the heat hoping for shade, or running through the rain wanting to stop and soak yourself cool. Like you did. But I've never wanted to go to the *wastelands*. I can't believe you do either, really."

Amanda sighs, her eyes hot with the pressure of tears. "It's too hot. I'm going to the root cellar."

"Do you want me to come?"

"No, I'm going alone."

She can picture Andrew's hurt expression as she turns her back. She knows he will sigh and rub the starred wrinkles by his eyes, run a hand through his hair again, and wonder what to do about her. He won't say anything to his brother. He'll laugh and report the small aches and concerns of pregnancy like any husband would. He'll worry about her and try to think of ways to make her happy, and his concern will only make her feel worse.

In the humid darkness of the root cellar, Amanda starts to gnaw at a carrot. Then she thrusts her nails into the muddy floor, scrapes up a handful of dirt, and tosses it into her mouth.

CHAPTER SIXTEEN

Amanda

Dusk is stretching and scrolling across the island like a drop of blue ink dissolved in water. Amanda stands staring out the kitchen window, biting the dirty nails of one hand and twisting the other in her sweat-stained dress. Finally she straightens, drops her dress, and goes to retrieve the netting Andrew gave her the night before.

It's an extravagant gift, most likely hard-won. The other men will tease him mercilessly for this. Women rarely receive netting in summer, because there is no need for them to be outside—the only exceptions being a visit to a neighbor, or a party, which the men do not see as crucial. Wives can beg their husbands for some, but most must resort to running as quickly as possible. Netting is precious, wasteland-only material, its intricate lines of soft metal dazzling the eye and confounding the blood-hungry mosquitoes.

Andrew kissed her softly when he gave it to her. "I'm not saying I want you to go stand in the rain," he said mock sternly, and they both giggled. "But if you feel, I don't know, closed in somehow, like I know you've been feeling, maybe you could go out a little bit. Where nobody can see you. I know it's not perfect, but it's the best I can give you." Touched, Amanda laid her head on his chest for a few moments, listening to his heart thump steadily.

She has not quite learned how to swathe herself effectively, and she thrashes inside it to bring her arms up and fold the top end down to her head. She must wrap it tightly around her ankles, and ends up toddling about in a ridiculous shuffling gait, always one misstep from falling over. And yet it gives her more freedom than most island women have dreamed of: the freedom to emerge from her house in summer and walk leisurely to her destination. She is quite sure the wanderers wouldn't approve. "Fuck the wanderers," she murmurs, her lips tingling pleasantly with blasphemy.

Her steps stuttering and mincing, Amanda clumsily walks through the door. She has one pair of shoes, and she has gone three steps before she kicks them away. Not only do they drench her feet with sweat, but the wooden soles mean she can't feel the ground at all. Her vision dulled by gray veils of wire, she is in severe danger of tripping and falling—and probably being unable to rise until someone finds her swaddled like a new loaf of bread in the morning. She groans, picturing the summer children discovering her, gravid and exhausted and half dipped in mud. Her pace slows even further as she struggles to move while keeping her balance.

The mosquitoes settle upon the netting like smoke, drawn by the heat of her exertions. The netting keeps them at bay, but their hum and whine grow louder and louder, until all Amanda can hear are seething high-pitched notes, shrieking endlessly near her hair and hovering in needle-sharp clusters at the ends of her fingers. She lets her filthy feet slide toward the beach, toward the place where, every summer, Janey likes to build her forts with Mary.

Janey rarely sleeps in summer; Amanda remembers her own moonlit, gleeful exhaustion as she would beg Janey to just stop talking or building so she could rest, sometimes simply leaving Janey in midsentence and moving toward a quieter place to curl up on the sand. As the muck between her toes turns to grass, to pebbles, to sand, she squints and tries to determine whether the two girls and the skeletal hut in the distance are real, or merely a blissful memory.

As she shuffles toward the vision, the taller girl spins and crouches. "Who's there?" she calls. Amanda sees Mary's smaller, wider figure stand up and move sideways toward Janey. As she nears, Janey folds into herself, as if to spring. "Who are you?" she snaps. "What are you doing here?"

"It's me," she says softly as she approaches. "It's me, it's Amanda."

"Amanda?" Janey gawps and then stands still, staring, uncharacteristically unsure. "Amanda? That's you?"

"It's me," says Amanda, close enough to see the way the moon outlines Janey's sharp cheekbones, her brilliant hair.

Janey stiffens and then lets out a volley of laughter, bending forward in mirth. "Amanda," she howls.

"What?" says Amanda, offended.

"You're all wrapped up in netting, and women never...I thought you were a short fat man."

There is a pause, and suddenly Amanda and Mary are laughing too, their peals rising toward the dimming sky. Suddenly exhausted, Amanda bends at the hips and thumps her rear into the damp sand. The netting rides up, and she feels the pricks of eager mosquitoes on her insteps. Their laughter joins together in a medley of raucousness and slowly, comfortably fades away.

"Janey, I need to talk to you," says Amanda. "I, I really need to—"

Janey stops laughing abruptly and crosses her arms, glowering at Amanda as if she has just remembered her anger. "You shouldn't even be talking to me," Janey says harshly.

"It's not my fault that I became a woman," retorts Amanda. "I didn't have a choice."

"That's debatable," snaps Janey, and then, "Go ahead. Talk." In past summers, Janey would sometimes smack or punch Amanda to make a point, and Amanda wonders if she is about to be pounded again.

Amanda's ankles flame with a needling itch, and she can almost feel the infinitesimal golden feet of mosquitoes dancing. "I can't. Not here. Can we please go to my house? Andrew isn't home, Mr. Aaron the weaver's roof practically fell in, he's working through the night with Mr. Balthazar and Mr. Joseph, and I just can't, I'm getting bitten

Jennie Melamed

and can barely move and can barely see—I can't think with all these mosquitoes!" Her voice rises with desperation.

"Fine, fine," says Janey, holding up her hands. "Fine. Let's go, Mary."

"I—I need to talk to just you," says Amanda, and flinches as Mary draws back, surprised. Dear Mary. Amanda remembers the shine of her young face when the three of them used to race around together, Mary's sweet naïveté and high, hopeful voice balancing out Janey's rages and rants. They would sleep, the three of them, curled together like puppies, and Amanda often woke with Mary's dark head on her flat chest, rising and falling as Amanda tried her best to breathe slowly and preserve the moment. To let Mary dream peacefully until the rays of the sun broke through their eyelids.

"I'm sorry, Mary," she murmurs. "It's—" She tries to think of the words. "The things I need to say to Janey are—" *I want to protect you,* she thinks, but cannot bear to say the words out loud for fear of sounding like yet another condescending woman deciding what's best for the children.

"It's fine," says Mary with feigned lightness, "I can wait here," and Amanda winces at the hurt in her voice. She glances at Janey, who pauses and then nods once.

Quietly they move under the moonlight, pacing the short distance from the beach to Amanda's house. Janey must slow her long strides to match Amanda's struggles, and silence stretches long and awkward between them. When they are near her door, Amanda tries to run and ends up on her face in the muck. Without a word, Janey reaches over to hook an arm around her belly and haul her back upright.

Panting, they enter the house, and Amanda immediately sheds the netting and lights a candle. Janey looks around uncomfortably before settling down on a kitchen chair, one knee drawn up to her chest. Amanda gazes at her and shakes her head. "I can't believe you're here."

"You came to fetch me, didn't you?"

"I didn't think you'd come."

Janey shrugs a shoulder. Dried flecks of mud sift to the ground like dirty snow.

"You're thinner," ventures Amanda. Janey's body is camouflaged with knobs and swells of mud, and it's difficult to tell a bony angle from a flesh-covered curve. Yet the difference between Janey now and two summers ago is plain. Janey has narrowed even as she has grown taller, and her thin, lanky limbs seem to trail on forever.

"I am," replies Janey. "I have to be."

"Why?"

"It's getting stronger. My body wanting to change. To bleed, be like yours."

"It must be hard."

"It is. Especially alone." Janey's eyes are accusing.

Amanda feels the sting. "What about Mary?"

"She doesn't have the will for it."

"Well, I guess I didn't either."

"You could have. You made a decision. But I don't blame you for it. Your father was disgusting, and your mother..." They both wince involuntarily. "Anyway. It wasn't the decision I would have made, but it was...understandable."

Amanda nods and shyly sits on a chair opposite Janey. Her wet, muddy dress clings to her globular belly, which Janey eyes with distaste.

"Six months," Amanda says confrontationally. "And it's a girl."

Janey shrugs a shoulder again.

"You hate me," says Amanda.

"I wouldn't have come here if I hated you," replies Janey. "I would have hit you on the head with a rock." Amanda ponders this statement and then sees the side of Janey's mouth quirking up, a dimple hidden underneath a cast of dry mud. They both giggle.

"So why did you want to talk to me?" asks Janey.

Amanda takes a deep breath. "It's hard to explain."

"Is it Andrew, is he terrible? Is it awful to be married?"

"I love Andrew," she says slowly. "I love him more than I ever thought I could." Janey frowns, looking askance at Amanda. "It's hard to explain," Amanda says again, lamely. "But I love him second only to her." She gestures at her belly.

Seemingly at a loss for a response to this admission, Janey puts her hands in her lap. Silence thickens the air between them while Amanda struggles to think of what to say.

"At first, I was scared when I wasn't pregnant," she says finally. "I was married, and that's what comes next, you know? It's what I was supposed to do. I didn't want to be a disappointment. I didn't think at all about having a baby. I mean, I know that's what happens after a pregnancy, but I forgot about it somehow."

Janey nods. Encouraged, Amanda continues.

"Then I got pregnant, and I felt so sick. I was so tired, I couldn't eat. But it seemed more like an illness than that I was going to have a child. I was so jealous of the other children. The ones who could run around with their bodies neat, without all these..." She gestures at her upper torso. "All this *extra*. When I was a child I never thought about it, but I was never lonely. Even with all the awful things about childhood, things I would never go back to, I wanted my body to be like a child's. I wanted to run like a child, have a child's summers."

"But you got away from your parents," says Janey. "That was always what you wanted."

"And then the baby started moving and I realized that I have a child inside me that's going to come. I was so hoping for a son, but I did the ritual, and I'm going to have a daughter, she's going to be mine, and I can't—I can't do this to her."

"Do what?"

"I can't make her go through what I did."

"As a girl, you mean? But what you went through wasn't unusual," says Janey. "I mean, your mother is terrible. But it's the way things are, we—"

"No. I, we, need to get away," Amanda croaks, her voice harsh and desperate and spiking through the dim room.

"Where would you go?" asks Janey innocently.

"Off the island."

Janey frowns. "What, you want to swim away?" She snorts.

"Janey, listen to me!" Janey's lips tighten, and she looks down. "Don't you understand? I can't stay here!"

"Why not?" says Janey. "All the others have."

Amanda starts to cry softly, her mouth gasping and twisting and her brows knotted into a tangle, hating herself for looking weak and foolish. "Janey, I can't do it again. I can't watch her go through everything I went through. When I married, I thought, okay, it's over, I'm free. But I'm not free. She's pulling me back. Seeing it happen to her will be ten times worse than going through it myself. And you know I barely made it through myself."

"Everyone makes it through," says Janey softly.

"I hate it," says Amanda savagely, clenching her fists in the cloth of her dress. "I can't even look at little girls sometimes, knowing what's happening to them. I'm so tired of what they do to us."

"What do you mean?" asks Janey carefully.

"You know what I mean! Since I was a girl. The love, the love that felt...wrong. It made me sick. Mother hating me, blaming me like it was my fault! The first time it happened, I hurt so badly I thought I was going to die. I thought he was killing me, that I'd done something terrible and was being punished for it. I didn't know what I had done. And then it was over, and I realized I would live, and I thought, at least I'll never have to do that again. And then every night. Or almost. The nights it didn't happen, I wondered if I was dead, if I had finally been able to die. There was nobody to help, nobody to save me. It became normal, like putting on my shoes or washing my face. And yet every time I lay down I would remember the first time, and I would freeze, and shake, and stare at the ceiling crying, and he didn't even notice. And then I realized that it happened to others—that it was *supposed* to happen, that it wasn't a punishment for anything, it was just how things were. And nobody else even seemed to mind, the girls, they didn't seem to care. And so I started running away, so I didn't turn into them. So I didn't stop caring, because that just felt . . . wrong."

Amanda wipes tears from her eyes with the heels of her hands and dares a glance at Janey. Janey's eyes are sharp and clear, but her dirty face is lined and heavy, like an old woman's.

"They care," Janey whispers.

"I saw how different it could be during the summer of fruition, I thought okay, now I'm free. It's over. It will never happen again. And then I did the ritual and found out it's a girl. And I'll have to watch, and to know. Maybe I can slip her a sleeping draft or try to distract Andrew but not all the time. I love him." Amanda is sobbing so hard she can barely speak. "I love him and I'm going to hate him, or worse I'll love him and hate *her,* and this man, this good man is going to turn into . . . turn into *Father . . .* " Her voice trails away in hysterical crying. Taking a deep breath, she tries to halt her sobs. "I love her—I already love her, I don't even want to but I do, and I can't stop it."

"So you want to leave?" asks Janey, staring intently at her.

"Maybe to the wastelands. I know they're terrible and burning and whatever Pastor Saul says. But they have to be better than here."

"But how?"

"I don't *know,*" she says, starting to cry again. "If I had a wanderer father, or knew somebody, someone. I know there's a ferry, that has to mean something. Maybe we can swim, who knows? Nobody's ever tried. But one thing is certain, I'm leaving. And I want you to come with me."

"Amanda, I can't leave Mary."

"So bring her with us."

"I know you want to leave, but—"

"I will leave. I don't care what I have to do. I'll kill people if I have to. I'll kill the ferryman. And if I can't find a way, I'll kill her. And myself. I don't care."

"Amanda," says Janey, suddenly stern, like she is the adult and

Amanda is a wayward child. Amanda looks at her stubbornly. "You will not kill yourself, or your baby."

"No," whispers Amanda. "I'm too scared of the darkness below." She laughs mirthlessly. "Everything I'm saying would put me there anyway. But I'm still scared. Isn't that stupid?"

Janey sighs. "I don't know what to tell you."

"Will you help me search? For a way out? I don't care what I have to do. I'll threaten the wanderers, talk to their wives. Someone must know something. Will you help me?"

After a pause, Janey nods.

Leaning forward, Amanda kisses Janey, like she is placing an imprint on Janey's dirty lips; a seal or some kind of vow. Janey sits up straight, her eyes turning to dark gray, flickering in the candlelight. Then suddenly they are black pits as her pupils dilate in alarm. Someone is there.

Amanda hears footsteps. A cough, a shuffle, the thump of something being dropped. Terrified, she leaps up from the table and runs into the main room. There is a pile of wood on the floor—a delivery for Andrew. She can smell unfamiliar masculine sweat, sawdust, leather boots. Dashing to the door, she sees a man in netting jogging away from the house.

"Janey?" she calls in a sudden panic. "Janey, it's not Andrew. Someone's been here, someone..." She trails off, and hears only silence.

Breathing quickly, she runs to the kitchen, but Janey isn't there. Through the window she can just make out a tall, gaunt figure blending deeper into the night.

CHAPTER SEVENTEEN

Amanda

One day toward the end of summer, Amanda is standing in the kitchen when she hears someone run up, panting, and slap something against the door. When she cracks the front door open, four or five mosquitoes hum in before she snatches the scrap of paper and slams the door shut. The note is written on the terrible, flaky paper they have this year. From the way it's falling apart, she can tell it's already passed through a number of hands. Squinting, she moves to a window to read the smudged charcoal.

Friends, let us meet before we die of loneliness. Bring something to eat. Wednesday at five in the afternoon. Come to Mrs. Betty Balthazar's. Chaperoned by Mr. Balthazar. Pass to your nearest neighbor.

It's Wednesday at four. The invitation must have taken a couple of days to make its way to Amanda. She can't be too upset, because it takes a lot of courage to go outside at the moment. Andrew is mostly busy from dawn until dusk, since even a tiny chink in the roof means swarms of mosquitoes. Amanda found the netting barely tolerable when she went to find Janey, but the thought of spending yet another day entirely alone with her constantly whirling thoughts makes her want to scream.

Sometimes in the warm days of spring or the crisp days of autumn, the women will organize get-togethers where they move from house to house, never going above the proscribed maximum of three women in one room without a man present. They are enjoyable, breezy, slightly drunken affairs, festivals of quick, pleasant conversations. In the summer, the mosquitoes render these roving gatherings impossible. So far Amanda has ignored the few invitations she's received; since nobody's going outside, she doesn't need to explain her lack of attendance to anyone. Amanda has spent most of the three weeks since she saw Janey brooding and alone. They haven't spoken since, and Amanda wonders if she should venture outside and try to find her again.

But for now, being left in the house by herself has become so stultifying that even the thought of a gaggle of women touching her belly and gossiping doesn't deter her. Maybe they'll understand how she's feeling, without her having to say anything.

Mrs. Balthazar's is quite a walk away, and so, sullenly wrapping herself in her layers of netting again, Amanda totters out the door. Sliding her feet one after the other in the mud, she finds a rather peaceful rhythm, warm muck collecting between her toes and falling away with each new motion. Bursting into Mrs. Balthazar's house, Amanda holds her belly and pants with effort. She spins out of her netting, shaking out her dress and turning around in a frenetic little dance just in case any mosquitoes infiltrated. Amanda heaves a big sigh and looks up to see Mrs. Balthazar smiling at her.

Mrs. Balthazar is quite old—nearing forty—and her granddaughter is only a little younger than Amanda. Because her husband has remained a useful carver, she has been allowed to stay alive along with him. Most elderly people on the island seem to be constantly angry—either at their failing bodies or at their impending death—but Mrs. Balthazar smiles serenely like a woman who has never known fury.

"Thank you so much for inviting everyone, Mrs. Balthazar," Amanda says as Mrs. Balthazar takes her hands.

"Please call me Betty," replies Mrs. Balthazar, the skin around her eyes wrinkling. Betty glances over her shoulder and then reaches out a hand to touch Amanda's belly. "May you have sons," she murmurs kindly.

The place is packed full of twittering women standing in circles, packed onto furniture, even sitting on the floor. Amanda gazes around for the chaperone and sees Mr. Balthazar seated at a lavishly carved table, looking annoyed at being pressed into service as the required overseer. Chaperones usually act in one of two ways. The first kind circles like a gull, immediately sliding over to bursts of laughter or enthusiasm in the hopes of catching something improper or blasphemous. The other kind can't stand being surrounded by a flock of women and often dozes off in self-defense. Mr. Balthazar is already blinking heavily.

There are a few children crawling around, those too young to emerge into summer. They cling to random legs and skirts to steady or amuse themselves, and at a sharp cry a pair of motherly arms will reach down and bounce, kiss, or feed one of them until they quiet down.

Amanda sees Pamela Saul, whom she hasn't encountered since the ritual. Peering at her, Amanda tries to make eye contact across the room, but Mrs. Saul gazes resolutely at a cup of tea in her hand. She looks sad, with deep lines wearing into her face; Amanda wants to go to her, but quails, remembering herself naked and bloody and weeping in the older woman's arms.

Dejected, Amanda spots Denise Solomon sitting in a chair, nursing her son. Amanda and Denise had their summer of fruition together, which always creates a bond, barring any squabbling over men. They hadn't spoken much that summer; Denise got pregnant almost immediately and was exhausted and puking the whole time. That baby, born in the depths of winter, was a defective. Amanda can't remember exactly what was wrong with it, but it was something like no head or no face. The next baby was healthy and sound, and is now busily drinking from his mother's breast, but Denise isn't looking at him—she's gazing at the wall.

Amanda remembers hearing from Andrew that Denise's younger brother, Steven, died right before summer started, of some sickness—Andrew wasn't sure of the details. It felled Denise's father too, and he had to take to his bed right as Steven died, although he survived. Given the mosquitoes and the possibility of infection, Steven's body was put in the fields quietly and without ceremony.

On an impulse, Amanda kneels next to Denise and takes her free hand. Denise jumps in her seat and then smiles faintly. "Hello, Amanda."

"Hello, Denise."

Denise touches Amanda's belly and murmurs something inaudible. Amanda sees that below Denise's close-set eyes are swaths of darkened, paperlike skin, like she hasn't slept in months.

"I'm sorry about Steven," Amanda says. "I remember him."

Denise nods, but Amanda isn't sure if she really heard her. Then she asks, "Amanda, after you left home, did Elias complain of anything to you?"

"Complain of anything?" Elias, mimicking his mother, always viewed her with simmering disdain, and she can't imagine him seeking her out to say anything.

Denise shakes her head. "Never mind. Forget I asked."

"Why?"

"Father made me swear."

"But John is the one you have to listen to, now," Amanda reminds her.

"John would agree if he knew." Her voice quavers.

"Knew what?"

Denise shrugs. She switches her son to the other breast, leaving her left one open and exposed, hanging there like a white bulbous fruit. Across the room, Mr. Balthazar looks more awake, and stares at Denise's breast until she folds the cloth up.

"What was going on. Amanda, I'm not sleeping, between the mosquitoes and this little one, I can't think straight. Fuck, I just... Please don't ask me questions I can't answer."

"I'm sorry." They both sit silent and glum. "But why did you ask about Elias?"

"I was just wondering."

"What was Steven complaining about?"

"Impossible things. It doesn't even make sense. I don't see how it would..." The baby falls asleep. She puts her other breast back into her dress, hikes him to her shoulder, and starts patting his back. "He died so suddenly, just like that. He wasn't even sick, just alive one minute and dead the next. I never saw his body. What happens to the sons, when the daughters leave?"

Amanda forces a laugh. "Is that a riddle?"

"A riddle? I think it might be. I don't want to talk about this anymore." Denise gives a small, mirthless chuckle and shifts her baby to her other shoulder. "Tell me how you're doing."

"Me? I'm ... pregnant." They both sigh, and start talking about the small annoyances of pregnancy. Amanda can't help but worry that she'll have a defective, but she's not going to say that to Denise.

Eventually a couple of other women join them, trading home remedies and ideas for sick babies, and Amanda breaks away and heads for the food. Betty has made her famous honey cake, although the whipped cream on top has quickly melted into a gooey mess. Amanda takes a huge piece and eats it messily from her hand. The sweet richness is heavy and intoxicating, flushing her body with satisfaction.

"Amanda." Betty comes up and puts a hand on her shoulder. "I'm so glad to see you well and breeding. Remember what a terror you were your last summer with the children? You were almost as bad as Janey Solomon. You broke Margaret's nose, remember that?"

Amanda blinks. "No."

"Well, how is your first summer as a woman? Miserable, isn't it?"

"Yes," Amanda says gratefully. "I don't know how I'll do it. Why can't we cover ourselves with mud and go run around?"

Betty laughs. "No running with that belly. I do understand,

though. We're trapped in our houses, and the children get to run free. I suppose we had our time, though."

"I suppose."

"At least we know autumn is coming." The season that used to be Amanda's biggest torment has quickly become a promise of relief.

"And a winter, and a spring, and then another summer."

"It can't be any other way," says Betty, laughing again.

A few women, picking at honey cake and talking with their mouths full, move toward them.

"Denise, Amanda," says Alicia Saul. "Your first adult summer."

"It's terrible, isn't it?" says Isabel Joseph, and they both chuckle.

"How is your Frieda?" Betty gently asks Isabel. She sighs.

"She was still having trouble before summer started. Crying all the time, not eating. Summer came just in time; she took a whole plateful of bread and cheese that I put out when I saw her creeping around the garden."

"You can't run about like that and not be hungry," says Alicia.

"It's his fault for waiting," says Isabel. "He waited a long time, and she had to be sent home from school, she was so upset, remember? It's best started before they're old enough to really understand it. Then it's just part of life."

"Oh, I completely agree."

"I can't believe Rita isn't having her summer of fruition right now," says Anne Abraham, who has wandered over. "She gets the pains, the moods, everything except actual bleeding."

"She'll be one of the older ones next summer, then."

"Oh, yes, that's always good, she'll have another year of being a child. As long as when the blood does come, you know...the shalt-nots are respected."

"Well, of course they would be!"

"I remember Mother used to say that the chickens could smell the blood, and it would make their eggs bigger."

"Really?"

"Mother told *me* I would spoil butter, so I snuck to the churn once and stuck a finger in some butter. Nothing happened."

"Speaking of butter, did you try this butter bread?"

"No, is that Ada Jacob's? I swear her husband got lucky. Her mother said she used to hate cooking and once made bread burned to a solid rock. She's certainly improved."

"Well, I used to hate little children, and I certainly don't hate mine now."

"Children are different."

"So is butter bread!"

Their laughter flutters upward like a flock of sparrows. Amanda looks at Denise and sees she is dreaming, somewhere else. Betty has scolded Amanda before, for having so few women friends, but this party is reminding her why she doesn't want any. She tires quickly of talk about bodily functions, sweet foods, the smugness of women with children. Of course, talking to a man besides Andrew or Father is frowned upon, and the girls she used to run around with treat her like she's invisible.

A few children, muddy and completely unrecognizable, streak by the window. Amanda stifles an urge to shatter the glass with her fists.

The cake feels burdensome in Amanda's stomach, and her teeth ache from sweetness. Circling, she looks at the happy women and snoozing chaperone, and feels a sudden longing to be alone in her own house, crouching in the cool, silent root cellar.

Jane Jacob comes to stand by her. "How are you feeling, Amanda?"

Amanda stutters. "I'm—I'm fine. Just, you know. Feeling a little ill."

Jane absently takes Amanda's hand, and Amanda recoils from her palm. It's soft, and damp, and sticky like the cake. Smiling and making gabbled excuses, she fetches the precious sheet of netting and begins winding it around herself, spinning like a top as she spurts forth wordy nothings about feeling tired, having had a wonderful time, the cake was marvelous, so nice to see everyone. She catches a glimpse of Mr. Balthazar staring intently at her like she is a madwoman. Hurtling out the door, she enters gratefully into the humid summer air, the scents of butter and the breath of women clinging to her skin. Inhaling deeply a few times, she immediately feels better and begins her shuffle toward home. Andrew has been pulled away for another all-night repair, and Amanda will sit in the kitchen with her head between her knees, legs splayed to allow for her stretching belly, and stare at the floor.

Near the path that leads to Amanda's home, there is another, smaller path through the grass that leads to the seashore. Amanda thinks pensively of the echoing emptiness waiting for her at home. Hesitating, she changes direction and shambles down the increasingly sandy path until she can see, blearily, the stretch of windblown sea before her. The rising moon hangs heavy, low and swollen, the golden color of butter.

"Amanda."

She whirls, squinting through the veils of gray across her face. A man is in front of her, clothed in netting like herself, so close to her she has to raise her head to see him. His face is a sparkling mass of points, wire pocked by moonlight, and no matter how she turns her head, she cannot see his features.

"Amanda."

His voice is deep, and he pronounces her name slowly, like it's an incantation. Her lips start to tremble. He advances toward her, slowly, inexorably, and she stumbles backwards. The waves hiss against the shore like hushed, fevered breathing. He says her name again and she tries to reply, but her lips are numb and clumsy with dread, and mumble shapeless sounds. Her heels creep back into damper and damper sand, until she feels salt water lick her ankles.

"Come here," he says, but she continues walking backwards into the cold sea, step for step, staring at his glowing face as it approaches her, suspended in the darkness.

CHAPTER EIGHTEEN

Vanessa

Vanessa can't quite understand what is happening to her this summer. It's like she has morphed from the bright, popular wanderer's daughter into a loner, not so much down the social ladder as on a different structure completely.

Father likes to say, "Each child has his own summer, but each summer leaves a different child." Father is always saying things that sound poetic, hoping other people will start repeating them—and to be fair, they often do. He says things about summer so often Vanessa believes that, deep down, he's really mad he doesn't get to have summer anymore.

This summer, Vanessa is happiest alone. She sways contentedly up in her tree, walks the shore with her feet in the muddy shallows, wriggles under netting and squats in herds of goats, enjoying their animal scent and the comforting rub of their rough skins. She sees other children often, and sometimes joins them in raiding a food supply, or in one of the organic games that spring up over a piece of shingle or a puddle of water. But when the game ends, instead of adhering to a group, she retreats to solitude. She wonders if it would be different if Ben were older. It might not.

This may be her last summer to spend luxuriating in freedom. She's already thirteen. She doesn't have some of the signs that other girls have that indicate fruition is coming: the thickening at the middle, the chest of an overfed toddler, the faint tangle of hair under the arms and between the legs. She remains neat, straight, and smooth, and wants to stay that way. At night, she even prays to the ancestors for this, even though she knows they have no interest whatsoever in her staying a child. But she persists, because she doesn't know what else to do.

One night she joins a group spying on the summer of fruition. She sees Hannah Joseph, who used to be her friend, being mounted from behind by Allison Saul's older brother. From the sounds she makes, Vanessa can't tell if Hannah is having a very good time or a very bad time. It looks like it would hurt. Vanessa always feels bad for the she-goats and ewes when they have to deal with the weight and penetration, the scrabbling hooves. Staring at Hannah, Vanessa imagines herself in her place and immediately feels sick. She vacates the window for another eager spy, trying not to retch. That night she sits in the water up to her waist, half wishing a sea monster would loop a slimy tentacle around her leg and drag her underwater to her doom. She pictures the sudden breathlessness, the gaping vacuum in her lungs, the thrashing of her body slowly becoming more peaceful as water fills the empty spaces inside of her.

She can't see the point of the repetitiveness of it all, people living to create more people and then dying when they're useless, to make room for even more new people. She's not sure why they keep making new people to replace themselves, except—of course—that the ancestors said to. In a year or so some man will mount and marry her, and she'll push out two children, assuming she is fertile and doesn't have defectives. She'll raise them to be like her—obedient, if smarter than most—and eventually she'll take the final draft and die. She sees her life before her like a dim pathway leading around and back into itself.

She finds herself envying the children who run and scream and play in the mud, fighting and eating and not caring one bit what will happen in autumn when the ground freezes, or even what will happen tomorrow. She watches Mary, Janey's sister, who they say disobeys the ancestors and the wanderers and even her own father. She searches for some difference in Mary, something that sets her apart from Vanessa and the others, a sign of regret or joy at having escaped her father's embrace. She watches her with hatred, wondering what it might be like to sleep through the whole night without her body, even in slumber, tensing for the possibility of a hand reaching under the sheets. And yet Vanessa also pities Mary. After all, Mary has never been as special to her father as Vanessa is to hers. Nobody will ever love Vanessa more than Father. *Our Book* says the father-daughter bond is holy. Does that mean Mary and Janey are blasphemous? Looking at Mary's laughing, trusting face staring at Janey, her graceful jaw and sharp cheekbones the only resemblance between them, Vanessa thinks she looks happy. But it's summer, isn't everyone happy?

In her tree, Vanessa dreams. She dreams of a world where she has something to do like a man does. She dreams she's a wanderer, importantly striding into the wastelands to search for goods and people and secrets. She dreams she lives in the wastelands, in the flames of sin, killing for her breakfast and running around with her clothes on fire. She dreams she's a mud monster, slithering slickly through the muck, spying the white soles of little girls spotting the slime above her and gleefully choosing her prey. She dreams she's Janey Solomon, and she doesn't need to eat to stay alive, and she terrifies everyone. And then she wakes up and she's Vanessa, small and unimportant.

FALL

CHAPTER NINETEEN

Caitlin

The end of summer is here.

All the children could sense it coming. The mud cooled and made them shiver in the morning. The afternoon rains had a new, potent chill. The sky collapsed into nightfall just a little bit earlier. Knowing that their summer was almost at an end, the children grew sadder and meaner. Janey and Mary, who spent the entire summer defending a wooden fort they built on the beach, gathered up some cousins and led a small army across the island. Everyone they encountered, instead of running away, lunged into the fight. Davey Adam hit his head on a rock and fell asleep for a few hours, Theresa Solomon broke her finger, which now crooks to the right, and Peter Moses was bitten in the knee by little Rita Moses, who is only four but managed to draw blood. Laughing, Janey scooped Rita up into the air and paraded her around on top of their crowd, the little girl's glee rapidly fading to frightened sobs.

Caitlin stays away from summer violence. Now she is staying away from the inevitable return home. She walks on the frosted-over mud near the shore, swinging her knees high with every step as the freezing muck stings and sparks her feet. Soon her toes will turn blue and she really will have to go back home. They've all heard the stories of the children who lost their toes, or their feet, and Caitlin wants her feet attached to her. But she also wants to stay outside and walk just a little longer.

The first frost means that summer is over. She can't deny that the frost exists; it's lacy and glistening and has draped a breathtaking veil over every field, rock, and tree. But still, just a little longer.

Most of the crops have been harvested and are lying in barns and cellars. The extra puppies and kittens have been drowned in buckets of water and used as fertilizer. The lambs and kids will soon be sheep and goats, ready to be slaughtered, shorn, or milked. The netting is being taken down from paddocks. A delicate, sparkling layer of dead mosquitoes carpets the ground like an infestation of minuscule golden flowers.

At Caitlin's house, Mother will be waiting, in an old dress that she doesn't mind getting dirty. First Caitlin will stand out in front of the house while Mother digs her fingers into cracks in the mud covering her, peeling it away section by section like she is stripping the shell off a beetle. Then she'll dump buckets of water over Caitlin's head, until she is pink and naked and shivering. Only then will Mother wipe her with a towel and drop a dress over her head. Combing out Caitlin's limp brown hair will take a few hours of wincing and grimacing from both of them. Then Caitlin will once again be bare and shiny, like she has been burned. At dinner, Father will be drunk and Mother and Caitlin will be careful. That night, she will lie awake in bed, half dreaming of muddy races and bare legs in the sand. When Father comes in and lays his hands on her, she will get up and walk over to the other side of the room. Crouching there, she'll watch the girl on the bed and feel sorry for her. It's always so hard for her to breathe, and she bruises so easily. When he's done, Caitlin will fall asleep against the wall, and in the morning she will wake up back in bed. All the marks she's watched him paint on another body will be on her own. She will go to school and try to hide the stains on her skin without success. He's had a whole summer without her.

All the other children have given up, headed back home to be cleaned and dressed and put back in their place. Mother must be wondering where Caitlin is. But she can't stop walking on the icy ground. Away from home, near the trees, around the shore.

Rounding a bend, Caitlin sees a group of men. She quickly darts behind a bush, its muddy branches camouflaging her easily. Caitlin's body becomes colder as she squats still, her breath smoking in the chilly air. Peering through a spray of mud-caked leaves, she sees the wanderers, a cluster of them, all wearing dark clothes. Two are in the water, pulling something to shore. *They killed a sea monster,* thinks Caitlin, *and now they're going to butcher the body.*

A gathering of wanderers all together, rising from the sea. Like tall, dripping crows, they shift in a rough circle. Faint masculine voices, voices of command, carry in the wind. She can't understand why, but of all the things Caitlin has ever seen in her life, this is the most terrifying.

Creeping closer, shivering, she squints to see what they've found. They've pulled the thing onto shore now, their circle tightening around it.

Two dark-clad bodies part, and through the brush, Caitlin sees a blue-white, limp hand and arm. A fall of dirty hair. Blue lips and blue fingers. One of the men presses down, and the indigo lips part to eject a gush of dirty water. The eyes stare, dead and white like pebbles. One of the wanderers—Mr. Joseph?—kneels down and pushes the hair back, gently closes the eyes with his fingertips. Another one kicks the sand and throws his long arms out, his terse volley of words jumbling into nonsense on the wind.

They put their heads together again, their arms on one another's backs, muttering. Then two stride off away from her while two others kneel at the body's ankles and shoulders. Hoisting it, struggling under its sodden weight, they follow the men who left. Five wanderers stand on the beach, looking at each other, looking down, making comments. One seems to be delineating something to the others. A stray wanderer, a little back from the rest, raises his head and, Caitlin is sure, looks right at her.

Someone grabs Caitlin by the throat and jerks her backwards in time.

They are pulling a dead woman by her feet from a swath of white sheets, revealing slack legs of violet and blue flesh. Slowly they peel bleached cloth from her, layer upon layer, until she lies naked and exposed, a rotten stamen at the heart of a stripped lily, sprawled lifeless on a pile of snowy petals. Her feet are near Caitlin's face, thick blue toenails like pieces of ceramic, delicate layers of dead skin peeling back in halos from the heels. Caitlin is not supposed to be there, and so she does not say anything, and hunches near the bed, pretending to be invisible.

She can hear sobbing, a woman, and the angry words of a man. The trickling of water into a bowl. Two female hands are washing the body. The washing woman's swift but tender movements make a soft sound that ends with a flourish at the apex of each stroke. Caitlin is sure if she got very close to a bird unfurling its wings, it would make the same sound. The woman squeezes the cloth into the bowl and the water swirls crimson and pink. Then the sounds start again. The bird brandishes its wings over and over, never quite taking flight. Moving in little jerks, Caitlin slowly raises her head over the top of the bed and sees the dead woman's slack breasts falling to each side, the riotous garden of bruises under her skin, the way her flesh gives like old meat in advance of the cleaning strokes.

Hands land on Caitlin's shoulders, unfriendly hands. "What's this brat doing here?" asks someone with incredulity.

"Learning life's lessons," says a woman tartly.

"No, come now, she shouldn't see this, not yet," another woman replies, and Caitlin is picked up and hurled outside the room, onto a dusty wooden floor.

Caitlin returns to herself with a croak, staggering, and falls to her hands and knees to gasp for breath. She puts her hands to her throat and whirls to look behind her, but nobody is there. Turning back, she freezes. The wanderers are still in sight, one raising his head to look back for the source of the strange sound. Panic floods her groin with sick heat, branching through her bones until her fingertips burn. She feels hot, salty urine lick her thigh. Caitlin takes off running, convinced that if they see her they will kill her. But the dead girl's face is burned into her memory, as much as she tries to wipe it clean. The blue hand beckoning her, the head turned to the side with its eyes open. The belly humped convex, pasted with wet cloth. The dark blue mouth a scar in front of Caitlin's eyes. The wanderers, flocked around her like hungry birds of prey, and the small smile on the girl's face that says, *You can do nothing to me.* Caitlin feels something like jealousy burn deep in her gut.

Then she's in front of her house, which is still dirty and falling down. She stands, a lone, small, muddy figure, staring at the structure rearing up before her like a nightmare. She suddenly feels the weight of Amanda's corpse slump onto her shoulders, heavy and cold and wet, and she staggers. Dropping to her knees, she puts her head down as if in prayer and waits for someone to notice her.

CHAPTER TWENTY

Janey

Mother is waiting with a bucket of water out front, but Janey pulls Mary past her. Giggling, they run up to their bedroom and dive into the freshly made bed, rolling around and smearing dirt on the white sheets like overexcited infants. Janey kicks her legs frantically until the sheets are in a tangle, drapes herself over Mary, and then falls into a dark and sudden sleep. She wakes up with a gasp in the morning, initially confused by the still air and the sun streaming in through the window. Mary's dark head is pressed against her chest. Breathing in and then exhaling, Janey makes Mary's head rise and fall. Squirming and grumbling, Mary puts a hand on Janey's breastbone to feel the pulse beneath. Janey's pulse is slow, beating strong and low like dragging footsteps.

The red clay from the shore has dried on the sheets, and it looks like they've been murdered in their bed. They're valuable wasteland sheets, which Mother must have laid out in an ill-calculated gesture of welcome. Janey thinks of all the sheets on all the beds in the wastelands, skeletons with shreds of dried flesh curled up underneath them like dolls. Or blood, perhaps, long dried, the sheets stiff and maroon like they've been caked with mud.

School always starts the day after summer ends, unless it's a Sunday. Janey knows the intent is to shock the children back into regular life as quickly as possible, like splashing cold water on fighting dogs. Janey and Mary clean themselves early, before Mother can get at them, and purposely do a bad job of it; they leave smears of mud behind their knees and between their fingers, and Mary's hair is one big snarl. Then they sneak into the cellar, Mary devouring an entire cold chicken and swallowing a raw egg while Janey nibbles on a potato.

When they emerge, Mother is cooking an unnecessary breakfast, although Mary might be hungry again in a few minutes. A summer supervised by Janey always leaves her ravenous. Mother hugs Mary tightly, kissing her forehead, and awkwardly pats Janey's arm. Janey doesn't like being touched by adults, and Mother is constantly dancing between wanting to show affection and fearing Janey's rejection.

"You two look like you're in one piece," Mother says. "Mary, did you eat the chicken I was saving for dinner?"

"Not all of it," Mary lies.

Father wanders in and looks pleasantly surprised. "Welcome back, girls," he says. Mother rushes to serve him some cornmeal porridge with berries, and Mary and Janey slip upstairs to get dressed.

Janey often feels a faint guilt about Mother and Father. She knows that, with a normal child, they would have been normal parents. Quiet and passive, they have always been bowled over by Janey's stubbornness, unsure how to respond to her. Since she was a child, Janey has ruled them. She loves Mother but pities her hesitant nature, treating her faint commands and tentative decrees as mere suggestions to be ignored at her own whim. As for Father, Janey has always held him at arm's length, with Mary safe behind her. She sometimes catches glimpses of thoughtfulness, of strength, in his personality, but the rule of father and daughter on the island keeps her steadfastly on guard against him. Father appears, somehow, to understand, and he skirts her and Mary with distant affection. The only time Janey lets him touch her is when she is sick, and unable to mount her usual defenses. When Mother has to sleep, or care for Mary, he holds her hand, bathes her forehead with cold water, sings to her, or tells her fantastic stories of flying girls and talking animals. Upon recovery, Janey treats these episodes like a dream, for fear of warming to Father and letting her defenses fall away.

Up in the girls' bedroom, Janey's skirt is too tight on her, and she swears and throws it to the ground. "I shouldn't be growing," she mutters.

"You don't look any different to me," Mary says to reassure her.

Janey turns away and leans her elbows against the window frame. Her vertebrae stretch and swell against the tight skin of her back, rounding upward like they are waiting to break free. She runs her hands through her damp hair. "I can't do this forever," she says out the window.

"Nobody can do anything forever," Mary says.

"You're right," says Janey. "Let me try on one of your dresses."

Mary is shorter than Janey but about twice as wide, and they both laugh as Janey swims about in too much cloth, striking ridiculous poses.

Eventually Janey finds a dress of hers that still fits. They slip on their shoes, which feel so strange that they have to take slow, careful steps to avoid falling over. Father is gone already, to see how their vegetables survived the first frost. The world seems new and chill and sparkling, although they know it will thaw to muck as the sun moves higher in the sky.

Mary dawdles, and they walk too slowly to get to school on time. Mr. Abraham might be angry, but Mary resists Janey's tugs on her arm, arguing that she would take a whipping right now if it means they get to be outside a little longer. Nobody's whipped Janey in ages, perhaps because they're afraid she might grab the stick and begin whipping them back.

At school, the children are uniformly miserable, pulling at their clothes, twisting in their seats, and picking at dirt under their fingernails. Their eyes roll red and wild, naked hands reaching to peel scabs and pick at sores. They avoid one another's gazes, trying to recollect themselves from the summer mobs, embarrassed at the way their skin shows, hair combed tight, wrapped and trussed in clothing that won't seem normal for a few days.

Janey always enjoys school, and even today she seems a little cheerful. At her age, she's learned all she needs to learn, so she rotates around to different classrooms, performing duties as a surprisingly patient assistant. Her thin fingers will grasp the end of a pencil over smaller, plumper ones, and she'll guide it around in careful swoops. Even the slow children, the ones who really can't ever learn to read or write but are eager to try, she approaches with optimism and interest.

While she can work forever with an intent child desperate to please her, Janey cannot stand impertinence or laziness. If any of her charges are feckless, or irritable, or do not properly appreciate her help, she loses her temper and rains a volley of smacks on his or her head and shoulders. Once, in a classroom of younger boys, she even grabbed the teacher's switch and thrashed an obstinate Frederick Moses until he howled.

It's early enough that the mud is still frozen in peaks and whirls and valleys, like dollops of filthy whipped cream. The air is strangely silent, the sibilant hum of mosquitoes vanished overnight. The entire world is brown except for the crop fields and gardens, where farmers are extravagantly stretching and moving very slowly, simply because they can. Women are sitting on steps, eating breakfast with their fingers. Pushed outside and left alone for the first time since the beginning of summer, dogs scrabble against the door in fear before suddenly realizing the air is clear. Then they lurch around like heavyset lambs, waving their tails and barking with joy. A dog knocks into Janey midleap, and she falls to her knees, giggling.

"I almost don't mind coming back from summer," she tells Mary, "if I can see the dogs." She pushes her face against the dog and blows into its ears. "The end of my freedom is the beginning of yours, isn't it?" she asks the dog. "Would you like to trade places until next summer?" The dog barks.

CHAPTER TWENTY∕ONE

Vanessa

That night, Vanessa sits at the kitchen table and drinks glass after glass of rich, musky goat's milk while Mother fills her in on what happened over the summer.

Grady and Karen Gideon took their final draft, as Grady couldn't walk well since the accident. Their son Byron took over the house with his wife and child. A slew of girls a little older than Vanessa are to be married, naturally, and a few are pregnant. Lots of women had babies, and lots had defectives. Jana Saul had her third defective, so her husband decided to take another wife and conveniently chose Carol Joseph, who was widowed last year. Now Jana and Carol are fighting like angry cats, and if Jana doesn't stop trying to eject Carol, she'll get a shaming. Amanda Balthazar bled out from a defective and is dead, and her husband, Andrew, is walking around like somebody hit him in the head with a brick. Ursula Gideon had twins, both healthy, which hasn't happened in so long that people are lining up outside the house to see them. Stella Aaron was caught talking to a man alone and will be shamed, and so will Ursula Saul, who blasphemed the ancestors to her sister.

Most surprisingly, there is a new family on the island. Their names are Clyde and Maureen Adam; Clyde is a skilled carver, and Maureen is pregnant. Father is having them over for dinner tomorrow night, and Vanessa has to be on her best behavior.

Vanessa is bursting with excitement about the Adams. She was a baby when the second-newest family, the Jacobs, came to live on the island. She's always felt cheated by not remembering what a family from the wastelands looked like, staggering in. This news is a bright spot in a generally dim return to home and regular life. Father won't stop hugging and kissing Vanessa and telling her how much he missed her, which makes her tense. Her face, clean and bare, feels skinned.

Mother notices Vanessa's discomfort and sings with her, "Summer Rains" and "Arthur Balthazar" and "Night of a Thousand Meteors." It feels all right to sing church songs, now that she's back.

For dinner there will be chicken, roasted with new potatoes and beans. With the chill in the air, hot food sounds wonderful to Vanessa, even though she'd trade any hot meal in a minute for a meal of filthy bread eaten outside. Father likes to say, "The seasons change, whether you like it or not." That night, after he leaves, she cries helpless tears of frustration into her pillow, thinking of the next summer nine months away—or, for her, perhaps never. In the morning, she makes sure her face is composed, even if her eyelids are swollen and her complexion mottled. She doesn't like Father to see her cry.

Walking to school with dragging steps, Vanessa watches the dogs run and play, wishing she could join them. She makes it on time, although Grace Aaron gets whipped for lateness. Her hitching sobs, disproportionate to the force of Mr. Abraham's blows, seem to cry for every dismal, uncomfortable student in the class. They read out loud from a book about metals and the layers of the earth, which makes Vanessa yawn and squirm. The only metal the island gets is brought in by wanderers, and the only layer of earth she cares about is the mud outside, slowly thawing.

During recess everyone huddles together, both because it's still chilly and because they're wretched. There are clots of younger children sluggishly circulating around the school, playing slowly and clumsily like they forgot how. Vanessa sees Janey Solomon's copper head and creeps closer to hear what she's saying. There's a group of girls around her, and Mary is stuck to her side as usual.

"Having two babies at once is ridiculous," Janey is saying, wiping a strand of bright hair off her forehead. "I'm surprised she's alive; she should have just ripped in two."

"But now she can stop," points out Mary. "She's had her two children."

"Maybe," chimes in Fiona Adam. "Father says they might only count them as one child, and let her have another."

"I read once about twins who were born stuck together," says Vanessa, her confident voice carrying over the group. "Two legs, but two heads. They grew up and lived until they were old." Vanessa's library is invaluable; she can almost always tell people something they don't know.

Everyone turns to face her. "That's impossible," says Fiona, scowling darkly.

"I saw a picture," says Vanessa defiantly.

"It's just a different type of defective," says Janey, and Vanessa feels a small leap of pride at being defended by her. "Except they lived. I didn't know they had defectives, before."

Not all defectives are born early, and some do continue to draw breath. Vanessa saw a defective delivered once that was quietly placed facedown in a bowl of water while its mother cried. It had no legs, just a tail that trailed off into nothing. Vanessa always wondered if it would have lived, had it been allowed to continue breathing.

"They both lived. Or it lived, or she lived," said Vanessa. "At least old enough to be a child."

"So if you marry her, are you marrying one wife or two?" asks Letty, and everyone giggles.

"What other defectives did you see in that book?" demands Janey.

"None," Vanessa admits. "Only those. They were dressed up in weird clothes and had paint on their faces."

Everyone nods wisely, as if they know what this signifies.

"I think it was a story," says Fiona. "Somebody made it up. How could something like that eat? Does it use both mouths or one? If you punch it, does it hurt both of them or just one?"

"Some of the defectives are bled out," Carla Adam points out. "And sometimes they have more than two legs, although I've never heard of two heads."

"I heard once," says Letty, "that a woman gave birth to a defective that was a fish. It had gills and scales and everything."

"Ha! Who did she spend the night with?" cries Fiona, and everyone doubles over laughing at the thought of a woman lying down under a big fish. They become breathless with giggling, their laughter echoing around the glum field.

As their mirth wanes, there's a pause, and then Diana Saul says thoughtfully, "Alicia is pregnant." Diana used to be Alicia's best friend, before Alicia bled and had her summer of fruition. Now Alicia is married to Harold Balthazar and her belly is swelling. She looks strange to Vanessa when they pass each other at church, with her skinny legs sticking out of a woman's dress.

"It'll be your turn next summer," says Letty to Diana, and it's hard to tell if she's trying to be comforting or threatening. Diana presses her palms against her flat chest, as if to test for new growth, and then runs her hands contentedly down her ribs. Nobody looks at Fiona, who missed her summer of fruition by about two days. Her body is pushing against her dress in all directions, fighting to emerge from the straight shift.

"Amanda Balthazar bled out, I heard," says Lily Jacob. "All of a sudden, her blood just all fell out and she dropped dead on the floor."

Everyone glances at Janey, who loved Amanda. Her face is turned away toward a cluster of boys playing with a frog. "She—" she says. Her voice is heavy and trembling, and she continues looking studiously away from them. Mary puts a tentative hand on her arm, and Janey lashes it off with a violent motion and then becomes still again.

"Anyone can bleed out," Diana says. "Sometimes it's a defective, but sometimes it's just bad luck."

"My mother almost bled out once," says Letty, "when I was younger. Her skin looked like chalk and she had to lie in bed for weeks."

"I heard that it's your monthly bleeding that will tell you," says Diana. "If you bleed a lot every month then you won't bleed out, but if you don't bleed much then the blood builds up in your womb, and then suddenly you bleed out the baby."

"I don't think she bled out," says a voice so soft Vanessa has to search for the speaker. She sees tiny, bedraggled Caitlin Jacob standing awkwardly at one side of the group. Vanessa finds Caitlin annoying, with her hunched-over frame and shyness; she acts like a frightened mouse.

"What do you mean?" demands Letty. "Of course she did."

Caitlin shakes her head, but she's already backing away slowly, admitting defeat in front of Letty's indignation.

"Wait," says Janey, turning and holding out her hand. Caitlin stops and looks at her. Janey's face is pale beneath her freckles, and her eyes are hooded and glassy. "What do you mean?"

Caitlin glances around as if waiting for someone and then shakes her head so her braid falls over her shoulder, hiding a bruise on her neck. "Nothing."

"Come here," says Janey in a sweet tone Vanessa has never heard before. Caitlin hovers indecisively, but then slips in next to her.

"Now," says Janey, putting a hand on her shoulder, "why do you say she didn't bleed out?" Vanessa has a sudden picture of Janey and Amanda running together two summers ago, muddy and bloody with their teeth bared.

"Because I saw her," says Caitlin so quietly that they have to lean in to hear her. "I saw her in the water. She drowned."

"In the water?" exclaims Fiona, but Janey silences her with a wave of her hand.

"When did you see her?" asks Janey.

"It was yesterday," says Caitlin, and suddenly Vanessa notices how

135

tired she looks, with purple half-moons under bloodshot eyes. There's a pattern of small bruises up her forearm. "I saw them take her body out of the water. It was all blue. Her body."

"Who took her body?"

"The wanderers. They were standing there in their black coats. They pulled her out of the water."

"Are you sure?" says Janey.

"Even if that was true, you don't know she drowned," says Fiona. "She could have bled out and then..." She trails off, trying to think of a reason Amanda's body would have been in the sea.

"There was water coming out of her mouth," says Caitlin.

Everyone is silent for a moment, and then Fiona glares at Caitlin. "Liar."

Caitlin shakes her head, and everyone looks at her frail, marked body. There's an awkward silence.

Letty sighs dismissively. "Why would they tell us she bled out?"

But Janey's face is stony, her hands trembling. She takes Caitlin's shoulder and peers at her intently. Caitlin, surprisingly, stares back, looking weary but determined. Inhaling, Janey releases her and walks off, leaving the school grounds. Mary is shifting her gaze from Janey to the other girls, trying to decide what to do, when Mr. Joseph, who teaches one of the younger classrooms, comes to call everyone back into the school. He looks at Janey's retreating body, but then shrugs one shoulder and turns away.

Back in the classroom, Mr. Abraham starts talking about types of metal in the wastelands, and Mary puts her head on her folded arms. Caitlin is staring vacantly out the window. Vanessa looks around, trying to catch someone's eye, but all the girls are resolutely faced forward.

CHAPTER TWENTY-TWO

Vanessa

For dinner, the wanderer Adams are expecting the new Adams. Vanessa knows she should be wild with anticipation, but she can't stop thinking about Janey's freckled, blazing face gazing at Caitlin's small, exhausted one. She would normally resent Caitlin and her whispery voice for taking everyone's attention away from her story of stuck-together twins, but she's too puzzled by what that whispery voice said.

Why would somebody put Amanda Balthazar's body into the water after she bled out? Dead bodies are buried deep below the farmlands. She's heard people say that they fertilize the crops, and others say that they stay whole until summer, when everything turns to muck and they sink like stones through endless layers of earth. Amanda couldn't have gone into the water and then suddenly bled out, because adults don't go out during the summer. Or if they do, they don't go in the water. The only explanation that would make sense is that her husband, crazed with grief, tried to wash off the blood in the sea. But why drag her all the way to the sea if he wanted to wash her? The mosquitoes would have sucked him dry. It doesn't make any sense to Vanessa, no matter how long she turns it over in her mind. Finally, she decides Caitlin must be a very good liar. But it doesn't seem right for Caitlin to be a very good anything.

Vanessa stays in a daze throughout her cool bath, fresh dress, and Mother rebraiding her hair. She is sitting at the table, still musing, when Father opens the door to greet a man with a deep voice. Starting,

Vanessa perks up and walks to the door, where Father is shaking the hand of an enormous man; not fat, but tall and wide. *Whatever is going on in the wastelands,* Vanessa thinks, *there must be food somewhere.* She peers around him for his wife, but doesn't see a new woman anywhere.

"I'm sorry," says the man, smiling. "Maureen is feeling ill tonight."

"The pains of breeding," says Father, smiling back. "I do hope she's doing well overall?"

"Yes, yes," says the man jovially.

"Well," says Father, "a shame she can't make it, but we're pleased to have you."

The man looks over Father's shoulder and sees Vanessa lurking by the wall. He gives a funny little bow at the waist. "This must be your daughter."

"Indeed. Vanessa, this is the new Mr. Adam."

Staring at Mr. Adam, Vanessa tries to pinpoint the traces of the wastelands in his face. She is not sure exactly what she is looking for: scars, maybe, or features arranged in a pattern foreign and new. She searches his eyes for emptiness or a bleak knowledge. Finally she gives up; Mr. Adam possesses blunt features and a friendly expression that could be found on any island man. The only unusual thing about him is that his eyes are a dark brown, and they are staring at her face as intently as she is examining his.

Vanessa goes forward and shakes Mr. Adam's hand, which is large and damp and squeezes too hard. "A lovely girl," says Mr. Adam, still holding on to her hand. She wonders if he's going to hold it all night. "Absolutely lovely."

Father's hands settle on her shoulders. "I agree, of course." He pulls Vanessa slightly backwards against him, breaking Mr. Adam's grip. "Irene has made a beautiful dinner for us."

Father sits at the head of the table with Mother to his right, Vanessa and Ben to each side, and Mr. Adam across from him. Vanessa breathes in the scent of the steaming food appreciatively. There are biscuits and roasted potatoes out already, and chicken cooked with onions. "We have carrots also, and baked apples," says Mother, drifting into the kitchen. She eyes Mr. Adam warily, like he is a strange new animal too unfamiliar to deem harmless.

"So, Clyde, how are you settling in?" asks Father as he passes him a plate of biscuits.

"Well, very well," says Mr. Adam. "A beautiful place here, very beautiful. Much different from what I'm used to, of course."

Ears pricked, Vanessa waits hopefully for him to say what he's used to, but he stuffs his mouth full of biscuit. She glances at Father, whose lips are tight. Sighing, she accepts a platter of roasted carrots, orange and purple and swimming in butter, and scrapes some onto her plate.

"It's a shame you arrived during summer," says Mother. "You hardly got to see anything, kept inside your house. Now it's safe to walk around outside."

"Safe from mosquitoes or safe from dirty children?" Mr. Adam chuckles. "No, no, a charming summer ritual you have. Let the children out to play. Keeps them obedient the rest of the year."

"You must be very excited to have your first child," says Father. "I hope Maureen isn't ill often?"

Mr. Adam shrugs, chewing. "She does like to rest a lot."

"Sleeping for two," says Mother, smiling stiffly. "She had better sleep while she can." Leaning forward, she wipes butter off Ben's chin with her thumb.

"This is a lovely house." Mr. Adam looks around at the well-maintained walls, arched rocking chairs, and soft, clean rugs. "Who lived in it before you?"

"My parents. It's been in our family for generations. We lived briefly in another one right after Irene and I were married, while my parents were still alive. Two Josephs had died, and the house was free."

"They both died at the same time?"

"Of course they died together," says Mother.

Mr. Adam frowns. "What, one killed the other?"

139

"No," says Father, coughing a little. "Remember. Here when somebody is no longer of use—no longer contributing, and their children have children—they take the final draft. It, well, I'm sure they must have told you before you came."

"Right, yes, right, I'm sorry," says Mr. Adam. "Clean them out when they've got no more purpose. Good idea."

"What, in the wastelands do people just live until they die?" blurts Vanessa.

Mr. Adam looks surprised, and Father looks worried. "Vanessa, please don't interrupt."

Mother smiles again, and Vanessa sees tightness around her eyes and the corners of her mouth. She doesn't seem to like Mr. Adam very much, or perhaps she's simply frightened of him.

"It will be so helpful to have another carver on the island," says Father. "It's a wonderful skill. We try to reduce our dependence on metal as much as we can."

"You seem to have some good wood on this island," says Mr. Adam. "Good trees. I think I can make some useful tools."

"Wonderful," says Father. "We bring in wood from the wastelands too. We have to be careful and make sure our trees keep up their numbers. There's a whole area of the island we haven't cultivated at all. It's perfectly wild. The children love it in summer." Mr. Adam nods, and everyone sits and chews for a bit. Vanessa bites into a biscuit and inhales the yeasty steam that emanates from it.

"Have you seen the church?" Mother asks Mr. Adam politely.

"Yes, the ever-sinking one. I can't imagine wasting all that labor on a building that sinks, but John says it's the way the ancestors wanted it. Have you ever thought about how tall it would be if you drew it back up from the mud? It would tower over everything!"

"It would fall over," points out Vanessa.

Mr. Adam laughs. "True, it would fall over. Anyway, it's quite beautifully designed, although the thought of it is a bit eerie. All those church rooms, all the way down, all empty and dark. It's scary, isn't it?"

"Why?" asks Vanessa. He winks at her but doesn't answer.

"That is Vanessa's favorite word," says Mother.

"A smart girl, are you?" says Mr. Adam.

"I do believe she's read almost all of my library," says Father. "She's an expert on many matters, although most of them are useless here."

"You let her read books from outside?" says Mr. Adam, looking surprised.

"Some of them," says Father defensively. "She's quite intelligent."

"That seems dangerous."

"No harm so far," says Father.

"I've seen the school, and I must say, I don't see the point of any of it," says Mr. Adam.

"What do you mean?" asks Mother. She is cutting her food very slowly, as if the task requires intense attention. "It's a school. For children. The first ancestors built it. The first school, I mean, not the actual building they use now."

"Why do the girls need to learn to read? Hell, I'd bet only a quarter of the boys need to read. There's no point." Vanessa isn't sure what "hell" means, but it sounds fun to say it the way Mr. Adam says it. *Hell.*

"Reading is a valuable skill," says Father. "Instructions, records, procedures...Many wives help their husbands with their work."

"And how many of those men need to read?" says Mr. Adam.

"What about *Our Book*?" offers Mother. "Everyone should be able to read *Our Book*."

"Not to mention that the schools teach skills," continues Father. "They teach about farming, forging..."

"I suppose that's useful, but why must the girls read *Our Book*? They can memorize passages—that should be enough."

"You don't think girls should read?" says Vanessa in a too-loud voice.

"No need for it, sweetheart," says Mr. Adam. Vanessa rolls the word "sweetheart" around in her mind. It sounds like he's going to eat her organs. "You'll get married, have children, help out your husband if you need to. Why waste the energy learning to read when there's no use for it? It's like all these clocks. Why do you need clocks? Why do you need to know what time it is? Why do you need books?"

There is a long silence around the table. Then Father sighs and says, "I believe in knowledge for its own sake."

"Well, I believe that teaching girls things they don't need, when they could be helping their mothers, is a waste of time," responds Mr. Adam.

Father nods curtly. "That's not a new idea. There are many on this island who agree with you. It's something the wanderers have discussed for a long time."

"Good!" says Mr. Adam, laughing. "I hope they agree it's a bad idea. The schooling you do here is more tradition than anything else. You need to break with the mainland—the wastelands, for good. I wouldn't send any daughter of mine to school."

"Maybe you'll have sons," Vanessa says irritably, and they all turn to look at her.

Mr. Adam raises his eyebrows, furrowing his forehead. "Different rules around this table than what I'm used to, I see."

Her irritation wars with her curiosity. "What *are* you used to?"

Father half smiles, but his eyes are hard. "You'll need to be more careful than that, Clyde."

Mr. Adam winces. "Sorry. I know."

"People eat at tables in the wastelands?" Vanessa persists. Her ideas of the wastelands don't include tables. "There are tables, and rules, and people eat there? What do they eat?"

"It's a figure of speech," says Mr. Adam, which she doesn't understand. "Where I come from, it's just a thing people say. It doesn't mean anything."

"But you do come from somewhere," says Vanessa.

"Vanessa," says Father sternly, and then Ben spills his milk all over the table and starts screaming. By the time it's cleaned up, the talk has moved to farming and the types of crops on the island. Vanessa tries to move the topic back to the wastelands, but every attempt she makes is neatly foiled by Mother or Father.

"Ben's done," she finally says, giving up. "So am I. May we be excused?"

"Of course," says Mother, nodding. "We'll call you when it's time to clear the plates."

Vanessa plays with Ben as he pretends to be a dog, yapping and wagging his little behind. "What a good dog," she croons, smoothing his tangle of curls. "Shall I give you leftovers from dinner for being so good?" Ben barks. Absently, Vanessa watches him turn in circles. She must get Mr. Adam alone.

When Mother calls, Vanessa puts Ben back in his chair and begins deftly gathering plates and utensils, putting them in the washtub in the kitchen. She takes a handful of gritty, slimy soap to mix with some water and swishes everything about quietly. Mr. Adam and her parents are talking about water and rainfall.

She pops her head in. "Excuse me, Mother," she says, "have you shown Mr. Adam the kitchen? He may want to build one like Father did."

She fears being reprimanded for interrupting, but Mother beams. "Yes, let me show you. James built it for me, and it's just so clever. A lot of houses are imitating the way he set the stones from the cooking fire."

Mother, Father, and Mr. Adam enter the room, followed by a curious Ben. As Father is explaining the way he set the stones and how the metal was forged from scraps, Ben becomes bored and fractious. Vanessa leans toward Ben and whispers, "I'm so sorry, I'm so sorry, I promise I will give you all my cookies forever." Then, closing her eyes and wincing, she gives him a sharp pinch on the arm.

A wail erupts from his small face, his mouth squared in a scream. The adults jump. Ben is pointing an accusing finger at Vanessa, but Mother doesn't notice. She swoops down and picks Ben up, cooing to him, and then shoots an apologetic glance at Father and Mr. Adam. "Excuse me for a moment. It's time for Ben to go to bed," she says, and walks away as Ben starts hiccupping, "Vanessa *pinched* me!" She knows Mother won't believe him, as Vanessa is never cruel to Ben. But her insides feel dirty and stained, and she wonders if she can ever think of herself as a good person again.

Taking a deep breath, she stills her mind and returns to her task. Mr. Adam and Father are chuckling about the trials of motherhood. She hovers around their perimeter, absorbing Father's story about Elizabeth Saul, whose son was so difficult to soothe that she once tried dunking him into the ocean to see if she could freeze him calm. Mr. Adam says he hopes Maureen's baby will sleep through the night early, and Father wishes him luck.

"Father," says Vanessa, when there is a lull in the conversation, "perhaps I could show Mr. Adam our library?"

"I don't think Mr. Adam is particularly interested in books," replies Father, with a slight bite to his tone.

"But, please, Father, it would make me feel so"—she casts around for a word likely to affect him—"so *knowledgeable*."

"It's fine, James," says Mr. Adam, his eyes now bright and blinking rapidly. "I'm actually curious to see what you've got."

"She can't show you the ones that are locked away," he says, "but perhaps you don't want to see them anyway."

"What do you mean, locked away?"

"They're not for everyone," he says. "Not for anyone, really, who has never been to the wastelands."

Mr. Adam looks stunned. "Why would you keep those?" he asks. "The risk! I'm surprised they let you have them."

"And what *they* would be forbidding me?" Father inquires irritably.

"Why, the other wanderers, I suppose. What's the point of having them?"

"Go, Vanessa," Father says, waving his arm. "I'll be here, enjoying some peace." He aims a dark look at Mr. Adam.

Her heart skipping with glee, Vanessa says politely, "This way, Mr. Adam," and leads him through the passage to the library.

It's almost dusk, and the irregular window Father placed in the ceiling emits a gray, dull light. Vanessa steps in and feels hushed by the quiet, dim air and the stately lines of books on their shelves. "Here it is," she whispers, "the library."

"Huh." Mr. Adam looks around halfheartedly, then gazes at her. "You've read all of these?"

"No," says Vanessa, "some of them are boring." Mr. Adam snorts.

Cubist Picasso catches her eye, and she pulls it out carefully. "This is a book of pictures," she says. "We don't have many with pictures."

"I see," says Mr. Adam as she opens the book to show a calm, satisfied-looking woman whose eyes are on the same side of her face, one resting on her nose while the other marches across her cheekbone.

"The pictures are strange," she says. "But see how smooth the paper is." She runs her fingers over it. "I don't know how he made the pictures that way."

"Those are pictures of pictures," says Mr. Adam. "Not the picture itself."

"Like the picture of the first Mr. Adam," she says. "Capturing time on paper."

Mr. Adam looks confused. "No, just a picture," he says.

"Did you know him?" asks Vanessa. "Cubist Picasso?"

"I think he's dead," says Mr. Adam.

"Did he make this book?"

"I doubt it. I guess he was a famous artist, so people took pictures of his paintings and put them in a book."

Vanessa considers this. There are artists on the island—Mr. Moses the brewer carves lifelike birds and people, and Mr. Gideon the shoemaker draws with charcoal on paper, making portraits almost akin to the miraculous photographs. Vanessa imagines using a magical contraption to catch Mr. Gideon's images and making a book out of them. The idea is so ridiculous she suddenly laughs out loud. Mr. Adam laughs too, even though he can't read her thoughts.

"I think it's...I don't think he's very good," says Mr. Adam.

"I don't either," says Vanessa. "Nobody looks like this, but at the same time it's interesting."

"I suppose," says Mr. Adam. "Which is your favorite book in here?"

"Oh," says Vanessa, overwhelmed at the difficulty of this question. "Oh, I don't know. I think...well, I love *The Call of the Wild.*"

"That's about a dog, right?"

"A dog, yes, in a place called Alaska, and they pull people around on sleds for gold. Some of the men are very mean. The only gold I've seen is on Mr. Solomon the wanderer's plate that he collected from the wastelands. It has flowers on it too." Vanessa isn't sure why people would fight and kill and freeze for something shiny and yellow, but at the same time, it is so brilliant and beautiful that she can almost understand it. "I can't imagine a place where you eat off something so precious."

"See, this is why it's a mistake to let everyone read things like this," says Mr. Adam. "You shouldn't know what Alaska is, or gold, or anything like that."

"But I just said that there's gold on the plate," replies Vanessa. "And I don't know anything about Alaska except it's cold and there's gold there. And there are big dogs, huge strong dogs, stronger than the dogs here, and you can make them do things."

"There are certainly a lot of dogs on the island," Mr. Adam says slowly. "Cats too, although not so many as the dogs. But I suppose you need cats to keep the rats in check. And dogs make for good company."

"Do you have a dog now?" asks Vanessa.

"Oh, not yet, though I'm sure I will eventually. Everywhere I look people are drowning puppies, so I assume they can spare one for us."

"Would Mrs. Adam like that?"

"I suppose. She had a dog back—back in the wastelands, a yippy little thing."

"Oh?" says Vanessa carefully.

"No bigger than a loaf of bread, barked at everything."

"A puppy?"

"No, no, a full-grown dog."

Vanessa has never seen a dog the size of a loaf of bread. All the dogs on the island are more or less the same size. "What did Mrs. Adam do with it?" she asks.

"Oh, she just carried it around," he says. "Like a baby. Now she'll have a real baby."

"Yes, when is the baby coming?"

"Oh, not long. Two months at the most. She's terrified of having it, poor thing."

"Terrified?"

"That something will go wrong."

"That she'll bleed out or have a defective?"

"Well, I suppose. No defectives, though." He snorts. "Not my child. We don't have that problem."

"But...there are no defectives in the wastelands?"

"Oh, well, there are, I suppose."

"You suppose?"

"I mean, yes, there are. It's different, though."

"What's different?"

"Well, it's not...I mean, there aren't the same kind of rules that you have here."

"What kind of rules did you have?"

"None, really. I mean, I couldn't go around killing people or anything like that."

"What about children?"

"What about them?"

"Do people kill them?"

"Kill them? It's—" He glances at her. "You know I'm not supposed to be talking to you about this."

She remains quiet.

"You're a sneaky little girl, Vanessa," he says, wagging his finger at her. "Do you know what I do with sneaky little girls?"

She stares at him. "No." She wasn't aware that people had procedures for such things. Perhaps they do in the wastelands.

He inhales to say something, then exhales and smiles at her. "You're very smart. Too smart. But you're such a lovely girl I think I'll forgive you."

She's not sure what to say, so mumbles a quiet "Thank you."

Suddenly she realizes she has never been alone with an adult man besides Father in all her life. She glances at Mr. Adam, who somehow seems larger and darker than he was before, like the dim light has obliterated his face, his hands swelled to gargantuan proportions. He appears to be moving closer to her, although his legs and feet are still, like he is expanding and his flesh is advancing on her small frame. She looks away, her breath quickening. Suddenly she is sure that if Mother knew she was alone with Mr. Adam, she would be furious.

"You're an obedient girl too, aren't you, Vanessa?"

"I suppose," says Vanessa carefully. She blinks a few times, but he still seems to be towering above her, wrapped in shadow. He moves closer.

"You do what you're supposed to."

"Yes."

He is quiet for a moment, and then says, "I like that about your island. That children follow the rules."

She says, "They don't, in the wastelands?"

"Not like here." And she knows she could parse the meaning of those three words for days, weeks, the rest of her life.

"Tell me," she says desperately, "please tell me."

"Sneaky little girl," he says again, and she feels an impotent fury well in her chest.

"Mr. Adam, please tell me *something,*" she says. "Anything."

He gazes at her for a while, taking her measure, and says, "In the wastelands..." He stops, obviously thinking as hard as he can. "In the wastelands...children can...No. In the wastelands..." He stops. "I'm sorry, Vanessa. I truly am. But I honestly think it's better for you, for everyone here, to know nothing."

"At least tell me about the fires."

"Fires?"

"The fires, the fires of the wastelands. Do they burn up everything?"

His mouth forms a vowel, then flattens. A pause, his eyes searching Vanessa's pleading stare. "I want you to tell me about the island instead," he says finally.

Something inside her falls down, down around her gut, the clattering remnant of her hope of knowledge. She feels angry at herself, for thinking she could engineer such a thing, angry at Mr. Adam for being so stupid, angry at Father and Mother and the wanderers and the ancestors and everyone she has ever known. She balls her fists and stamps her foot, and feels Mr. Adam's hand suddenly on her shoulder, his bulk rearing toward her face, and she takes a deep breath and tells herself not to punch him.

"Vanessa!" a sharp voice says, and it's Mother, standing by the entrance of the library and looking furious. "What are you doing here?"

"Father said I could show Mr. Adam the library."

"Mr. Adam," says Mother, courteously but with a chill vibration in her voice, "please come have a cup of tea with us."

"Of course," says Mr. Adam. "Thank you, Vanessa, for the tour."

They sit and sip tea while Father and Mr. Adam talk about dung, of all things, the collection of it and fertilization of the fields. Mother rolls her eyes at Vanessa, who smiles slightly into her teacup. Mr. Adam keeps staring at her, as if he wants to move closer to her again and have her beg him for answers. Finally it is full dark. The candles are lit, and Mr. Adam gets up and moves around clumsily in preparation to leave, although he did not bring anything he needs to retrieve. Vanessa has a headache and wishes he would just go.

"Good-bye, Vanessa," says Mr. Adam after bidding farewell to Mother and Father. Mother is hovering over the table, pretending to be rearranging the cloth. He lowers his voice. "I hope you're not angry with me for not answering your questions. I just have to follow the rules like everyone else. I do hope to see more of you."

"Good-bye," she says. They shake hands again, and again his hand holds on to hers for an uncomfortably long time. There's a funny quiet all around the room. Eventually she slips free; his hands are coated with an amalgam of sweat and butter.

Later, when Vanessa is supposed to be asleep, she hears Mother and Father talking in their bedroom. Stepping hesitantly and softly, she crouches by their door and puts her ear to it.

"He's not very bright, is he?" says Mother. "I mean, he's…cunning, I suppose. Sneaky."

"By the ancestors, I hope he doesn't turn into another Robert Jacob," says Father. "What luck that would be."

"I'm sure he won't be that bad," replies Mother. "He's just—"

"Did you see the way he looked at Vanessa? After they'd been in the library? By the ancestors, I'd never have let her go in there with him if—I just wanted to get rid of him for a few blessed moments. But then after, his eyes were…They were before, even, I think. I just didn't notice, I just thought he was strange."

"Well, when you invite someone new to the island, I mean, they have to…"

"They have to have some self-control. Perhaps we should stop having these new families come in, just go on on our own."

"You know we can't. Think of all the defectives this year."

"I know, I know. Where are the men like the ancestors? Where are they?"

"Perhaps there are no more men like the ancestors anymore," says Mother.

"Perhaps," says Father. He sounds broody and fretful, and it's a tone Vanessa recognizes. She goes back to bed and lies awake, waiting for him. He'll want to be held, to be soothed. When she finally falls asleep, she dreams of Amanda Balthazar rising up from the water, holding a defective that's half fish, half baby.

CHAPTER TWENTY#THREE

Janey

Janey carries Amanda's kiss on her lips, sweet as a slick of honey, relentless as a disease. She will hear a faint echo of Amanda's voice, or catch the scent of her skin on the air, and whirl abruptly to see nothing.

Ever since Janey found out about Amanda's body being pulled from the sea, she hasn't slept. Her nerves are kindled, each strand blazing at both ends. At night, she paces, everything she knows whirling in shimmering patterns in her brain. The hard sensation of the wooden church pews against her bony rump. The pastor's rants against disobedience. The morning fog, obscuring the horizon as neatly as a shielding hand. The wanderers, stalking the island like tall, grim predators. Amanda's face, her look of terror as she heard someone in the house. The vortex of the summer of fruition, sucking in girls and spitting out wives. Muddy children pushing each other over for sugar-sweet morsels. The ferryman, gliding in and out like a slow tide. The wasteland glass, sturdy and crystalline in ever-rotting houses. The church, falling down into the darkness below, forever sinking under its own weight while islanders scramble to build up a series of dark rooms replete with the stale, imposing words of dead holy men.

As she paces, she snatches at the floating pieces in her mind, trying to make a structure that stands. The wanderers. The water. Amanda. The wastelands. Mary. The shalt-nots. Every time she tries to create an integral pattern, a clear picture, it shatters and falls into mist. But her will is ever-flowing, unquenched. If she thinks hard enough, she can solve this puzzle. She can solve everything.

At first Mary scolds her affectionately. "Janey, I can't sleep without you!" she whispers. "And stop *walking*."

"You were sleeping," retorts Janey. "You can do it again."

Then Mary tries appealing to her. "Janey, I'm cold. Come back to bed, it's freezing."

Janey pads over, deftly doubles their quilt into a thicker, narrower one, and ceremoniously drapes it over Mary. Giving it a little pat, she goes back to pacing.

Mary tries arguing with her. "Janey, this is ridiculous. You and Amanda weren't even that good friends." She knows this is a lie; Amanda was Janey's only real friend. During summer, they would wrap their arms around each other and simply sway in a slow dance, holding their bodies close, murmuring into each other's hair.

Janey bristles. "I loved her," she says, and then forgets about Mary completely, returning to her pacing. Six steps up, four steps over, six steps down, four steps over. It becomes a poem, a rhythm in her head. Janey becomes brighter and more awake with every passing moment, until something inside her is luminescent, sharp and alien. Mary squints at the light pouring out of her, although the room is dark and Janey is just a shadowy figure.

"Women bleed out and die all the time," Mary whispers to Janey as she paces the room. This isn't really true, although it seems to be increasing in frequency. "There's nothing special about Amanda."

"If she bled out, why was she in the water?" A pause. "Have you ever seen a woman after she bled out and died?"

"No," says Mary. "So what? I've never seen a woman die while birthing either, but it still happens."

"Do you remember Jill Abraham?"

"I guess. She died a while ago."

"I heard she wanted the summer of fruition changed. So the men and women were the same age."

"Ugh, the boys!"

"No, she wanted to wait until the girls were older."

"But...what would they do while they waited?"

"I don't know. Do you know how she died?"

"No."

"She bled out."

"Oh."

"I think there are others."

"Oh."

"I don't know." Janey goes back to pacing, sighing loudly every now and then. Mary yawns, mutters, and falls asleep. The moon is full, limning the room with edges of silver. Sitting on the bed, Janey realizes that she herself is absolutely exhausted, bone-weary, shaking with the effort of days awake. Suddenly she begins weeping silently, tears sheeting down her face and pattering onto her lap. She has a vision of Amanda's face when they heard the intruder: pale, her eyes wide, her hands frozen in midair. *I could have saved her,* thinks Janey, *instead of walking away.* Her lips retracting to bare her teeth, she brings her slender palms to cover her face in shame.

CHAPTER TWENTY*FOUR

Vanessa

The night after the dinner with Mr. Adam, Vanessa wanders outside. It's a warm day, and her shoes sink into the mud with a satisfying squelch. No longer foreign, the rough hem of her dress brushes her shins with every step, and her fingers play with the edge of her reddish-brown braid. Summer, the girl in the tree, seem years away.

The Jacobs' dog Bo comes to greet Vanessa for the first time since summer started. They are old friends, and Vanessa smiles to see her. She scratches Bo's ears, and the graying hound leans into her hand contentedly until she catches sight of a rat and immediately takes off. In fall and spring, it isn't even necessary to feed dogs and cats, as they can live off rats. Vanessa has always wanted a dog or cat, but they make Mother itch.

Slipping and sluicing through the mud, she heads toward the new Adam house. It is a popular location lately; Vanessa has seen many people slowly wander by, some blatantly staring through the windows to catch sight of the new Adams. It's almost dark, and nearly everybody is inside now, so Vanessa can lurk alone. Stepping around back, she sees a figure by the garden too small to be the new Mr. Adam.

"Are you Mrs. Adam?" Vanessa says softly, drawing closer. The woman doesn't answer, and Vanessa wonders if she's found another woman sneaking about, hoping for a glimpse of the new arrivals. "Mrs. Adam?" she says more loudly.

There's a pause, and then the woman turns. "Hello, I'm sorry," she says. "I'm not used to that name yet."

They stare at each other. "What was it before?" says Vanessa.

"Oh, never mind, nothing," she says. "There's just so much to get used to here." Mrs. Adam is thin, with poor posture, her long arms hanging down and crossing across her belly. Vanessa remembers Inga's mention of what happens to pregnant women in the wastelands, and she feels sorry for Mrs. Adam. She is about to reassure her that nobody here cuts open pregnant women when Mrs. Adam says suddenly, "What's your name?"

"Vanessa Adam. What's yours?"

"Maureen Adam, of course," she says, and they both laugh.

"What's different here?" says Vanessa. "From what you're used to, I mean. That you have to get used to. Or want to."

"Well." Mrs. Adam waves her hand vaguely around her. "The trees, so many of them! The people, the customs. You know."

"No."

"Well, of course you don't. I was told I wasn't supposed to say anything about—about—back there, you know. I mean, the wanderers know, of course. But nobody else does."

"Why can't you say anything?"

"They said it would poison everything," she says. "That's the word they used. Why, do the wanderers talk about back home? I mean, back there?"

"No. And the Jacobs, their daughter doesn't even remember anything."

"I see. Well, we're not supposed to either."

There's a silence. "What are you planting?" asks Vanessa.

"Nothing, just trying to take care of what was already here. I don't know much. So many women have offered to teach me."

"When will you have your baby?"

"Oh, a couple of months."

To Vanessa's eye, Mrs. Adam looks too big for seven months. Perhaps she will have twins. It's hard to make out her long face in the dim air, but she looks awfully old for her first pregnancy.

"My father has books," says Vanessa. "Wasteland books. He's a wanderer. He'll lend you books, if you want."

"Oh, I don't read well," Mrs. Adam says. "I don't garden well." She gives a little laugh. "I don't know what I'm good at!"

"Maybe you'll be a good mother."

"I hope so." She pats her belly. "I hear I can only have two."

"How many do people have in the wastelands?"

"The waste—now, you know I can't tell you anything."

"It can be a secret."

"I've been *strictly* told."

"What did you eat there?"

"Vanessa."

"I'm sorry. It's just so rare to get someone from the wastelands. I mean, the wanderers, but not someone who lived there."

"If it wasn't for your wanderers, we wouldn't be here. I must be thankful to them."

"And the ancestors."

Mrs. Adam sighs. "Yes, I suppose. My ancestors too now, although not by blood."

"They take care of everyone on the island. They're always watching us."

"Isn't that a little scary?" Mrs. Adam tugs on her ill-fitting dress and laughs nervously. "So tell me, Vanessa, what advice would you give to someone who's just moved here?"

Vanessa stares at her and tries to think of something Mrs. Adam might not have been told. Something every woman knows, but doesn't usually say. "Have sons?"

Mrs. Adam nods as though this isn't a surprising suggestion. "That's it, with daughters..." She pauses. "Clyde was very excited to come here. Not for that, for..." She shrugs. "You know. The new start. Nature, community..." She pauses, thinking. "What you've done here is impressive. The wanderers really explained how the whole society here...I had to know about it, or it would be too late. They don't want anyone leaving. And it's necessary. I mean, you know men. You have to keep the population down. And I guess there's drinks you can give, medicine, if they can't control themselves? Clyde wants to be here so badly, and he's my husband. There's nowhere I'd survive, anyway, on my own, I'm not good at being on my own. And if everyone does it, it can't be too bad, right?"

She stares pleadingly at Vanessa, leaning toward her eagerly as if Vanessa is about to pardon a crime. Vanessa has no idea what the jumble of words tumbling from Mrs. Adam means. All she can think of to say is "Right."

"Are you happy here, Vanessa?"

"Yes," says Vanessa, although she's not sure. Nobody has ever asked her that before.

Mrs. Adam hugs her. "Thank you, Vanessa. You've eased my mind. Clyde keeps saying it's just society, how people react. And I know, I know women want sons, who wouldn't? Some have only sons. I don't know what those fathers do. I'm sure I'll find out eventually. And being young is never pleasant. I think there's a better childhood here than back—than out there. Loving parents. A strong community. But it's good to hear. It's very good to hear." She pulls back and stares raptly into Vanessa's face, her eyes almost manic in their intensity.

Vanessa is beginning to think that Mrs. Adam is a little bit crazy. But she hugs her back anyway. "I'm sorry," she says into Mrs. Adam's lank, mouse-colored hair, even though she's not exactly sure what she's sorry for.

CHAPTER TWENTY-FIVE

Caitlin

At night, Caitlin has trouble finding a comfortable place to rest. The summer bruises are fading but still sore, and the autumn bruises— finger-sized, handprints, straight-out blows—are blossoming like rotten ivy across her body. She knows Father doesn't really beat her, he's just getting rid of all the tension that built up over the summer, but she wishes he'd let her sleep more. Mother gives him a double serving of pungent mash-wine every night at dinner, and Caitlin knows she's trying to make him slumber through the night. A small part of her glows at this exhibition of love.

She's dozing off after an exhausting evening when she hears tapping on her window. Jerking awake, Caitlin thinks for a moment that it's spring, almost summer, and Rosie is tossing pebbles at her window. She blinks, and it's autumn again and she has no clue why anyone outside would want her, but the thought of Father waking fills her with panic. Rushing to the window, Caitlin opens it quietly. There's Rosie, perched on her roof.

Caitlin scoots down toward her across the dry, flaking shingle. "Rosie. What is it?"

"We're all supposed to meet at the church."

Caitlin stares at her, trying to decide if she's dreaming. She looks upward to a clear, cold sky striped with alabaster stars.

"Well?" says Rosie. "Do you want to go together?"

"Why would we go to the church?" asks Caitlin carefully, as if Rosie is raving.

Rosie shrugs. "Linda told me about it. Janey wants us all there at midnight."

"Who's *us?*"

"The girls. The older ones, anyway."

"Why?"

"Do I look like Mary? I don't know why Janey does what she does."

"Well, I don't have a clock in my room. The only one is downstairs."

Rosie rolls her eyes. "Go watch it, then. I'll watch mine too. I'll wait for you a little before midnight."

"Do you know what time it is now?"

"About eleven."

"Okay," says Caitlin slowly. "Are you playing a trick on me?"

Rosie's face darkens. "That would be a stupid trick!" Caitlin can't tell if Rosie is offended at being accused of lying or of playing an inferior prank.

"Well, I'll try to get downstairs. If Mother or Father wakes up, I won't be able to go."

"I was scared your father was in there with you. He's so scary. Lots of girls won't be able to go. Make sure he doesn't come to your room and find you missing."

"How do I do that?" Caitlin asks.

"I don't know. I don't know everything. Why don't you just sit there and count out fifty minutes by seconds."

And so Caitlin goes back into her bedroom, kneels on her scratchy bed, and does just that. She counts too fast; when she creeps downstairs to look at the clock, it's only eleven thirty-five. She sits, nervously staring at the clock, watching the hand slowly creep toward midnight, worried that Father forgot to wind it and she'll miss the whole thing. Eventually she can't take it anymore, and she rushes outside. Rosie is waiting in the cold, shifting her weight from foot to foot on the frosty ground. It's a full moon, and Caitlin can see the outline of Rosie's thin body through her illuminated nightgown.

"You're late," says Rosie. "We have to hurry." She reaches out and grabs Caitlin's hand. Surprised and pleased by the strong hand gripping hers, Caitlin starts running with Rosie beside her. Their panting breath fogs, and Caitlin giggles at how cold her feet are on the stiff mud and wet, shining grass. Rosie remembered shoes, but they're too big, and she keeps losing one and then rushing back to claim it.

They hear other footsteps and slow down to see three girls jogging toward them.

"Do you know what's going on?" Natalie Saul hisses. "I heard Janey wants us in the church."

"I don't know," says Rosie, and Caitlin shrugs in agreement.

"This is all a trick," says Linda Gideon as they hurry along together. "There's going to be a bunch of boys there, and they're going to laugh at us."

"I don't think so," says Alma Joseph. "Janey would find out and beat them up."

When they arrive at the church, there's a small group of girls gathered around the entrance who hail the newcomers with relief, hoping vainly for further intelligence.

"I'm not going into that dark church," says Letty firmly.

"Me either," says Rosie. "Something might be in there."

"What if there's something waiting to eat us?" pipes up Joanne Balthazar, who's only five. Her sister brought her along.

"We're not going into the dark," says Rosie decisively. "We can wait here for a while and then leave if nothing happens."

"My toes feel like they're going to fall off," says Violet Balthazar.

"We can throw them down the stairs for the monster," giggles Letty, and the rest of the group laughs nervously.

"Look," says Ophelia Adam, pointing, but they all see it at the same time. There's a faint tawny glow coming from inside the church, illuminating the windows and seeping out through the door.

"There's somebody in there," says Linda.

"Or some*thing*," replies Natalie. The glow grows brighter. There are more girls gathered around the doorway now.

"Someone's lighting candles," says Nina Joseph. "I can see them through that window."

Rosie pokes Caitlin in the side. "You go first." Caitlin shakes her head rapidly, backing up a little in case Rosie decides to push her down the stairs.

"I'll go," says Vanessa Adam, looking annoyed. Playing with the end of her braid, she peers into the doorway and then takes a few hesitant steps down. "It's all right. It's Mary and Janey," she calls back. "Nina's right. They're lighting candles."

Confident that Janey and Mary wouldn't be lighting candles if they were fighting a monster, the girls tumble down the steps and into the church. Empty and shadowed, it looks cavernous compared to its familiar state, replete with worshippers and dim daylight. The orange glow of the candles lends light to the room, if not warmth. Mary is sitting calmly next to the altar, her shimmering dark hair loose around her shoulders. At her feet is Janey, looking impatient and twisting her fingers together.

"What is it?" cries Gina Abraham excitedly. "What are we doing?"

"I wanted to talk about... important things," Janey says. "Forbidden things. I didn't know how else to get us together without some adult looking on."

The girls glance around at one another as the silence lengthens and they wait for her to say more. Then Mary says, "Go on, get behind the altar."

Janey rolls her eyes. "I'm not Pastor Saul," she says.

"What?" calls a girl from the back, and then more softly, "What did she say?"

"See," says Mary. "We'll hear you better if you're higher up."

"But it's stupid," says Janey.

"If you have something to say," says Vanessa, "and you want us all to hear it..."

Janey unfolds her spindly body and walks up to the altar, almost as tall as the pastor but slender as a blade of grass. When she speaks from behind the podium, her faint voice is suddenly strong and echoing. With a start, Caitlin wonders if Pastor Saul's sermons are really deep and thundering, his voice driven by otherworldly power, or if it's simply a result of the way the church is structured. Janey coughs. "I...thank you for coming here. I just wanted to—I was talking with someone before she died. And she was talking about leaving the island. Maybe going to the wastelands, but I thought, maybe there's another island. Another island to go to."

A voice whispers, "What does she mean?"

"What I *mean* is what if we're not the only one? If you can go on an island and avoid the scourge, surely others did too."

Caitlin thinks of another island, perhaps with a similar church, perhaps with a red-haired girl admonishing the others at midnight.

"I mean, the world is big, right?" Janey asks. Caitlin sees Vanessa, who knows all about the world, nodding.

"Mr. Abraham showed us on a map," says Letty. "He said the island wasn't on it, but told us where we were."

"And for all we know, there's more world, not even on that map."

There's silence as everyone ponders this uncharted world. The littlest girls, already bored, have started a game to see who can jump the farthest. Cheers and whoops carry from one corner of the room, providing a jarring score to Janey's words.

"But Pastor Saul says that everyone else got stuck in the war," pipes up Wendy Balthazar.

"Well, what if he doesn't know everything about the entire world?" snaps Janey. "He's a pastor, not an ancestor. Or God."

Wendy shakes her head at her sister to indicate her disapproval of Janey's comment.

"Why would we be the only ones to escape the war?" Janey continues. "What's so special about us?"

"The ancestors," Nina says. "They had foresight."

"Well, maybe other people's ancestors had foresight."

There's a collective gasp, and then a mutter. The ancestors aren't just ancestors, they're *the* ancestors, chosen by God to start a new society. Janey slams her fist into the altar so hard that Caitlin wonders if she's dented it. "Are you seriously saying it couldn't ever happen anywhere else?" she asks. "That it's impossible anyone else might have survived?"

"She's right," says Vanessa. The others quiet and turn to her. "There must be pockets of people somewhere, on islands, in valleys…places where the scourge didn't reach, or didn't reach as badly. I mean, we can't be sure, but it wouldn't make sense for us to be the only ones." Caitlin isn't sure what a valley is, but she trusts Vanessa.

"It doesn't have to make sense," says Paula Abraham nastily. "It's the ancestors. And God."

"Other islands," continues Vanessa as if Paula hadn't spoken, "and they might be completely different."

"What do you mean?" asks Fiona. "Different how?"

"However you like," says Vanessa thoughtfully. "It depends on where they are. Different plants and animals and weather. Hotter, colder. Different trees, or no trees."

"What do they carve out of, then?" demands Paula.

"I don't know, I don't live there," Vanessa replies, and everyone laughs.

"What if on that island, it never gets warm enough for a summer?" asks Letty, and someone else says, "What if there aren't any dogs or cats?"

"What if women wear pants and men wear dresses?" says Fiona, and everyone laughs louder.

"What if nobody ever gets married, or knows who their father is?" says Millie Abraham.

"What if there aren't any men at all?" says Wendy.

"Then there'd be no babies," answers another voice.

"What if," says Lana Aaron, who is only six but more alert than her shrieking, tumbling counterparts, "what if the children are head of the family, and the parents have to do what *they* say?"

"What if they're all defectives, and they all live in one big defective family?"

"This isn't time for storytelling," insists Janey, although the ideas keep whizzing through the air, each girl eager to add her own. "This is a time to ask serious questions." Her voice becomes louder. "If there are other islands, where things are done differently, can we go there? Or can we change things here?"

There is a blank silence. "Change what?" ventures Nina.

"Change anything. Not just dogs and dresses. Change things that matter."

Another silence, and then a few girls turn to mutter to one another. "Like what?" asks Nina again.

Janey sighs. "If you could change anything about the island, what would it be?"

There's a pause. "More cookies," someone whispers, and a trail of giggles blows through the group like wind on grass.

"*Think* about it," says Janey, slamming her hand into the altar again. "What if we didn't have to get married? What if we didn't have to obey our fathers?" A spark in her eyes. "What if we could make it like summer all the time? Wouldn't you like that?"

The silence this time is full of doubt.

"But," says Fiona, "what about the ancestors?"

"What about them?" demands Janey.

"Well," says Fiona, as if explaining something to a very small child, "we live this way because the ancestors tell us to. So we don't fall to the darkness below."

"But then," says Vanessa, over another girl who is trying to speak, "what's the use of thinking about it? What if we didn't have to obey our fathers? That would be nice, but the truth is that we have fathers and they make us obey them—with their fists if they need to." Caitlin can feel everyone's eyes on her and wishes she would shrink into the ground.

"It would be nice to have summer all the time," continues Vanessa, "but we don't. We never will—the frost comes at the end of summer, and we have to go home. Otherwise we'd freeze or starve. They're going to make us get married whether we like it or not. We're small and they can force us to do anything they want." Her voice is grating and bitter. "And our mothers would help them. And when we are mothers, we'll feel the same way, no matter how much we think we won't. You want us to lead some kind of revolution?"

The girls look at one another helplessly, unsure what the word means. Even Janey looks puzzled.

"We have no weapons, nothing. We're like a herd of goats plotting to overthrow the humans that keep them. It's laughable. What's the point of thinking about it differently?" Vanessa's teeth are bared. Caitlin feels the room deflating, shrinking back.

"Because," says Janey, "they can't stop us from *thinking*. They can force us to do anything they want, but they can't stop us from thinking. And maybe if we think, we'll think up a way to..." She pauses, sighing. "Amanda is dead. You know that. But she was seeking a different way. A way to leave to another place. Amanda—" She stops herself, actually biting her lip to stem the flow of words. She glances at Mary, who shakes her head almost imperceptibly.

She stares around the room. "Think about it. Think if it was different."

There's a snort from a corner of the group, and someone whispers, "What if on the other island, it's your summer of fruition *all the time?*" There are giggles and groans of disgust.

"What if all there is to eat is spinach?"

"What if the freaks in the wastelands invade and kill everyone?"

"What if all there is to eat is cake?"

The chorus of what-ifs continues, and Janey looks tired. "This isn't the point," she says, but the idea has run away from her, galloping around the room like a playful dog. She looks sad, and frustrated, but also unsurprised. Caitlin wants to go comfort Janey, tell her she understands, but she isn't sure she does understand. Inching closer—invisible as ever—she hears Janey murmur to Mary, "They're too young. The adults keep them too young. Or too stupid."

Mary puts an arm around Janey and says, "They're how the adults made them. You told me that."

Caitlin wants so badly to be different, someone not young or stupid, so she might grasp the significance of what Janey is saying. But Vanessa made more sense. What difference would it make, if there were other islands? They can't get there. They can't talk to the other islanders to get ideas. The other islanders aren't going to come beat the adults until they agree to whatever Janey wants.

Janey walks over to Vanessa, looking intent. Everyone falls silent, and so Janey's whispered words are clear, echoing off the walls. "You have your books, and your cleverness, and your wanderer father," Janey says softly. A muscle near Vanessa's ear twitches, but she doesn't say anything. "You need to remember," Janey continues, "that one day soon, unless something changes, something big, you're going to bleed, and marry, and raise two children, and die, just like everybody else. Nothing will be any different."

"You think I don't know that?" hisses Vanessa in a sharp fury. "And what about you? You're a freak, an overgrown freak, and you think that will save you. Well, I've seen you with no clothes on—you're getting close and soon you're going to bleed like the rest of us."

They stare at each other, anger flaring in Janey's ice-gray eyes and mirrored in Vanessa's rich hazel ones. Suddenly Janey slumps. "Then we're both doomed, aren't we?" she says with a crooked smile, looking like she's going to cry.

Janey moves away, and Vanessa puts her head in her hands. Walking over to Mary, Janey whispers something to her, and they leave up the long staircase. The girls fall back to talking, telling the story of the other island, where people live in snow houses or grass houses, and they eat spinach always or never, and they have cats as pets or cats have people as pets. Faces are filled with mirth, alarm, confusion. Nobody leaves until the sky starts blushing with dawn, and then Caitlin feels dizzy as she hurries back home.

The next day at school, Mr. Abraham rails about how lazy and slow the girls are. Yet at recess, the girls who made it to the church fly around to the others like bees, depositing reports of what was said and gathering disbelief and confusion.

Despite the strangeness of what Janey said, and all the unanswered questions, the girls walk a little bit taller for the next week or so. They feel a little more satisfied leaving the dinner table. They know something. Or, at least, they might know something. Slowly, the doubters begin to believe in other islands, simply to have something new to believe. Something dark and mysterious, something exciting. Something forbidden.

Caitlin still whimpers and cries before Father, sits hunched and shivering in the classroom, wanders alone at recess, but she feels just a little bit different. She knows others can see it too; girls who used to tease her for her smallness, her shyness, her ugliness, now meet her eyes like she's a person.

Caitlin can tell Janey's not done. She still looks angry and deep in thought most of the time, as if she's heading toward something that needs to be beaten into submission.

CHAPTER TWENTY-SIX

Vanessa

For the next few days, all the girls can talk about is the Other Island. To Vanessa, this shows that their perspective is weak, for there could be dozens or even hundreds of islands. She still feels depressed by the prospect, as it leaves her as impotent as she's ever been, but the other girls adore the concept. Each has made up an island in her head and claimed it as her own.

Letty's is cold all year round and covered in snow. People live in snow houses and eat squirrels and winter berries. There's no summer, but it doesn't matter, because only the children are brave enough to go out into the cold. They hunt and gather while parents and babies huddle inside.

Nina's island is up in the sky, floating. If you get too close to the edge you might fall off and smash into bits.

Rosie's island has only women, and they can have babies without men, just by deciding to. The mothers farm, cook, carve, and hunt while the daughters take care of littler daughters. At night they go to a special part of the woods, where they sing and tell stories, and then sleep in a big pile together. There's always someone awake to watch for danger while the others sleep.

Leah's island is overrun with dogs that live with the inhabitants, keeping them warm and catching them food. On her island, nobody ever drowns puppies, and they are all allowed to live and have their own families. Each child has two parents and ten dogs. The dogs eat at the table with the children, sleep on their bed with them, protect them, and escort them around. When there is a new litter of puppies, everyone celebrates like a baby boy was born, and then decides who needs more dogs.

Vanessa can't conjure up a dream world. All she can think of is Janey's voice whispering "Nothing will be any different." She doesn't know why the church meeting bothers her; she never expected to do anything but get married, have two children, and send them off to summer. She will persuade Father to give her his library, or at least some of it, and she'll read all the time. When she is old, she and her husband will take a final draft and die. Her children, or perhaps someone else's children, will take over their house, and her body will rot in the fields. She's never been thrilled about any of it, but it always seemed inevitable, so she never considered any other option.

Now that there might be different possibilities, the idea of this ordained future keeps circling back to vex her. She tries to comfort herself with the idea that once her childbearing is done, she can read whenever she wants, but she still feels a sense of staleness and boredom. *Nothing will be any different.* All of their futures are interchangeable. Other than the defectives, they will all grow up, marry, have children, die.

The other girls are bubbling with creativity and laughter, which only makes Vanessa feel even sadder. In the evenings, she doesn't eat much dinner. Mother fusses over her a bit and fixes her some tea with a drop of precious honey. It's sweet on her tongue, but her thoughts remain bitter.

After Vanessa splashes her face clean from the small basin in her room, she starts to do her usual check, starting at her ankles. Craning her neck, she softly pats at her legs, running her fingers over the skin, ensuring it is smooth and her thighs are straight. Her hips are smooth and straight too, in line with her waist. She sticks her fingers between her legs, where everything is neat, bare, and dry. Resting a finger in her navel, she surveys her belly, which is flat, and then she carefully presses on her chest.

Vanessa has been wondering for a while if it was getting bigger, but dismissed her concerns as imagination. Tonight, she is sure she can feel some substance, and her heart starts beating faster. Pressing down with two fingers until she can feel the ribs beneath, she gauges the depths of each pad of fat. They're soft like wet wool, and her stomach flips over violently. She does not want to be soft, she wants to be flat and hard as a board. There must be a way to get rid of them.

With her fists, she grinds at one of the protuberances as hard as she can, pinching and compressing it to lie flat against her chest. She counts to a hundred, and then releases it and compares it with the other one. They look the same, although the one she worked on is reddened. She vows to do this every night and every morning, first just on the right to make sure it works, and then on both. She tucks the loose cloth of her nightgown under her armpits, pulling it tighter so her chest looks flat. Father is surprised when he comes in, to find her standing in her nightdress with her hair uncombed, instead of in bed waiting for him.

CHAPTER TWENTY-SEVEN

Janey

Janey is curled up with her back facing Mary, cold and still in the pale moonlight. She wishes Mary would fall asleep, but she can feel her staring at the back of Janey's head, patient and worried. Janey wants to roll over, put her arms around Mary, and drift into sleep, but this seems as impossible as growing wings. She needs to be awake. Her mind is racing, always racing.

"Janey," whispers Mary.

"What?" snaps Janey.

"You have to tell them what you told me."

Janey is flooded with a sudden wish that she had no more to tell. That Amanda were alive, lumbering around with an abundant belly, that there were no suspicions and theories and fears spiking blackly into her brain every second. That she could simply sleep like a child.

"How long are you going to wait?" persists Mary.

Janey rolls over to face her. "I'm not a pastor," she says. "I'm not an ancestor. Why do I have to gather everyone together? Why do I have to try to change things?"

"You're Janey Solomon," says Mary, with a touch of reverence. "You *know* things. You can't just run around stupidly like the rest of them. You know you can't."

"Feel this." Janey puts a hand on her chest, and Mary feels her heartbeat.

"What about it?" says Mary.

"Compare it to yours."

Mary puts her other hand on her own breastbone. "Yours is slow. It always is." Two pulses in rapid succession strike against Janey's ribs, then a pause, then the regular rhythm starts again.

"My chest hurts sometimes. I think I might be dying."

"Well, do something, then!" says Mary angrily. "Stop acting like you're helpless. Start eating. That will help. Won't it?"

"I can't."

"You can, it's easy. Take food, put it in your mouth, chew, and swallow."

"I can't, I can't... become a woman."

"You'll become one anyway, eventually. You can't put it off forever."

"No," Janey says.

"Just become a woman and don't do your summer of fruition. You'll figure out a way."

"Of course I won't. Remember how Alberta Moses screamed and fought, and they made her drink something, and every time she started screaming again they made her drink something again, until the summer was over and she was married to Frank? And then, I heard, she kept screaming and they kept giving it to her, and then she bled out and that was that, that was her life." Janey pauses. "If she even really bled out." Suddenly, violently, Janey bursts into tears. Mary wraps her soft arms around her.

"They wouldn't treat you like Alberta," Mary says soothingly. "They wouldn't dare."

"They'd like nothing better."

"They're scared of you."

"That's why they'd like nothing better."

"So just go through it, everyone does. You could have children. You'd love them."

Janey convulses at the thought. "I'm never having children."

"You might have boys."

"That's even worse."

"So you're just going to kill yourself. You'll go to the darkness below, you know."

"I know."

"Why won't you eat? I would do anything for you, why can't you do that for me?"

"Mary, I can't. I mean really, I *can't*."

"You have teeth." Mary sticks a finger in her mouth, taps her teeth to make her laugh. It doesn't work. "You have a belly." She tickles her and it's like poking something dead. "You have everything you need."

"I don't," Janey says. "I'm sorry." There's a pause. "I love you, Mary."

"I love you too. I won't let you die. Don't worry. When you get too weak, I'll feed you eggs and honey."

Janey smiles a little and hiccups. "That sounds disgusting."

"Cheese and honey, then."

"You think too much about food."

"You don't think about food enough," fires back Mary.

Janey sighs. "I think about it all the time," she says quietly. She pushes her body into Mary's, feeling her bones imprint on soft skin. "You don't understand."

"I never understand anything," Mary replies. "Not like my sister, the great Janey Solomon."

Janey blows air dismissively through her teeth, ruffling the hair at the back of Mary's neck. Mary shivers, and giggles a little.

"You have to talk to the girls again," says Mary. "You have to talk to them about everything you know. Everything."

"I can't. They're too . . . too young."

"Wait for them to be old enough to understand," yawns Mary, "and they'll be adults. And then you can't do anything."

CHAPTER TWENTY-EIGHT

Vanessa

A few days later, Vanessa is leaving her house in the morning for school; the grass is still slightly frozen and crunches satisfyingly under her feet. Suddenly someone leaps forward, grabs her arm, and pulls her around to the side of the house, where she falls over and lands with a thump on her back. Looking up, she sees gray eyes in a freckled face.

"I need to talk to you," says Janey rather unnecessarily, still holding on to Vanessa's arm with both hands.

"About what?" asks Vanessa, sitting up and rubbing her lower back. "And why are you jumping out at me? I could see you at recess."

"No!" says Janey, pounding the wall of the house with a thump. "It's too important for that."

"Oh," replies Vanessa, shakily getting to her knees and then her feet. "Well... I'm here. I'm listening."

"Vanessa?" Mother calls from the door. "Is that you, banging?"

"Yes, Mother," she calls back. "I, um, I fell. Right here. Against the wall." She glares at Janey, who gives an apologetic little shrug with her bony shoulders.

"Are you all right?" asks Mother.

"Yes," says Vanessa. "I'm off to school now."

"Be good, dear," says Mother, and Vanessa hears the door close again. She and Janey stare at each other uncertainly.

"Well?" says Vanessa.

"Well," says Janey, "we can't really talk here." She looks around exaggeratedly, as if people are creeping toward them to hear their every word.

"I need to be in school. Mother will know if I don't go to school."

"Tell her you fell asleep."

"I fell asleep walking to school?"

"Tell her you fainted."

"I fainted and lay unconscious all day and then woke up after school let out. And came home."

"Well," says Janey again. "Can you promise to meet me after school?"

"Meet you after school," says Vanessa slowly. "Where?"

"By the shore, near the shelter Mary and I built. Do you remember where that is?"

"It's a long walk, but yes."

"Promise."

"I promise."

After school, Vanessa wraps her sweater around her as she walks through the fields toward the beach. She rarely goes to the perimeter of the island unless she is naked and covered in mud; it's not forbidden to visit the sea during autumn, but she considers the shore to be a summer place.

They all know the spot where the shelter was built; the water stays shallow for ages, and even the youngest children can wade around, hunting sea creatures or flopping on their bellies. She has fond memories of being a little girl, pleading with the older girls to pick her up and toss her into the ocean with a huge splash. The water always welcomed her in a rain of bubbles and droplets, slipping cool ribbons between her toes and fingers and into her ears, wrapping her body in a chilly, playful embrace.

The water seems different in autumn, angrier, even though its soft swells haven't changed. Perhaps it is the color, the gray of charcoal smeared across paper, reflecting the sky above. Seagulls have gathered on the childless beach, stark white and soft drab with vivid flame-colored beaks and feet. They toss back their heads and keen in sharp, halting sobs.

Crouching, Vanessa runs her fingers through the cool, damp sand. The gulls shift uneasily and glance at her. The skeleton of Janey and Mary's structure remains, although the twigs woven throughout have frayed and blown away. It reminds her of the altar at home, but stranger, frozen and broken and meant for worshipping something inhuman. She approaches it and runs her hand down one of the supports. A splinter catches in her palm, and she winces and pulls it out with her teeth.

"You came," says Janey, appearing from nowhere and making Vanessa jump. "I thought you might not come."

"I promised," replies Vanessa, wiping the streak of blood from her hand on her dress before she can think better of it. "You said you wanted to talk to me."

"I do," says Janey. "I wanted to talk to you after the meeting at the church."

Vanessa sighs. "I'm sorry I called you a freak," she says. "But you shouldn't have reminded me that I'll end up like all of them. I try to forget it, most days."

"You reminded me of some things I don't like to think about either," says Janey. "I'm sorry too."

They smile shyly at each other and then shift uncomfortably, shouldering the weight of renewed amity.

"Where's Mary?" says Vanessa suddenly.

"She's playing with someone," says Janey vaguely. "Or helping Mother."

"She's always with you," replies Vanessa.

"I love Mary," says Janey, "more than anything. But she's not..." She fingers the cloth of her dress. "She's not..."

"Like you."

"Lucky her," says Janey wryly. "I just felt like she wouldn't be able to add much. To what we have to talk about." Catching Vanessa's gaze, she says uneasily, "I'll tell her when I get home, of course."

"So, what do we have to talk about?"

"I've been thinking about what you said in the church."

Vanessa snorts, a bit self-deprecatingly. "I say a lot of things."

"What you said about us being unable to change anything. Like we're goats waiting to be slaughtered. Something like that."

Vanessa nods. "Right."

"And that got me thinking. You say it isn't worth wondering if there are other islands, or about the wastelands, because it doesn't make a difference."

"Yes." Vanessa puts a fingernail in her mouth to chew, then snatches it away. "I didn't say that about the wastelands, but yes. That's what I said to the other girls."

"But you love knowing things," argues Janey. "All those books? Why read them? They won't make a difference, but you do it anyway."

"What am I supposed to do?" says Vanessa despairingly. "Just clean the house, and go to school, and watch women have babies, and listen to Pastor Saul go on and on, and wait...wait for my body to change."

"That's what everyone else does," says Janey.

"Not you."

"Those books won't change what happens to you."

"They're...windows. Even if the place they let me see is impossible."

"They teach you things."

"They do," says Vanessa quietly.

"Why don't you want to think about other islands?" says Janey. "You say it's no use, but it might be a window too."

Vanessa rolls her eyes. "Because I'll never know if it's true," she says. "Whatever I think of *could* be true, and so could the islands where they live on honey and babies grow on trees."

"What if you could know something?" asks Janey softly. "I think we should *try* to know more. Even if in the end, it doesn't change anything."

"Know more about what?"

Janey arranges her skirts around her knees and then sits down on the wet sand. Vanessa imitates her and feels the cold dampness invade the backs of her thighs. As Janey leans forward, her braid swings into Vanessa's lap like a flaming rope. "We need to know," she says, "about the wastelands."

CHAPTER TWENTY-NINE

Vanessa

Janey thought she was the first of the children to seek out the wastelands. Vanessa didn't mention that ever since she first heard of them, she has been trying to find out more. The enticing vision of a world on fire intoxicates her. She imagines the grass, the trees, the houses of the island exploding into flames: the warmth, the brightness, all she knows turning to tinder and shattering, sparking, collapsing into ruin and dust. She pictures sifting through the soft, sable ash for the clean white bones of her kin, walking with gray feet to survey the fallen stones of a dead church. Daydreams like these make her wonder, sometimes, if she is marked in some way, a hidden defective but a defective all the same. A streak of rot across her mind, staining her thoughts pitch-dark.

When they met on the beach two days ago, Janey suggested that Vanessa try harder to inveigle information from Father, but Vanessa knows this is futile. She has spent her whole life using everything she has—her body, her voice, her words, her smiles—in order to find out more about the wastelands. Father knows how to push aside her questions with a calm, easy voice, as if he had been taught from an early age to deflect the curiosity of daughters. Perhaps he has. Perhaps soon he will begin to indoctrinate Ben in the art of closing off the world to those who seek it.

Father is a dead end, but Vanessa has other sources now. Perhaps the new Adams do not know, yet, how to turn away those who are persistent. Vanessa has to beg or trick Mrs. Adam into telling her of the wastelands. She shies away from the idea of more time with Mr. Adam, remembering how he swelled darkly over her in the library. He seems like he would extract something vital from her in exchange for information, like her lungs or her teeth.

On the other hand, Vanessa quite likes Mrs. Adam. She is hesitant and gentle, with the mannerisms and speech of a child. Unlike most adults, she looked at Vanessa with a bright face, like she couldn't wait to speak with her. If Vanessa could talk to Mrs. Adam without Mr. Adam interfering, she would do it even without an ulterior motive. She thinks she knows how.

For a week's worth of afternoons, Vanessa lurks about the Adam household like a hungry dog lured by the promise of scraps. Finally she sees Mrs. Adam drift vaguely toward the garden and rushes to meet her. "Mrs. Adam!" she says breathlessly.

Mrs. Adam starts. "Vanessa!" she says just as breathlessly. "How nice to see you. How are you?"

"Well," says Vanessa, feeling almost shy. "Are you going to garden?"

"I'm going to try," says Mrs. Adam, laughing a little. "The women have been trying to explain to me what to do, but I'm just hopeless. I hope I don't kill everything."

"You won't," says Vanessa encouragingly, "I'm sure you won't." She pauses. "Would you like me to help you?"

"That would be lovely," breathes Mrs. Adam. "Are you good at gardening?"

"Oh, yes," lies Vanessa, who is so averse that Mother doesn't even bother forcing her anymore. "I love it."

"Oh, good," says Mrs. Adam. "I was going to weed."

Even though Vanessa rolls happily in the mud every summer, she can't stand pulling spiky plants out of rich, fertilized muck. "I love weeding," she says with flagging conviction.

Pulling up the skirt of her dress and the ends of her thick-knit shawl, Mrs. Adam kneels on the cold ground. "How do you tell which one is a weed?" she asks.

Vanessa also kneels, her kneecaps becoming frigid within seconds. "Well," she says brightly, "it takes *practice.*"

Carefully, Mrs. Adam begins pulling strips of plants from the garden that seem like they might not belong. Vanessa, trying to appear patient and calm, does the same. They make a little pile of greenery between them. "How are you settling in?" asks Vanessa.

"Oh, everyone is so kind," says Mrs. Adam cheerfully. "People are helping us with everything. I don't know how to sew, or, or scrub things with sand, or cook over a *fire,* goodness no. Everyone is so willing to show me things, twice, usually."

Vanessa instantly realizes that this means that people in the wastelands do not sew, or scrub things, or cook over fires. She wants to interrogate Mrs. Adam immediately, but has learned from her interaction with Mr. Adam in the library. She simply says, "Oh?"

"Oh, yes, I either burn things or they're raw. Luckily Clyde is patient with me. More than usual, since he's learning so much too. It's so different here."

Vanessa has to bite her tongue, hard, until her questions slide back down her throat and can be swallowed. "I'm sure," she says.

"It will be normal in no time," prattles Mrs. Adam. "It just takes time. That's what Clyde says. He was so eager to come here, and I've never seen him happier. And it is so lovely here, *so* lovely. Like nothing I've seen. It was hard to come here, to leave everything behind, but the beauty of it—the trees!—that helps."

Vanessa sorts carefully through a variety of responses and checks to make sure Mrs. Adam is distractedly peering at a plant before saying, "Who do you miss most?"

"My grandmother," says Mrs. Adam. "I'll never see her again, and that's hard."

Vanessa sits up on her heels, her hand full of leafy vine, and gapes at Mrs. Adam. "Your *grandmother?*" she says.

"She was—is—such a love," murmurs Mrs. Adam. "Her name is Elizabeth. Now, *she* could have sewn things."

"How old are you, Mrs. Adam?" asks Vanessa softly.

"Me? I'm twenty-seven," replies Mrs. Adam.

Vanessa's head reels, and she reaches out and pulls out a plant at random, trying to keep her face neutral. At twenty-seven, Mrs. Adam should be a grandmother herself. How old must her grandmother be? Why didn't she have to take a final draft? Could her husband be supremely useful in some way?

"And your grandfather?" she says in what she hopes is a light tone.

"Oh, he died years ago," says Mrs. Adam. "He was wonderful too."

"I see," mutters Vanessa, pulling out bigger and bigger handfuls of foliage and trying to control herself.

"Vanessa," chirrups Mrs. Adam suddenly, "I think you've pulled out a carrot."

Vanessa jumps, and looks at a tiny orange root growing from a flock of green stems. "Oh," she says.

"At least I think so, let me see." Mrs. Adam runs her fingers over the root, brings it to her mouth, and then says, "Oh," and puts it down.

"What is it?" asks Vanessa.

"I...I forgot what you use to fertilize plants here," says Mrs. Adam.

"What of it?" replies Vanessa, confused.

"Well, it's, let's just say, the *humanness* of it...I just don't want to eat it."

"A carrot?" Vanessa peers at the root, sniffs it, and takes a bite. "Yes, it's a carrot." Looking up, she sees Mrs. Adam looking faintly ill.

"I'm sure you get used to it." Mrs. Adam gulps. "I mean, I think I'm almost used to the smell. I must say, when I first arrived I couldn't stop, you know, puking. Maybe it's the baby. Clyde didn't mind as much, but me, I would wake up, take a breath, and puke."

"I guess it does smell kind of strong," agrees Vanessa. "You don't notice it after a while."

"Strong," says Mrs. Adam with a brave smile. "That's the word."

They grin at each other for no reason.

"So," says Vanessa. "What did you like to eat? In the wastelands?" But at the word "wastelands" Mrs. Adam's face falls, and Vanessa feels her heart sink.

"I can't tell you anything about the wastelands," whispers Mrs. Adam dramatically, like that very inability is a secret that must be guarded. "Clyde says I mustn't. And the wanderers, they were so . . . forceful. From the time the one came to see me at—in the wastelands."

"Of course," says Vanessa. "How stupid of me."

"Oh, but I'm sorry," says Mrs. Adam in a normal tone. "You must be just *dying* to know. I would be dying to know!"

Vanessa smiles tightly. "Just *dying*," she agrees. She rises and goes to kneel near Mrs. Adam, their thighs pressed against each other.

"Which wanderer was it?" asks Vanessa, after a time. "Who came to see you?"

"I don't—I don't think I can say. But he was so, so tall and sure of himself and dressed in that black coat. He asked me so many questions."

"Like what?"

"Was I prepared to take the ancestors into my heart, was I prepared to accept Clyde's authority and his authority. He told me a lot of things too."

"What did he tell you?" asks Vanessa eagerly.

"Well, about the island, of course. How things are. Not everything, but most things, you know? And we were so happy to be chosen. Although Clyde said a lot of people wouldn't go, because of the final draft and the daughters, but it didn't bother *him*."

"What daughters?"

"You know, he saved me, he really did, I was such a wreck and he saved me. So I couldn't say no to anything he wanted. Plus, it really is so beautiful."

"Saved you from what?"

"Just...not a good life. I was doing things I shouldn't have done. I mean, I didn't have any choice, but all the same, they were bad things."

Vanessa stares at Mrs. Adam's wide, shallowly set brown eyes. "What things?"

"Oh, no," says Mrs. Adam, shaking her head. "Even if I could tell you everything, I wouldn't tell you that. It's not for children."

"I'm not a child," snaps Vanessa.

"But you are," says Mrs. Adam, smiling in bewilderment at her. "Of course you are."

Vanessa is silent for a moment, and then says, "So Mr. Adam saved you. And then brought you here."

"Yes," she says, eager again. "He's such a good man, really."

Slowly, Vanessa says, "He saved you from the fires."

"Fires?"

"Pastor Saul says everything is on fire," murmurs Vanessa, less to Mrs. Adam than herself. She is surprised to find a cool, dusty palm on her cheek.

"Vanessa, Clyde told me about how you tried to get him to answer your questions," Mrs. Adam says fondly. "How much you want to *know*. I've never been like that, but I admire it."

Vanessa puts her hand over Mrs. Adam's, and waits.

"There's..." Vanessa can see Mrs. Adam struggling to string words together. "You're so bright. I'm not surprised you want to know everything you can." She pauses. "But it's not a good thing. It won't make you happy." More silence. "My whole life, I've learned to not question things. It doesn't do any good, really. You usually learn what you didn't want to learn, and still don't know what you wanted to know." A sigh. "I mean, knowing things, it can really hurt."

"But Mrs. Adam," whispers Vanessa, clinging to the hand on her jaw, "what if the hurting isn't the most important part? What if it's not even worth considering?" She swallows. "What if you were going to hurt anyway?"

Mrs. Adam blinks, and a tear crawls down her face. "Are you hurting, Vanessa?" she asks softly.

Vanessa can't answer. Suddenly she feels that she is the adult, and Mrs. Adam is the child who needs to be protected. "Not all the time," she gasps, and it's the most comforting thing she can manage. She digs her fingers deep into the earth and closes her eyes, as if she can feel the soil groan and settle under her numb knees.

CHAPTER THIRTY

Janey

It's a drizzly day, soft ash-colored mist lying heavily on the bare branches of trees. Mary shifts and shivers, but Janey can tell she is trying to bear the cold and wet without complaint. They are ankle-deep in muck at the edge of the shore, gazing at the spot among the reeds where the ferry comes and goes. Near the dock is a huge, hunched, arthritic willow whose branches slump to graze the surface of the water. Janey and Mary stand half crouched with their hands on its dry, pimpled bark, watching for the raft to come to shore.

"They're going to see us," whispers Mary. "You know we aren't supposed to be here."

"They won't see us," replies Janey curtly, "they would have to be looking for us." But then, glancing at Mary again, she lifts her sweater so it shields her bright hair, and suddenly there is no vivid color anywhere.

When they hear the slow, sucking sounds of the ferryman's pole, they crouch further, so the muddy water grabs hold of their hems. The ferry hisses to a stop among the grasses, and two wanderers disembark, draped in black. They nod to the ferryman and then begin striding across the grass in their leather shoes toward their homes. One has a bundle wrapped in cloth under his arm.

"Let's go," whispers Janey.

"We have to wait until they're out of sight," murmurs Mary back to her.

"They won't look back. Come." She grabs Mary's elbow with a strong hand. They want to run, but the wet grass and mud make them slip and slither, and eventually they clop along in their wooden clogs as quickly as the ground will allow.

The ferry is floating on soft swells like a dozing seabird, the ferryman sitting on a strange box on top of the boards. He appears to be breathing fire. Smoke billows out from behind his cracked white hand, but then his fingers move to reveal that he is pulling with flesh-less, sallow lips on a cylindrical piece of paper. He breathes in, the paper burning redly at the end, and then opens his mouth and emits a rolling, graceful flood of oyster-colored smoke.

Janey walks toward the raft, more hesitant now, and he looks up at her abruptly. He is wearing his strange hat with a brim just on the front, beaten and weathered to the point of colorlessness. His iron-hard face is all slabs and angles: broad sheets of cheekbone, a once-broken nose that shies away toward the right, a thin mouth pulled up into a sneer by a scar on the upper lip. His eyes are all but hidden by the shadow of his hat and by the dimness of evening.

Janey opens her mouth, then closes it and waves the man forward weakly. The man stares at her, his eyes shrouded in black, and then shrugs more slowly than she thought it was possible for a man to shrug. Languidly, he picks up his pole and pushes once more toward shore. Janey turns to Mary and holds out her trembling hand.

Interlocking fingers, they walk slowly to the ferry: two girls, one tall and red-haired, one small and brown-haired, leaning into each other like they could not stand without the other. When the ferry touches the reeds, the ferryman spreads his hands as if to gesture, *Well?*

With a deep breath, Janey and Mary take off their shoes. The water bites frozen at their calves as they wade to the ferry and awkwardly clamber on. Janey wonders if she is dreaming, if this vessel only occupied by wanderers and exiles is real beneath her feet.

Up close, the ferryman smells of smoke and metal and something rotten. His face is swathed with small scars, from the slice on his upper lip to a smattering of pockmarks roughening his cheeks. The gray light catches his narrow eyes under the brim of his hat.

"Hello," says Janey in a shy voice she has never heard emerge from her throat. "I suppose you're not used to having girls on the ferry."

Frowning, the ferryman stares at them.

"You see," she says, growing louder, "we want to talk to you. We think...we think that you have valuable things to tell us."

He coughs wetly into his fist and resumes gazing at them.

"About the wastelands," continues Janey. "You're from there. You live there. Unless you live on this raft, but that seems unlikely. We need to know things."

Bringing the strange paper cylinder to his mouth, which Janey can now see is filled with what look like wood shavings, he inhales and then blows a cloud of gloom over them. She inhales to speak, coughs, and then starts again.

"You see, it's..." She pauses. "We're trapped here. We don't know anything. About what happened, or how things are now." She shifts and the ferry moves alarmingly under her. "We need to know what it's like. In the wastelands. We have...questions."

The ferryman sighs impatiently.

"I said we have questions. Will you answer them?"

He stares.

"No, that's not—you need to—so my first question is about the scourge. What..." And she trails off because he is opening his mouth to speak.

Underneath the current of fear that consumes her, Janey feels a thrill run through her skin like the tingle before lightning strikes. Whatever this dark prophet says will be something new, uncharted, forbidden. She leans forward into his smoke-and-rot smell, his charcoal stare.

He is opening his mouth slowly, shakily, as if struggling against some unseen force that binds it shut. His lips splay wider and wider, and now Janey wonders if his jaw will dislocate, or if his cheeks will split and ooze like the skin of a smashed fruit. She feels an urge to run, but her morbid fascination is stronger. The ferryman gestures at his open mouth with a crooked finger. As if in response, a ray of sun splinters through the clouds to bathe the island in light.

Janey follows the ray into his mouth and then croaks, a strangled indrawn breath. She sees a carcass, a rot, obscene folds of flesh.

The ferryman has no tongue.

It is not a clean cut; half of his tongue was shorn at the stump, but a few trembling muscles bound by scarred flesh remain and twist dumbly, like a trapped, eyeless creature straining toward the light.

Mary shrieks. Janey manages not to, but gives a guttural moan, and they both turn and leap off the ferry into the icy water, their legs raw and shivering, and splash frantically toward shore. Forgetting their shoes, they take off barefoot, their soles sliced by half-frozen grass as they race away from the water. Janey's lungs smolder and her skin erupts in chill sweat. "Home," mutters Mary unconsciously, and at that Janey stops her.

"No!" screams Mary, turning to look back wildly over her shoulder, even though they are far out of sight from the ocean, from anyone, and are standing in a field next to Mr. Balthazar's plum trees.

"Stop," says Janey, also out of breath. "Stop. We're safe."

"Who cut out his tongue?" cries Mary. "Was it the wanderers? We *spoke* to him, what if he tells—what if he tells—"

"Breathe," commands Janey shakily, her face nearly bloodless. She tries not to think of the tongueless ferryman exhaling fumes. "Just breathe in and out." Mary starts to cry, falling to her knees. Janey kneels and wraps her in a tight embrace. "Breathe," she says again.

"What if he *follows* us?" asks Mary suddenly, whirling to see behind her.

"He won't," says Janey.

"He could. He could be going to the wanderers right now, to tell them. He could be furious—"

"He doesn't know where they live. And he's not furious. Didn't you hear as we were running away?"

"Hear what?"

"He was laughing at us. It was hard to tell, but that's what it sounded like."

"Laughing at us? Why?"

"Because we were afraid." Janey tucks a windblown strand of hair behind Mary's ear.

"What kind of thing would make someone cut out your tongue?" sobs Mary. "What if he does it to us?"

"He's old, isn't he," says Janey, more to herself than Mary. "Very old. He's survived out there a long time. Did you see his clothes?"

"No," says Mary, sniffing. "I didn't notice them."

"They were filthy, and old, but well made. Very well made. And his shoes were...complicated."

"Do you think he's still sitting there?" whispers Mary.

"No," says Janey brusquely. "I don't. I think he's gone back to out there." She sweeps her hand in an extravagant gesture.

"We need to tell the other girls—"

"No." Janey's face is hard and cold, and her eyes burn into Mary's. "We will never tell anybody."

"Why?"

"It just...If we don't tell anyone, it stays between us, it's our secret. I just can't have everybody knowing."

"But why?"

"Because it was—" And Janey's lower lip quivers until she has to catch it in her small white teeth, and bite hard. "They're so young, and the way he—" She wraps her arms around herself. "Besides, if someone found out we'd been on the ferry, if it got back to a wanderer...Just don't tell anyone. Please."

"Janey," whispers Mary, "now how will you find out about the wastelands?"

Janey shakes her head. "I don't know. Please stop asking me

questions. I just want to go home too." They stagger toward their house, feeling contaminated by their new knowledge. It drags on them like shackles as they try to forget it ever happened. For days after, Mary wakes up screaming in the middle of the night, from nightmares of rank, infested earth slowly opening up beneath her to swallow her whole. And Janey simply doesn't sleep.

CHAPTER THIRTY ONE

Caitlin

Caitlin is eager for the next time Janey will call the girls together. She's not the only one; Rosie tells her that a few hopeful girls even went to church the next night, but were met with only darkness inside. After a few days pass, it seems like a dream: Janey behind the altar, everyone looking at her, the captivating notion of new islands. Caitlin feels a little foolish to have thought she knew something exciting.

But then, about two weeks after the first church visit, Rosie taps on her window again. This time, Caitlin doesn't even crawl out on the roof, she just opens the window and nods. She puts on her shoes, recalling the freezing ground, and then takes them off again, remembering the tap they make on the floor. She remembers to bring a blanket, though, and Rosie has a shawl.

This time, nobody hesitates at the church door; they can see the soft, coral glow filtering up through the dark stairway and hovering faintly in the night air. Janey is at the altar already, pacing like a skinny, freckled Pastor Saul, scowling fiercely at them. Mary hovers near her, quiet as a graceful shadow. There are more girls here this time. You can tell the new ones, because they're only in their nightgowns, while the girls who attended the last of Janey's sermons are wrapped up and shod. Clutching one another and hopping up and down, the underdressed girls giggle and wince at the cold on their skin. Their collective breath turns into fog, wisping up toward the black, invisible church ceiling. There's a smell in the air Caitlin's never noticed before, a smell of rich earth and dank wetness. She wonders if the walls are slowly caving in. Suddenly she has a vision of all of them writhing under a pile of rubble like trapped white worms.

Janey says, "Diana, you can't bring your brother."

"But he's only three," says Diana Adam, who is holding a sleepy William in her arms.

"He can still talk."

"He cried every time I tried to leave the room. What was I supposed to do? Look, he's falling asleep already."

Janey frowns at her for a moment and then says, "Make sure he keeps quiet."

Diana shrugs, bouncing William on her hip.

"Last time, I was trying to talk about an idea, but it didn't go how I wanted. I feel—well, like I'm running out of time. But there are some things I do know, and even if... Well, if I tell you, you'll know them too. I want to talk about Amanda Balthazar," Janey says. "She didn't bleed out."

Caitlin's skin freezes and crawls. She feels like she's been dragged out of the shadows for everyone to see. Slipping into a pew, she sits down, touching her chin to her chest and wrapping her arms around herself. What has she started? Why couldn't she stay quiet?

She thought everyone had heard about the dead girl in the water, but apparently not. Gina frowns and says, "What do you mean? She bled out. She's dead."

"She is dead," says Janey. "But she didn't bleed out. I think she was murdered."

There's a long silence. "By Andrew?" whispers someone in a tone of scant belief.

"No. By the wanderers. They pulled her body from the water. Caitlin saw them," Janey says. Caitlin shrinks into herself even more and suppresses an urge to crawl under the pews on her belly. Heads swivel to look at her and she pretends she isn't here, she is somewhere else, asleep in bed with Mother, perhaps, or walking the shore in summer. She has never had so many eyes on her.

"Caitlin could be lying," says Gina. There's a murmur of agreement.

"I don't think so," says Janey. "Caitlin saw what she saw. She isn't a liar."

"How do you know?" demands Gina.

"Because if she was, she'd make up something about the wastelands. Something she remembered from when she lived there. But she never has." Caitlin remembers her vision of the dead woman, but she would rather die than tell a soul.

"Maybe she isn't smart enough," remarks Harriet Abraham.

"She is plenty smart!" cries Rosie, and Caitlin feels a warm glow in her chest at the unexpected defense. "She's *memorized Our Book* and everything Pastor Saul ever said." This isn't quite true, but Caitlin would never correct a whole roomful of people.

"Let's have her recite it, then." Harriet laughs, and Janey glares at her until she looks down, cowed.

"So I was wondering," says Janey, her voice louder, "if Amanda was murdered . . . how many other women have been murdered?"

She looks at everyone expectantly, as if she's asked a simple question. There's some shuffling and glancing, and finally Violet says, "What do you mean?" Pressed breast to breast for warmth, she and her sister Sarah have their arms twined around each other like slender ropes.

"I mean that if Amanda really was killed and didn't bleed out, maybe the other women who supposedly bled out were killed too."

"But I've seen someone bleed out," objects Rosie. "In front of me. She died. It was disgusting."

"Me too," says Harriet. "I saw Mrs. Jacob die. Anna Jacob, the soapmaker's wife. Or, she *was* his wife."

"But sometimes you can't find anyone who saw them die," says Brenda Moses. "If it happens at home, or . . ." She gestures. "Like, Mrs. Gideon the farmer's wife, the young one, she bled out at home, but her daughter Kelly said she didn't see it, and Mr. Gideon didn't see it, she was just home alone and then she was dead and there was no blood anywhere and her body was ready to be buried. Kelly said it was very strange." Kelly Gideon is now Kelly Abraham, married and unable to be useful to them.

"That doesn't mean she was murdered," says Lillian Saul. "That doesn't mean anything, maybe they just cleaned it up real well. Even if she didn't bleed out, how does it mean she was murdered?"

"But what if she was?" says Fiona. "Remember, she was one of those who used to say that girls and men should have their summers of fruition when they were both the same age. Nobody listened, but she said it." Someone giggles shrilly at this notion.

"But if they were killed, then..." mutters Diana.

"Who killed them?" says Letty just as Fiona asks, "What if she just fell into the water?"

"Wait," says Rosie. "It's not like the sea is full of dead women. It's just Amanda who was in the water."

"Remember Mrs. Joseph," says Brenda slowly, "Alma Joseph. She was crazy, remember? She said that fathers shouldn't... that girls shouldn't... remember how crazy she was? Mr. Joseph had to marry her because there wasn't anyone left, but, remember? And she bled out real soon after? Did anyone see her bleed out?"

Everyone starts speaking at once. Girls turn to each other, sharing theories and memories with their friends. Slowly, Janey leaves the altar and sits on the edge of the pulpit, swinging her skinny legs.

Without the promise of an island full of kittens, or snow, or honey, the youngest girls have lost interest again; a few are playing a clapping game in the corner. The staccato of palm against palm clatters like rhythmic raindrops as they chant in time:

One-two-three-four-five-six-seven
Drink a draft and go to heaven
Grandmother can't, Grandmother won't
Push that poison down her throat!

There's a crash, and laughter.

Another girl from the back of the room says, "You're not supposed to murder people, it's against the shalt-nots."

"The wanderers make the shalt-nots," murmurs Gabby Abraham.

"No, the ancestors did," corrects Ellen Joseph.

"But the wanderers add to it," says Fiona. "Maybe you don't have to follow a rule, if you're the one who's making it."

"But if they did kill Amanda, if they kill women, what if they kill me?" asks Ellen with a note of panic.

"We're not sure they killed anybody," says Linda soothingly.

"I was with Amanda," says Janey, standing up again, and the pale faces turn to her. "I was with her a few days before she died, and she was talking about changing things. Looking for a way out. Trying to get help. And then we heard a noise, and then... there was a man."

"And he killed her," breathes Brenda.

"No," says Janey, annoyed. "He was just there, he listened, he ran away. The things Amanda was saying, they were blasphemous, I guess. They were dangerous. And now she's dead. Do you understand?"

Another group of little girls is now racing around the church with an occasional shriek. Caitlin hears the brief, keening wail signaling a bumped elbow or skinned knee. A fight breaks out. They're more restless, more irritable than at the first meeting. It's strange, these echoes of summer when summer has already died and is lying comatose, waiting for the months to pass until its resurrection. The further it recedes in the past, the harder it is to control the young ones.

Janey looks exasperated. Caitlin suddenly remembers how much older she is than the other girls, those key three or four years between her and even the oldest of them. It means, by rights, that Janey should have shrieking children of her own. Her glimmering, flyaway hair should be pulled back and knotted on top of her head, her dress longer and looser, her movements heavy and sedate. This vision of adult Janey clanks jarring and wrong in Caitlin's head, and she lets it fall away gratefully. It's easier to imagine Janey dead than married.

"So you're saying the wanderers are all murderers," says Vanessa bitterly.

"I'm saying there is something happening," replies Janey. "I didn't say they were all murderers. I don't know how they work, not like you. It could have been one of them, all of them, I don't know."

"And your proof is that Amanda spoke some blasphemy and bled out?"

Caitlin looks at Vanessa, and it suddenly occurs to her that if Janey didn't exist, Vanessa would be the girl everyone stared at and spoke about. She's so tall, and beautiful, and she spends hours reading her father's books about ancient magic. She uses long words and nobody ever knows what they mean.

"Her body was dragged from the water," says Janey. "What do you think, she happened to be waist-deep in the sea, in summer, and then just bled out then and there?" Vanessa looks away.

"Think of the women who've disappeared, the women who were odd or blasphemous, maybe they got shamed and it didn't change them at all. Think about it. How many men mysteriously disappear? Just drop dead, without anybody seeing them die?"

Caitlin thinks back on the men who have died of injuries, of sickness, of slow wasting diseases. Men don't die as often as women, since they don't have to give birth, but they still die. Mr. Aaron the weaver woke up one morning recently and his legs didn't work, and now the uselessness is spreading up his chest. Mr. Joseph the carpenter fell off a roof and broke his neck. Mr. Solomon the farmer died of swamp lung. But for all these men, there were those eager to tell the story of their suffering and death, those who witnessed the pain and shock of it all. Whereas many women simply bleed out and are buried quietly and swiftly; such a commonplace end that recounting the tale would be mundane.

"Women are being killed," says Janey slowly and loudly, and suddenly Rhonda Gideon, the wanderer Gideon's daughter, shrieks, "My father is not a murderer!"

This sets off a hubbub. Gabby says, "They'd kill a pregnant woman with a baby?" "Are you saying Mr. Joseph would kill someone?" asks Gina. "Are you saying that June Abraham was murdered?" says someone else. "What's wrong with you?" demands Violet, as Leah says, "She's right, though. Mrs. Joseph. Mrs. Gideon. Mrs. Adam, the one who said men shouldn't take on other wives. They're all dead. They're all dead."

"I'm going to the beach," says Janey loudly, over the clamor. "I'm going to the beach, and you can come if you want."

"For the night?" says Letty.

"Forever. I'm going to the beach. We have to find another way to live. I'm going to the beach, and you can come. It will be like summer, but all the year round. Leave your fathers. Come with me. They might kill us, but at least—at least—" She doesn't finish the sentence.

In the uproar, Caitlin sees Janey stepping back, and then quietly descending the altar steps. Mary follows her, hands clasped, peering back at the noisy clot of girls in the center of the church.

"Janey," calls Vanessa peremptorily, but Janey doesn't stop. "Janey!" Janey leaves the church, not looking back, Mary trailing anxiously behind her.

Nobody follows Janey, but nobody wants to go back home. The promise of the beach hangs heavy in the air like a mist. Girls stand in little clusters, slowly talking over what Janey said, until Caitlin's feet turn white and everyone's teeth are chattering. Girls run to the stairway, shivering, and then turn back to the light and company of their friends and foes. The girls who have been playing games double their efforts, throwing their limbs about and screaming in the unexpected freedom of the dark church.

Caitlin huddles with Rosie, Linda, Violet, and Fiona. They are gathered close to one another for warmth, murmuring about Janey's dark idea. "I can't say it doesn't make sense," says Fiona. "Not everyone who bleeds out, of course, but it just makes sense."

"They don't even need to kill me. I'd kill myself right now if it wasn't for the darkness below," says Violet, and they look at her with shock.

"You would?" whispers Linda.

"My sister told me that after she got married she felt like nothing would ever change for her again," said Fiona. "Especially after she had her daughter. She said she loved her daughter, but also couldn't stand her, and that after she was born, she kept having nightmares. She said she wanted to die. Not that she would kill herself, but if she got swamp lung or something and it killed her, she wouldn't mind. She used to go out in the cold, sometimes, in light clothes, to see if she could catch it." There is a long silence as they digest this information. "She wasn't the type to say anything to others, but she said things to me. How she wanted everything to change. How everything was wrong. She said it to me. Maybe if she said it to other people, she'd be dead."

Everyone is silent for a minute.

"I can't feel my feet," says Rosie finally. "I cannot feel them." She leans over and pokes at the skin of her instep. "My toes are blue."

Caitlin suddenly realizes she is shivering heavily and is feeling sleepy. "Your lips are blue," Rosie informs her.

"We need to go back," says Linda. "It's almost dawn anyway."

"We don't need to go back," says Rosie, and Caitlin sees new conviction dawn in her eyes.

"You're going to go," she whispers.

"I think...I think I'm going too," says Fiona. "Not right now. Maybe tomorrow, when I can bring something warm to wear and some food. Will you go?"

"I—I don't know," says Caitlin, her head spinning.

Clutching themselves, they ascend the church steps and run home on numb feet, tripping and falling, catching themselves with cold hands that prickle with pain, thrusting fingers into their mouths for warmth. Caitlin sneaks into bed, rolling herself over and over so she is wrapped in layers of quilt, and immediately falls into a deep sleep.

The next day, Fiona and Rosie are missing from school, as are Letty and Violet. Caitlin feels envy stab her in the gut so sharply it's hard to walk upright.

CHAPTER THIRTY‑TWO

Janey

Mary and Janey work through the night to build a large shelter, held up by birch branches and woven through with bark and dead grass. Janey's fingers fly like narrow white birds as she twines strands together, looping and winding. They are companionably silent in their task, with only the sounds of bark scratching against bare wood, and their feet shifting in the sand.

Fiona arrives first in the pearly gray early morning, looking petrified, along with Rosie, who looks fierce as usual. Mary welcomes them with embraces. Fiona holds on for a long time, shaking, and Rosie irritably accepts a few seconds of Mary's arms and then shrugs her off.

"So what are we going to do here?" asks Rosie.

"Live," says Janey simply.

"They'll never let us."

"We'll figure out what we need to," replies Janey, her confidence burgeoning outside but weak and thready inside. Rosie is right; the adults will not tolerate defection. She needs time to discover some advantage, some strategy for resistance.

"My father will come for me," whispers Fiona. "He'll beat me."

"Then why did you come?" snaps Rosie.

"I couldn't *not* come," says Fiona. "It's ... it's my only chance, you know."

Letty comes later in the morning, saying she simply walked out of school. "The teachers don't really know what to do when you look like you know where you're going," she reports. "What are we doing here? What are we going to do here?"

"We're going to live together on the beach," says Mary, her sweet voice full of joy.

"For how long?" says Letty. "They'll come for us."

"We'll figure it out," says Janey. "For now, welcome."

Violet comes running up breathless, laughing and sobbing with exhaustion. "I ran the whole way here!" she cries. "I ran the whole way! I'm going to stay here with you!" Her breath is rapid and her voice a little hysterical; Letty goes over and rubs her back in circles until she's breathing more normally. "I brought a bowl," says Violet, "I thought we might need a bowl." Then she bursts into laughter, and so do the others.

Over the next three days, the girls come to join Janey one by one: apologetically, triumphantly, so quietly that she simply wakes up to find them there. They bring food, sisters, buckets of rainwater. Their eyes are disbelieving, like this is the dream, and tomorrow they will wake up in their regular lives, mourning a vision of freedom. They are mostly Mary's age, teetering on the brink of fruition, although some have younger girls in tow. Abigail Balthazar, who is only three, cries so hard for her mother that her sister, Lila, must grumpily go leave her on the doorstep. Janey had hoped to see Vanessa Adam, but she remains obtrusively absent. Perhaps she is upset because Janey intimated that her father killed people. The rest of the girls slowly move into the motions of life. There are basic problems to solve: food, warmth, fire.

The supplies the girls bring dwindle quickly, and Janey forbids theft. "I don't know why they haven't come for us already," she says. "Maybe they're trying to figure out what to do. The last thing we need is to be stealing from them." They dig for clams, nibble on different kinds of seaweed to discover which are edible, daring the others to try the slimiest specimens. Despite the prohibition on stealing, Dava Gideon sneaks home in the middle of the night and takes her little brother's fishing rod and hook. Her bounty is scant, bony fish barely the size of her palm, but the act of catching them makes the girls whoop and cheer. When the rainwater runs out, Janey agrees to have Rosie steal a small rain barrel. After all, she says, there are plenty of unused barrels and an endless well of rain waiting in the sky.

Fires must be small and innocuous, ideally walled with sand, and when darkness comes the beach springs to life, small flaming blossoms opening on delicate wooden skeletons, warming hands and half cooking fish flesh that will be sucked from needle-sharp bones. When it is deep night, stars plastered across the sky and frost beginning to form on the ground, the girls retreat to the shelter, where they curl up and stretch out and form patterns of limbs meeting together to create a breathing, slumbering, murmuring mass of dirty cloth and tangled hair and still faces.

During the day, the more industrious girls hunt for food, care for the little ones, and tend to the shelter. Most of the others simply hitch on to whatever amusement catches them. They build castles and moats out of sand and reverently transport minnows, crabs, and snails to pools, where they are named and fed everything from seaweed to spit. Girls strip naked and wade into the water to have vicious, laughing fights, the drenched losers and winners alike warming themselves by sunlight and wading back in again. Dogs run by to investigate this new island population, wagging and barking in greeting, and often staying for a game of chase or tug-of-war before they head back to their home for more reliable food. The one exception is Roro, the apple farmer Saul's dog, who is enormous and shaggy and gray and seems quite content to spend all day with the girls. With his tongue lolling and tail wagging, he plunges into the water, then rolls in the sand and stretches luxuriously in the sun, only to crash back into the water again. This infuriates Dava, who is always yelling at everyone to be still and not scare the fish. Vera Balthazar, whose father weaves, makes endless garlands of wildflowers, evening blue and golden yellow and blushing pink, and places as many on Roro as he will tolerate, so he springs around the beach shedding glorious scraps of color as the stems come undone.

When the girls are tired, or lazy, they sit and talk, heads on each other's stomachs or thighs. They talk about the girls who aren't on the beach and what they must be doing, and they talk about the girls who are on the beach, and they talk about what they will name their sons and daughters, and they talk about which hurts more, burning or freezing, and if being gathered into the ancestors' arms involves literally being hugged for all eternity. They proclaim their disgust with boys, and pregnant women, and parents, and everyone who isn't a girl with a straight, neat body and long sand-caked hair and more freedom than she's ever tasted in her life. Each hour, it seems, another girl shows shyly at the beach and is welcomed with kind words and shouts of "What took you so long?"

Everything seems brighter, the colors of the island sharper and more vivid. Janey sees the violet undertone in each ripple of water, the amber shimmer of sun-warmed sand, the dulcet, garnet gleam in each strand of Mary's damp hair. Janey's own flesh seems lovelier, creamy-white with sea-green veins buried beneath her pigment-flecked forearm. The sky arcs gracefully above them in washes of blue, the dense, pillowy clouds pearlescent and peach-toned along their bulging bellies. They reflect in the sea like giant, harmless beasts, slowly drifting toward the horizon.

Janey wakes early the third morning, at the first tint of crimson shattering the black night sky, as if someone had shaken her from slumber. She takes the precious moment gladly and watches the girls sleep peacefully. *Let this last,* she prays, she knows not to who—certainly not the ancestors, or their puppetmaster God. *Just for a little while, let them have this. Let me have it. Please.*

CHAPTER THIRTY-THREE

Vanessa

V anessa," says Father, "I need to talk with you."

It's late at night, but Vanessa is still awake, and he knows it. Ever since the meeting with Janey she has been thrumming with indecision, with excitement, alternately preparing to run out the door barefoot and then sitting down to carefully plan a list of supplies she will bring to the beach. Vanessa has thought through her mundane future, and dreamed of the power to alter it, but she never pictured this.

Obediently, Vanessa follows Father downstairs in her nightgown. She can hear Mother moving restlessly in her and Father's bedroom. Ben is the only one sleeping well tonight. She pictures his golden hair spiraled out in wild tufts, his baby mouth drooling innocently on his pillow.

Father sits at the kitchen table, the yellowing, mealy remnants of an apple core lying next to him. Vanessa avoids his eyes, staring at the clean-swept floor and her small bare feet.

"Vanessa, I know about the girls on the beach," he says.

"I thought everybody would know by now."

He shrugs. "True enough. It's unprecedented. At least since..." She waits, confused, but he makes a motion with his hand like he's throwing something away. "Vanessa, what Janey Solomon is doing is..." He searches for the word, then stops. Catching her gaze, he sighs. "I know. I know. But Vanessa, hear this now, hear me clearly: you will not join her."

She stares at her feet again.

"Do you hear me?"

She nods, feeling like a ghost in her nightgown, transparent, without will or agency. And yet she could disobey him. She could walk out that door tonight, when the house is dark, after he has left her room. Suddenly, a surge of power boils in her chest, so astonishing that she gasps out loud. He cannot stop her.

"Vanessa, please look at me."

She doesn't want to. She stares at his chest, the rough-woven, stained cloth, the slight rise and fall of his breath.

"*Look at me,* Vanessa," he says, and she reluctantly brings her eyes to his. With him sitting, their gazes are level. His eyes are so like hers, hazel with gold and green, a dark splotch on one iris, slightly narrow and fringed with thick burgundy lashes. Slipping away from his gaze, she looks at his set mouth, also like hers, the deep-cut notch in the full upper lip.

"I know what you did," she whispers.

"What?"

"I know what the wanderers did."

He stares at her, his brow furrowed. "What did we do?"

She leans forward and hisses, "You killed Amanda Balthazar."

To her surprise, he looks bewildered instead of guilty or enraged. "Vanessa, what in the ancestors' names are you talking about?"

Vanessa blinks and shifts from foot to foot. "It's true," she murmurs.

"Vanessa, who on earth have you been listening to? Of course we didn't kill Amanda Balthazar. She bled out. It was very sad, but the wanderers had nothing to do with it."

"She didn't bleed out. They pulled her body from the water."

"*What?* Vanessa, are you...are you awake? You're not making sense."

She stares at him intently, trying to elicit a gleam of knowledge from his eyes, a shade of shame in the twitch of his lips. He looks at her, confused, and she sighs. "It's true," she insists again.

"I am sure you heard something, Vanessa, but I would know if that happened, wouldn't I?"

She nods slowly. Could the wanderers have excluded Father from their darkest workings?

Father shakes his head, as if to clear the accusation, and then says, "We were talking about you staying home, where you belong."

"But Father—"

"I want you safe and alive," he tells her softly. "We're going to wait until the girls get hungry and cold and come home. The others are certain it will happen in a few days, but I'm not so sure. If time passes and they're still out there, I'm sure the plan will change and we'll start searching."

Vanessa crosses her arms under her chest, puts her hand on her throat. "Are they going to kill them?" she asks. "Kill the girls on the beach?"

"Please don't be ridiculous. Of course not."

"Well, then, why can't I be safe and alive with them?"

He sighs. "I know it's selfish, Vanessa. But if you can't see why you shouldn't run away from school and your mother and your home, then do it for me. I need you here with me. I have done so much for this island, so much for this family. I just need you to be good. I need you to be the good girl you are. Please, stay here for me, and be good for me. Please don't go." He takes her hands in his strong, hard ones, then pulls her into his arms.

She resists slightly, meets his eyes with her mirror ones. "Don't you want to me to..." She can't find the right words, although she discards many—*be free, run, fight, rebel, be a child one last time.* A precious few seconds pass, and the moment of opportunity is lost. Her hope of escape drains into the floorboards.

"Who is my little wife?" asks Father in a sweet tone.

"I am," whispers Vanessa.

"And what do wives do?"

Vanessa hesitates. He's never followed up with this question before, and a multitude of answers mill through her mind.

"Do wives stay with their husbands?"

She sighs. "Yes, wives stay with their husbands," she echoes dully.

"Be a good girl," he whispers again. Her heart is clamoring and screaming to go, run out the door, but his pull is stronger, and the weight of him on her shoulders drags her to the ground.

CHAPTER THIRTY*FOUR

Caitlin

Countless times over the next few days, Caitlin steps out her front door and walks a few strides in the direction of the beach. Each time she stops, sighs, and turns on her heel, returning to her stultifying existence of cooking and sewing and trying to fade into walls and tables.

A foreign, previously undiscovered part of Caitlin is waking up. It burgeons and yawns and stretches under the blanket of her ribs, sealed in soft sheaths of slimy muscle. It breathes and shivers. It terrifies her to no end.

She puts her hands on the rotting frame of the back door and surveys the unweeded, blackbird-savaged corn lurching crookedly from its stems. Father is nominally a corn farmer, but all of their barter comes from his mash-wine, which doesn't require corn that is whole or even unblackened. His vats, set aside from the house, brew a concoction so burning and strong it must be watered and honeyed heavily before it is potable.

Caitlin has a strong aversion to the vats. Once, when she was younger, Father found her dropping pebbles into the searing brew, to see if they would dissolve before they hit the bottom. He wrapped his hand around the back of her skull and shoved her head under the conflagrant liquid. She saw the color of pain inside that vat, red-black and flaming brighter than any fire. He left her weeping and vomiting acid, wondering if she was blind, if the crimson surge had burned out

213

the hollows of her eyes. She was sick in bed for a week after. When Mother asked, she obediently told her that she'd fallen in while playing. She could just see Mother's face, blurry through her stinging eyes, and watched the smudges of her features contract and change shape. Caitlin could tell from the way Mother wept and kicked the wall that she didn't believe her.

Suddenly the smell, so familiar and pervasive, makes her eyes hurt. She walks quickly to the front door and stands there, breathing fresher air. She mulls on Mother's impotent grief.

A thought that Caitlin has been trying to suppress abruptly rises to the surface: if she leaves, if she is not there to stand in front of Mother and absorb Father's violence, what will happen to Mother?

But another voice, one that has been driven down even deeper, suddenly sings forth. *She should be standing in front of me.*

She stares at the horizon: the trees wave, the clouds pass.

Caitlin leaves that night.

CHAPTER THIRTY⧸FIVE

Janey

It is dusk, blossom tones seeping across a graying sky. Kneeling in the damp sand, Janey is digging for clams while the others finish their slumber. Mary is curled up back to back with Ruth Balthazar, her face inches from the lightly snoring Frances Adam, everyone unconsciously snuggling closer for warmth in the crisp air.

Scanning for pinpoint airholes, Janey uses two long fingers to dig small vertical tunnels until her nails hit a shock of wet shell, and then she scrabbles to catch the burrowing creatures before they escape. Clamming was never one of her skills before the beach, but she has become quite good at it and enjoys the bloodless hunt. As the stars come out, the girls will rise, yawn, and take to smashing the huddled clams with rocks and sucking out the salty, slimy insides. Sometimes, if the moon is dark enough that the smoke won't show, the girls make small fires, put a rock by the flames, and boil the clams in their own juices until their shells creak open reluctantly, leaking clear seawater like tears of grief.

There are snuffles and snorts as the girls wake, see the lilac sky, and roll over for another few minutes of dreaming. They are nocturnal now, sleeping during the crisp fall days and rising at night, always moving their chosen sleeping spot lest habits give them away. Their shelters are flimsy and hastily made. Janey already recognizes the danger of this communal sleeping and suspects soon each girl will need to choose her own hiding place in which to doze during the day. And yet it is hard to deliver that edict, for watching the girls sleep in a pile like puppies, soaking in a more peaceful hibernation than many of them have ever known, gives Janey a sweetness in her chest that rises to the back of her tongue and makes her lips curl upward with pleasure.

There is a sharp rustle to her right, and she freezes. A large figure emerges from the brush, and Janey's breath pulses in her throat. "Janey?" whispers a familiar voice.

Janey half crouches into a fighting stance, although there is no way she could prevail against Father; he is a large man and she a spindly, exhausted girl. But then she notices that he is carrying a basket smelling of fresh bread and festooned with wildflowers, and she straightens, feeling foolish. "Father," she says.

"Your mother insisted on the flowers," replies Father, looking at her kindly. "I said that living outside, you could probably find your own flowers if you liked." Coppery glints glow in his cropped hair and square beard, the same shades that smolder on Janey's skull.

"They're pretty," says Janey softly, staring at the tiny golden blossoms. "Tell her I liked them."

"She made you bread. She said she can't imagine what you're eating out here. It's not like it's summer and there are offerings on every doorstep."

"Well, we eat," says Janey lamely. "Tell her not to worry."

He chuckles at that, glancing at her handful of button-sized clams. "I don't think me saying that will do much good."

"It's true," insists Janey. "We eat well. We had chicken yesterday." She doesn't mention that after Mildred Aaron had triumphantly carried back the squawking, bristling chicken, nobody wanted to kill it.

"It's so pretty," little Evelyn Jacob had said. "Look at its feathers." They all stared at its snowy, fluffed feathers like thistledown.

"It could be our pet," suggested Mary.

Janey didn't want to kill the bridling, noisy bird either. However, she knew that the other girls were hungry all the time, and that they didn't have her fierce determination to keep their hunger at bay. Biting her lip, she snatched the chicken by its fluttering, gulping throat and snapped its neck, which gave like a salt-bleached twig. A few girls burst into tears, but Minnie Saul, obviously used to this process, grabbed the carcass and began expertly plucking the feathers in a flurry of snowfall. Half the girls swore they wouldn't eat it, but once the smell of the skin curling and crackling in the fire began disseminating through the air, everyone ate a small slice of meat and sucked the bones clean.

Janey blinks, feeling an unaccustomed wash of guilt. "I'm fine," she says determinedly. "Tell Mother I'm fine."

"I know," he says, holding out the basket. She takes it and cradles it in her arms. The bread is still warm, and the gentle heat radiates into her rib cage. Unable to resist, she pushes a fingertip through the firm golden crust into the soft, spongy bread below. Mother used to get angry at her for doing that as a child; she would leave an intact loaf of bread to cool and come back to a pockmarked, half-eaten mutation with Janey nowhere to be found. Janey raises a fingerful of hot, grainy, barely cooked dough to her mouth and swallows without thinking about it. Unused to such richness, her body shimmers with pleasure.

"She's been trying to do this for days, but I haven't been able to find you," he says.

"How did you find me today?" she asks tensely.

"Janey, the island isn't huge," he replies. "They can find you, as soon as they want to. And they'll hurt you."

They gaze at each other, and Father blurts suddenly, "I've been unhappy here since I was born."

Janey blinks. "What?"

"I just...I'm not a very good man, I think. At least, I don't follow the ways of the ancestors well. I suppose I don't believe in them. I know everyone thinks I'm scared of you, but that's not it. It just never felt right to me. I know it's supposed to be good for you, good for Mary, a father's duty. I know I'm supposed to believe, supposed to pray, supposed to...do a lot of things. It's a sin, disobeying the ancestors and the wanderers, but God gave me a mind too, and the way we do things never seemed right to me. Ever since I was a boy. Lots of things. I'm not a fighter like you, but I can still think."

Janey is taken aback; this is the most she has ever heard her father say. It never occurred to her that Father could do anything but passionately believe in the ancestors' ways.

"It's going to get colder," he says. "You and Mary can come home whenever you need to. Your mother and I will welcome you."

"I can't come home," says Janey.

"How long do you think you can stay here?"

Suddenly she feels exhausted, like the weight of her own body is dragging her to the ground. "I can't think about that."

"You will need to," he says gently. "It's getting colder." His eyes are glistening. "You are getting thinner and thinner. You can't keep doing this without starving. Dying."

"Mary," she murmurs. "You have to protect Mary."

He snorts joylessly. "Protect Mary?" he says. "Do you have any idea how many men are waiting for her to come to fruition? How many are desperately putting off their own until she's ready? She's on her way, Mary. I can try to counsel her on which of the men will be the gentlest, the least likely to cause her pain, but Mary will have her summer of fruition soon, and she will marry, and she will have children if she is able."

"I don't want that for her," Janey says brokenly, tears coursing down her cheeks. "I want her to be happy."

"Some women are happy, with their husbands and their children," he says.

"She never will be," says Janey, "and it's all my fault. I've ruined her for it. I should have left her alone."

"You couldn't," says Father. "You need her. And whatever happens, the days she had with you will always be the ones she remembers and longs for."

"And she'll never be happy again," finishes Janey, and they both bow their heads at the truth of this.

Father takes her slender hand. She jumps at the unexpected contact, but doesn't pull away. Then suddenly he laughs.

"What?" says Janey, suspiciously.

"I'm just trying to think of a man who wouldn't be petrified to marry you," says Father. "And I can't think of a single one."

"I would end up with the one too drunk to know what he was doing," offers Janey. "He would sober up and take one look at me and run straight into the sea." Holding hands and inhaling the smell of fresh bread, they tilt back their heads and laugh upward at the emerging starlight.

CHAPTER THIRTY‑SIX

Caitlin

Caitlin doesn't sleep. She is terrified of waking up back at home, in her own bed. At night she lies listening to the collective breath of sleeping children. If she drifts off, she snatches herself awake immediately and lies in a state of peaceful torpor, inhaling the dark and salt and rich smell of sea-stiffened dresses softened by sweat and play. At dusk and dawn, when the sun is hovering in the sky, sometimes she feels safe enough to curl up on the sand and doze. Sometimes Roro decides to stretch out beside her, and she wakes up with a mouthful of wet sandy fur, his huge heart thumping against hers.

A day or two after Caitlin's flight, Fiona is the first to be caught. She is last seen at twilight, chasing a rabbit into the brush with a homemade slingshot, then simply disappears. Shaken, the girls debate whether she was captured, or just decided to leave and go back home. Fiona returns to the beach two days later, her body painted in lush bruises of indigo and gold, her lip split and stuck together with clotted blood, her hands shaking.

"It was Father," she says thickly through her swollen mouth. "He just... *took* me. But the wanderers were there too. They said he had to punish me properly. They said if he didn't, they would. And so he beat me, and then left, and then came back and beat me some more. Mother cried and put me to bed and I left as soon as I could walk again, but they know where we are. They knew where to find me."

Caitlin, staring at Fiona's damaged face, feels a sense of sinking,

221

filthy inevitability. She had gotten carried away by the utter joy of these past sweet days and nights, but of course they won't be allowed to stay on the beach. There are houses to be scrubbed, dishes to be washed, animals to be fed, men to be married, children to be borne, and the fathers have had enough.

"We're not stopping," Janey says in a voice so low and grating that Mary jerks in surprise. "They can't have us. I won't let them. Not yet."

"What do we do, then?" asks Diana.

"I don't know," says Janey. "They're going to find us one day and take us. Hurt all of us."

"Not if we kill them," growls Rosie.

There's a shocked silence, and Violet says in a horrified tone, "I don't want to kill anybody!" just as Mary says, "We're not killing anyone."

"There's more of them than of us," says Janey, sidestepping the question of violence to focus on practicalities. "And the men are stronger."

"Even if they weren't, we're not murderers," says Mary slowly and intently, staring at Janey, who holds her gaze for a long moment, then looks away and nods slightly.

"*They* are," Rosie mutters, but nobody answers, and the idea trails off into the darkness. Shoulders loosen, lungs sigh with deep breaths once more.

"We can't sleep together during the day. It isn't safe. We need to hide. We can still be together at night, but we'll change where we meet each time and set girls to watch for intruders. It's not perfect, but it's the best we can do."

"But what if they find us during the day?" asks Helen Abraham.

"Then we'll be taken, and beaten, and maybe never come back," says Janey. "I don't think they'll kill us, there's too many of us out here, and we're children."

The weight of this statement, with all its possibilities, settles heavily over the girls. Joanne Adam starts to cry. "I don't want to be beaten," she says.

"Then go home," advises Janey. "Say you're sorry and start going back to school and living with your parents."

"I don't want to do that either!" wails Joanne.

"It's not like we haven't been beaten before," Fiona points out to Joanne, talking slowly and painfully. "It's worse, but it's the same. Hasn't your father ever beaten you for something?"

Joanne sniffs, nodding.

"Well, me too. Not this badly, but almost, that time I—well, it doesn't matter. They're not going to stop me by beating me. I'm going to hide, and if they catch me and beat me again I'll come back anyway." Fiona tosses her head, then looks at Janey for approval.

Janey sighs. "It's best if we sleep alone, or in pairs. Try to choose places people won't find you, even if they're looking. That means no sleeping on the beach—it will have to be inland. The woods where there's no houses will be good, but then again they'll be looking for us there. Choose as best as you can. We'll be together at night. Please don't lose hope."

"What's...what do you want to happen, out of all of this?" asks Violet.

"I want something to change," says Janey, "and I'm not even sure what could or would change. But I want things to change for us. Maybe a big change, like going to the wastelands. Maybe a small change, like we have a little more freedom, not just in summer."

"How would this bring us to the wastelands?" asks Fiona, confused.

Janey sighs. "I don't really know," she says, "but Amanda died for it." And there is silence.

The next day, Caitlin sleeps in the brush next to the Saul orchards, curled up under the thicket in the hopes nobody will find her, and nobody does. That night they meet at the beach off the Gideon cornfields where the two willows meet, and excitedly exchange sleeping locations: a thornbush (from a Helen covered in scratches), a haystack, a roof. Violet brazenly snuck into her house and slept in her own bed after her father left, exiting in late afternoon. "I think Mother might have known," she confessed, "but I never saw her."

That night, Diana is missing, and she returns the night after, beaten bloody. "I pretended I couldn't move," she says spitefully, "and then I just walked out."

"Who beat you?" whispers Caitlin.

"The wanderer Solomon found me and took me to my father with instructions for a beating," she says. "Father seemed happy to do it."

"But now what if they catch you again?" asks Isabelle Moses fearfully.

"Then they'll beat me again. And I'll come back again," says Diana, and spits. One of the girls, farther into the darkness, gives a little cheer.

One by one, not every day, but often, the girls are discovered, and each time the beatings seem to get worse. Nina comes back missing a patch of hair, Natalie with a broken finger, and Letty doesn't come back at all. Rosie sneaks to her house during the day and peers into a window, and reports seeing Letty in a bed with the covers pulled up over her dark hair. "So at least she's alive," says Rosie. "They wouldn't put her in bed if she was dead."

Marks from the beatings become badges of honor. The girls compare injuries, competing for the deepest-black bruise, the grisliest swellings, the most blood dried to crackling brown on their faces. Elsie Jacob waits to return to the beach and a circle of girls before she triumphantly removes a tooth knocked almost out of the gum, displaying the long-rooted, blood-slick piece of enamel in her fingers like a battle trophy. Helen, with two immobile fingers swollen like sausages, walks with her hand held before her like it was draped in ostentatious jewelry, making sure the girls see the damage thrust in front of them. Fiona, with her iridescent face, is envied and admired, and she walks around, tilting her head up toward the sun, so her skin glows in navy and violet and gold. Diana doesn't wash the blood from her body, spending the next few days looking like a thinly coated summer child. And yet Caitlin hears them at night, when darkness renders them unknowable: sobbing quietly, creeping to the sea to immerse fingers and feet, wrists and faces, and numb the agony of their suffering bodies. When Helen slinks away to the woods, Caitlin knows she will drop to her knees out of sight, hold her fingers to her chest, and rock in silent affliction.

Since Caitlin arrived on the beach, she and Janey have become closer. Janey seems to like her, although Caitlin isn't sure why. They talk softly sometimes, about little practicalities or nothing in particular, and often move close to each other in the moonlight and watch the other girls, or the sea, or the star-soaked sky. Sometimes they simply sit in silence and look at the dark. Caitlin enjoys the lines of energy that seem to radiate from Janey's form, even when she is quiet and still. At one point, Janey puts a bony arm around Caitlin's back, and Caitlin freezes as if a bird had landed on her shoulder, wanting the moment to last.

"I don't know what we're going to do about winter," remarks Janey.

"What do you mean?"

"It's almost here," says Janey. "It's getting colder and colder, and we're half freezing already. Some of the girls don't even have shoes. And it would be too dangerous to try to steal our winter clothing. We'd all have to go home." Caitlin has a sudden vision of barging into her house, rushing to the cupboard, and running out, streaming sweaters and blankets behind her like a river of warmth.

"So what will we do?" ventures Caitlin after some prolonged silence.

"I don't know," says Janey, deep in thought. "We can build fires at night, at least small ones, but even that is dangerous. I suppose we could build them during the day, wherever we find to sleep, but I don't trust some of the little ones not to burn the entire island down."

"I've never actually heard of someone freezing to death," says Caitlin tentatively. "I mean, they say you will, but I've never known it to actually happen. Maybe it's not true, that people freeze. Maybe you just get colder and colder."

"I've never known anyone to leap off their roof, but that doesn't mean they wouldn't break their bones," replies Janey.

There are watchers at night, for movement, for sound, and they crouch in the cold sand, often falling asleep until Janey begins rotating them more often. Fitful and nervous, they envision the wanderers swooping in like birds of prey, seizing the girls with their talons and carrying them off to break their bones and tear their flesh. The wanderers, who have always represented majesty and order, now resemble monsters. And yet the only intruders to break their peace are boys: a runaway pleading to join them, or a little brother seeking the solace of his sister.

And then, the next night, they come. The girls are alerted by Sarah Moses's shrill scream from the edge of the woods. Sarah comes flying toward the girls, who flutter and flurry like a flock of hens, until Janey runs straight toward the wanderers with her arms outstretched. "Run!" she cries. "Run down the beach and into the fields!"

She collides with the men, and Caitlin can't tell if they're trying to contain her or she's trying to contain them. All she can make out is a tangle of dark, twisted limbs like fallen trees in a storm.

"Run!" yells Janey from within the scuffle, and cursing herself for her cowardice, Caitlin does.

CHAPTER THIRTY╱SEVEN

Vanessa

One morning, as Vanessa is leaving for school, Mother stops her. "There's a shaming today," Mother says, sounding confused. Usually everyone is informed of both the infraction and the punishment well before the day of a shaming arrives, and school is always canceled so the children can watch and learn.

"Who?" Vanessa asks.

There is a pause, and then Mother says, "Janey Solomon?"

Vanessa shakes her head. "No, that can't be."

"No, it can't," says Mother, sounding more confused. "I don't know what's going on."

But nothing makes sense lately. Half the girls are missing from school. Letty showed up last week with a broken arm splinted to her side and two black eyes that she refused to talk about. She spoke about the beach, though, as if she would go back soon. "I did whatever I wanted," she said dreamily. "I slept in the sand and fell asleep by counting stars."

Mr. Abraham, usually such a stickler for attendance and rules, seems to have given up. Vanessa has the feeling she could get up and walk out of class at any time and he would barely react. Most of the time he has them reading from textbooks, or *Our Book*. He didn't mention a shaming when he dismissed class yesterday afternoon, as he usually would.

Vanessa does not look forward to shamings the way some children do, those who love the unique opportunity to mock and jeer an adult. They are simply part of island life, a punishment for those who blaspheme, or have secret meetings, or refuse their chosen profession, or a hundred other reasons. They tend to be fairly perfunctory, unless the crime is something particularly scandalous, like when Jonathan Balthazar lay with June Gideon before her summer of fruition; they were both shamed and then exiled.

When Vanessa arrives at the field, it is milling with people, most of whom are taking the opportunity to catch up with friends and neighbors. Mrs. Joseph the beekeeper's wife is exchanging some vats of honey for fluffy, peeping chicks from Mrs. Aaron the weaver's wife, and there is a flock of teenage boys by the edge of the field, voices swelling like there is about to be a fight. The small scaffold is empty, nine wanderers standing nearby in a line, looking solemn. Usually all ten are present, but Vanessa has heard that Mr. Gideon is badly ill and confined to his bed. Father tries to catch her eye, but she gazes in another direction.

Pastor Saul ascends the scaffold and clears his throat to silence everyone. When that doesn't work, he cries, "Attention!" People quiet and turn to him, although the teenage boys remain distracted until some women hiss at them.

"My brethren, we are attending the shaming of Janey Solomon."

Vanessa freezes, and there is a buzz of shock. So Mother *had* heard correctly. But children are never shamed, no matter what their infraction—it is a punishment reserved for adults. Before she realizes what she is doing, Vanessa runs up to Father, ignoring the gasps from the crowd and glares from the other wanderers. "Father, it's a mistake," she whispers.

"Vanessa, please go back with everyone else."

"But she's not an adult! You can't shame her."

"It's done, Vanessa," he says in a dull tone she doesn't recognize, and she backs away. Looking around wildly, she sees her teacher, Mr. Abraham, who appears as stunned as everyone else. Running over, she tugs on his sleeve.

"Mr. Abraham," she hisses. "Stop them. They can't."

He looks at her for a few moments, as if he doesn't recognize her. "What do you want me to do?" he says finally.

"Stop them! They can't shame Janey, they don't shame children, children belong to their parents—"

"Janey doesn't belong to anyone," he says coolly, but then sees her distress and takes her hand in his.

A moment later, Janey walks calmly toward the scaffold, her dress mended, her hair braided, looking like an amiable child tailing an adult. Vanessa stares at her eyes, searching for the glaze of a drug, but Janey's eyes are darting around—not wildly, but with slow purpose. She catches someone's gaze and shakes her head sharply, lightly, so it simply seems like a quiver. Then, staring harder, she shakes her head slowly from side to side like a tree swaying in a storm. Vanessa follows her gaze and sees Mrs. Solomon in the crowd, her hair a mess, both hands to her tearstained face. *Mary,* mouths Janey to her mother, and then looks away. Mrs. Solomon starts searching the crowd. Vanessa stands on her tiptoes to look for Mary but can't see her, or Mr. Solomon either.

Janey steps neatly before the stake, calm and sedate as they tie her wrists to it. The sound from the crowd is growing and swelling, some voices angry, some pleased, some alarmed. The girls, the good girls who have stayed away from the beach, glance at one another, hoping to find some signal or meaning from one of their peers.

Pastor Saul steps forward. He has performed enough shamings that he doesn't need *Our Book,* but he holds it in his hands anyway, for performance's sake.

"My brethren, we are attending the shaming of Janey Solomon," he says again. "Philip Adam wrote, *For those for whom the fear of the darkness below is not a deterrent from evil, let them fear the shame and disdain of their neighbor. We here on the island are all interconnected, and none could survive without the other. Let the poor opinion, the disgusted glance of family and friends, be the punishment and the terror that perhaps may sway their path, and save them from the darkness.*"

Pastor Saul puts the book down by his side. "Janey Solomon, you have blasphemed. You have lied. You have encouraged others in blasphemies and lies. You have disobeyed your wanderers. For shame."

"For shame," echoes the crowd: not the lusty yell that normally accompanies this phrase, but a tentative whisper.

The wanderer Mr. Balthazar comes forth with the lash; the crowd's voice swells fuller. People seem to be arguing, remonstrating, encouraging—the din falls on Vanessa's ears, and she flinches. Then Mr. Balthazar tears Janey's dress down to her waist, and a sudden hush falls upon the congregation.

Janey is so thin that Vanessa wonders how she continues to breathe. Her body is graceful in its starvation, posed in arcs and wings of bone, her collarbone soaring upward against her skin like a loosed bird. The hollows between her ribs are so deep that the shadows loom gray and blue, and the sockets of her shoulders are neatly encased in skin and little else. Vanessa thinks she can see her heartbeat, the tiny tremor of it, against the triangle of her sternum, and the pulse in her long, stemlike throat. Where her dress hung, Janey's skin is so pale it glistens silver, her freckles faint amber motes.

Mr. Balthazar pauses before this skeletal apparition and shoots a questioning look toward the wanderer Mr. Joseph, who stands at the head of the line of wanderers. Mr. Joseph looks annoyed and nods his head exaggeratedly. Even so, Vanessa can see by the way that Mr. Balthazar brings his arm back halfway, how he bends from the elbow and not the shoulder, that he does not intend to give Janey the lashing others have received. Possibly he fears she would fall apart.

Janey's beautiful speckled-eggshell skin is suddenly severed, cracked open, a rosy welt with a spine of crimson wrapping around to embrace her fluttering rib cage. She jerks, but her expression doesn't change. Mr. Balthazar peers around to look at the front of her and make sure she is still alive. Wincing, he sends out another lash, this one striking her shoulder.

"No!" From the crowd, from the trees, from somewhere, emerges

Rosie, her dress in tatters and her hair matted and loose. Vaulting onto the scaffold, she sinks her teeth into Mr. Balthazar's hand near the thumb. Hissing, he drops the whip and stares at her in utter befuddlement. "They're liars!" Rosie shrieks wildly. "Don't listen to him!"

Janey stares at Rosie. *Go,* Vanessa sees her mouth say, and when Rosie doesn't move, she shouts, "Rosie, get out of here!"

"They killed Amanda Balthazar!" screams Rosie, pointing at the wanderers. "They killed Alma Joseph! They killed others too, but I can't remember their names. They say they bled out, but they're dead! They're murderers, they're liars! They're the ones who should be shamed, not Janey!" She coughs and bends around the middle as a male arm snaps around her. "They're liars," she cries, gulping, and starts to cry. Mr. Joseph hauls her up against his waist and she goes limp, sobbing. "Liars!" she shrieks, and he strides away, carrying his tearful burden with him.

Everyone is silent, wide-eyed, including Janey. There is a long, weighty silence before Mr. Balthazar picks up the whip and delivers Janey's remaining eight lashes. Janey appears so astonished and lost in thought that they barely seem to register. When she is untied, Mrs. Solomon runs up to take her weight. They put their heads together and start whispering. Vanessa looks up at Mr. Abraham, and he stares down at her in disbelief.

"What's going to happen to Rosie?" she whispers.

"Vanessa, I have no idea," he answers, and she leans into him as they watch Janey shake free of her mother, pull the top of her dress back over her shoulders, and slowly shuffle toward the beach.

CHAPTER THIRTY EIGHT

Janey

Mary is carefully laying cold seaweed on Janey's broken, wounded skin. Janey, facedown in the soothingly chill sand, winces. "I don't see how this is supposed to do anything," she says. "The salt stings."

"It feels better, though, doesn't it, when the sting dies," says Mary. She is right, and Janey feels icy silk crisscrossing her back, numbing the pain of the welts wrapped around her like hot wires.

Janey sighs deeply. "Mother was there," she murmurs. "Poor Mother."

"I wish I'd been there. Instead of on the beach, crying, wondering if they were going to kill you."

"You would have done something stupid, like Rosie," says Janey. Mary nods ruefully.

"Father wasn't there," Janey continues. "I wonder if they held him back or he just didn't want to go. He never liked shamings. He might not even have known it was me."

"He knows now," says Mary. "I'm sure everyone is talking about it. They're not supposed to shame children. I think you were the first."

"I'm not a child. Not really."

"You're not an adult either. Father is supposed to manage you."

"Well, maybe they thought he was doing a bad job of it."

Mary snorts. "I'm sure they've thought that for years."

"I wonder what they'll do to Rosie," says Janey. "She's probably being beaten right now."

"And she'll get up, no matter what they do to her, and come right back here, angry as ever," predicts Mary. Janey imagines Rosie barreling across the island, brows lowered, trailing blood and pieces of bone, and shivers.

"Was it terrible?" whispers Brianna Joseph, sitting nearby. "Them taking down your dress? In front of everyone?"

"It's hard to explain," says Janey. "I felt embarrassed, but not for me. For them, the wanderers. For the people watching."

After Janey was taken, the girls remained on the beach, ignoring the sunrise. At first they clustered together for support in her absence, but they have remained there ever since her return. They squat and sit on the sand in varying distances from Janey, watching Mary tend to her. Some look anxious, some furtive, some furious, some tired.

"What do we do now?" asks Mary, voicing the question in everyone's head. "Carry on like we did before? If this continues, Janey, they'll kill you. They already found us once."

"We could stay separate all the time," says Brenda. "Never gather, just hide."

"Please, no," says Brianna. "If we can't all be together, I can't do it. I'd have to go home."

"We won't separate," says Janey. "Being together is the only thing we have. And we have to keep going as we were before, after what Rosie did. She shouted the truth to everyone—she did what Amanda wanted to do—we can't just go back now." Janey pauses and sighs, her face growing longer. She hadn't meant to mention Amanda.

"But nobody will believe Rosie," says Fiona. An incandescent sheath of fading bruises sweeps across her face and throat. "It doesn't matter that she said it—they won't believe her."

Janey is silent for a long time, as the truth of this washes over her. The girls shift uneasily. Their feet, chill and bloodless, look as if they are made from wax.

"Maybe she planted a seed," Mary finally says. "Maybe someday—"

"If we go back," says Janey gravely, "it means we agree, that it's not the truth, that it doesn't matter. We keep going. It's daytime: we should be hiding, we should be sleeping. Tonight we'll meet at the beach—" She thinks. "Meet at the stretch behind the fields next to the spinner Saul's house. Maybe they'll find us again, I don't know. Right now, you should sleep."

"I can't sleep," says Violet.

"Well, you can't stay here," snaps Janey, and slowly, painfully, rises to her feet. The slices of seaweed draped around her writhe in the wind like snakes, and suddenly she resembles some sort of arcane goddess, a silvery, flame-crowned deity wreathed in serpents and blood. Power crackles from her like electricity as she stalks forward, parting the girls, and they scurry to do her bidding.

CHAPTER THIRTY‹NINE

Vanessa

Vanessa was never particularly fond of Rosie, annoyed by her constant brashness and resentment. Yet she can't help but admire her courage in trying to stop Mr. Balthazar's whip. Vanessa is sure she must have suffered a harsh beating after her removal from Janey's shaming. She wonders if Rosie has already returned to the beach, or if, like Letty, she is having a long and painful recovery at home.

She cannot stop picturing her last glimpse of Rosie, being carried limp and sobbing by Mr. Joseph like a dripping side of meat, her limbs swaying, her filthy hair covering her face. Over and over again, Vanessa sees Mr. Joseph's rapid, purposeful strides, Rosie bumping against the side of his knee, disappearing into the fields.

After a couple of days, Vanessa stops by Rosie's house after school. It's a small, tightly built structure, and yet it shines like a palace next to the Jacobs' ramshackle house slouching almost drunkenly next door. Vanessa knocks, waits a minute, and then knocks again.

Mrs. Gideon slowly opens the door, her pretty round face splotched with weeping, her eyes scarlet. Vanessa draws back a little and then whispers, "I've come to see Rosie..."

Mrs. Gideon begins sobbing in loud, hiccupping heaves. Tears wash down her face, laminating her cheekbones. She continues to cry, like a bleating sheep, while Vanessa stands there with her mouth slightly open and her hands half outstretched. Suddenly there are loud, angry footsteps, and she catches a glimpse of a furious Mr.

Gideon, his dark, scowling face resembling Rosie's, before he slams the door shut.

Vanessa stands shocked for a few moments and then makes her way home, so lost in thought that she has to redirect herself a few times after absentmindedly walking into random fields.

The next morning, instead of walking to school, Vanessa takes the path back to the Aarons'. Settling in the grass near the Gideons' house, she watches for activity. For what feels like hours, nothing happens. Vanessa yawns, thinks vaguely of food, pokes at an anthill with some dry grass, daydreams. In the early afternoon, her patience is rewarded as Mr. Gideon leaves the house with a bag of tools. The hammer clenched in his hand makes her doubly glad she didn't attempt the door again.

She waits a little longer, in case he forgot something and decided to return home, and then creeps to the Gideons' door and knocks. There is no answer, despite her continued knocking. Finally, taking a deep breath, she simply opens the door and walks inside.

Mrs. Gideon is sitting at the kitchen table, her frizzy light hair haloed in sunlight, and she slowly raises her head and stares at Vanessa as if she were an apparition. "You again," she says.

"Hello," says Vanessa awkwardly, crossing her arms in front of her and shifting her weight to one hip.

"You wanted Rosie," says Mrs. Gideon.

"I just wanted—"

"Rosie is dead," hisses Mrs. Gideon. "She's dead and you can't see her."

They stare at each other, Mrs. Gideon's light blue, flooded eyes meeting Vanessa's shocked stare.

"Brian says they were beating her," says Mrs. Gideon. "They were beating her and she fell and hit her head. He says it was an accident."

"An accident."

"But I don't believe him," whispers Mrs. Gideon, her face suddenly contracted and ugly with hate. Her eyes narrow and radiate fury.

"No," says Vanessa. "No."

"They never showed me her body," she cries bitterly. "They never let me see her. I wanted to dig her up and say good-bye but he won't tell me where she is. He won't tell me—" She breaks down in sobs, her tears falling gracelessly, splattering onto the kitchen table. Vanessa rises to comfort her, and realizes that her embrace would mean nothing, worse than nothing. She stands for a moment, respectfully witnessing Mrs. Gideon's savage grief, and then walks quietly out of the house.

Vanessa knows who to tell at school. She whispers the news to Letty, whose face is now amber with old blood. She tells little Edith Aaron. She tells Dorothy Abraham, a year older than her, slow and unpopular and constantly trying to win affection with secrets. She tells Mildred Balthazar. She tells Frances Joseph. She watches the sadness and anger and confusion bloom on their faces.

Vanessa's promise to stay home latches to her feet, weighs them down like shackles, like animals with their teeth cleaved to her ankles. She finds she cannot break it. And yet she is not completely powerless after all.

CHAPTER FORTY

Janey

They leave their homes, creeping out in the milky light of an early morning, slipping away during recess, simply walking out of class during the day. These are not older girls, like the first wave of Janey's followers, but those Rosie's age—eight, nine, ten years old: her friends, her allies, her peers and her enemies. They leave in twos and threes, clutching hands tightly until their knuckles are white. They blindly walk through the brush, kick through fields, peering behind rocks and under hedges, until they find a girl who has already left, who can tell them what to do and where to meet at night. They carry knowledge of Rosie's death to the girls on the beach, spreading the dark news, eliciting stunned stares and tears of grief and confusion. Caitlin, who had begun to emerge from her shyness to talk and laugh with the other girls, endlessly wanders the beach, pale and silent in her sorrow.

Unexpectedly more practical than their older counterparts, these new girls also bring blankets from their beds, flint and steel swiped from their kitchens, pots of fermented dough and wheels of cheese from their family stores. These supplies are heaped in hiding places, or dragged from the night beach to their daytime sleeping locations, becoming filthy and damp but still useful. Shoes and sweaters are shared with the other girls, often with giggling pairs shimmied tightly into the same sweater, high-stepping clumsily with one shoe each.

Parents come out during the day, the injunction to ignore their daughters disregarded. They search, eager to drag them back and

241

punish them, frequently hauling any child they find back to her home and depositing her there to be beaten, hugged, or lectured. The wanderers are busy, going to and fro from the wastelands, marshaling adults and holding their secret meetings, but they too search the fields, wrestling children home and demanding they receive a harsher beating than most parents would give otherwise. Sometimes the children, secretly relieved to be back with their devoted mother and doting father, in a warm bed at night, eating hot food until their stomachs bulge, will stay. More often they wait, recover, and flee again to their intoxicating, firelit existence.

"It's nice, having the young ones, isn't it?" says Mary to Janey one night, and Janey sighs like an overworked mother. The supplies these girls bring are vital, and will hopefully keep them from freezing at night. And yet they are troublesome, crying on Janey's shoulder for their mothers, squabbling and expecting her to adjudicate, forgetting the rules and frolicking on the beach during the day like wild animals. They cry and wail over scraped knees and hungry evenings. They eat the wrong berries and squat all night with diarrhea. They fret about the darkness below and look to her to argue them back into complacency. Janey wanted to lead the girls to freedom, not to end up being the counselor, comforter, and pastor of a gaggle of children. She tries to share the burden with the older girls, but they are still years younger than Janey and lost in their own play.

It is not only the young ones who left home after hearing of Rosie's murder at the hands of the wanderers. There are older girls who were shyer, more frightened, but were spurred into action. They are still learning how to sleep during the day and live on clams, bloodberries, fish bones, and scraps of cheese. While they are able to rely on one another and themselves more than the little ones, they are little help apart from the supplies they carry with them.

It is getting colder and colder. The sea has changed from a welcoming blue to a stippled, threatening gray. The grass frosts later into the morning, the sky fades icy and white. Trees turn yellow and brown, with leaves falling like a papery rain when the wind blows. Slowly, despite prior restrictions, the girls build their night fires larger and higher and hotter, returning to them to steep in the flaming warmth when their fingers or toes become numb. They sleep in bigger groups, layering themselves under damp blankets stuffed with chicken down, huddling together like skinny featherless hens. They discover previously unknown reserves of strengths even while battling chilblains, constantly running noses, and the threat of frostbite. And yet the chronic pain of their cold bones and whitened skin wears on them. Janey hears sobs at night, frantic whispers while girls chafe each other's fingers and toes or plaster themselves body to body for warmth.

"Do you think we can make it through the winter?" Mary asks Janey. "It's still autumn and it's so cold."

"I don't know," says Janey. "But what's our other option? Going back for the winter, coming out again in spring?"

"We'd definitely be let out in summer."

"Would we?"

Mary looks appalled at the implication and says no more. A light drizzle begins falling from the sky, scattering sparking jewels on her skin and hair. She snuggles into Janey's ribs. "If you can survive the cold, surely we can," she says. "You've got no fat on you at all."

"I burn hotter," says Janey with a laugh, neglecting to mention that she is cold, deathly cold, cold beyond shivering, all the time. The night fires are utter bliss to her, and during the day her bones ache and creak with icy chill, her flesh hardens and complains bitterly, her mouth feels coated with ice, and it is only when she puts cold fingers on her tongue to warm them that she realizes it is warmer than the rest of her. Sometimes, when a little girl comes to her for succor, Janey wants to keep that girl on her lap for hours, sucking in her young heat like some enormous winter spider with fresh, hot prey quivering in her web.

CHAPTER FORTY-ONE

Vanessa

Vanessa is woken in the middle of the night by a strange sound, like a high wailing. Rising quietly in her off-white nightgown, she glides downstairs carefully, in case a monster is lying in wait. The sound is now a howling cry emanating from the library, and she recognizes the voice: Father.

Opening the heavy door, she sees him sitting on the floor, curled into himself, sobbing savagely like an angry child. Something is wrong, perhaps she is dreaming; men do not cry like this. Children cry like this, over anything from a broken cookie to a sister dying, and women cry like this when they deliver defectives or are beaten, but men simply shed a tear or two and are done with it, even if they are burying their own son. Something has gone wrong within Father, and part of her is so bewildered that she wants to creep back upstairs and pretend she never heard him. Steeling herself, she whispers, "Father?"

He opens his arms, and she goes to them, only to find herself constricted in an embrace that crushes her ribs together so tightly she cannot breathe. Heaving, Father buries his face in her bare neck, tears and spit streaming out of him and dampening the shoulder of her nightgown, wet strands of beard sticking to her flesh. She pats him automatically, knowing this is what she should do, but something inside her quails. Of all the acts she and Father have ever performed together, this feels the most intimate, the most raw. It makes her want to shrink inside herself, so she can't feel her own skin.

Struggling to breathe, she waits for the intensity of his sobs to lessen, for him to raise his face and wipe it on his arm and apologize, but he simply continues to cry, his body convulsing and twisting with grief. "Father," she says eventually. "Father, let me get Mother."

"No," he gasps, loosening his hold so she can take a few deep breaths. "No. Please."

"What is it?" Vanessa asks, still tangled in a tearstained, muscular embrace and aching to disengage herself. "What happened?"

"Vanessa," he whispers, "my father was a wanderer, and his father as well."

This is beyond obvious, but she says nothing.

"The things I have seen in the wastelands, the things I have seen . . . what I have protected us from. I have shepherded the island, I have carried on the teachings of the ancestors."

"Yes," she says after a pause.

"It is my life's work, it is holy work, but—" Here he breaks down sobbing again, his forehead on her collarbone. "Vanessa, I'm not the only one who didn't know, and . . . I don't know how . . ."

Suddenly Vanessa understands. "You found out," she says. "You found out they killed Amanda and Rosie. You didn't believe it at first. You thought the girls were lying, and then the rest of them, the wanderers, told you the truth. They waited this long . . ."

He pulls back and stares at her. "When did you find out?"

"I've known for a long time."

In an instant he is standing, rearing back, a creature of rage, but somehow she feels no fear. "You knew," he says. "You knew and you didn't tell me."

"I did tell you."

"But not so I'd believe you, you didn't *convince* me!"

They stare at each other, Father with tears streaming down his face, Vanessa calm and pale. Suddenly he collapses, sits on his haunches with his face in his hands, no longer weeping, but frozen like a trapped animal. Vanessa knows she should go to him. She has never seen him so defeated. She will have to soothe and comfort him for nights to come, but for now she turns on her heel and leaves the library, quietly mounts the stairs, climbs into bed, and falls into a dreamless sleep.

WINTER

CHAPTER FORTY-TWO

Vanessa

It starts in church.

The next Sunday. Vanessa is sitting between Mother and Father, half listening to the pastor talk about disobedience and the darkness below, when Mrs. Gideon, the farmer Gideon's second wife, starts coughing. People are always coughing as the weather cools, but she coughs for so long that people start frowning in her direction. Vanessa turns around just in time to see her spray the face of Mrs. Saul the fisherman's wife with flecks of blood.

Everyone freezes, except for the pastor, who drones on. Mrs. Saul blanches, suddenly resembling Janey, with too-white skin and a smattering of dark freckles. Mr. Gideon puts his arm around Mrs. Gideon, who is dabbing at her bloody mouth in shock, and they stand up and stumble toward the stairs. Alma Gideon, the first wife, sits stock-still for a moment before following. Then everyone stares at Mrs. Saul, who wipes at her face with the edge of her coat, her eyes wide and horrified. Someone else has started coughing far in the back rows of the church, and all heads swivel in unison to see. Eventually that coughing quiets and the crowd's attention drifts back to the pastor, who looks annoyed at the disruption.

Later that evening, Mother tells Vanessa that Mrs. Gideon is dead. Vanessa is shocked; plenty of people die of sickness, but sickness usually takes a while to claim its victims. That night, Vanessa lies awake in the dark and thinks of Mrs. Gideon, who was nondescript and boring, but is now interesting because she is dead.

251

The next day Hannah Adam's baby dies. Mrs. Adam goes to feed her and finds the infant sprawled in a rictus in her cradle, her face azure and her tongue swollen. Vanessa's house is too far from theirs to hear the screams, but Father tells them of the scene later. When Vanessa leaves for school, he warns her to keep her coat on, like coats can protect you from dying bloody. Or blue.

Five more girls are missing from class: Edith, Leah, Mildred, Deborah, and Julia. In an already decimated class of only twelve girls, the absence looms hugely. Have they all gone to join Janey? The children look at Mr. Abraham out of the corners of their eyes, trying to read his expression, but he merely looks bored and launches into the day's lessons.

After school, Linda tells Vanessa that Mildred hurt her arm. Leah's brother tells her that Leah is sick, but not that kind of sick. But then two days later, Mr. Abraham wipes his eyes and tells them that Leah is dead. Mildred is still absent, and Linda looks quiet and pale.

The pastor likes to talk about the scourge, and Vanessa can't help but wonder if it has come to punish the island for the girls' disobedience. True, nothing is on fire, but surely this is the disease that scoured the wastelands. She asks Mother, who shakes her head but stays quiet.

By the end of the week there is no school anymore. Mother tells Vanessa that she will stay at home and help her until the sickness has passed. She talks about it like a fun party, but her voice is strained and there are violet circles around her eyes. She cycles between offering an uncomfortable surfeit of affection and ordering Vanessa to mend seams and scrub floors. After a day of this, Vanessa bitterly thinks that she would gladly be in bed coughing up blood, given the alternative. The next day Mother seems to regret holding her captive, and she lets her outside to run around the house. Vanessa sees a few men checking on gardens or crops, and a few women hanging out laundry to dry. She waves at Jean Balthazar through her window, and Mrs. Balthazar waves back.

Vanessa visits the chickens and watches them squabble, laughing as they peck one another on their tufted rumps, and then goes to throw rocks into the water at the beach, enjoying the serenely expanding circles on the calm surface. She is pretty sure this doesn't count as running around the house, but after all, it's not like she's gone to join Janey.

She ends up thankful for her brief disobedience. When she returns home Mother, uncharacteristically frantic, smacks her across the face, and then tells her that two more people are dead and she can't go outside anymore.

CHAPTER FORTY&THREE

Janey

The girls have become accustomed to dodging roving parents and wanderers. The majority of them have been chased across fields, plunging into seas of muck or thick hedges to hide. Some have even clambered up trees to cling to high branches and wait out baying adults. And then, almost overnight, the hunt stops. Suddenly they are able to sleep through the day instead of jolting alert to crackling footsteps, and the quick, panicked scatter of night vigils becomes a thing of the past. The bolder girls walk freely through cornfields and orchards, taking large steps and swinging their arms in wide brash arcs, almost daring someone to come and snatch them. Nobody does.

Most of the girls simply assume that the adults have given up. Laughing, they recount their most hair-raising tales of pursuit and beatings like veterans of a consummated war. Gathering in larger and larger groups, they sing songs loudly and hop about in frenetic games, celebrating their victory over the adults, the wanderers, the entire island.

But the older girls remain uneasy, aware that this cease-fire could mean something other than triumph. "They're plotting something new," Mary tells Janey. "Do you think... do you think they would kill all of us?"

Janey shakes her head. "That would be too much. That would turn people against them, if they killed a bunch of children."

"They've already killed a child, and that didn't seem to change anything."

Janey shrugged. "They probably lied about how she died, and people didn't know any better. But dozens of children, they can't hide that."

Rosie's death is lodged deep within Janey like a sharp black thorn. She is always aware of it; it cuts her flesh when she moves. Her impotent grief and guilt branch throughout her at unexpected moments, almost doubling her over. Whenever she sees the stunned, miserable Caitlin, Janey imagines how she could have prevented Rosie's death. She could have screamed the right words. She could have overpowered the wanderers and sprinted away with her. Rosie, her unwanted protector. Rosie, the hopeful truth teller, presuming that adults would believe the tales of children and turn immediately against their guardians and idols. Rosie the angry, the rebellious, churning with fury she could never fully release. Rosie, cold and dead, bones broken, suspended in mud under someone's winter field.

"Well, if they're not going to kill us, then what are they planning?" asks Mary.

Janey shakes her head. "I don't know. If I were the wanderers, I would arrange for every adult to come out at the same time, take all the girls they could, watch them constantly so they couldn't go back, and wait for the rest of the girls to give up and come home."

"What do we do then, if they do that?"

Janey shrugs. "Who knows? We might be at home, with someone watching us."

"They'd probably plant a wanderer outside your door. You're the most dangerous."

"Very dangerous," says Janey, smirking.

"I'm serious."

Janey looks at her bony, dirty lap and snorts. "I'm hardly in shape to fight someone."

"It's your mind."

"My mind." Janey massages her temples, as if to soothe it. "My mind is tired."

After a few days, some of the intoxicating rebellion of strolling around during daytime fades a bit, and the sharper girls notice something odd: there are no adults outside. It might as well be summer. There are no women dipping buckets of water from the rain barrels, feeding chuckling white hens, or walking over to visit a neighbor. There are no men at work—no farmers pulling winter weeds, no fishermen fringing the beach with their wooden poles, no builders repairing roofs or windows. Even the children who did not come to the beach, who are much derided and pitied, are not walking to and from school, or chasing one another around in their thick sweaters, or toddling after their mothers and falling on their rumps. There is simply nobody in sight.

"What if everyone's dead?" asks Fiona. "What if the ancestors killed everybody except us?"

"That would mean they decided we should be the only ones here," says Sarah, looking intrigued.

"But that goes against everything, *Our Book,* the wanderers, everything," points out Violet.

"Not to mention that if we were the only ones left, we couldn't have children, so after us there would be nobody," says Mary.

"The island would be cleansed," whispers Fiona, who tends toward the dramatic.

"We need to figure out what is happening," says Janey. Inwardly, she worries the wanderers are planning their mass murder, but she keeps her tone mild as she continues, "We need to go look into houses, see what's going on."

"But then they'll take us!" wails eight-year-old Eliza Solomon, who has inched forward to hear the conversation.

"We have to know," says Mary, looking troubled. "We have to know what's happening."

And so Janey gathers Mary, Fiona, Sarah, and Violet, and leads a small expedition. There is nowhere in particular to go, so they simply walk through fields and grasses, trying to decide which door to knock on, where to find someone willing to give information without looping them into a beating and detention. As they skirt a hedge between the Balthazar cornfields and the Joseph potato plot, they hear a moan. Alert as a hound, Janey swivels her gaze around, and it alights on what looks like a dead body.

Quietly, slowly, they move toward the corpse, flinching when it suddenly flings out an arm. Stepping closer, they see it is Lydia Aaron, the young wife of Mr. Aaron the dyer, lying slumped on the ground.

"Mrs. Aaron?" says Mary anxiously. "Mrs. Aaron?" The woman's hands shake frenetically. Kneeling, Mary lifts the sweaty head to her lap. "Mrs. Aaron?"

Mrs. Aaron's eyes roll back in her head, the orbs shining like tide-soaked stones, and a thread of blood slowly zigzags down her lower lip. She coughs, a deep hack like there is mud in her lungs, and flecks of blood hang in the air like tiny red stars before collapsing to the ground.

"By the ancestors," whispers Violet. "She's sick."

"She must be very sick," murmurs Janey. "I've never seen someone cough blood like that before."

"Mrs. Aaron?" says Sarah hopefully. Mrs. Aaron groans.

"She needs help," says Mary. "Janey, get her some help!" Nodding and rising, Janey motions to the other girls, and they run toward the nearest house, the farmer Josephs.

Janey pounds on the door, but there is no reply. Frowning, she pounds again. "Hello!" she calls, but nobody comes.

They move to the next house, the weaver Gideons, and she knocks, then pounds, then calls, but the house stands silent, its windows blank and lifeless as dead eyes.

Finally, at the fisherman Moseses' house, they hear someone coming toward the door. "Who is it?" calls a woman.

"It's, well, it's Janey Solomon."

The door creaks open, and Mrs. Moses stares at them. She looks haggard and underfed, her hair greasy and her eyes underlined with stippled gray skin. "What are you doing here?" she says in disbelief.

"It's Mrs. Aaron. Lydia Aaron," says Janey. "She's outdoors, she's sick, she's coughing up blood. She needs help."

Mrs. Moses gazes at her, blinking. "So why did you come to me?"

"We tried other houses and nobody answered. We came to you because she needs help!"

"My husband is upstairs. He's sick too. He's coughing up blood. He's so feverish I can barely stand to touch him or he'll burn me. I've been tending to him for . . ." She slumps. "I don't know how long."

"Everyone's sick," says Janey slowly. "That's why they disappeared."

"Well, not everyone, obviously," snaps Mrs. Moses. "I don't have it. Yet. But yes, everyone's sick. And it's a bad sickness. People are dying. We're not supposed to go outside, or talk to anyone. I shouldn't be speaking to you."

"But Mrs. Aaron still needs help," ventures Fiona. "She can't just lie there."

"Why is that my problem?" exclaims Mrs. Moses, her voice rising. "I'm not her family. I have my husband to take care of."

"Well, can't you at least help us get her home?" pleads Janey desperately.

"There's four of you!" yells Mrs. Moses. "What do you need me for? I'm not going outside, I'm not getting sick for her. You take her home, they'll take care of her, if there's anybody left. You're a disgrace, all of you, running off like that. If I had children like you, I'd thrash you until you couldn't walk. You can just leave me alone." And the door slams shut.

The girls stand before the door, stunned by Mrs. Moses's tirade. Then Violet says, "Do you think we can carry her home?"

"I—I suppose we can try," says Janey. They walk back, quiet. Janey thinks of Pastor Saul at her shaming. *We here on the island are all interconnected, and none could survive without the other.* Is Mrs. Moses a particularly bad specimen, or are all adults like this when there is danger in the air? Janey would help a sick girl on the beach, even if she didn't know her, even if she didn't like her.

"When this is over," says Fiona suddenly, fervently, "we should tell the wanderers about Mrs. Moses."

Sarah giggles suddenly. "Yes. Let's go tell the wanderers all about it!"

The rest of them start laughing as Fiona turns red. "I mean—I mean, you know what I mean!" she says, starting to snicker herself.

When the girls return to the field, Mary still has Mrs. Aaron's head on her lap, where it rolls feverishly. Suddenly Janey remembers Mrs. Moses's words about contagion, and the fear that flashes from her groin at the thought of Mary getting sick is so white-hot and agonizing that she frantically puts it out of her mind. "We have to take her home," Janey tells Mary.

"What? There was nobody who would help?"

"There was Mrs. Moses, but she didn't feel like helping," says Violet darkly, and Mary shakes her head in disbelief.

They hoist Mrs. Aaron up, stick their shoulders under her armpits, and wrap arms around her waist. With heavy, stuttering steps, they begin the walk to her house. Suddenly Violet gasps and drops her arms, which had been holding Mrs. Aaron's hips.

"What is it?" asks Mary.

"There's something inside her." Violet's face is white and terrified. "Something is moving!"

"She's pregnant," says Sarah in the flat, brass tones of annoyance, and Violet flushes and puts her arms around Mrs. Aaron again. Mrs. Aaron moans and coughs, but her legs move, and she seems to be trying to help as much as she can.

"If her husband won't take her in," mutters Janey as she knocks on the door, "I swear I'm taking her to a wanderer's house and they can deal with it."

When they arrive at the Aarons' house, the door flies open after a single knock. Mr. Aaron cries, "Oh, thank the ancestors." His skin is the color of slate and running with sweat, and his body shakes and shudders like a speared rabbit. "I wanted to look for her, but

I couldn't..." A blood vessel has broken in one of his eyes, and it screams scarlet from his face. "Lydia..."

"Can you...can you take her?" asks Mary.

"Yes, I mean, I think I can, I need to get her in bed." He looks behind him despairingly at the staircase and then says, "Or at least inside. Yes, at least inside." He reaches out and lifts Mrs. Aaron from them.

"Thank you, girls. Thank you. I don't care what they say, you're good girls." He makes a vague gesture toward them, which Janey guesses to be one of gratitude, and he closes the door, weeping.

Mary bursts into tears.

"Come on," says Janey, embracing her. "Come. Let's go back to the beach."

Hiccupping, Mary nods through a sheen of tears and snot, and they all walk slowly back toward the sea.

Later that night, Janey gathers the older girls, the ones she trusts, and they sit in a ragged circle by the shore. She tells them of what happened with Mrs. Aaron, and Mrs. Moses, and Mr. Aaron. "There's an illness," she concludes. "A bad one."

"It's the ancestors," breathes Catherine Moses. "They're punishing us for running away."

"Oh, shut up," snaps Mary with uncharacteristic irritability.

"They'd make us sick instead," explains Caitlin dully.

"Unless they wanted us to watch everyone else die first," replies Catherine, stung.

"Shut up," says Mary again. Leaning into Janey's cold, thin neck, she whispers, "Do you think Mother's all right?"

Janey takes in a deep breath, her ribs pushing into Mary's side, and then lets it out very slowly, like she is breathing the life out of herself. "We have to go see," she mutters softly.

"We have to go see," echoes Fiona. "We can't leave them alone."

As if she had heard Mary's whispers, Violet pipes up, her voice breaking. "What if my mother is lying in a field somewhere? And nobody will help her?"

"We can't go back," murmurs Sarah. "Then it's all been for nothing."

"They killed Rosie," chimes in Vera Saul.

"Rosie is dead," says Mary. "The wanderers killed her. But my mother didn't kill her. And your little sister didn't kill her either. And we need to make sure they stay alive. That there's someone there, if there's no one else there... We can't leave them alone."

"When I had the pox," says Violet slowly, lost in memory, "I couldn't see. Light hurt me. I couldn't think. I couldn't breathe. Mother stayed with me for weeks. She didn't even cook for Father or clean or do anything. She kept hauling up cold water and putting it on me. I was seeing things. Father said he thought every day I would die."

"Someone needs to tell the other girls," says Brenda.

"They don't have to go. Nobody has to go anywhere," says Janey.

"But you're going?" says Mary, staring into Janey's face intently.

"But I'm going," Janey agrees, her gray eyes dark and full of sorrow.

"But..." The word hangs on Caitlin's lips, heavy and painful like an open wound. She doesn't have to say the rest. Without Janey and Mary, the girls' rebellion will shatter, fall to the ground in meaningless pieces.

"I know," says Janey. "I'm sorry." Mary bursts into tears again, burying her head in Janey's lap while Janey strokes her dark, oily hair.

"We can always come back," says Fiona, and her sentence hangs in the air, heavy with untruth. "We could!" she cries as if someone has argued with her.

Caitlin, her mouth still slightly open, her face hanging downward, shakes her head slowly. Fiona starts to cry.

The girls look toward the younger ones, hopping and laughing and playing near the sea, and suddenly Janey feels like she's murdered something that was fresh and budding and alive. *I'm sorry, Amanda,* she thinks. *I'm sorry, Rosie.* And her bones feel so heavy when she rises that she waits to collapse like a corpse onto the sand.

CHAPTER FORTY-FOUR

Caitlin

Caitlin tiptoes in past midnight to find Father snoring with his head on the kitchen table. Moving slowly, like a rodent skirting a dozing dog, she climbs the stairs and slips between the blankets next to Mother. Mother wakes with a gasp, throwing her arms out to shield herself, and then whispers, "Caitlin? *Caitlin?*"

"It's me."

Mother lets out a soft cry of joy. She gathers Caitlin into her soft, warm arms and Caitlin breathes in Mother's scent gratefully. "You're alive," Mother whispers. "So many are sick. I thought you might be dead out there."

"Father will kill me."

"He's been so drunk he probably thinks you left yesterday."

"Mother, I . . ." Caitlin tries to think about how to tell her of her journey, of the beach, of Janey. "There was a dog," she says, "and he ran into and out of the sea." And then the sudden, sure realization that she is never going back to live on the beach with Janey strikes her, heavy as a load of stones, and she begins shaking and keening like a child lost in a nightmare. Mother cannot soothe her, although she holds Caitlin in her bruised arms until dawn.

CHAPTER FORTY·FIVE

Caitlin

Coming home from the beach is like coming home from ten years of summers. She doesn't mind the clothing, and welcomes being washed in hot water. But at night she wakes with a start and panics, trying vainly to remember the capture and punishment that led to her reinstallment in everyday life. It is only when she is fully awake that she remembers she came back of her own volition. It is a bitter draft to swallow. When Father comes into her room she closes her eyes and removes herself back to the beach. She walks barefoot in damp sand, sits close to Janey Solomon, sucks hot clam flesh from a jagged shell, squints into an early morning sunrise that promises rest. Sometimes it takes her so long to come back to herself that cold midmorning light is shining steadily in her window.

Mother's obvious joy at having Caitlin back, however, warms her like a summer sun. Mother's face, usually shadowed and afraid, glows with delight whenever she catches Caitlin's eye, and she keeps Caitlin close by her side. They lean into each other, hug, touch each other briefly as they pass. Even during Father's tempers, Mother keeps her head a little higher than usual, and her hands shake a little less. Luckily, Father treats the command not to leave the house as a suggestion and often stalks outside, leaving Caitlin and Mother to take their first deep breath of the day and smile at each other.

The women of the island have set up a way for information to be passed along. Mother has a line of communication with the nearest neighbors. On one side is Mrs. Gideon, Rosie's mother, or at least she used to be; Caitlin keeps remembering with a sick, painful jolt that Rosie is dead and Mrs. Gideon has no children now. On the other side is Mrs. Adam the dung collector's wife. Mother goes outside the house to face Mrs. Gideon, keeping as much distance as possible between them, and Mrs. Gideon shouts the news to Mother. Then Mother walks to the other side of the house, howls for Mrs. Adam, and yells the news to her. Caitlin hears everything twice, and loudly.

Everyone says that disease is spread through the breath of a sick person, and while Caitlin isn't sure how far away one need be to avoid sucking in the kiss of illness, she is sure that Mother's yawning distances from their neighbors are safe. She wonders exactly who the ancestors are trying to punish and if their final aim is to wipe out all of them.

The pastor has always said that disease is punishment for everyone, although he usually assigns extra blame to the women, who go home and rock and weep for afflicting their children. Punishments come regularly with the seasons: colds and gripes in the winter, flux and fevers as it gets warmer. Every child must wade through the poxes, the lumps, the rashes, and the other hardships of the young. Usually they make it through more or less intact, though some are sucked under and delivered to the ancestors early. There are drafts to calm fevers, pastes to soothe itching, tinctures to paint on erupted pox to help the pain, but these remedies work fitfully and inconsistently, mostly leaving the sick to bite their pillows, scratch their lesions, and pray for relief.

But Caitlin can't remember a sickness like this, and Mother can't either. So many people are sick that the names all blur into each other, except the girls Caitlin knows, like Letty and Heather Aaron. It's hard to tell whether or not everyone is dying; some shouted news tolls the end of everyone, and other times optimistically reports recoveries. One theme never changes: the pregnant women and babies are all dying. Mrs. Gideon yells, "It's the cruelest sickness!" to Mother, and

Mother shrieks, "It's the cruelest sickness!" to Mrs. Adam. Caitlin also hears that if the fever breaks and the sick person becomes damp, they are going to live, but if they get so hot you can't touch them, they will die. A paste of oil and salt helps earlier in the day, to Mrs. Gideon's relief, but later in the day it's reported to be useless. A small amount of final draft, usually never touched until the end of life, is said to lead to a refreshing sleep, but might also kill you.

And then, Mrs. Gideon isn't there to tell Mother anything, and so the chain is broken. She isn't there the next day either, and Caitlin wonders if she's dead. Mother is too frightened to walk past the Gideon house to see. Caitlin finds life more peaceful without the regular screeching updates. She and Mother sit in the house, which is already clean from top to bottom. Even the sprays of mold have been scrubbed as faint as possible. Mother sings, and they eat bread and pray.

The next morning, Mother falls over while she's wiping up crumbs from breakfast. Father is sleeping on the floor by the front door, reeking of wine. When Caitlin runs over to help her, Mother mumbles, "There, there, dear," and her nose starts bleeding.

Mother is too big for her to carry. Caitlin pushes, pulls, and coaxes her into the bedroom, where Mother falls onto the bed and starts coughing. Mother never goes to bed dressed, so Caitlin pulls the dress over her head and leaves her naked and shaking. The warmest blanket is in Caitlin's room; she runs for it and throws it over Mother's trembling body, but Mother casts it off her. "It's cold," Caitlin tells her. "You're naked." Caitlin has curled up before to Mother's body in the night many times, but never seen her without clothes in the daylight. There are silvery stripes crawling up her belly, and her breasts are sagging and soft like barely cooked eggs. She's missing a patch of hair between her legs, the skin covered by a smooth pink scar. Mother has bruises too, in places people can't see. Caitlin tries to pull the blanket over her again.

"It's hot," says Mother. "I need water."

The cistern in the kitchen is empty, so Caitlin runs and scoops some from the rain barrel. Mother tries to drink it, but most of it spills down her chest. "Ah," she says, as if refreshed, and then falls asleep. Caitlin remembers hearing somewhere that you shouldn't let a sick person sleep, so she shakes and pokes her. Mother only frowns and continues sleeping, her eyeballs rolling back and forth under purple eyelids. Her nosebleed has stopped, the blood smeared on her upper lip like dried mud. Her body is covered in a thin sheen of sweat that seems to glow.

Caitlin considers going down to wake Father, but immediately abandons the idea. Waking Father when he's sleeping on the floor never ends well. She puts the blanket over Mother again and then brings over a cold cloth to lay on her forehead. Mother bats it away, and Caitlin starts to cry. Mother always knows what to do when Caitlin is sick, but now Caitlin can't remember any of it. Her head hurts.

Crawling into bed, Caitlin puts an arm over Mother's chest and falls asleep there. When she wakes a few hours later, her bones are twisting and cracking and it's become a snowy winter. She crawls down beneath the blanket by Mother's feet, curling herself into a ball. When she opens her eyes, the dust on Mother's soles dances and sparks. Caitlin flexes her fingers and then crunches them into fists, trying to relieve the pain. Needles of frost prick her skin. Gasping, she chokes on a sea of warm slime ascending her throat. She falls asleep coughing.

On waking, there is cold water trickling into her mouth. It's hard to swallow around all the coughing, but the water feels wonderful. She sees a wavering face above her and tilts her head from side to side to figure out who it is. The face swims into focus as Father. Caitlin chokes on the water and starts coughing harder. Using her elbows, she drags herself under the covers, coughing and spitting and coughing more. Her feet feel naked in the cold air, and she wonders if Father will cut them off. Her face is next to burning branches, and she gropes them curiously until realizing they are Mother's legs. As she wriggles upward to see her, the world gets blurry and she falls asleep again. She wakes up on top of the blankets, shaking and coughing again, an old song. Inhaling is a battle, like someone is holding a pillow over her face, and she wonders if Father is trying to kill her. Perhaps this is her punishment for running away. "Mother!" she screams, but it comes out as a hoarse growl. She can't get the breath to call out again. Grabbing her ribs with her hands, she pumps them to make herself breathe faster.

Then she is at the foot of the bed, and Mother is up and well, wearing a lovely blue dress. Mother holds out a spoon and says, "I made you some jam, since you were very good." Caitlin doesn't want jam, but she wants Mother. She leans in and water goes down her throat again. Gagging, Caitlin keeps swallowing, feeling her stomach turn delightfully icy. "That's good," says Mother, but her voice is rough and deep. Then she disappears, and Caitlin rolls over to find Mother in the bed next to her, asleep. Where is the blue dress? Another coughing fit comes, and everything goes black. Caitlin is asleep, but she can still feel herself coughing. Someone has put her in a hot bath, but it's still summer and she should be outside in the mud. "I don't want to wash my hair," she whispers, and then shudders so hard she's afraid her bones will snap. "Help!" She gags, smelling Father behind her. She tries to run, but trips over Mother and falls off the bed. "Help! Help!" she keeps saying, until Mother puts cool clothes on her and sings. "Away, past the shore," she croons, "I will meet my evermore." Caitlin doesn't know that song. Breathing becomes easier, and Caitlin lets her head fall on Mother's cool breast.

CHAPTER FORTY⚜SIX

Vanessa

When school is canceled, Vanessa takes the opportunity to hide in Father's library, carefully turning pages and drinking in the words of her favorite books. Her pleasure is soon overcome by sick guilt, however, that she's somehow profiting from death. Father hasn't mentioned their night meeting in the library and seems so nonchalant that Vanessa wonders if it was a particularly lucid dream. He goes to meet with the wanderers every morning, bringing back names of the dead. And in every heavy deposit of death, there are names of girls she once knew, played with, hated, ignored. So many names. Vanessa puts down the books and takes to her bed.

She discovers that grief is a liquid. It passes thickly down her throat as she drinks water and pools soggily around her food. It flows through her veins, dark and heavy, and fills the cavities of her bones until they weigh so much she can barely lift her head. It coats her skin like a slick of fat, moving and swirling over her eyes, turning their clear surfaces to dull gray. At night, it rises up from the floor silently until she feels it seep into the bedclothes, lick at her heels and elbows and throat, thrust upward like a rising tide that will drown her in sorrow.

As Vanessa enters her second week in bed, Father comes into the room and pulls her into a rough embrace. It is not a prequel or an invitation, but rather an attempt to wrest his daughter out of her despair. "Vanessa," he whispers, "you must let yourself live. You are alive.

I am alive, Mother and Ben are alive. You must focus on the living and not the dead. It was my fault, I put my sorrow on you and Mother and I should have kept it to myself. The girls, everyone who is lost, they are in the arms of the ancestors. Don't listen to what anybody says. They came back, like good children. They were all good children. Dying of sorrow when everyone around you is drowning in blood is understandable, but not forgivable. Do you understand me?"

She tries to understand. She tries to let the names pass through her mind like water; not thick or sticky but clear running water, like the rain that pelts the rooftop. If she stays in the house, someone being dead is the same as them being alive, she tells herself. She feels cold glass under her hands, looks out her window at branches and dead leaves. She sits at the kitchen table in her nightgown and watches Mother's face, the absentminded contentment as she cooks. She watches Ben while he sleeps, innocent and free, like a lamb resting after a day of gamboling. Eventually the names of the sick and the dead milling in her brain begin to blur into an opaque wash of gibberish. Nothing seems to make sense, but she'd rather be confused than dying. She lets grief drain from her eyes as she weeps, seep from her fingers and soles into the floorboards as she walks, rise from her stomach in a cleansing rush as she falls to her knees and heaves.

Vanessa idly wonders what the wanderers will bring back from their next wasteland voyage. Mother hopes it's something to help with the bodies. Corpses are usually buried swiftly, deep in the fields, but now there are too many bodies and not enough people to dig. Next door, Mrs. Aaron died, and all they could do was drag her body outside and cover it with a blanket. There have been rains the past few days, and occasionally Vanessa will inhale the fresh smell of rain and dirt laced with a scent so indescribably horrible that she has to rush to the kitchen and bury her face in something fragrant to wash it away. Mr. Aaron is recovering, Father says, and while Vanessa feels sorry that he has to bury his rotting wife, she is also impatient for him to hurry up and recover so he can take the body away.

Mother is anxious and fretful. She asks, "What did we do to deserve this?" as if Vanessa knows the answer. Vanessa wants to sit, bar her grief from her mind, and reread her favorite books, but Mother barely leaves her side. She makes Vanessa sit and talk to her while she sews, finally mending hems and darning holes that have marred the family clothing for months. Vanessa finds the closeness of their bodies, the constant questioning tone of Mother's voice, unnerving. Once Mother coughs into one hand, and Vanessa doesn't even think until she is flat against the far wall. Mother sighs and rolls her eyes, and Vanessa guiltily goes back to her seat, leaving a few extra inches between them.

For a long time, as long as she can remember, one of Vanessa's favorite daydreams has been that everyone on the island, except her, would die. Even Father, even Mother. Not die in piles of stinking bodies, but simply be swept away by some unknowable force, leaving the entire island to Vanessa. She would walk naked by the water, letting the sun warm her skin, not caring if her body started to change. She would go into other people's houses and take whatever she wanted, whatever gewgaws caught her fancy, or perhaps the collections of wasteland detritus in the other wanderers' houses. After she took them, maybe she would smash them. Maybe she would break all the windows in all the houses—except hers, so the wind wouldn't get in. All the dogs and cats would be hers, in one big furry pile begging for her attention, walking by her side like protectors, like guardians. She could read for days and nights, every book, not just the ones Father thought were good for her. She would sleep in a pile of licking dogs and purring cats, and wake up with the entire day and the entire stretch of island all to herself, morning after morning.

Late one night, Vanessa remembers this daydream and feels choked, nauseated by guilt. How could she have dreamed of losing Mother and Father? Is she a defective, not in body, but in mind? The ancestors can be severe in their punishments; what if the entire island dies to show her the consequences of her fantasies? Every minute she closes her eyes and begs the ancestors to stop. She tells them she didn't really mean the daydream in the first place. She begs them to save Mother and Father and Ben, at least. She steals a knife, cuts her hand, lets her bright blood drip onto the floor as tribute, like in church. *I repent.* She rubs the bloodstains with her toe until they are a rusty smear. *Please hear me.*

Days pass as she hides in Father's library whenever she can, not reading but just staring, her arms crossed around her rib cage. Eventually Vanessa decides that the ancestors wouldn't kill everyone to punish one girl's daydream. That would mean they are cruel and capricious, but Pastor Saul says they are kind and that all punishments are deserved. She almost manages to convince herself.

They have enough to eat, thanks to the wanderer tributes. Despite the commandment to stay home, people appear to be sneaking out of their houses at night to leave food on their doorstep: filthy carrots, ears of corn, a dead chicken. The island can't try to appease the ancestors with anything tangible, so they seem to be thrusting food at the wanderers in hopes they can somehow intervene. It used to be that families brought by a load of vegetables, a loaf of bread, or a cut of meat with a smile. Mother would chat with whoever came by, invite them in for some tea. Now the food waits, sparkling with dew in the morning, half ravaged by dogs and rats.

After a week spent mostly in silence, Father leaves at dawn for a trip to the wastelands. The next day, he returns in a long coat Vanessa hasn't seen before. He looks furtive and anxious, glancing over his shoulder every few seconds. After hugging Vanessa, he touches Mother's shoulder and says, "Vanessa, can you leave us alone for a moment?"

Hurt, she creeps up to her bedroom. Why should Mother know secrets she can't? When Father comes in, she rolls to turn her back to him.

"Vanessa," he says, perching on the edge of the bed. His tone is brisk, like he hasn't noticed she's angry. "I need you to pay attention."

"To what?" she mutters.

"Sit up. Look at me."

Vanessa slowly pulls herself into a sitting position. He's holding his hand like there's something precious in it. Peering into the palm, she sees a small white pebble.

"I need you to do something for me, but you can't tell anyone."

"What is it?"

"I mean, your mother, but you can't tell anyone outside the family. Ever."

Vanessa frowns. She has been so long confined to the house that she can't imagine seeing anyone besides her family ever again. "What is it?" she repeats.

"I need you to swallow one of these every day."

Vanessa looks into his face to see if he's joking, but doesn't see a smile. Examining the pebble further, she sees that it's not a pebble at all: it's too round and regular, with a faint line dividing it into two equal halves.

"What is that?"

"It's medicine."

Medicine is a syrup, or tea, and tastes murky and terrible. "It doesn't look like medicine."

"I can't explain."

"But I'm not sick." She makes herself cough once or twice, experimentally, but all feels as it should.

"It will keep you from getting sick. Mother and Ben will take them too, and me."

Vanessa stares at Father. "Thank the ancestors! You can give them to everyone now."

"No, I can't."

"Why not? Why is it secret? Why can't we give it to everyone?"

Father sighs heavily. "I can't discuss that with you."

"Why?"

"Because the decisions of the wanderers are not for little girls to judge," he says stiffly.

"But you could save everyone."

He shakes his head. "Not the dead. Not even the sick. I can't save everybody. I don't have enough of them."

"But how do you decide who gets them?" He's silent. "How many are there? How do you decide?"

"You and Mother and I and Ben, and that's all I can tell you."

"The other wanderers, their families are getting them?"

He doesn't answer.

"It's true, isn't it? They'll get them. But who else? Anybody?" His face is rigid. "Nobody?"

"I can't discuss that with you."

"Where did they come from?"

"The wastelands."

"Who made them? Somebody must have made them, was it the defectives? Or are they from before the scourge? What's in them?"

"I don't know, Vanessa. I need you to take it."

"Are they making things in the wastelands?"

"Enough. Please, just take it." Father's tone is firm and he sits tall, but he cannot seem to look at her.

"No." Vanessa crosses her arms over her newly soft, abhorrent chest.

"Vanessa."

"I want to know why there aren't enough for everyone, and who made them, and how you found them, and how you know what they're for."

"This is not a discussion. I am telling you what to do, and you will do it."

"You can't make me."

"Vanessa, I will not stand aside and watch you die."

His face hardening, Father grabs her face and digs his fingers into her jaw. Clenching her teeth, Vanessa plunges her face into the pillow. She feels a tearing pain in her neck as Father tries to turn her around, but she brings her arms up over her head to keep it hidden.

He grabs the span of her shoulders and forcibly twists her about, and she shoves her fingers into his face. They wrestle hotly, and finally he pins her wrists under one hand and forces his fingers into her mouth. Some deeply planted instinct keeps her from closing her teeth on him. The pebble slips in over his fingers, bitter and powdery, and when she tries to spit it out, he clamps a hand over her lips. Back arched, hands trapped, his palm pushing into her mouth, she feels a surge of nausea and a flicker to another time, long ago. Inhaling sharply, she starts coughing.

Immediately Father is off her, sitting her up and pounding her back. Vanessa chokes and gags and brings forth the remains of the pebble, ragged and slimy, into her cupped hand. Father slips his hand under hers and slowly but firmly guides it to her mouth, his eyes on hers. She swallows the bitterness convulsively and then curls up in a ball on her bed.

"Go away," she says. "I took it, so please just go away."

"If you won't take it tomorrow, we'll do this again."

"Go away."

She feels the weight of him on the bed for a while. His footsteps recede, then come back. Quietly, he lays a copy of *Just So Stories,* one of her favorites, on the bed and leaves again. Vanessa waits until she can't hear his steps anymore and then screams impotently into her pillow and kicks the book onto the floor.

CHAPTER FORTY-SEVEN

Caitlin

Caitlin wakes up in Mother's bed alone, with a faint memory of Mother feeding her a thin soup. The sheets are damp and smell of sweat and blood. Raising her hands, she feels the curves of her face, and then her neck, trying to ascertain if she's still alive. She is weak, her hands floating like feathers, but she's fairly sure she's not dreaming. Carefully, she swings both legs over the side of the bed and tries to stand. She has to wheel her arms to get her balance, but after a moment can stay upright.

The effort of standing drains her, so she crawls back under the sweaty sheets and falls into sleep. She wakes to Father's voice saying, "How are you feeling, Caitlin?"

Opening her eyes, she sees his face inches from hers. His beard is straggly, the whites of his eyes bloodshot and yellow. Blossoms of small, dark veins begin at each side of his nose and twine into his large-pored cheeks. Alarmed, she flips and rolls away from his heavy foul breath, sliding on the sheets and falling on the floor on the other side of the bed. Curling into a ball, she waits for kicks and slaps, but all she hears are footsteps. "Are you all right?" Father says, standing over her.

"No," she says carefully, peering at him from between her fingers. He stands above her, legs planted firmly.

"Well, get back into bed, then," he says. Moving slowly and watching him carefully for sudden movements, she crawls back into bed.

279

Closing her eyes, she waits for a touch, or a weight, but nothing happens. Opening them again, she sees he's still staring at her with tired blue eyes.

"Where's Mother?" asks Caitlin. She remembers snuggling into Mother's delicious coolness and falling asleep, but can't remember her getting up.

"She's out," says Father.

"Out where?" Mother never goes out.

"She's taking care of someone," Father says. "She'll be back soon."

Caitlin feels betrayed that Mother would leave her alone with Father. She's always in the house somewhere. But maybe he's been sick, or maybe everyone else is so sick he made Mother go.

"Are you hungry?" asks Father. Caitlin shakes her head. "Thirsty?" She realizes she is thirsty, and nods. Father leaves and comes back with a pitcher of water and a clay cup. Caitlin gulps the water, feeling its cold nourishment trickle down her throat and into her gut, drinking cup after cup until her belly feels tight as a drum. Her fingers are shaking with effort.

"Try to sleep," says Father. "You were very sick."

This quiet version of Father, who does not weave or yell or swear, seems like a stranger. "Yes, Father," Caitlin says obediently, and he nods, but keeps standing there. She closes her eyes and finds she can't sleep with his presence in the room. Behind the darkness of her eyelids, he blares like a spotlight onto her brain. She stays still, closing her eyes almost all the way yet watching him through needle-thin cracks in her eyelids. She sees him look down at the floor, sigh, wipe his face, and eventually shamble off. Pushing herself to the head of the bed, Caitlin piles the stinking sheets on top of herself and falls gratefully into cool, black sleep.

She wakes fitfully, and it's either dark or light out, and sometimes there is soup next to her and sometimes bread, and sometimes nothing. Mother is keeping the water pitcher full, but Caitlin never sees her. There's a pot so she doesn't have to use the outhouse, but Mother keeps forgetting to empty it, and eventually the room stinks of stale urine. Caitlin begins practicing standing and taking steps around the room, and starts feeling stronger. She hears Father's footsteps sometimes. Mother must be keeping him away.

Soon she is strong enough to leave the bedroom. The sour sick smell permeates the house, but Caitlin barely notices it anymore. She walks slowly down the hallway, and suddenly Father appears like a creature from a nightmare. Caitlin stumbles backwards a few steps.

"You're up," he says.

"Yes," she says, peering around him for Mother.

"That's good."

"Where's Mother? I want her."

Father looks down. "Caitlin, she..."

"Is she out again?"

"No."

"Good. Mother!" she calls, looking past him.

"Caitlin, she's not here."

"You said she wasn't out?"

"She's not."

"She has to be somewhere."

"She is."

Caitlin's breath is starting to choke her, high up in her throat, and she swallows and gulps a few times. "Where is she, then? Where's Mother?"

"She can't... she isn't..."

"Is she sick? Is she still sick? I can take care of her now."

"She's not sick."

"Where is she?"

"Caitlin, she died."

The words fall heavy onto her head, like blows, and she raises her arms to ward them off. "She can't die," says Caitlin. "You're a liar."

"She did. She got sick and died."

"You killed her. You murdered her! I knew someday you would hit her too hard and now she's dead!" She has never screamed at Father before, and it feels like punching through a sheet of glass, a shattering of a wall thought unbreakable; she bleeds relief from between her clenched fingers.

"I—" Father chokes. She sees something unfamiliar on his face. "I promise you..."

"Show me the body, then, if she's dead. Prove it." Caitlin knows she isn't making sense, but doesn't care. "You say she's dead? Show me the body. You have her locked up somewhere, don't you? Locked up to punish her for being sick."

He takes a deep breath and kneels down to be closer to her face. She leans backwards. "Caitlin. Your mother is no longer with us. She's gone to the ancestors. I'm all you have left."

"That's not true!" shouts Caitlin. She sees a flash of anger in his eyes and instinctively cowers close to the floor.

"I did the best I could!" Father shouts back, rising. "I tried to help her eat and drink and I washed her when she needed it and she still died! And then I helped you! Who do you think was bringing you food and water? Who do you think washed you when you pissed yourself? She's *dead*, Caitlin, and you can't do anything about it."

Fury rushes through Caitlin like a storm, so loud and hot that she can barely see. "Liar!" she screams, and hurls her whole body and head into his belly. He falls over like a rotten tree in a strong wind, and she runs over him and out the door, into a cold drizzle of rain. Weakened by her sickness, she can only run like a very young child, tottering along with her arms waving, slipping and falling, but she doesn't take the time to look behind her. Reaching the sea, she collapses to her knees, out of breath. Father isn't over her shoulder, so she pushes herself up and starts walking down the shoreline, the cold dark sand sticking to her feet, the windswept water raging blackly at her. Eventually, when she's too tired to walk anymore, she curls up by one of the structures Janey built. Caitlin closes her eyes and hears the faint echoes of children giggling, breathes in the clean smoke of burning wood, feels the soft shiver of sand as small excited footsteps whisk by her. When she opens her eyes again, she is utterly alone. Her nightgown is drenched and stings her cold skin. Pushing her head down on the sand, she falls asleep. She dreams that the branches spiking upright to form the shelter skeleton gather around her like sentries, multiply and flourish into a forest that hides her from Father when he comes looking.

CHAPTER FORTY‑EIGHT

Janey

A few weeks after Janey returns home, she and her family begin to notice people outside. The first time Mother sees a group of people through the window, she yells and waves until they come within shouting range. They call that they were sick, but they survived the sickness and so now can leave their houses without fear of contagion. It's the first time Janey hears that living through the illness is possible.

She knows that there were some girls who didn't leave the beach when she and Mary did. Not many; the combined blow of losing Janey and hearing the story about Mrs. Aaron sent most of the girls anxiously fleeing to their families, a mass exodus weeping bitterly— at the loss of their rebellion, at the dead or dying parents and siblings who might be awaiting them in their long-avoided houses. A few of them, however, refused to leave, declaring obstinately that they didn't care if their mother and father dropped dead, they were staying on the beach. Janey thinks about them often. Are they still there, those few brave, heartless ones, running down the shoreline and piling together under a mountain of blankets, eating fruit from untended orchards and playing whatever savage games take their fancy?

Janey spends the next few days gazing out the kitchen window. Occasionally two people meet in the distance, and after a brief shouted conversation they move close, hugging and talking, touching each other's arms and face as if patting clay into a wall, as if making

285

sure nothing is broken. Janey, yearning to be in open space, finds it harder to watch than an empty landscape.

Father sits in the front room and sleeps all day. Janey whispers to Mary that he must have secret activities at night, because she's never seen a man sleep so much. When she's tired of watching Mary, she watches Father, the way his eyelids are finely lined with small purple veins, the tapering of his fingers from knuckle to fingertip. Normally Father stays away from the house, preferring to tend to their farm, and he usually makes himself small and unobtrusive at night; apart from his visit to her at the beach, she has rarely spent time alone with him. She sees the way his mustache floats slightly upward with each breath, the small smile on his face when he wakes up and sees her gazing at him, the calm, fond glances he shoots at Mary when she is turned away. When he thinks nobody is watching, he puts his fingertips on his face and cries quietly. Once again, she is struck with the suspicion that she should have trusted Father earlier.

Every evening, Father prays to the ancestors to protect his wife and daughters, which is nice, as he usually prays for the crops or the weather. But the sweet prayers can't mask the awfulness of dinner. Thanks to the late-summer harvest, they have ample stores of corn, but Mother and Father have always traded for everything else they eat. Butter, cheese, most vegetables, meat, and fruit are all paid for in corn, and now they must sit and eat what they would have traded away. Corn mush for breakfast, dense corn bread for lunch, and bowls of corn soup for dinner. As usual, Mother vainly coaxes Janey to eat more than a mouthful, but she undermines this encouragement by picking listlessly at her own food. Janey wonders what the other families are doing, those who trade labor or cloth. You can't eat sweat, or wool.

Janey argues endlessly to leave the house. "Do you realize," she says to Mother, "that we lived out there with no adults for weeks and weeks?"

"And now you're here. And I will keep you alive if I can help it."

"But we came home to keep you alive!"

"Well, then we'll just have to keep each other alive. But I am your mother, in this house—"

"I could go back anytime!"

"You'd freeze, Janey. I'm surprised you haven't already, all of you."

"We kept warm," says Mary. "We had fires, and we slept cuddled together." Janey glares at her. The details of their freedom are cherished secret's, not to be handed out thoughtlessly to adults.

Janey is irritable, thwarted, tired. The girl who once led a rebellion of daughters is trapped at home like a buzzing insect in a box. The last few weeks seem like one long dream, distant and impossible now that she is obeying Mother and grumping around at home. Sometimes she slips out of the top of her dress to examine the healing lines of pain that drape around her body like filigree. Ironically, she finds the proof of her shaming comforting, a concrete reminder that she did not simply imagine her time on the beach.

"I wish I'd been sick," complains Janey pettily as she and Mary sit one afternoon and watch two people run toward each other joyfully and fling themselves into each other's arms. "Then I could go out."

"You do not," says Mary, and then, "What if we can never leave?"

"Leave the house? Of course we can leave the house. We're not trapped in here forever. We have legs."

"How long would you wait to leave? To make sure the sickness was gone?"

Janey looks uncertain. "It depends," she says finally. They watch another person—a woman, it looks like—walk across the landscape.

"But if we never get sick and survive it," says Mary, "how can we be allowed out where the sickness is?"

"I don't know," snaps Janey. "I don't know everything."

"Oh, really," snorts Mary. Janey scowls.

The next morning, Janey leaves before dawn.

CHAPTER FORTY-NINE

Vanessa

Now that people are emerging alive from the illness, Vanessa wants to go out too. Father tells her she can't, despite the magical medicine that won't let her get sick.

"I can't be positive it will work," says Father, looking down and away, which means he's lying. "Besides, you don't look like you've been ill. It would seem strange."

"What do they look like? The people who've been ill?"

"Thin. Pale, like they've lost all their blood." Father's look is distant and weary. "They're weak, and they cough and have to catch their breath."

"I could pretend."

"No." He shakes his head. "No, you couldn't."

Vanessa stays in the house with Mother, alternately cuddling and sniping, trying to amuse a bored and fretful Benjamin. They have exhausted his favorite songs, stories, and games, and he repeatedly asks to go out, confused at their lack of response. At one point, Vanessa smears butter on her face for him to lick like a dog. Infuriated by the waste, Mother smacks Vanessa, but her hand slides greasily away and lands on the wall with a satisfying slap.

Vanessa finds it ironic that those who almost died can walk about freely, while the healthy are still rattling about their houses like trapped mice. "Are they going to just take over?" she asks Mother.

"Will the people who never got sick stay in their houses forever, and become a race of hidden people?"

"Don't be dramatic," Mother says. "As soon as Father says there are no more people getting sick, we can go out."

"How long does there have to be nobody sick? A day? A week? A year?"

"A week," says Mother, sounding uncertain, but Vanessa grasps at her words. Father keeps them updated when he comes home in the evenings. Two days. Three days. After five days, Father silently shakes his head.

Let pain pass through your mind like water, she tells herself firmly, her eyes flickering closed. *Let it fall away like a dream.*

Eventually Mother persuades Father to let her roam, and spends a whole day and most of a night away, visiting houses and speaking with friends. Vanessa sulks and worries, Benjamin screams. And then, on the sixth day with no new illness, the new Mr. Adam comes over.

Vanessa is upstairs, trying to read, when she hears the door close. Thinking it's Father, who went to meet the wanderers, she jumps up and speeds downstairs for news. Instead she sees Mr. Adam. He is shirtless, weaving through the door, his face flushed, his eyes wet and scarlet in their sockets. At first she thinks he's sick, but then the smell reaches her and she realizes he's drunk.

"Father's not home," says Vanessa.

"Good." He coughs and spits out some phlegm. "My wife is dead."

Vanessa pictures Mrs. Adam laughing, her hands in the dirt, and feels like she's been struck in the chest. Pain flares in her throat, and she chokes for a moment. "I'm so sorry," she manages lamely. She will not show Mr. Adam her grief, but she feels it running under the floor like a river, waiting to permeate the skin of her soles. "When . . . when did she die?"

"Two days ago," he mutters.

"Did the baby die?"

"It wasn't old enough not to die with her," he says.

"Of course not," Vanessa says awkwardly. He continues to stand there. She feels dazed, bewildered. "Would you...would you like some tea?"

"I don't want any tea."

"No." She stands there with her hands folded and suddenly wonders what happened to his shirt.

"I know what you do with your father," says Mr. Adam.

Vanessa's breathing quickens as she realizes he knows about the medicine. "It wasn't my choice, I didn't have any idea."

"But you went along with it."

"I fought. I mean—"

"Soon it became the way things were."

Vanessa remembers Father's fingers depositing the pebble in her mouth and doesn't know what to say.

"My wife is dead," Mr. Adam says again.

"I'm so sorry," mutters Vanessa wearily. She needs him to leave. She needs to sit alone in the library and cry. "So sorry," she says again in a dull voice, like a drowsy, miserable child repeating a rhyme.

"It's terrible to lose someone you love."

"Yes."

"None of the wanderers died, or their families. How do you explain that?"

A streak of fear shoots upward like a flaming bird, tearing through Vanessa's throat. "I...don't know."

"Your father loves you, doesn't he?"

"Yes?"

"All those nights in his arms."

Vanessa looks around, vainly hoping that Mother has returned. "Father's coming back any time now."

"No he's not. He's at one of those wanderer meetings. Secret, of course."

"Of course."

"You like what he does, don't you?"

"I don't really know what he does, I mean..."

"You know. I know. Everyone knows."

"Knows what?"

"I heard some girls try to fight it, but not you." He is swelling again like he did in the library, blocking the light. Her breath quickens, and she tries to calm herself, putting a hand on her belly.

"I told you, I did try."

"That you *like* it."

"No I don't. It's bitter."

Mr. Adam laughs loudly for a while. "I'm sure it is."

"I think you should go."

"Such a pretty girl. I don't even know if I was going to have a girl."

"I'm sure you'll have one later," she says stupidly.

"It's why we came here, you know."

"To have a girl?"

"So to speak." He smiles crookedly.

"What?"

"I've seen you watching me."

Startled, Vanessa pulls back, crossing her arms over herself.

"Look at you now, in that pretty dress."

Vanessa looks down to her drab dress, spattered with stains. "Uh...thank you."

"Why should I have to wait years?"

"For what?"

"You're used to it already. It's genius."

"What's genius?"

"You. You in that dress."

He marches up to Vanessa, quicker than she thought he could move for how drunk he smells. He puts a hand on her arm and kneads it painfully. "Such pretty white skin."

Suddenly Vanessa feels like an animal about to be slaughtered. She moves back a few steps, but he advances until she's trapped against a wall. "Pretty girl," he says, and tries to put his mouth on hers. She cringes away, and he smears saliva against her ear.

"Stop, Mr. Adam. You can't. They—they'll shame you. They'll exile you." She inhales his sour, drunken smell and wishes she didn't have to breathe. "It's against the shalt-nots."

"But why do you *care*? Why do you care? You get it every night."

"I don't. Leave me alone."

"From your *father*. Do you know how sick that is?"

For a second Vanessa thinks he's talking about the illness. Then she's not sure what he's talking about. Every girl lies down under her father, even if nobody talks about it. Like picking your nose, or scratching your bottom; it's not something to be discussed in public, but you know everyone does it in darkness, when nobody else is looking.

His hand is on her, pulling, and it hurts. Taking a deep breath, she ducks down, then darts to the side. Vanessa runs up the creaky stairs with Mr. Adam huffing behind her. "Go away!" she screams as she runs into Mother and Father's bedroom. "Leave me alone!"

"Why should I? Why shouldn't I take what I want? He does. My wife is dead. His wife is alive. He takes what he wants." He grabs at Vanessa's dress, and she pulls away. The sleeve rips off. She should have run out the front door, she knows now, and curses herself for her stupidity.

"That's different!" she yells.

"Oh, it's different."

"Father loves me! And I love him. And I hate you!" This time it's a piece of the skirt.

His hands close around her waist, and he's got her against him with one arm, undoing his pants with the other, heaving his stinking breath into her face. Wriggling, she sinks her teeth deep into his arm until she tastes meat and copper. He roars and lets go.

"Bitch!" he says, dabbing at the welling marks. Vanessa casts her eyes around and sees a rock that Mother brought home a long child-summer ago, black veined with blue. As Mr. Adam comes for her again, she swings it and smashes the window. Grabbing a shard of glass with her palm, she hurtles around and slices at Mr. Adam's belly.

Blood beads onto his skin, and he stumbles back, looking comically surprised. Vanessa slices him again, and this time the blood pours. He lets out a yell, hoarse and gurgling, and closes his meaty hands around her throat.

Without air, Vanessa desperately thrusts the glass into him and jerks it out, shuddering at the stretch and give of the thick skin that leads to his soft flesh beneath. His hands weaken, and he takes a step back. She is warm and sticky, and he falls heavily to his knees.

Behind him is Father, suddenly there, swinging a length of wood and smashing it into Mr. Adam's head. He turns to take hold of Vanessa, who slashes and pushes wildly with the shard of glass. "Vanessa. Vanessa. *Vanessa!*"

She stops. Father's arms are covered in cuts, and the glass has sliced into her hand so a thick stream of blood spirals down her wrist. "Vanessa," he says again, pale as paper. He steps forward and unwinds her fingers from the shard one by one, setting it on the floor carefully like it's alive. The glass is coated with blood and globules of fat. "Vanessa, what happened?"

Mr. Adam is moaning and writhing and holding his head, but Father doesn't seem to care. As soon as Father lets go, Vanessa snatches for the shard, holds it to her chest with her uninjured hand, and backs against the wall. "Vanessa, he won't hurt you," Father says. She sinks down into a crouch, the crimson glass in her slippery grip.

Father stares at her and then turns to Mr. Adam, whose eyelids are fluttering. "He's got so much fat that I don't think you hurt him very much," Father says thoughtfully. This surprises Vanessa, as Mr. Adam is lying in a dark red lake of blood. "Vanessa, you had better leave."

"What happens now?" she whispers.

"Now he's exiled. I'm almost glad his wife is dead." Father kicks Mr. Adam in the ribs, eliciting a groan.

"What if—what if—"

"Nothing more will happen, Vanessa. I promise. It's over."

Still she crouches with the glass in her hands. When Father moves forward and puts a hand on her shoulder, she screams.

He jerks back, stares at her, and leaves the room. She doesn't know how long she squats there, panting, until Mother comes in. She puts her arms around Vanessa, who relaxes her hands and drops the glass on the floor. Mother has to help Vanessa from the room; she can't tell which way is up, and the floor heaves left, then right. Pulling out the battered tin tub, Mother lights a fire that reflects in coral shards on its rippled surface, and heats pot after pot of water until the bath is steaming. When Vanessa steps in, it's so hot it hurts, and she has to wait before putting in the other foot. As she sinks down, the water turns pink, and when she submerges her hand the pain stings so sharp and vivid that she bites her lip and whimpers. Mother murmurs soothing words as she gently sponges Vanessa's back and face, wringing out scarlet water into the reddening bath. Heating another pot of water, she helps Vanessa stand up to be rinsed off. The sponge traces the water down her body, and Vanessa feels as fresh and weak as a new puppy.

Lifting Vanessa's arm, Mother sponges from wrist to armpit and then freezes. Vanessa looks at her questioningly, and Mother hastily puts her arm down by her side. Vanessa turns her head and raises her arm again, despite Mother saying, "Not now, Nessa." There in front of her eyes are a few fine, dark hairs marring the pale smoothness where her arm meets her body, coiling and thrusting angrily like blades from her skin. Collapsing back in the tub, Vanessa starts to cry. Mother hugs her fiercely, soaking up pink water with the cloth of her dress. She's crying too.

CHAPTER FIFTY

Caitlin

Caitlin wakes up in the darkness, shivering, her bones jostling against each other. A harder rain is falling, and the leftover sticks from the old shelter do nothing to protect her. She thinks briefly of trying to find something to drape over them for a tent—surely there is a blanket left somewhere—but it's so dark she can't see.

Lying on the wet sand, she listens to the sounds of the water. Eventually she can't take the cold anymore, and she stands up and starts running in place. It helps, but she tires soon, coughing a deep, rasping cough. Sitting back down, she tucks her knees and elbows and feet into the shell of her curved torso and wonders if she'll die.

She remembers the heat of sand in summer and digs down with a ragged fingernail to see if the sand below the surface is warmer. It's not. Then she thinks that if she could make a coat out of wet sand, it would be warmer than just her threadbare nightgown. She doesn't know how to sew together sand, but she starts digging in earnest, stopping only to pant and cough every now and then. Finally she nestles her curled body into the deep, chilly hole, so just her head and hands peek out, and scrapes in more sand to fill the empty spaces around her. She's still cold, but she stops shivering after a little while, and the weight of the sand feels comforting. Her head falls forward over and over, and she isn't sure if she's falling asleep or freezing to death. Dreams bloom in her head, weaving out from her thoughts, slow colorful dreams that snap her briefly awake. Then they get thicker, and she drifts away from the freezing sand and the beach altogether.

Caitlin wakes to someone calling her name. Her forehead is against gritty sand, and her neck hurts. Lifting her face up to daylight, Caitlin narrows her eyes. Someone is standing over her, talking in a girl's voice. The glare fades, and it's Janey Solomon, wearing a coat over a nightgown, her red hair falling toward Caitlin like a rain of fire.

"I've been looking for you for hours," says Janey. "Your father's staggering around drunk, telling everyone to look for you." She imitates his low, slurred voice: "'My little girl, she's all I have left, I'll make it up to her.'"

"How did you know I was here?" croaks Caitlin, trying not to cough.

"I didn't. I just said I've been looking for hours. I thought you might be at one of the hiding places, behind a rock or something. Then I thought of the shore, but I didn't know where, so." Janey shrugs. "And now you're drowning."

"I'm not in the sea."

"No, just in the rain. That's a great hiding place, under the sand. Your hair blends in. I almost looked right at you and passed by."

"Oh."

"There's nobody else here anymore. I thought maybe a few of the girls might have held out, still be somewhere out here, slinking around. But they're not. Why are you here? I'm sorry your mother is dead. I'd be out here too, if I was left alone with your father."

She looks at Caitlin, who doesn't say anything.

"I brought you food," says Janey, leaning down to a pile Caitlin hadn't noticed. She brings out a damp loaf of bread and tosses it to Caitlin. Wiggling her arms free, Caitlin tears into the bread with her teeth, barely chewing. Suddenly her stomach stabs with pain, and she stops and swallows, trying not to vomit.

"Thank you," she says after the nausea has passed.

"I brought blankets too. They'll get wet, but they're better than nothing. You might be able to use them to block the rain."

"Thank you."

"I'll try to come every day. Mother will try to stop me. I was able to sneak out today, though, and I heard you were missing."

"How many people are out?" asks Caitlin around another mouthful of bread.

"The only ones out have been sick already," says Janey, "so they aren't worried about being sick again. So many people are dead. *So many people.* The girls too. The children." Her face clouds, but then she shakes fervently, whipping her head from side to side as if to dislodge the fog of sorrow. "I'm trying not to think about it." She pauses. "It was worst for the pregnant women. I think all of them died, or at least most of them."

"That's bad," says Caitlin, feeling like she should say something, but unable to muster any true sadness. When she learned Mother died, Caitlin's emotions faded to a dull gray hum.

Janey shrugs. Her whole body is frenetic, her shrugs and stretches sudden and almost violent. "Some people haven't had it, and they're still in their homes. Like us. When are we going to come out? Nobody will tell me."

"You're out," says Caitlin.

"I know, but I'm not supposed to be," she says. "But it's not like I'm going into rooms with sick people, or... I don't know. I just had to get out."

Caitlin nods.

"There's not much food around, so few have been farming or baking or making cheese. But there are fewer people. I don't know. Maybe we'll all starve." Janey shrugs again, her shoulders jerking upward like startled birds, then swiftly falling back into place. It looks like the prelude to a fit of convulsions. Caitlin lets out a sudden, very loud belch. Janey giggles. "They'll all find you now," she says.

"I don't want anyone to find me."

"Maybe you could come home with me," Janey says thoughtfully. "Your father would look for you, but maybe he'd let you stay with us.

You need a mother. There are so many of us without mothers now. The wanderers will work it out. Someone said they will just match up wives and husbands. I'm not sure that would work. Can you imagine any woman agreeing to marry your father? He'd cut them in two. Here, I brought you water. You can fill it up in anyone's rain barrel."

Janey hands Caitlin a cup and she gulps the water down. Taking it back, Janey sets it on the sand. "It'll fill with rain soon."

Caitlin nods.

"Can you get out of there?"

Struggling a bit, Caitlin stands up shakily. Janey smiles. "I was worried you were stuck."

Caitlin shakes her head, and reaches out and wraps one of the blankets around her. It's scratchy and wet, but warm, and she gives a little sigh.

"I don't like you staying here alone. Why don't you come home with me?"

Caitlin shakes her head hard.

"What are you worried will happen?"

Caitlin's mouth quirks, and then she bursts into tears.

"Well, I'll come see you every day. We'll think of something." They sigh in unison. "What else do you need?"

Caitlin shakes her head again.

"You're very brave." Janey hugs her, hard, and Caitlin leans into her bony shoulder and wishes she'd stay. "I'll see you tomorrow. Try digging a hole and lining it with the blankets, and then gathering everything at the top."

She does try, that night, but it doesn't work. She rolls up in blankets and sleeps badly, waking to numb feet and a racking cough. Waiting all day in the same place, Caitlin watches the water advance and recede, and builds little shapes of sand, but Janey doesn't come. That night Caitlin wakes up coughing so hard she vomits slime streaked with blood. "Janey?" she mutters, squinting to see a tall spindly figure coming toward her, dancing like a flame.

Then Mother's soft hands stroke her brow like a mist of cool water, and Caitlin sighs with relief.

"Mother, I dreamed you were dead," she says. Mother doesn't answer, but keeps caressing Caitlin's face with cool damp hands until Caitlin wakes up sprawled out in the rain, feverish and alone.

CHAPTER FIFTY-ONE

Janey

When Janey returns at nightfall, sandy and soaked and flushed, Mary moves to hit her. But before she can raise an arm, Janey pulls her aside and starts talking about how they have to take in Caitlin, and when Mary cocks her head in confusion, Janey paces around the room, throwing her hands in the air and making stifled half-exclamations. "Janey," says Mary. "Janey, I can't understand you."

Janey shakes her head and staggers. Rising, Mary darts toward Janey, who sinks warm and shaking into her arms.

"Mother," says Mary. "I think Janey's sick."

Janey tries to protest, but time stops, stretches, and twists away like a plume of smoke. Her tongue is slow, pushing against heavy air as she tries to form words. *They cut it out,* she thinks thickly, *so now I can go, to and fro.* Then she laughs a little at her rhyme. Her body is made of water, and she pulls from Mary's arms and splashes to the floor.

Then everything happens very quickly, in flashes. She is in Father's arms, being lifted toward the ballooning ceiling. Mary's face is near hers, smearing and blurring like streaks of paint on a rain-swept window, and then suddenly snatched away. She is in bed, the sheets thick and silky and coiling against her skin like live snakes. Everything is swaying and shuddering. *Something's wrong,* she thinks slowly, and then, *I am sick.* "Mother," she says heavily. Mother turns toward her.

"Don't let Mary in," whispers Janey urgently, trying to make each word separate and easy. Her mouth feels numb. She has to speak quietly; she doesn't want another lashing.

"I won't," promises Mother tautly, stripping Janey of her damp dress. She gathers Janey in her arms and lifts her easily, slips a warm nightgown over her aching head and down her slender body.

"You'd better get out of here," croaks Janey.

"If you think I'm leaving you alone for a second, you're a fool, Janey Solomon," snaps Mother, and Janey sinks back, intimidated and a little impressed. Mother's hair, sleek like Mary's, falls out of her topknot in slices of darkness, and her freckles shift around on her face as Janey stares blurrily.

"Mother, your face," says Janey, and a cool cloth is laid on her aching forehead. It's the most wonderful thing she's ever felt in her life. The coldness sinks into her brow bone, flows down her temples in pulsing waves, cooling the inferno in her brain. It cuts past the sourness in her throat, the throbbing pain in her eyes, the trembling ache in her bones. "Thank you," she gasps, and slips beneath consciousness.

CHAPTER FIFTY TWO

Vanessa

Vanessa's hand is healing, although Mother bound it so tightly to keep the edges of her wound together that the flesh swells between the cloth strips. She makes Vanessa hold it in the rain barrel regularly, and gives her a bitter tea that sleeps away the pain. Mother says her hand won't work perfectly again and will probably always pain her, but that Vanessa should be able to do everything that a woman needs to, except perhaps sew. Vanessa is no lover of sewing and can't help feeling that this news is a ray of light in an otherwise dark prognosis.

Two of Father's cuts needed a stitch from Mr. Joseph the weaver, but Father tells Vanessa they don't hurt. She responds that he needs to go put his belly in the rain barrel, which makes him smile.

A few days later, the wanderers meet in Father's library. Vanessa is accustomed to wanderers gathering in her home, but now they seem like alien beings, murderous and predatory. She thinks of them sitting uncomfortably on the floor, or leaning against the bookshelves and dirtying the books with their black coats, and shivers.

She can only assume they are trying to figure out what to do now that everyone is dead. Curiosity proving stronger than fear, she inches away from Mother when her back is turned and sets to eavesdropping.

"The fields will be admirably fertilized, but there is nobody to farm them."

"No, that's not true. Quite a few farmers survived; we can simply broaden some of the fields that we made smaller before. We'll divide them again, when we need to."

"We have nobody to make paper now. Only one carver left. We've lost a lot of skilled—"

Mother finds Vanessa and pulls her into the kitchen. Once she stops glowering at Vanessa and becomes lost in her work, Vanessa creeps out to listen again.

"More widowers than widows. All the women with child died. We need everyone to marry, but we're short on women. A few men could take on more wives, but in the past that's only been if their first wife can't have a healthy child. Is that something we want to change?"

A sharp, nasal voice. Mr. Solomon? "Ah, says a man who won't have to deal with a furious wife!"

Laughter.

"Let some of the older men go to the summers of fruition. The younger men can wait a year."

"We've never had older men or widowed men at the summers of fruition. For good reason. That could be a catastrophe."

"That also doesn't fix the problem, and we don't want unmarried young men roaming around."

"If we could bring in couples with older daughters—"

"Remember what happened to the Josephs all those years ago, the new ones, and she was only eight!" That's Father.

"But in these times—"

Mother swats Vanessa's behind and sends her to her room, threatening severe punishment if she stirs again. Vanessa waits a few minutes, then darts past Mother's back toward the library once more.

"We have the room to bring in new families. Many new families. This is a very unusual opportunity."

"We don't want to throw everything out of balance. The carver Adams were a complete disaster and they were only one couple. We can't make sure everyone is suitable, and if they outnumber us..."

"The Adams were a disaster, but almost every family we've brought in throughout the generations hasn't been."

"And the Jacobs?"

"All right, they haven't been perfect, but they've stayed. We need people."

"The ancestors came with ten families."

"We are not the ancestors! Nor are there any like them to choose from out there."

"That many people, all at once, their knowledge will spread. It can't be kept when half of us are—"

"Not half."

"No, listen to him. Can we persuade everyone not to discuss the wastelands among themselves, when they've all come in from outside at the same time? Can we keep it from spreading?"

"Yes, if we choose the right men."

"But do they have the right women?"

"All women can be taught what is right."

"They most certainly cannot. Look at what our daughters did. That Janey Solomon, she didn't just lead them all out onto the beach, did you know she gave secret sermons?"

Vanessa's heart contracts with a painful jerk, and she has to breathe deeply and remind herself that nobody knows she's there.

"What's this?"

"My daughter was acting so strangely, I had to force it out of her. Janey is saying that there are other islands, she knows about Amanda Balthazar—I thought it was just the Gideon girl and that nobody would believe her, but—"

A long exhale. "That's why they went to the beach, then. I thought it was just Janey Solomon convincing them they didn't need parents."

"It *was* Janey Solomon. But how did *she* find out?"

"I don't know how these girls thought they could do such a thing. They are going to be the next wives, in a year or two. We can't have them going to the beach to escape their husbands. Nothing like that has ever happened. If it wasn't for the illness, they would still be out there!"

"Nonsense, as soon as it got cold enough they'd have crawled back, whimpering for mercy. It was a game, but it's over."

"You call that a game? They wouldn't listen! I had to beat my daughter so badly that—"

"I don't know why you take the Solomon girl so seriously. In a year she'll be dead or married."

"Yes, let us fear the girls! They will bring war against us!" There's general uneasy laughter, but some sighs of frustration.

"And the sickness?" asks one wanderer bitterly. "Their disobedience brought it down from the ancestors, worse than war."

"Who knows what more Janey will tell them in a year? She's already sown distrust and disobedience. She's the only one old enough to piece anything together. I say we—"

"You underestimate the older girls, thirteen and fourteen. I always said we should marry them younger."

"The ancestors said—"

Mother digs her fingers into Vanessa's arm, marches her upstairs, pushes her into her room, and drags a table over to block the door. Sitting with a frustrated snort, Mother does her sewing right there, sitting at the table.

After peering out the door a few times to see Mother either yawning or scowling, Vanessa catches her nodding off. Eventually Mother sighs and puts her face in her hands. Quietly, Vanessa squeezes through the door, crawls around her, and heads down the stairs on her hands and knees.

"I'm sorry, James, you're outvoted." James is Father. "We need new people. We need parents to take on the children who have no parents!"

"There are only ten who lost both mother and father, and we have enough families who lost children to take them in," insists Father.

"We need to replenish our stock anyhow. More and more defectives each year, women bleed out—have freaks—and sometimes they die of it. The ancestors warned us of this, and we've ignored the warnings. Remember what Philip Adam wrote about diseases, how they flatten a herd unless—"

"People aren't goats," interrupts another wanderer.

"They breed like them, and we've had as many generations of the same people breeding as we can stand. We're starting to breed wrong. For all we know, this disease could have been avoided. We need new blood."

"Fuck new blood and fuck breeding. This is a message from the ancestors. We have slipped, and our standards for everyone have slipped. How can you think that now, *now*, when the girls have rebelled beyond anything we've ever seen, when they are asking dangerous questions—"

"It has to be done, the defectives are the ancestors' way of—"

"James. We already voted. The decision is made. We will take in new families, as many as we can find."

"Then," says Father, "this is the end for us. This is the beginning of the end of everything we've ever worked for." His voice sounds bleak and ragged.

"Don't be ridiculous."

"Do you remember what I said about the Adams, first thing? And that man—"

"What he tried to do to your daughter was terrible, but he didn't succeed. And he's been more than adequately punished."

"That's not my point."

"We need your help. We don't need your arguments, we need your help."

"So what about the men and women who remain?" says another voice. "Do we assign husbands and wives?"

"Perhaps we should have a second summer of fruition for them."

There's a bark of laughter, and someone else clicks his teeth.

"I think it's best—"

Father interrupts. "I can't believe you don't see what you're doing, what you're risking."

"James, I'm sorry to say this, but you are a weak link among us and it has to stop."

A long, incredulous pause. Vanessa's jaw drops. And then Father says darkly, anger brimming in his voice, "What did you say?"

"You are faint of heart. We have to keep decisions, actions, secret from you, telling you after the fact, when you should be helping us! Your reaction to Amanda Balthazar's—"

"If you had told me, we could have found another way!" Father pleads. "She was with child! She—"

"Sometimes you have to dig the weed out by the root," another voice says.

"Everything we have done is within the ancestors' teachings. You need to reread the secret writings of Philip Adam—"

"I *know* his writings."

"Then why this hesitation, this—this—rebellion? You nearly had a fit when you found out what needed to be done with the Joseph woman, and then Amanda Balthazar, and Rosie Gideon..."

"She was a *child*."

"And what kind of woman would she have made? What is the point of waiting to find out?"

"You didn't even bring it to us, you just did it yourself!"

"He's right, you know," says another wanderer. "I never would have disagreed, but—"

"You don't hesitate to kill a dog that bites," snaps the first wanderer.

"I agree," says a bass voice. "We have to be able to act on our own judgment. *Everything* doesn't require a meeting, a vote."

"The murder of a child," says Father indignantly.

There is a moment's silence, and then two voices rise up and battle for primacy. The louder one wins. "Philip Adam said—"

"I don't care what Philip Adam said!" cries Father, and there is an appalled silence.

"James, we are going to change," says the sharp, nasal voice. "We will not be allowing what happened this year to ever happen again."

"The plague?"

"Well, that too," says someone else. "If we bring in new families—"

"*Not* the plague. We will be...better enforcing the shalt-nots. Things will never go this far again. Daughters who escape, who try to live without their fathers' guidance, will be punished severely, and if they continue not to listen...they must be uprooted too."

"You think their fathers won't care?" asks Father softly.

"I think their fathers will listen and *obey*, unlike their children. I think that once we show what the response is to any kind of rebellion, the daughters will listen and obey as well. Perhaps our mistake was keeping Amanda Balthazar and Rosie Gideon and the others secret. Perhaps we should have—"

"But the husbands, the fathers," says Father. "These are women and girls who are beloved. If you do this, don't you think that the men—"

"*They. Will. Obey.*"

"And *your* daughter..."

"What about my daughter?" whispers Father through his teeth.

"It's the way you've raised her. We never should have let you have books."

"How is it different from your collection of things?"

"Now, now," says a soothing voice. "The subject isn't James's library right now. And Vanessa didn't run away to the beach. How many of you can say the same of your daughters?" A pause, sighs, and embarrassed shuffling.

"So what does this mean for Janey Solomon?" asks someone else.

"It always comes back to Janey Solomon," says a third voice, with a halfhearted laugh.

"Now, *her* father—"

Mother smacks Vanessa across both cheeks, her face betrayed and wild. The voices stop at the sound of the scuffle. Someone chuckles, someone else murmurs concernedly. Shaking her head and taking a deep breath, Mother pushes Vanessa to the table and makes her practice sewing with one shaking hand, which is impossible.

CHAPTER FIFTY-THREE

Caitlin

Caitlin waits for Janey to come back, but she never returns. Caitlin can't count how many days it's been. Sometimes she thinks it's been only hours, and sometimes she thinks it's been weeks. Time stretches and blurs and warps in front of her. Her cup fills and she drinks it. Her bread is gone. When she wakes up it's dark, but Caitlin can't be sure if she's waking up every night, or it's all the same night. She can't stop coughing.

She knows what a normal person would do is get up and go home. Father might hit her, but he might not. She could even go to someone else's house. They would let her in. They would feed and dry her, while someone went to get Father.

She knows she can get up because she practices, every now and then, to make sure she still can. She stands under the weight of soggy blankets and moves her feet up and down. Then her knees fold again, and she is back inside her sandy hole. Cold body, burning face. Sometimes she shivers and sometimes she doesn't. Caitlin has grown to like the feeling of cold on her body. It feels clean and fresh and new.

Her mind skips, dreaming, then not; sometimes a daydream turns into a real dream. She dreams she's in school and Mr. Abraham is throwing pins at her. She dreams she and Mother are digging a garden for plants that eat people. She dreams that dogs with giant white teeth are biting her feet. She wakes, coughs, and spits; her spit is dark and glistening under the moonlight. The echoes of little girls racing, laughing, giggling, rise up from the sand like they left their ghosts behind them.

Caitlin's mind slides back and forth over her life, like someone running their finger over and over a frosty window, making patterns. If she could start her life over again, she decides, she would shout more. She would bite like the dream dogs. She wouldn't be so scared of everything all the time. She wouldn't come when Father called, she would stay where she was. She wouldn't lose her breath when Mr. Abraham said her name, but speak boldly. She would stomp and yell and be loud and big, eat until she grew six feet tall and then run away.

She rolls into a vision, instead of being yanked or lulled toward it. It is as easy as falling from a high place to a low one.

She is perhaps three or four, closer to the ground than she can ever remember being, reaching her hands forward to another little girl. It's hot, not the moist heat of an island summer, but a parched, sucking heat that makes her lips feel like dry canvas when she presses them together.

Their dirty hands meet, their forearms marked with black and purple fingerprints and fading golden traces of yesterday's blows. Their dresses are breathtaking, marvelous: the other girl is wearing a pink Caitlin has only seen in garish sunsets, spotted with bright orange flowers. The embroidery is so fine as to be undetectable, like the cloth itself is branded with the pattern. Looking down, Caitlin sees that she is in stained white, whiter than any cloth she has ever seen, and printed on her dress are tiny words, black and busy like ants, but she doesn't know how to read them.

The girl's face is familiar, brownish teeth bared in a smile and brilliant dark eyes staring happily into Caitlin's. She looks thin, almost as thin as Janey Solomon, but her hair is bright and shining. They laugh at each other in joy and start slowly revolving in a circle. "Ring around the rosy," *they chant in singsong, "pocket full of posies." Caitlin hears Father yelling at Mother, but Wasteland Caitlin doesn't fret about this. She is used to it.*

"It's the only choice!" screams Father. "It's our only choice! I will not stay here!"

And Mother, surprisingly, screams back in a robust voice, "No! I will not go!"

"Ashes, ashes," the girls chant, "we all fall down!" And Caitlin drops to the ground like her bones snapped. Laughing at their own cleverness, the girls roll around in the dust, which is silky on her toes and spotted with rocks, and strange, small metal circles with crimped edges. She doesn't know what the song means, but it doesn't matter. What matters is the spinning and falling. Caitlin stares up into a hot yellow sky.

Sitting up, the girl coughs wetly, spraying dark flecks into her palm, then says, "Again!" Brushing off their strange dresses, they begin circling and chanting again, Caitlin already laughing with the knowledge of how their rhyme will end.

And then she is back on the beach, back in her trembling freezing body, years older. She feels the ache of not being with that girl, whoever she was, of not being little and brave, even if everything around her was burning.

Caitlin stands shakily, the rain turned to needles of chill metal, the night turned into poison that chokes her as she struggles for breath. She knows this is the end of her short life, her small life, small in all ways. She knows what she is about to do is a sin, but at the same time she can't imagine anyone—celestial or mortal—would want her to do anything else.

She has heard a lot, too much, about the darkness below, but she doesn't think that the ancestors would send her there. She's always done exactly what she was told to do, except for going to the beach—but so many girls went to the beach. And she went back home. She thinks that must be enough to join the ancestors in heaven.

Does she want to join them there? Maybe there's another place to go.

Her feet are numb and she stumbles a little when she walks. The waiting water embraces her softly. It's like a safe bed where nobody will ever bother her again. Bending her knees, Caitlin sinks down into the water, then bobs up. Her skin pricks and chills in the wind. She slides back down into the sea's warm grasp, the current a soothing tongue against her belly, walking straighter as she goes deeper. When she's up to her neck, she holds her breath and lifts her feet off the ground, and stays there like she's flying.

CHAPTER FIFTY-FOUR

Janey

Janey wakes to find Mary by her bed, slumped forward, her rump in a chair and her head on Janey's arm. "Get out of here!" Janey hisses at her. "Get out! You're not supposed to be in here!"

Mary blinks, yawns, stares at Janey with weary eyes. "It's all right," she says. "Mother says you don't have the sickness. You're not coughing, there's no fever." Mary must be right, for her face is sun-warm on Janey's cool forearm.

"Get out of here anyway," says Janey spitefully. But instead Mary crawls into bed next to her, all soft warm skin and clean dry cloth, and Janey is too tired to protest. She drifts into slumber, and when she wakes, Mary is asleep, her eyes darting back and forth restlessly under her pearly eyelids. Janey's hands and feet feel like blocks of ice. She fears she is sucking away Mary's precious warmth and guiltily moves away, almost falling off the bed. But then she is so cold she snuggles close to her once more and dozes off.

She wakes to Mother coming in with a bowl heaped high with corn mush. "All I have is corn," Mother says angrily.

"She won't eat it," says Mary.

"Oh, yes, she will. She will eat every single bite."

Janey inhales the thick, yeasty smell and rolls over in bed, away from them.

"Janey," says Mother.

Janey doesn't answer.

"Start with one bite," Mary says, smoothing Janey's brilliant hair. Janey catches Mary's hand and puts it under her face like a small pillow. "You need to eat," Mary says. "If you'd been eating, you wouldn't be in bed. You would be up, out of bed, doing things."

Janey opens her eyes, but stares at the wall instead of looking around. Streaks of water roll from the insides of her eyes toward the bedclothes. "Janey," Mary says. "Janey?"

"It's your fault," Janey rasps.

"Mine?" says Mary.

"All of you. You, all of you. All you mothers and fathers with your ancestors and rules and secrets. You can blame me if you want, but it's all your fault."

"Janey," says Mother, "you have to live in the world as it is. Starving yourself—"

"It's that way because you let it be that way," mutters Janey. "Leave me alone."

"You need to eat," insists Mary, freeing her damp hand from under Janey's cheekbone. "You fainted, and you aren't making sense." Janey doesn't answer. "Janey, this is important."

Janey's eyes stare glassily at the wall again, skimming over the little imperfections in the wood, the scratches and dents and knots. Her bones feel like a bundle of dry sticks as she curls into herself, poking and scratching her from the inside.

"I will make you eat," says Mother.

"No," whispers Janey, "you won't."

"A little?" says Mary. "Please? What will I do if you die?" She takes the bowl from Mother and indicates with a movement of her head that Mother should leave the room. Exhaling a frustrated snort, Mother does. Janey feels Mary's finger gently push a ball of corn mush into her mouth. She scornfully spits it out.

"Caitlin's dead," Janey says.

"What? How do you know? I didn't hear."

"She died by the water. She was waiting for me."

"How do you know?"

"Because I was the only one who knew where she was. Alone in the cold. I promised I would come."

"Janey," whispers Mary after a moment. "Janey, did they kill her?"

Janey shakes her head. "No," she says. "It was me."

"But you were here. You've been here for days."

"Exactly."

Confused, Mary sits with the bowl of corn mush against her knees and waits. Eventually Janey pushes aside the bedclothes and, her arms shaking, lifts herself into a seated position with her bony hip poking into Mary's softer one. Her face is pale and slightly luminescent, a small dim moon suspended in the room. "Mary," Janey says, swaying slightly, "if I need to get to the church, will you help me?"

SPRING

CHAPTER FIFTY*FIVE

Vanessa

Yesterday was the first day nobody cried in school, and Vanessa feels the full gravity of this. Ever since school started again, children have been constantly breaking into sobs in the half-empty classroom.

First everyone was crying for the dead people, the mothers and fathers and brothers and sisters. There are so many to mourn that choosing just one seems random and meaningless, like plucking an ant from a teeming hill. Vanessa, unable to hold grief at bay when it was washing over everyone else, wept with them.

Then the wanderers remarried everyone.

It's not unusual to lose a husband or wife. Widowers, especially, sprout up as women bleed out or die in childbirth, and hapless men are left with cooking, cleaning, and parenting they are utterly unprepared to do. There is usually a mother, or sister, or aunt happy to take care of a bereaved man, especially if they themselves are barren. But the wanderers encourage remarriage, and while there has been the rare man who prefers to set up housekeeping with a sterile, set-aside sister, most seek out new wives avidly; widows are in high demand. Courtship is no-nonsense but friendly, the weddings cheerful and jokey. Remarriages breed the occasional household with three or four children. These rich, chaotic families cause ripples of envy even if the husband and wife soon grow to dislike each other, or the children beat one another with fury in the shadow of evening.

This time, after the sickness fully ended, the wanderers took all of

323

the bereaved into a cold field, commanding them to pair up and get married before the day was out.

People wept and trembled. For some, their dead spouses weren't even buried. As the wanderers loomed around them, they shakily, obediently tried to pick the person they thought would be best. A few men fought over Mrs. Moses, the young pretty one, and nobody wanted to marry old Mrs. Adam, the dung collector's widow, who still smelled like an outhouse. Caitlin's father didn't even show up. There were more men than women, and a few were left wifeless.

The couples got married then and there, and negotiation about houses immediately followed. Now there are empty houses for the new families from the wastelands. Many daughters got new fathers, and cried and cried. The boys who got new fathers grieved too. Those who saw strange women installed in the place of their mothers sobbed. For days, everyone on the island seemed to be constantly weeping, eyes swollen and seeping constantly like festering wounds.

Mr. Abraham's son died, and so every time anyone cried at school he would struggle not to join them. The tears in his eyes were visible anyway, and that made more children break down.

And yet yesterday, nobody cried in class. Today, so far, nobody has cried. Mr. Abraham has delivered a dry-eyed lecture on arithmetic and then the many uses of tree bark. Emily Abraham, who sits across from Vanessa, absently picks and scratches at a scab on her leg, and Vanessa watches a thick bead of blood slowly descend in a stripe from her knee to her ankle. The squeak of charcoal on slate is almost unbearable.

The normalcy of it all makes Vanessa feel oddly guilty. When she could finally leave the house, the weight of the dead came crashing down on her, multiplying with each name until the breath was pressed from her. Letty, Frieda, Rosie, Lily, Caitlin, Hannah—the names didn't seem to end. The slick black grief entered her once more, flowed across the ground and rained from the sky, turning everything dark and dull. All the pregnant women died with their babies inside them.

There are so many bodies, most of them rotting already, and a disgustingly sweet stench hangs in the air and coats Vanessa's skin with a film of death. She heard there is such a glut of bodies that some had to be chopped up and dumped off the ferry so the crops wouldn't be overwhelmed with rot.

Now it feels like they're pretending it didn't happen, these dry-eyed children. Vanessa fears they're letting down the dead, and yet they're all so close to dead anyway. Everyone is pale and slow, and half of the children are still coughing. Vanessa feels tired and sick all the time, even though she never actually had the sickness. At recess, the girls just sit. They stare into space, they sigh, they lean on the friends who are left. Slowly, Vanessa can see the younger children recovering, like flowers regaining their height after a cold snap. They unbend and blossom, have moments of laughter and play, before the cold stares of their elders turn on them and they sink guiltily back into the shadows. And suddenly, Vanessa seems to be one of these elders. The children's laughter infuriates her, their bold resilience when she is broken and dead.

Everyone is eating better now. People exchange stores, and there are rabbits and milk and berries. Every day after school, Vanessa finds Mother sitting with some woman in the kitchen, or having just returned from someone else's house. Dust collects in the corners, and stains grow on the tabletop. Everyone is so busy consoling each other, and yet nobody speaks to the children. Vanessa is pretty sure they don't know what to say.

Father is also gone, meeting with the wanderers, planning, plotting. They're not going to bring in the new families until autumn. Father talks about "recruiting" and Vanessa doesn't know what it means. He's always irritable, and sometimes just angry, snapping and making Ben cry. Vanessa saw a bruise on Mother's leg the other day, which made Vanessa think of poor, dead Caitlin Jacob. Now that Caitlin is gone, Vanessa remembers her small braveries, and she weeps for ever thinking her weak and useless.

Rachel Joseph reaches back to scratch her shoulder and then drops a folded piece of paper on Vanessa's desk. Her posture is so similar to Letty's that Vanessa stares for a while, unsure if she's dreaming. Vanessa's hand has healed to a pink, puckered scar, but it still hurts to move her fingers. Clumsily, she opens the note; written in minuscule letters is "Church. Midnight. Janey." Vanessa stares as if the words are gibberish, remembering the thrill that would have run through her, back when she was young and people were alive. Right now all she can muster is a faint flare of curiosity.

Janey hasn't come back to school, but Vanessa knows she's still alive. She assumes they have just given up on educating her, since Janey knows more than anyone already. She misses her keenly. Vanessa thought a lot about dream islands, lying in her bed at home waiting for the world to start or end. She wondered if the wastelands were just another island, a big one, with stockpiles from the world before. She wondered if maybe she could swim to another island, if anyone has ever tried.

Maybe Janey will tell them. Maybe she's been to another island, and that's why they haven't seen her. Maybe she's been going to another island all along, and she brought the sickness back with her. With Janey, anything is possible.

Feeling a stab of excitement for the first time in months, Vanessa can't suppress a happy sigh. Rachel twists around when Mr. Abraham isn't looking and half smiles. Vanessa smiles back at her, expecting her face to crack from it. The air feels foreign and cold on her teeth, and her cheeks ache. Then tears fill her eyes, and she crumples and puts her head on her desk.

CHAPTER FIFTY*SIX

Vanessa

Janey looks like some kind of insect, with a thin middle and spindly legs and huge, dark eyes. The circles under her lower lids are so black that Vanessa fears she's been beaten. Her hair is still sparkling, the braid alive down her back. Mary stands by uncertainly, facing Janey with her arms half held out, like she's waiting for her to fall into them.

There are so few of them, even fewer than Vanessa had expected. Many girls must have had trouble getting away, and then so many are dead. The girls who did make it stand oddly staggered and spaced out, as if to leave room for all the bodies that should be there but are instead underground, or floating in the ocean in pieces.

Janey steps up to the podium. The glow catches the stray hairs on top of her head, the thin, brittle down on her arms, bathing her in golden light. "You came here," says Janey quietly. Mary whispers in her ear, and she speaks louder. "This is the last time you'll come here. For me, I mean. Thank you."

The girls shift uneasily and glance at one another across the darkness.

"I just wanted to say I think it's all a lie."

"What is?" says Caroline Saul, biting her fingernail.

"The scourge. There was no scourge. There are no wastelands. There's people, living out there, living however they live, and there's us here. Living how we live. Everything, *everything* they told us, that

327

they told our parents and grandparents and all the way back to the ancestors. They lied about all of it."

There's a long silence. Mary stares at Janey in a way that makes it clear this is new to her.

"Why?" says Rhoda Balthazar.

"Because they could," answers Janey quietly.

The room is silent again. Vanessa stares at a shadow in the corner of the ceiling. If she believes Janey, then her life is a lie. If she doesn't believe her, then her life is nothing. This would have angered her, once, made her desperate and terrified, but now she's too tired to feel much of anything.

"I'm not sure of it," says Janey, "I'm not sure of anything. But we need to stop believing everything we've been told. And I don't just mean *us*."

There is a long silence. "Well, that's all," says Janey, and steps back. Stalking, starving, her limbs straight, thin lines, she slowly moves toward the stairs like she's moving through water. Mary stands up, arms wrapped around herself, and watches her go in a kind of bleak horror.

"Wait," says Vanessa, but Janey keeps going and disappears.

CHAPTER FIFTY-SEVEN

Janey

Black. Dead. Burnt. Each kindled nerve end is starting to fray, burning to a jarring stop as her limbs become heavy. Janey is no longer Janey, but shades of gray bones lying piled in a bed.

This is the other side, this is the dark side, of all her bright and shining moments. This is the part where she kneels down alone, in the dark, and inexorably continues moving downward, disappearing into the dirt, her eyes and ears and throat stoppered with black. She has never sounded such depths before, never felt such despair, silent and heavy as all those stone churches sinking endlessly through the muck, to where the pressure is enough to crush a girl to nothing.

She may survive this. She may die. It doesn't matter either way. She will never again sit on her heels on the damp sand, warming her chilled white fingers by a small fire. She will never again laugh at a soaked, sandy dog garlanded with flowers of red and yellow and white. She will never sleep in a halo of small children, shifting and murmuring and pushing against her in the night. Never listen to young girls argue endlessly over the best way to break a clamshell, or how to describe the color of the sea. She will never again sleep under a pile of thorny brush with Mary's dear form clinging close to her. But she simply does not care. She does not care about any of it, anything. The part of her that cared has expired, and she is too weary to try to resuscitate it.

Over the next few days, Janey seems to be slowly dying, and she welcomes it. She doesn't unfold her body, instead releasing dark urine into the sheets. Her words are slow and garbled and her eyes dead. Her starving body slows, her heart jerking and stuttering, her fingers turning cold and prickling and blue. Her breath is acrid, like rotting fruit, her eyes sunken and shadowed with violet and ash.

Mary is quiet and gentle with her, almost courteous. Her fingers on Janey's skin are trembling and careful, her lips on Janey's brow swift and soft as a bird's wing. Janey can tell Mary wants to be angry, to rage and sob and howl, but fears her fury could be the gust of air that blows Janey out of life and into death. And so Mary cleans her quietly, changes her sheets, and then tells her stories of their long-ago childhood to make her smile. Janey's gray eyes close and open, open and close without meaning or pattern. She turns her face away from nourishment. She hears Mary murmuring to Mother, and she is already halfway to slumber when Mary's fingers, coated with honey, enter her mouth. She twists, but doesn't quite wake, and when Mary removes her fingers, she swallows in her sleep. The next few hours, Janey consumes the entire Solomon stock of honey, one fingerful at a time, sucking at Mary's finger like a slumbering, ravenous baby. She wakes glassy, dead-faced, miserable.

"I killed Caitlin," she whispers to Mary. "And Amanda. And Rosie."

"You didn't kill anybody," Mary insists.

"Well, I didn't save them." She settles into staring at the wall, her eyes seeing beyond the wood and into the gathering darkness beyond it. Mary slips beside her under the clean sheets, her warm form huddled against Janey's cold, sharp one.

"Is it true, Janey?" she whispers in her ear. "What you said in church?"

"I don't know," Janey says. "I don't know anything. But I think it's true."

Mary puts her head on Janey's chest, listening to her heartbeat speed up, then slow down.

"Are you . . . are you all right?"

Janey coughs a weak laugh. "No."

"What should I do?"

"Stay here with me."

Lately, everything has been bathed in a beautiful mist, as if the morning fog that hangs massive over the gray water has snaked onto land. It dulls Janey's vision with its billowing smoke. Every now and then Janey sees a black wing fluttering at the edge of her vision. She is sure that there are no birds in the house, but cannot resist checking now and again, swiveling to squint at the corners of the room in case a horde of blackbirds has swarmed in through a new hole in the roof. But she sees nothing.

Mary climbs on top of Janey to stop her shivering. Janey wraps a chilly arm around her and murmurs, "I wanted to change everything." Her voice is grating and hollow.

"You did."

"I didn't. I couldn't. I was trapped."

"The island."

"No."

Mary's face seems to emit a soft glow in the gloom of night. *If there is a God,* Janey thinks mistily, *I bet he looks like Mary.*

Mary falls asleep with her ear on Janey's collarbone, waiting for her to say something else. In the morning, when she wakes, Janey's limbs are still and cool. Nestling in beside her, Mary watches the blue and white colors change in the contours of Janey's face as the sun rises. Mary doesn't move until daylight is streaming in the window, and Mother is screaming.

CHAPTER FIFTY-EIGHT

Vanessa

Ever since the incident with Mr. Adam, Vanessa has been having nightmares of blood. Blood wells out of Mr. Adam, covering the floor in a slick, wet sheet, rising to cover her ankles in summer-warm fluid, grasping her clothes and licking her waist. It pours out of a crack in the sky, pounds the island red, rises in a scarlet mist from the early morning ground. She drinks water to find her mouth ringed with crimson and thick, salty blood running down her throat. When blood begins spotting her inner thighs one afternoon, Mother weeps, but Vanessa is unsurprised. Surely so much blood can't live in her dreams without finding its way to her waking life.

Since that day, Father still comes to her room occasionally and climbs into her bed, but only to talk, or to sleep. Vanessa can tell Mother doesn't like this, and sometimes she hears her listen closely by the door, or tiptoe into the room to stare at them. Father seems amused and then annoyed by Mother's snooping, but in the morning he looks away from Mother's gaze and talks of something else.

One night Vanessa wakes up screaming from a dream of choking, a worm of blood coiled in her throat and slithering toward her lungs. She coughs and breathes gratefully as Father, lying in the bed, rubs her back and murmurs comforting words. Eventually she trusts the air enough to lie down against his chest.

"Father," she whispers, "when I killed Mr. Adam—"

"You did not kill Mr. Adam," replies Father. "I told you. We exiled him."

"When I cut him, then."

"Yes?"

"I couldn't help thinking of Mrs. Adam's baby."

"The one that died with her?"

"Yes."

"What about it?"

"It might have been a girl."

"Well, yes."

"If it was a girl..."

"Yes?"

"It would have had Mr. Adam do to her what he tried to do to me."

"Well, it would be different."

"And then I thought, what if I were Mr. Adam's daughter?"

"You would be a completely different person, Vanessa."

"Perhaps. But what if you died in the sickness—"

"We had the medicine."

"Fine, what if a big rock fell on your head, and Mother had to marry again, and Mr. Adam was there—"

"Mother would never marry him."

"What if the wanderers told her to? Or he was the only unmarried man?"

"But that wouldn't happen. I mean, at the worst, she'd become a second wife—"

"It doesn't matter. I'm saying, what if Mother had to marry Mr. Adam, and I was suddenly his daughter?"

"But I'm telling you that wouldn't happen."

"Everything that happened that day would have been different. He wouldn't have been breaking any laws. I would have been wrong, for cutting him. *I* would have been punished. They probably would have killed me."

"But—"

"Think of all the daughters who got new fathers, after the sickness."

"Well, I should hope none of them are like Mr. Adam."

"But nobody knows, really."

"What do you mean?"

"Nobody knows what someone is like, unless they live with them."

"You think all men are like Mr. Adam, behind their walls? Am I like Mr. Adam?"

"No. But I think you want to think Mr. Adam was a strange mistake, something that never happens, and I'm not so sure."

"I don't understand."

"I've been thinking about it." She pauses. "The last new family, before the Adams, was the Jacobs."

Father is silent.

"You know what Mr. Jacob is like. You just had to look at Caitlin to know what Mr. Jacob is like. Mr. Jacob could take a new wife at any time. That wife could have a daughter."

"I don't think he will live that long. He's poisoning himself with drink."

"But what if everyone from the wastelands is like that?"

"Like what?"

"Like Mr. Adam, like Mr. Jacob."

"They can't be."

"Remember that meeting you had with the wanderers?"

"Where Mother said you were listening at closed doors?"

Vanessa flushes slightly, but continues, thankful for the darkness. "What if all the new families we bring in are like him? You're right, all the people in the wastelands can't be like him, but what if all the men who want to come here are?"

"Like Mr. Adam?"

"Yes."

"That isn't possible."

"What if it is? What if I marry someone like that?"

"You'll be married by the end of the summer. We won't be bringing in unmarried men."

"How do you know Mr. Adam was like Mr. Adam when he was a young man? How do you know Mr. Jacob was? What if the new families bring in, somehow, something that turns island men into that kind of man? Like a wasteland sickness?"

There's a long silence. She takes a deep breath. "What if—"

Then Father says angrily, "That's enough, Vanessa. I know you're clever, but you're still a child." He gets out of bed and stomps down the stairs, not bothering to be quiet. Vanessa lies in the dark for a long time, holding her breath.

CHAPTER FIFTY-NINE

Vanessa

W e are choked with death," Pastor Saul says, his voice trembling. His wife and both his children died, and his new wife sits in the front pew, staring at him like someone struck her over the head. It's been weeks since church has reconvened, and his messages of gratitude have slowly become more and more sorrowful. "Death has smothered us. And yet we still live. There is no death without rebirth, and our island has been reborn. We thank the ancestors for our deliverance.

"And yet, why did this happen? Why did such a terrible plague fall upon our society? Perhaps the ancestors asked God to punish us for our sins. Perhaps the ancestors are displeased with us.

"As I look upon us, I can see the reasons for their displeasure. We have strayed from them. We have strayed from their vision and their holiness. We clot up the minds of our daughters with useless knowledge, instead of taking the precious time to teach them to be a solace to their fathers. Wives have forgotten how to be a support to their husbands. We let our aged live too long, past their prime years, for the simple reason that our hearts are soft. Men are swayed by the words of women, by the words of wives and daughters who refuse to submit to their will as wives and daughters should."

Vanessa sneaks a look at Mary, who looks incomplete without the tall figure of Janey next to her. Her face is white, her eyes closed, her lips still. One of her hands lies limply in the grip of her mother, who chafes it like she's trying to bring Mary back from the dead.

"With rebirth comes the chance to start again. We will have outsiders coming to fill our pews again, families who survived the scourge and have longed for this. We can start them off anew. We can teach them correctly. We can guide them the way we should have, all along. We will cleanse them of the filth they carry with them. The discarded relics of a sinful society, a society that set itself on fire and burned, burned until bodies littered the ground.

"We will cleanse ourselves. Our wanderers will show us the way. Discipline will be sharp, harsh, and yet what are we doing but cutting away the mangled, rotting fruit of a harvest and letting the healthy fruit live and flourish? What are we doing but following the will of the ancestors?"

The wanderers have been coming to Vanessa's house late at night. She wakes to hear them arguing through the walls. The first night, she crept downstairs to hear them and was shocked to recognize, strewn in a nest of vehement words, her own name. Unsure if they were aware of her presence or simply talking of her, she fled back upstairs and pretended to be soundly asleep, in case a troop of wanderers was about to storm into her room to question her. Now she is too scared to try to listen, and simply lies in her bed, while the tones of furious male argument drift up from downstairs.

Pastor Saul bows his head. "We must pray for our renewal."

There is a rustling of assent, or discontent, or grief. Vanessa starts to sob, and the people around her sit facing forward dully like they are deaf, or asleep.

CHAPTER SIXTY

Vanessa

Vanessa feels Father come to shake her in the night. She wasn't really asleep—she was lying half awake, thinking about Janey Solomon. They say she was so light that her mother carried her to the fields in her arms, that when she was dropped into the hole in the ground she floated like a feather.

It's late, but Vanessa turns down the blanket, lies back, and opens her arms like she's supposed to, before she remembers that she's no longer even allowed to.

"No, Vanessa," says Father. "Get up."

"What? What's going on?"

He has already moved back. "I need you to get some of your clothes and get ready to leave."

"Leave?" Vanessa sits up. "Leave for…"

"I don't have time," he says, and is gone. The moon is so full and glaring that she doesn't need a candle. She gathers some clothes in the dark. Then, gasping, she drops them in a heap and runs to the library.

"Vanessa," says Father when he finds her with an armful of books. His voice is stern, but she catches a glint of affection in his eyes.

"I'll wear Mother's clothes," she tells him. She's grown tall lately, her body disarranging and rearranging itself in new, messy, hideous patterns. Mother's clothes should fit her now.

Ben and Mother are standing by the door, Mother with a big

339

bundle in her arms. "What's happening?" Vanessa asks her, although she knows what's happening.

Mother shakes her head, her mouth pursing and stretching. Vanessa sees she's been crying.

"I need you to be quiet," Father says. "As quiet as you can be. If anybody wakes and finds us…Irene, I'll take the clothes, you carry Ben."

Wordlessly, Mother hands over the clothes and stoops to take a fretful Ben in her arms. She leans her head on his.

Father opens the door and slips out, and the rest of the family follow in a straggling line. The books drag heavily at Vanessa's arms, but she refuses to drop one and her arms grow sore, then numb. Her scarred hand aches. They're past the Abrahams' when she realizes she didn't put on any shoes, and her feet are needling with cold. There's nothing to do but walk on.

When they reach the ferry, Vanessa's sleepy mind suddenly jolts with the full recognition of what is about to happen. Her heart leaps up into her throat, and she bites her lip hard. Father goes up to the ferryman and whispers something. The ferryman doesn't move. Turning, Father beckons them on board.

Vanessa's numb feet step onto the flat planes of wood. The floor is dusty, splintery, and cool. Vanessa bends to release the books in a pile, and when she straightens the ferryman is staring at her. His eyes are like pools of darkness under the brim of his hat, and she looks away.

"Did you tell anyone?" Father demands of the ferryman, who merely gazes at him, swaying slightly. "Did they ask you anything?" Shrugging and looking away, the ferryman reaches for his long pole and sweeps it into the water.

As they pull away from shore Ben cries, and Mother sings a little song to him. Father is staring out at the water.

Once they're out of sight of the island, the ferryman pulls a cord and a terrible growling comes from under the raft. Vanessa grabs Mother's hand, trembling, and the ferryman laughs silently to himself.

"It's all right," says Father. "It's always like this." A waterfall pours from the back of the raft, and they begin to move quickly. With eyes on the horizon, Vanessa sees the gray sky turn pink. She sits cross-legged and watches the water go by.

Father squats next to her. "I'm doing this for you, Vanessa," he says.

"You're doing this because you didn't get to say what happens next," she replies, not looking at him. "You pretend it's about me, but it's really because they wouldn't listen to you."

There's a silence, and he says, "You don't understand."

"What, then?"

"They were going to burn my books. They still are. But I just couldn't stand there and watch it happen. It would be like watching my family go up in flames. You don't know how proud I was when I saw what you were bringing with us."

Vanessa is still for a moment, thinking of her father's library of beautiful words and pictures catching fire, crumbling to ash. "You left because of your books?"

"No." He is silent, then sighs. "I left because I was worried they might try to kill you someday." Vanessa hears Mother inhale sharply and looks up to see her wrapping her arms tightly around Ben, as if only he can save her from drowning.

Reaching out, Vanessa squeezes Father's palm, just for a moment. When his fingers try to wrap around hers, she draws her hand away. Squinting into the gray morning, she thinks of last summer, and how beautiful the island looked from the tallest tree.

Finally she sees the horizon's end: land turning bright with the sun. As they approach, she can see figures moving. Everything is in flames, blazing brightly, dark silhouettes outlined by flicker and glow. She can't tell if it's the wastelands burning their forever fire, or the sun catching light on human bodies as it rises behind them.

Acknowledgments

First thanks to Karen Siegel, who read an old high school friend's snippet of a novella and gave invaluable feedback. Bryan Melamed and Christopher Brown also provided helpful and incisive critiques.

I am new to this field, but I think it's safe to say that Stephanie Delman at Sanford J. Greenburger Associates is the best literary agent in the world. Thank you so much for your support, guidance, fantastic ideas, and for literally making my dreams come true.

I was fortunate and honored to have Carina Guiterman as my U.S. editor. Carina, I am so grateful for your astonishing skill in honing plot and prose. Thank you for making my novel a hundred times better than when it was passed to you. And thanks to everyone else at Little, Brown who helped my novel along its journey.

Leah Woodburn at Tinder Press was my U.K. editor and Carina's partner across the pond. Thank you for your spot-on observations, fabulous ideas, and insightful comments. Thanks to Leah's colleagues at Tinder Press for your help and contributions.

Deborah P. Jacobs, my copyeditor, has a mind like a steel trap. Thank you for turning your expertise toward my novel and catching everything I didn't.

Thanks to Stefanie Diaz, the intrepid international rights director at Sanford J. Greenburger, for introducing my book to new lands.

Thanks to Helene Wecker for reading my manuscript in her very scant spare time. Cookies forthcoming.

Thanks to Molly and Ember, my muses, who cannot read and yet still deserve recognition for their unflagging support.

And finally, heartfelt thanks to Chris, my captain, best friend, and true love. Next year in Palau.